RUNNING WITH THE GODS

RUNNING WITH THE GODS

SHAREN PITTMAN

For information contact:
Ink Dance Publishing, LLC
P.O. Box 1655
Holmes Beach, FL 34218
www.inkdancepublishing.com

ISBN: 978-1-956747-00-3 (pbk.)
First Edition: December 2021
Cataloging in Publication: https://lccn.loc.gov/2021949969
Library of Congress Control Number: 2021949969
10 9 8 7 6 5 4 3 2 1

DEDICATION

Dedicated to my wonderful children, Shaileah and Sean who
are the greatest joys of my life.

It takes a team to bring a book to life. Thank you to
Mary Schultz, Carol Caswell, and Sylvia Mills
for all of your love, help, and
support in making this novel a reality.

CHAPTER 1

This is the first time I've ever seen my father cry and it wasn't the kind that leaves little streaks of wet on one's cheeks. These are large teardrops that roll down his face like waves and drip off. Seeing him like this makes me cry that much harder. The doctor just told us that my little brother, Colson, has inherited the heart disease that runs in my mother's family. He's only 15.

This can all be fixed with a simple surgery but we are only Level 3 people. Our Level doesn't include the healthcare he needs. We watched this slow, painful, drawn-out death sentence with my cousin, Felix. He was such a hearty, robust young man with great promise for moving up a Level. But then he was diagnosed with this genetic disease. He was 19 when he died.

My father turns away from my mother and staggers toward the door, still completely devastated by the news. He looks at me and comes toward me. I think he wants a hug so I stand up but instead, he grabs my shoulders in an excruciating grip that lifts me off the floor. I gasp at the suddenness and pain of it.

"You must win!" he spits out between gritted teeth. Then he drops me and stumbles out the door.

My mother runs to my side. "He's not angry with you, my sunshine. He's mad at the world and at himself for not being able to move us up into a higher Level. But what he says is true, it really is up to you now," she says while caressing my arm.

I stare at her for a moment. Was that supposed to make me feel better? Because right now I just feel the pressure. Whether my brother lives or dies is in my hands. That is what they are laying squarely on my shoulders. My mother is smiling sweetly at me, then she gets up and follows my father outside.

I wipe my tears and go to my room to pack. I sit on my bed and consider what just happened. Colson has always been so tall and strong for his age. He's 7 years younger than I. I helped raise him. I love him so much. Why him?

Then the reality of my father's words hit me deeply. The fact is, my brother is going to die if I don't get through this race. I have to move my family up a Level so they can get the healthcare they need. We knew that my mom was showing signs of early heart stress, a side effect of the genetic disease she carries in her blood. While she doesn't get the full symptoms, she has struggled all her life with a weak heart because of it. Having kids almost killed her. My brother and I both had to be taken early.

I look down at my hands. Can I do this? I mean, really do this? I see my commemorative race book laying on the table next to my bed. A big blue ribbon that I used to mark my contestant page encourages me to open it one more time. My own face stares up at me from my contestant photo.

My mind begins to consider the upcoming race. I was really excited about it, feeling nervously jittery and thrilled at the same time. But now, now I feel numb. I have to win or at least be in the top three finishers to move my family up a Level. I have to do this or die trying. If I don't succeed, I'm allowing my mom and brother to die. It might as well be me also.

Next to my picture is the handsome stranger who is to be my partner. He's a "Specialist". They are partnered with each contestant as a sort of guide and escort through the race. They are also highly trained to keep us safe from harm. Since I was a young girl, my goal, and that of my family, had been for me to qualify for this race. I think it's the dream of every Foundations family, to hope that their child will one day qualify for the race and move them up in Level. As for me personally, I always dreamed of having a handsome swordsman by my side, like a pirate. It seems all so romantic and silly now.

I look at my partner's face once more. I should have met him two weeks ago at the ceremony where I found out I was chosen to participate in this great opportunity. He was announced, I mean, I know he's an Archer, but that's all I really know. When I think back to the Choosing Ceremony, I was astonished when they called my name instead of one of the other 11 finalists for Statsia. Now, I am just so thankful that I was chosen.

When the moment arrived to announce my partner, "The Archer!" boomed over the loudspeaker. The whole arena came alive. People stood up and cheered. I started clapping too. The Archer? I remembered thinking; I got a bowman? I also remember thinking that I guessed it didn't really matter as long as he was the best. I always pictured myself being paired with that swashbuckling pirate or someone like that. It's funny how things turn out.

Then at the celebration, instead of my partner coming out to greet me, 20 young Temple Archers ran out and around the stage to form a circle. "Archers! Start the celebration!" echoed from the loudspeaker.

They all walked forward in unison to a fiery cauldron, grabbed an arrow from their quivers and lit the tips. Next, they shot the arrows to the top of the arena that set fire to a large overhead platform. Within seconds, fireworks were shooting into the sky. Everyone was cheering and having a great time. It was fantastic. I remember looking around the stage for my real partner but he never did emerge.

The following morning at the Winner's Breakfast, where I met with past Statsia racers: Luke, Harlon, Rainia, Melia and Vell, they told me some more about the Archer and about the race in general. Luke competed in the race five years ago, Melia four, Harlon three, Vell two and then Rainia competed in it last year.

We were all sitting at a round table trading pleasantries. Luke was on my left and Rainia on my right. Once the breakfast was served and we were left alone in the room, Harlon opened the conversation.

"Okay, Liliana, what do you really want to know?" he laughed.

I smiled, "Tell me something that they don't tell you," I urged.

"They don't tell you how extremely difficult it is," Luke continued. "Out of this group, I'm the only one in the last five cycles to have completed it. I may have finished in the top three, but I didn't win. It's really tough to get through."

Everyone nodded.

Melia added, "Use the transport time to your best advantage. Read maps, read about places you're going. Try to get any advantage about what the cultural experience might be in that area."

Vell offered, "You'll never be completely prepared for what's ahead. One thing I learned was not to get flustered when other racers seem to be pulling ahead. You can pull ahead at the next juncture or find a shortcut they missed. I guess the point is, don't worry so much about what the other racers are doing. Focus on what you are doing and just keep going."

Harlon chimed in with, "Trust your Specialist. They really know what they are doing. I found out the hard way that they know the locations better than we ever will."

"Why is that?" I wondered. I realized I don't know too much about them.

"Specialists are trained their entire lives to be killing machines." Luke interjected. "They go over the entire world 'preventing' escalating problems. They are the reasons we don't fear war so much anymore. They take out the disturbance before it becomes real."

I had no idea. I knew they did "special missions" and such, but I guess I never thought about it much.

Harlon added, "During my journey, my Specialist was a Nandao. She knew the complete ins and outs of what our bodies could stand, how long we could endure at certain temperatures, our paces, the wind speed, the foliage, what bugs were safe to eat; she knew all that. They know it all. That's why it's important to trust them."

I smile. I think it is cool that Harlon had a swordswoman.

Melia commented, "The sleep deprivation and lack of food sometimes will make you crazy but just try to remember that the pain is temporary. Trust your Specialist, but DON'T trust anyone else. Everybody wants to win and they will lie, cheat, steal or whatever it takes to get ahead of you and knock you out of the running."

The others nod.

"I have one more question. When will I meet my Specialist? He wasn't at the ceremony last night."

Luke answered, "If he wasn't there, he was on a mission. You'll meet him at the banquet. Who did you get?"

"The Archer," I disclosed.

Melia let out a little gasp while the others nodded enthusiastically.

"What?" I questioned.

"If it's the Archer who I saw at the last Temple competition, you've hit the top prize," Luke divulged.

"Really?" I'm excited now. "Tell me about him."

"As past competitors, we were invited to the last Temple Challenge competition. It's where the young up-and-comers and the top guys from the other National Temples take on the Temple Master trying to get his spot. As you may know, Archer is the Temple Master here." I shrug my shoulders and shake my head as "I didn't know". He continues, "Well, there was no contest really because none of the challengers even came close. He was that good." Luke said.

"Yes," Rania added, "and he would give the young competitors pointers on why their tactics didn't work. He seemed like a good guy."

"He certainly is," Vell offered. "I spoke with him afterward and asked him if he was worried that one of these guys would take his place. He just said 'That day will certainly come, but it is not this day.'"

"He's very pleasing to the eye as well." Melia added with a wink.

"It's strange." Luke pointed out. "The Archer has been a top dog for several years but they have not sent him to this race competition. Either he was always tied up with missions or there is something special going on this year. He really can dominate the others."

"That's excellent news!" I chirp. I'm extremely happy about it. I may actually have a chance.

The rest of the time, the group told me stories of their adventures. Some were funny; some were absolutely frightening. I don't know what to expect now, but for my brother's sake, I have to find within me what it takes to complete this race.

CHAPTER 2

Sionatel

"I'll leave you now. We don't have much time; the crew will be here soon. Once you shower, remember to just remain in the dressing robe. After the virginity check, we'll give you the spa treatment to prepare you for the banquet. If you need anything, there is a communication terminal next to the bed." Miss Terry said while walking toward the door.

I'm stunned to have a virginity check so soon and find myself standing there looking at her. She turns around.

"Let's not stand gaping, dear, chop, chop," she says with two fierce claps of her hands. Then adds over her shoulder as she walks out the door, "The doctor will be here in 10 minutes." I run to the restroom and look at myself in the mirror. What have I gotten myself into? All I know is that I'm about to embark on an incredible journey. I'll be racing around the world with a stranger. I am my family's only hope. I must do this or die trying.

I hear a noise outside the door. I quickly strip and jump in the shower. Once I dry off, I put on the hanging aforementioned robe and walk into the bedroom. I'm still alone. I don't know what to do while I wait. I walk over to the table and grab a few grapes. They are so sweet and delicious, I grab a few more. I realize I haven't eaten much since I left Statsia. I spread some of the soft cheese on a small chunk of bread and toss it in my mouth. I moan involuntarily at how good it tastes.

Tonight, I will finally meet my partner. I have been waiting for this moment for two weeks.

My thoughts are brought back to the present with a loud bang at the door. I set the fruit down as Miss Terry and the doctor walk in, then shut the door. I'm instructed to sit on the edge of the bed and open the robe. The doctor inspects my body and listens to my breathing then has me lay back. The doctor proceeds with the virginity check.

I hate this. I should be used to it. I've had virginity checks since I was a child. Of course, they have gotten more frequent as I have gotten older. The political climate believes that those who are virgins have more self-control and are held in a higher respect. I wonder who came up with that?

In my history classes, we learned that The War of Powers wasn't about explosives. The biggest fear going into it was that it was going to be a nuclear holocaust and that everything and everyone would die from the fallout.

The War started that way, but there were only a few nuclear bombs that actually targeted something. I mean, sure, there were plenty of non-nuclear bombs and arsenals used, but as part of their war efforts, countries viciously attacked each other technologically and politically. People were placed strategically within governments to assist in bringing the citizens down by decisions disguised as help.

Others manipulated technologically by hacking into electrical grids, monopolizing food and water distribution and maneuvering financial markets. At the end, it had turned every country on the planet into a third world with no power, no money and no way to communicate. Most people died from starvation, sanitation problems and disease.

Governments had to start over. Every country was in chaos. Looting and rioting were widespread. There were no police. Anarchy was rampant. It was every man for himself. Killing to take another person's food became the norm. Bodies littered the earth. In cities, it contributed greatly to disease and pestilence.

However, it didn't take long for steam power to come back up, but generating real and consistent electrical power again was slow. Governments began to form and produce documents and laws that were completely new and different. Instead of countries, they made Regions.

Because of the lack of money and opportunities, all Regions designated a social order. The lower Levels are called the Foundations. Level 1 includes jobs such as digging and mining and various work crews to help rebuild. Level 2 jobs were those assigned to produce food, farming, harvesting, fishing, herding and the like. Level 2 also works on the social end by serving those who are mentally ill, homeless, fallen on hard times as well as reaching out to families in crisis situations. Level 3 are the merchants and distributors. They make sure resources get from place to place and that the people are able to buy food and products needed to live and survive. Once you get to Level 4, you are considered above the Foundations. Placements above a Level 4 are the most desired but are also the most limited.

For that reason, all Regions agreed to this race which is held every year. Only those chosen from each Region can compete to gain the best opportunities in order to help the world rebuild itself. That way the "most intelligent and competent could be spread around thus guaranteeing that no one Region has an edge on the others.

Competitors would not be restricted to their own Regions after the race but could pursue opportunities and technologies in any Region. Winners would have not only opportunities, but also top marriage selections as well as be allowed to take part in their marriage selection process instead of the usual, just being assigned a mate. Winners also get top housing, not only for themselves, but also for their families. Their wage cards would be filled twice before they ever receive their normal salaries. Winners become what would be considered wealthy individuals to the Foundations. However, all participants in the race get certain degrees of benefits and opportunities, since they are all the cream of the crop that year, unless you are disqualified by some disgraceful act, which leads to the importance of virginity.

It is very important that the winning contestant is a virgin. According to some history books, sex played a big role in bringing down governments. Sexual satisfaction was so rampant that even incest between siblings and cousins and other family relations was becoming the norm and people thought it was okay. There is a lot of gray area there that is not fully explained, but the whole virgin thing has remained and has had a huge impact on society.

One has to be a virgin before marriage. If it is determined that a person is not a virgin during a premarital virginity check, the "offender" is considered "Basal" and relegated to Level 1 in the Foundations with no chance of climbing out. Basal people are social outcasts and become homeless most of the time. It's tragic really.

Women heavily protested the virginity rule because it was gender biased until a protein was discovered in male testicles that is only there until he loses his virginity. The test is painful for men so it is limited. During the race, they have the qualifying test at the start, another at the finish and a random check at some point during the race unless there is "reasonable cause" to request other random checks.

The goal of the race, for Regional leadership, is that contestants experience the differing places and cultures first hand. They believe this makes for well-rounded professionals with a better understanding and empathy for the world in which they live. It also helps professionals to find solutions that may assist in better living conditions or other concerns for the indigenous peoples of different lands. They don't want to go back entirely to the lesson books of the past, fearing that the end game will be the same and most likely quicker to get to a world at war again.

There are still many areas that are "off the grid" meaning that those people are more rural. It was harder to bring some of the modern conveniences back to those areas. It must be awful to have to live like that.

There are major political implications of the race. They don't go too deeply into that with us. But if I were to guess, I think it has a lot to do with positioning as in all politics. The question always is, who is better? The "elephant in the room" question is, better at what? I never really understood what drives politicians and as a result, I don't consider it for too long.

I close my eyes and remember that I'm doing this for my brother, my family and also, I'm doing this because it's been in my blood my whole life. I've fought for this opportunity since I was a child. I have to win! I trained in school for a chance to be here. Many are dropped from the list early and some are dropped during later years in school. Only the top 5% of higher education graduates may try for a spot.

The top 100 then take the next year to train physically and mentally. There are 12 competitions leading up to contestant choice. They start at the local level, then, if they succeed, they continue to compete at higher levels until the last competition at a Region's Capital City. The final competition at Capital City is a grueling event. You are partnered with someone who stands in for a Specialist. This stand-in helps you navigate a 1,000-mile trek that you have to complete in three days including an arduous task. If you are one of the twelve finalists, the judges hold a banquet in your honor. Based on your final scores, they announce the winner. The winner is then paired with a real Specialist and will be able to compete in the world competition.

My partner for the trek was a ridiculously incompetent boob. I truly thought I'd lost because of him. He had the brawn alright but intelligent decision making was not in his wheelhouse. I barely got to the check-in points in the time allotment because of him. I let him tell me what to do because I thought he knew the best way. I'm not falling for that again. I suppose my "Archer" will be the same; more nerve than brains. I learned my lesson. I'll be the one making the final decisions. I'm not taking any chances on losing this thing. It's far too important to me, especially now.

Again, I'm brought back to the present by hearing the virginity testing tool beeping the "all clear" as the doctor finishes the exam.

"Bring the team in!" Miss Terry yells as the door opens and the doctor walks out.

CHAPTER 3

While my body and hair are being plucked, pulled, exfoliated, rubbed down, made up and prepared for tonight's banquet, I long for the tranquility of this morning's commute to this place.

I remember looking out the window of the commuter and seeing the purple light of dawn outside my window. It was so beautiful and peaceful. It helped to calm me. At the time, I was huddled beneath a flimsy transporter blanket freezing to death halfway across the world from my home. I was feeling scared and alone but also very fortunate to get to this place. I have spent my whole life dreaming about it and working toward it. Now I am finally on my way to either an incredible experience or my eternal doom. Everything I do over the next weeks or perhaps months, depending on how long I remain in the race, will affect the lives of my brother, my family and, my entire future. Since I'm only twenty-two, that could be a very long time.

It's the Race of a lifetime and I'll be running it with a man I've never met and don't know. I've never even seen or talked to him. We will be going up against the 13 other Regions that divide the world. Statsia, the Region I'm from, originally was called North America. During the rebuilding period, its cities began using trains powered by a magnet system. All Regions, after steam, adopted the use of solar or thermal energy too along with magnets as well as limited varieties of other power sources. Papa says that the cities of today are nothing like they used to be. They are scattered far and wide. I've been to some of the ruins. They are overgrown, but you can still see how majestic they once must have been.

There are 14 teams of two; one team per Region. Our race goes through each Region of the world so no one team ever has the advantage. Depending on how far a team gets, it could take months to get to the final.

During each Regional leg of the race, at some predetermined location, we must perform a task. Sometimes we do them alone. Sometimes we do them against an opponent. Sometimes we do them with our partners. Once we complete the task, we have to get to the checkpoint and not be last. The last team to the checkpoint is eliminated. The checkpoints could be at the complete other end of the Region which could cover hundreds or even thousands of miles from the starting point of the Region's leg.

That's where our partners come in. They are Specialists. I don't know much about Specialists. I understand they live their lives in vast, enormous temples where, I guess, they study their specialties. My grandfather calls them ninja assassins; he has such funny, odd ways of explaining things. He says they are the best weapons masters in the world and that he had the privilege of watching one in action years ago when he was a child and has never forgotten it. He says they can do things that most men can't. Grandfather says the temples are regulated and controlled by their Regional governments.

Here's what I do know about them. Specialists begin as children. All children are exposed to certain weaponry in school at an early age. If a child shows an aptitude for excellence in it as well as a certain amount of higher intelligence, they may be chosen to live in the temple where they are trained and study for life. If they excel, their families are well taken care of. If they fail, the family is thrown out of the postulant housing and must return to living at the lower levels. The child will only be allowed to work in the Foundations of the Region and the family cannot present another candidate child for seven years. It sounds so harsh. They claim it facilitates excellence.

I've never known anyone who has been chosen. When the tests were completed during my age year, the judges came but not one person seemed to show the aptitude in skills they wanted. It is very difficult to be chosen and is considered a significant honor.

As for me, this has always been my path. My parents nor any other member of family even came close to final selections. They were all eliminated early on in the process. My mother once told me that if she had understood the importance of the opportunity when she was young, she would have applied herself more diligently. She has pushed me in this direction since I can remember. She was tough on me when it came to my education. I thought she was strict and stern, but I understand her point of view now and I'm glad she pushed so hard.

If I complete the journey with my virginity intact, I will be eligible for the marriage selection. If I win, my marriage selection opportunities will have the best placement and I will be able take part of the selection of my mate. As a winner, I will receive the apprenticeship of my choice. My financial card will be doubled and filled two times as I start my new life.

Earlier today, when the international transporter landed in the neutral territory of Sionatel, this is where we start and finish the race, I looked out the window and laid my eyes for the first time on this "magical" place I've heard about since I was a small child. My first impression? It was extraordinarily beautiful. The sky was bright blue, the grounds were covered in lush green grass and in the distance, I saw sparkling blue water.

That was my first encounter with Miss Terry. She was dressed in a navy-blue suit when she approached me.

"Liliana?" she asked. "Liliana Ellis from Region Statsia?

"Yes," I answered. She motioned for a porter to take my bag.

"Welcome to Sionatel. My name is Miss Terry. I'll be helping you find your way around while you are here. Our first order of business is to get you showered and prepared for the banquet tonight." She continued to talk as we stepped into the glass-topped vehicle.

"We'll go to the competition transport and get you checked into your room. A small repast will be waiting for you. You will have approximately 20 minutes to eat and shower before the doctor comes in for your physical check. The people from hair and makeup will then arrive."

She looks at me and lifts my hair. "We better do a completely fresh haircut with some highlights, brows and nails, too. I'll have them include a complete leg and bikini wax also. They should probably look at that chin as well. This is going to take some extra time. It's a good thing I planned on it." My fingers immediately fly to my chin and feel around for long obnoxious hairs.

She pushed her wristband and said, "we'll need a few extra hands," then looks back at me. "How was your trip?"

I'm half stunned by everything that has transpired with her but manage to stutter through an answer. I mean, how can I concentrate when she has basically told me that I need a complete overhaul?

"Everything was very nice," I said sheepishly.

"Excellent," she said as the porter opens the vehicle door.

We stepped out in front of a very large black round building with a black dome roof.

"This is the Checkpoint transporter." This transporter is your home while you are competing in this race. This area here," she points to a large opening on the side, "is where you'll actually come through to be recorded at the Checkpoint."

She leads me through the black double doors to the inside of the building. From the austere look of the outside, nothing could have been more surprising. The inside is absolutely stunning. It is beautifully decorated. There are windows lining the ceiling all around the far end of this round room, while below there are a number of plush couches and tables around several open fireplaces.

Closer to where I'm standing are tables and chairs. Beyond that, I can see an area that looks like it leads into a kitchen facility. To the right of it is a sectioned-off open meeting room that has long bench seating all around the walls and a rather big meeting table in the middle. A green and brown area rug is on top of deeper green carpeting. It has the look of bamboo.

There are video screens dotted around all the rooms. I'm sure that makes for easy viewing and reviewing of certain parts of the race. At the base, there are 14 doors at different points lining the front and side walls. Miss Terry leads me to one of the doors on the far wall by the couches.

"This is your room," she announced as she opened the door to a beautifully decorated room that is surprisingly large considering that we are basically in an air ship. There is a very sizable bed at one end. Drawers and a mirror line the opposing wall with an outfit laid out on top of it. There appears to be a closet next to that. A large opening next to the bed leads to an immense bathroom.

There is a table on the far wall with a small plate of fruit, cheese and breads as well as a pitcher of water and a cup of ice.

"You have a few minutes to eat something and shower before the crew shows up," she says.

The porter brought in my bag and set it next to the dresser.

Miss Terry looked at it with a degree of distaste. "You won't be using any of your own things during the race." She moved to the dresser and opened a drawer. "All of your clothes have been provided for you," she says with a wave of her hand. "Your ball gown and outerwear are hanging in the closet. Your toiletries, including all personal hygiene products, are in the bathroom."

The porter looked at her, over at me and then moved my bag to the back of the oversized closet.

CHAPTER 4

My first look into the banquet hall takes my breath away. It's gorgeous. Everything is gold and white. Everyone is dressed in all their finery. The ball gowns are stunning. The ball gown that my stylist chose for me is a deep purple silk sleeveless gown with a very full skirt. The bodice, embroidered with gold and white leaves, is fitted and cinched at the natural waist. At first glance, I thought it would be gaudy from the initial look of it, but once on, I realized it is really quite flattering to my figure. My hair is styled such that it falls in long waves over my shoulders spilling also onto the dress. This dress is actually very suitable for a brunette like me. Now, in this setting as I finally let out my breath, I feel for a moment, like a princess.

There are so many people here! I look around wondering if I can spot my partner, the Archer. I have only seen him in the one picture so I have no idea what he looks like in "real" life. Looking around in the ambient light, I know I won't be able to pick him out in this enormous crowd of people, but it's fun to speculate. It's also slightly weird to be standing here by myself. A waiter walks by with a tray full of champagne flutes so I grab one. I definitely need a little something to calm my nerves and take the edge off.

A man is walking up to the podium. He's an older fellow, graying around the temples, but looks very sharp in his tux. He scans the room and taps the mic. The lights dim and the room goes quiet while a spotlight finds him.

"Good evening and welcome contestants, Specialists and honored guests. My name is Ruler Martinez. I will be the top official presiding over this year's race." There is a brief applause. "At this time, we ask that everyone find their tables and take their seats." He lifts his arms slightly as direction to move.

Contestant tables are located to the right side of the stage. Specialists are to the left. Because of the dimmed lighting, and then the bright lighting of the stage between us, I can't see much on the other side of the room where the Specialists are gathering, but I can see the contestants on my side. I find my name plate and sit down. We are all sitting alphabetically according to our Regions. I introduce myself to the woman on my right. Her name is Poppi. She is from Scoterie. She has flaming red hair and very fair skin. Her nose is dotted with freckles. She has a very athletic build. My first impression is that she is not here to make friends. She's very terse with her answers and doesn't seem to want to know anything about me. She is definitely a tough competitor.

To my left is Zara from Zealya. She is a pretty girl with long brown hair and a warm, happy smile. She is bubbly and friendly. I love her accent. She is nervously talkative and makes me laugh. She is as excited as I am to get to meet and talk to our Partners.

Ruler Martinez steps back up to the podium.

"And now ladies and gentlemen, I will ask that our Contestants and Specialists take the stage for the presentation of the Regions Racers."

All the contestants line up along one side of the stage. When they call our region, we are supposed to move to the middle of the stage where we will join our partner and then we exit the stage on our partner's arm.

Once we have our places on stage, the Specialists line up opposite us. Oh. My. God. I have never seen such a lineup of beautiful men and women. They are gorgeous with stunning looks and amazing bodies. They look like gods. No wonder they are the best of the Regions. How in this world did they get all these stunning people?

"From Abric, presenting Master Minsher representing the Hunter class and her partner, Lufti." Minsher is beautiful with wavy long dark hair, dark eyes and exquisite glowing skin. Lufti is a nice looking fellow. He too has the same dark hair, dark eyes and thick dark brows. He has a dark beard groomed very close to his face. Their eyes are kind of shifty and watchful. They greet each other by touching noses.

"From Carita, presenting Master Porra representing the Hammer class and her partner, Lyron." Porra has dark hair, dark eyes, and beautiful dark skin. She doesn't smile. Lyron on the other hand smiles a lot and seems very friendly. He has curly black hair, brown eyes and the same dark skin. His hair is longer than most of his race. He is good looking with a great smile.

"From Franka, presenting Master Byhed representing the Souka class and his partner, Elodi." Byhed is the tallest of the Specialists and has a little bit thinner frame than the Specialist men. His eyes are kind of squinty when he smiles but he has a full mouth and a dimple in his chin. Elodi has straight brown hair. She's wearing no makeup. She seems very timid and walks with her head down. She slouches a little too about the shoulders. The only time she smiles is at him and then very briefly when he offers her his arm.

"From Ingadeska, presenting Master Teever representing the Alchemy class and her partner Verandha." Teever is beautiful with very long black hair, large dark eyes and deep espresso skin. She has a jewel on her forehead. Verandha has thick black hair, brown eyes and a bit of a baby face.

"From Lachan, presenting Master Wuchi representing the Souka class and her partner, Ang." Wuchi is also beautiful with long straight blue black hair. Her eyes pierce through slanted eyelids and flawless olive skin. Ang seems like a happy go lucky fellow. He lopes onto the stage and reaches her quickly with his long strides. His eyes almost completely shut when he smiles. He has a big, happy smile and large white teeth.

"From Meditilli, presenting Master Kavalaris representing the Fetter class and her partner, Mirko." Kavalaris is a true beauty with thick dark hair, big eyes, thin nose and thin lips. Makeup is perfect. Mirko seems rather goofy. He's not bad looking or anything, but he looks like he just crawled out of bed. He seems like he is still in secondary school with all his dorm pals. He too, has dark hair, dark skin and eyes.

"From Mocombo, presenting Master Peago representing the Alchemy class and her partner, Banzi." Wow! Peago is stunningly beautiful. She has light brown hair that is pulled back but little whisps of it frame her delicately featured face. She has full lips and beautifully shaped almond eyes. She is the picture of grace. Banzi is a nice looking guy. He has dark hair cropped very close and his shadowy beard has jagged edges around his mouth and chin. He has thin lips and a very nice smile. He is covered in a variety of tattoos including a small dove at the corners of each eye. She curtsies to him and he bows.

"From Nosworef, presenting Master Langt representing the Long Blade class and his partner, Jannika." Langt is not just good looking, that man is stunning! He has long very dark hair pulled back and tied at the back of his neck with a ribbon, a gorgeous smile and light twinkling eyes. He exudes confidence but not quite arrogant. He definitely swaggers when he walks. Jannika is a beauty herself. She has thick, wavy, long, luscious (I'm totally jealous) light hair. She has pretty eyes and full lips that hold a flirty smile. She also has a very curvy, heavy bosom. Langt greets her by kissing her hand and then tucking it into his arm. With a small wave of his hand in the air, he turns and they walk off the stage to applause. You can't help but laugh. What a show that was.

"From Panill, presenting Master Kali representing the Hammer class and her partner, Roni." Kali is also stunning. She is very exotic looking. Unlike most of the other women, her gown is in two pieces. The top is cropped just below her ribs and the skirt clings tightly to her body at the hips but then lightly flares out. She has creamy tanned skin. I bet the men just applaud her presence. Roni is a big guy. His shirt also bears his midriff and very ethnic tattoos can be seen on his sides. He has thick lips and a heavy brow that makes him look angry. It contradicts his pleasant smile.

"From Razatina, presenting Master Espada representing the Long Blade class and his partner, Antonella." Wow! This guy is also spectacular and it seems like he knows it. He has thick black hair that he combs straight back on his head. It tickles the back of his neck with small waves at the ends. He has big dark eyes and full lips sitting on a perfectly chiseled jaw. Antonella looks like a normal very sweet pretty girl. She has long light ash curly hair. Her nose points down somewhat.

"From Ruska, presenting Master Kuzhan representing the Short Blade class and his partner, Galina." Kuzhan also has a very chiseled jaw. He is handsome with a heavy dimpled chin and heavy brow. He has big full lips. Galina is good-looking with light strawberry hair, very fair skin and dark eyes. She has an attractive smile with red lips. She seems very reserved.

"From Scoterie, presenting Master Foyver representing the Hunter class and his partner, Poppi." Foyver looks very intense. He has short red hair, red eyebrows and a light red beard closely cropped to his face. He is pale and freckled. He is nice looking verging on handsome if he would just smile. There is a bit of a wildman look in his eyes but he is all business. He formally bows to Poppi. She doesn't smile either.

"From Statsia, presenting Master Archer representing the Archer class and his partner, Liliana." My heart starts pounding. I'm so nervous I can barely move but I somehow make my way up to the stage to face him. He is magnificently handsome as well. He has longer, wavy blonde hair, blue eyes and an engaging smile. I glance up at him and smile. He's easily over 6 feet by a good two or three inches, I would say. His smile has a calming effect on me as he gently takes my hand and tucks it under his arm. His other hand then covers the top of my fingers as we walk off the stage. He seems very kind and thoughtful. He even smells good. At the bottom of the stairs, he gives my hand a little squeeze before we both walk in our opposite directions. My first impression is that he seems very warm and approachable. If truth be told, I think I'm going to like working with him and having him as a partner in this race.

"From Zealya, presenting Master Hamar representing the Hammer class and his partner, Zara." Hamar is rather scary looking. He is very large and bulging with muscles. All of the men are muscle-y but this guy's muscles have muscles! I can see tattoos peeking out from under his shirt. He has a thick face, solid nose and pronounced brow. He has dark hair contrasted by light eyes. He is not bad looking though. He simply seems a bit untamed. He offers Zara his arm. Her shoulders lift as she smiles at him in a nervous shrug.

Once we take our seats again, the governing Rulers take turns reviewing the rules of the race.

"The race is simple. Be the first to cross the Finish Line at the end of last leg of the race to win." There is applause as well as a variety of loud whistles and people excitedly yelling. A few call out Region names. Ruler Martinez motions his hands for silence. Once the room quiets, he continues.

"Here is how it works:

We will transport the Specialists and contestants separately to each Region. For the protection of the participants, the order of the stops for each Region has been randomly drawn and will remain confidential until race day. The teams will not know where they are going until 30 minutes prior to start time; at which time the Contestants will be given a map and any necessary funding will be loaded into their fund accounts. They will have 7-10 days, depending on the leg, to find the location of the Region's Task, complete the task and proceed to the Checkpoint. Expertise, guidance and protection will be provided by their Specialists.

We will now take a moment to review the rules. We understand the fierce competitive nature of humans especially when the prizes are so enticing. Rules are made for the protection of the contestants. Rules that are broken could lead to immediate disqualification up to and including criminal execution.

Number 1 - Triggered and exploding firearms of any kind are not allowed.

Number 2 - Specialists are not allowed to engage in battle with contestants unless the contestant attacks the Specialist or the Specialist's partner first. If contestants are engaged in battle, a Specialist can stop the battle but the Specialist is not allowed to wound the opposing contestant unless the Specialist's partner is in mortal danger.

Number 3 - Specialists are not allowed to permanently maim or kill contestants, even in the course of a contestant provoked battle.

Number 4 - Specialists are not allowed in the neutral task zones or in the Checkpoint transporters with the exception of Team specific tasks.

Number 5 - Tasks must be fully completed by contestants or teams and accepted by the Judge before a contestant can continue with the race or as noted on the Task Card.

Number 6 - The last contestant to check in at a given Checkpoint will be eliminated. There are 3-4 predetermined non-elimination checkpoints.

Number 7 - If a Specialist becomes injured or incapacitated during the course of the race, the contestant may try to continue on his or her own. If a Specialist is temporarily called away or in need of medical attention, they may resume the race with the contestant at a later time, place or leg if the contestant has not been eliminated.

Number 8 - If a contestant is no longer able to race for any reason, the Specialist will also be eliminated from the race.

Number 9 - The teams are comprised of one male and one female to provide a level playing field. However, all contestants must maintain sexual purity and integrity throughout the race. Random medical checks for sexual purity will be performed to verify that the contestants are still eligible to race.

Number 10 - No technological devices of any kind are allowed to be carried by either contestant or Specialist.

As a final note, with the exception of the no firearms rule, no other rules apply to Specialists who engage in battle with one another."

A hush falls throughout the audience at that comment and all of the contestants look around at one another in disbelief. The Specialists get very serious and focused, with tight-lipped looks on their faces like they have just been called to war. Did he just give Specialists permission to kill each other? The entire room fills with whispered murmurs.

"Please," he continues, and I think he's going to clarify that last statement, but he only adds, "enjoy your meal." He steps down from the podium and the lights are brought up slightly. Plates filled with delectable cuisine are set in front of us. Wine also flows freely.

After a few glasses of wine Zara turns to me and giddily says, "Can you believe that? It seems like he is telling the Specialists to kill one another. Do you honestly think things will turn that rough?"

"I know, it sounded crazy. I guess I never truly considered that side of it. I thought we'd just be having fun and seeing the world. I didn't realize the competition would get that fierce." I pick up my wine glass to take a drink. That is very scary. Killing people? Purposely murdering each other? They can't really mean that! What have I gotten myself into? It is actually starting to hit home. We will be starting this race in two days. This is getting real.

"What do you think of your Specialist?" she asks.

I look over at Archer. He has moved away from the table and is leaning against the wall drinking his wine. None of the Specialists seem to be conversing with one another. Then I see Langt swagger over to Archer, wine in hand, and the two seem to fall into easy conversation. At least both of them have genuine smiles on their faces. The two men are quite evenly matched as far as height and body size. Both are extremely handsome men. I wonder who would win if they had to fight each other.

"He seems nice," I answer, getting back to her question.

"I'm terrified of mine." I look at her with this surprising revelation. She laughs nervously and takes another sip of wine.

"Why?" I ask sympathetically. As I ask, I look over at her partner. He does have a bit of a roughness about him.

"Have you looked at him? I have been watching him all during dinner. He never smiles. I hope he's not an angry or mean person. I have to spend a lot of time with him. A drag of a partner could really make this a terrible experience," she says taking another gulp of wine.

I watch her for a minute as she nibbles a piece of bread like a rabbit. I let her words sink in. I guess I never thoroughly thought about that either. What if your partner is a total asshole? That would be awful. I look back at Archer. He looks very nice and all, but what if he is a jerk? I stare at him for a moment while he and Langt laugh about something. Then I remember the hand squeeze he gave me and the warmth of his smile. He must feel me staring at him because he looks over at me with a disarming smile. I smile back at him. He just can't be a jerk. Can he?

I turn back to Zara but something catches my eye and look back once again more covertly. As I watch, I see the Specialist Peago move with her very sexy sway over to the two men. Both of them look at her with appreciation in their eyes. She says something to them while running her hand lightly across Archer's chest, then smoothly along Langt's jaw. While they appear to appreciate the lady, there is something about both of them that seems as if they know they are being played. It makes me wonder if these two men have experienced a relationship with her in the past or if they are naturally leery of one another's motives whether male or female, especially in light of that death knell announcement that was made earlier.

After dinner, we all move to the ballroom. A woman dressed in white and silver starts a conversation with me. On her head is a white turban-type headpiece with a large white feather sticking out of it that moves when she speaks.

"You're from Statsia, aren't you?" she asks. She has a deep voice, a bright red mouth and throws her head back as she smiles.

"Yes, I am," I answer, also smiling.

"We're one of your sponsors. We're really rooting for you! Make us all proud." She laughs loudly and throws her head back again. I am humbled. She sponsored me? That's amazing.

"Thank you so much! I will work very hard to win this race," I respond sincerely.

"Of course you will, dear." She turns as a good-looking man walks up and hands her a glass of wine. "Look, Alec, this is the young lady we sponsored."

The man smiles and shakes my hand. "Good luck, young woman. The competition looks quite fierce this year. I won my year. Stay tough and don't quit," he encourages with a shake of his fist.

Ruler Martinez draws everyone's attention to the bandstand. He calls for all the teams to take to the dance floor for the team dance. I take a few steps away from the couple but I can hear that rude woman ask her husband if he really believes I have what it takes to win. I keep my back to them pretending to be looking for my partner. I don't hear the man say anything. He must have shook or nodded his head. Then she asked, "What is the hardest thing to overcome; the physical part of it or the mental part?"

"Every one of these teams will undergo more tests than they can imagine. Their relationship is going to be the toughest part of all," he answered.

"Why that's absurd! Do you mean if they can't get along it will be hard? Surely, they can all withstand spats and tension when they are trying to win such a prize," she spews.

"No, that's not what I mean. Think about it. You have a strong healthy male and a vibrant young woman, living in close quarters for months, sometimes half naked and sharing showers." I can feel his eye on the back of me.

"That can't be so difficult," I hear the wife say.

"Maybe not for you, you've never had to go through something like this. But look at her, she's lovely, intelligent, good figure. Did you see Archer? You don't think they'll be attracted to one another? Sexual purity is probably the biggest struggle because they can't touch each other. You don't think that is a great test? Believe me, I know first-hand. My partner was a beautiful woman. Only the strongest of body and mind will endure," he emphasizes.

I move away from them. So that man thinks a physical relationship between two people is the hardest part of the race. How can he think that? I mean, I know he actually ran the race before, but I don't think that will be a struggle no matter how good looking my partner is. I've never had any close male friends, but I think I can certainly keep any man in line.

I start looking around for my Archer for this dance, but I don't see him. Then I feel a hand on the small of my back. I look up as Archer's attention is turned away by a man talking softly in his ear. Archer nods at him and then turns back to me. He smiles, "shall we?" he asks.

He has a bit of a husky voice that suits him. He leads me to the floor and we face each other. He has such a pleasing smile. As the music starts, the men bow and the women curtsy. In this particular dance, we come together with our partner who lifts and turns us. Then we side step around each other and move down the row to the next person. It's pleasant because I actually get a chance to dance with all the males, whether Specialist or Contestant and see what they are like.

Archer has such an easy way about him that I am immediately comfortable in his arms as he easily lifts me and spins me around. He smiles at me and never takes his eyes off of me while we step around each other. What an attentive and thoughtful partner. He makes me feel like I'm the only person in the room. I smile back as I'm drawn away by the next man.

At the end of the dance, I'm back with my original partner, Archer. I think he was the best of them anyway. The only one who could have come close to him, by the smallest of margins, was the Specialist, Langt, with all his charm, winks and smiles.

Archer leads me to the champagne table where he offers me a glass. I take a sip then look up at him expecting some great conversation and maybe even chat about some race strategy. I'd like to find out what makes him tick.

Before we even say a word, I see him nod at someone over my head. He smiles, lifts my hand and lightly kisses my fingers. "I'll see on you on the field," he says. He bows tilting his head to me then walks to the entrance where the other man who whispered to him is waiting. I watch as they disappear through the door.

My heart sinks. I feel my shoulders slump in disappointment. I was really hoping we'd have a chance to get to know each other and talk for a while before the race begins. I look around and see that most of the other teams have paired off throughout the ballroom. I'm instantly jealous that they get to strategize and then mad that I feel like I'm starting off behind now. How could my partner put us at such a disadvantage already? Doesn't he realize how important this race is to me? To my brother? Did I end up getting another brainless muscle head? I'm getting angrier the more I think about. I look around again as the band strikes up another number.

With my partner gone, I decide to call it a night. I toss back the last of my champagne and walk out the door. The fate of my life begins tomorrow when we travel to our first location.

CHAPTER 5

Statsia

The commuter drops off all of us contestants in a valley where the air is very cool. Our Specialists are waiting at a nearby street close to a coffee stand. I find Archer on the right side of the stand looking at the area's map.

He looks at me and smiles. "Would you like some coffee? The day is only going to get colder."

"No thanks, I'm fine."

"Good, let's get moving then," he replies setting his coffee cup down.

"We have to catch the train here," he says pointing to a place on the map. "But to get there, we need to cross this river. There are some rapids. We'll need to be quick so we don't get sucked into them and taken downstream." He lowers his voice and bends closer to my ear.

"The others will probably want to get on here." He points at a narrow bend in the river. "But the best place where we might save a little time is here." He points to an area further back. "It's slightly wider, but the water is calm and shallow."

I look at him and grin.

"Let's go," he says. We begin moving away from the other racers, but they just start following us. Once the river is in sight, they all begin to run to the waiting boats. Archer grabs my hand, holding me back and moving at a slower pace. I take his cue and let the other teams rush ahead. Once they push their boats into the water, Archer and I sprint in the other direction upstream. I can hear the others yelling and wondering where we are going.

We find some boats waiting by our inlet and grab one. Archer bobs his head to signal for me to get inside. I jump in as he asks the attendant if he can borrow his water boots. The attendant agrees. Archer puts them on then pushes the boat with me in it. The water is very shallow here. In fact, Archer just pushes the boat all the way to the other side. It barely got to his shins. He puts the boots in the boat and waves back across the river to the attendant who waves back. We hail a taxi and head to the train station.

We beat everyone. Maybe this is a sign that Archer does know what he is doing. According to our instructions, we take the red funicular most of the way up the mountain. It's a narrow but amazing ride. There is a thick layer of snow blanketing the ground on the mountain. It is getting very cold just like Archer said. I can see my steamy breath as I breathe out. The sky has gotten quite gray and the clouds are low. Archer is quiet. He seems very thoughtful, like he's already two steps ahead. Just the kind of guy I need.

We step out of the car and into "Anchor Point Station". Cool name. Out of the windows I can see a road with little shops and homes. It looks like a normal northwestern town. Way north, I should say. Since I'm from a southeast town that ends in the warm Gulf waters, this is far from what I'm used to but I find it exhilarating.

Archer steps aside to talk to a few men, I'm assuming for directions, but since he's a guy, and it's about directions, who knows?

While he's gone, I put on my gloves and walk over to look at the large map of the local area on the station wall. A young man about my age approaches me.

"Hi," he greets me, "I'm Edrice. Can I help you find a place?" He's got a sweet smile and pleasing face.

"I'm trying to find the sled training track. Do you know it?" I ask.

"Oh yes, there is only one." He's so sweet with just a hint of a northern accent. "It is here," he says pointing to the map. "It is about a 10-minute drive from here up the mountain. Then you'll have to take a gondola the rest of the way up. Do you need a ride?"

I smile. "Oh no, I'm waiting for my friend. But thank you."

"It is my pleasure," he says and walks away.

Archer comes up behind me and rests his hand on my back while leading me to the door. "There should be a transport waiting for us outside," he tells me.

Once in the transport, he mentions, "This weather is extremely questionable. I don't know if we're going to get up the mountain today."

"But then the others will be able to catch up," I warn.

Archer only lifts his brows in agreement.

Once we reach the gondola, an attendant says we're on the last one going up before they close it down. Before we get on it, Archer asks if the track is open. The attendant looks at me and then nods. Archer looks at me and then slowly back at the attendant. I don't know him very well, but I can tell that something put him on alert.

The gondola ride is amazing! Visibility is a little low but what I do see is incredible. The mountain and the little villages all covered in white. It is breathtaking because I've never seen this much snow before.

I'm also excited since this is the last gondola up the mountain. The others will have to wait until tomorrow to make their runs. Archer is very quiet during the ride and isn't really paying attention. He only smiles at my excitement a few times, but his mind seems elsewhere.

When we get to the top of the mountain, we see that there is a path leading to the track. The attendant turns around and it is Edrice! I am very happy to see his smiling face.

"Hey, why didn't you tell me you worked here? This is my friend, Archer." The men nod to one another.

Edrice remarks, "It's good to see you again. Let's get you into a harness. I'll send you down first."

Archer steps in front of me, "We'll go together," he says.

Edrice is very kind with his reply, "I'm sorry, but this is a one-man sled. I can only allow one person at a time."

Archer says again more firmly, "We're going together."

Now Edrice answers more firmly, "I'm sorry, but for safety reasons, I can only send one at a time or no one goes. I'll send the girl first."

The two men square off. They take a step closer to each other and push their chests out in some primal man stance.

I step between them, "Archer, it's okay, I'll go first. It's okay. Or you can go first and I'll wait here. It's okay."

He doesn't take his eyes off Edrice as they both stare each other down. I continue pressing Archer's shoulder but it's like trying to move a boulder. He won't budge.

Finally, I plead with him. "Archer, I need to go. Please. If we wait, the others will catch up. I need to get ahead." I touch his face trying to get his attention.

The only sign of his relenting is an audible exhale through his nose. He steps back, but he doesn't take his eyes off Edrice.

Edrice, however, turns and gives me his full attention. "Let's put on this harness," he says as he helps me into it. Granted, his hands were a little slow when he needed to pull it over my body and he managed to get a quick feel of my boob as he clipped the harness. He has certainly perfected that move.

Archer is exceptionally fidgety. Nothing escapes his notice. He steps forward, grabs my arm and pulls me to him while he double checks the harness. I look up at him. He lowers his face next to mine.

"Something is not right here. I can feel it. Please trust me," he says in a low tone.

I look around. There doesn't seem to be anything untoward. I look back at him.

"Archer, I think it's okay. What makes you think something's wrong?" I ask because I don't feel anything weird about it.

"I can't put my finger on it, but it's not right," he says with a very serious look in his eyes.

"Archer, they seem quite friendly." I'm pleading. "I don't know what you're getting upset about."

"Just because someone smiles at you doesn't mean that person is your friend," he replies patiently. He looks around again. "In fact, we're leaving." He uses a tone of finality and grabs my hand.

I pull away from his grip. I'm through trying to convince him and can see that I simply need to take action. "Okay, well, I have to do this. It's part of the race. If you can't give me anything more concrete than that, I'm going to override your feeling. I'm going down the track," I grind out and turn back to Edrice.

"Okay," Edrice smiles. "Let's get you in the sled. I'll need to clip you in."

"Is that really necessary?" It seems excessive.

"Oh, yes. For safety reasons," he answers while clipping the belt of my harness to the inside of the sled.

I put on the helmet. I'm ready. This is so exciting.

"How long does it take to get down the mountain?"

"Generally, it takes about 4.35 minutes on a good run," he smiles. "Off you go!" he says as he gives the sled a big push.

I begin to move. It's slow at first but as the track makes a steeper angle, I start flying! It is fast and furious. I'm going around curves and angles. I'm having a great time!

Then I see an arrow hit the front of the sled, then another, and another, and another. Damn, he's really good. I don't know what's wrong but Archer is sending me a clear warning. I frantically try to unclip the harness but it is difficult when you're being jerked around and moving so fast. Now, I'm pulling and starting to panic. I tell myself to focus and get it done. Finally, I unclip. I try to pull up on the brake lever but I can't. It seems locked! I look ahead and see a break in the track. Shit! I maneuver from side to side trying to get the sled off balance. It starts wobbling and slamming into the sides. With all my effort, I push off and manage to clear the back of the sled as it goes around a turn.

My body is hurled in the air. I slam down on the track so hard I lose my breath. I'm gasping for air as I continue to slide, but slowing down. I look over to see the sled fly up in the air off the track and over the side of the mountain. I lie there trying to catch my breath realizing that my forehead was used as a brake to stop my momentum. I reach up to make sure there is no blood. There is no blood but it really hurts. How the hell did this happen? I could've been killed.

I stand up. My balance is wobbly and my head is quite painful but everything else seems to be in order. Nothing is broken and I'm not dizzy or anything. It's a miracle really. I look around. There is nothing and nobody around. I guess I'm walking down. Since Archer's senses were right, I owe him an apology.

I arrive at the point where the sled went over the side. The angle is too high for me to reach. I want to look over to see where it went. The good news is that I can see a small piece of sheet metal nearby. They must be using it to fix the broken area. Maybe I can sit on it and slide down the track. It won't be as fast or cool as a sled but maybe it will be better than walking down the mountain.

The sheet metal works surprisingly well. I am able to slide along the track fairly quickly. Actually, it is fun! I'm really glad Archer saw that break in the track. I wonder where he is.

The bottom of the mountain turns out to be a lonely place. There is nobody here. I look up at where I was. There is no sign of any kind of movement. There is nothing but snow flurries and metal track. At least I have a jacket and gloves on.

I see a man wearing a yellow "official-looking" jacket and walk over to him.

"Are you a race judge?" I ask.

"Yes, I am. How can I help you?" he encourages.

"I just came down the track. Do I need to check in with you?"

"I thought they closed the track," he replies.

"They did. They said I was the last one. It was broken but I was able to ride it down," I tell him.

"Oh really? That was the higher track. No one should have gone down that one. You're lucky you weren't hurt." He looks at me in my harness then continues. "I'll let you pass." He looks at my race card and checks me off the list. "But someone will have to explain why they put you on that track," he says sternly.

I just agree, take off my harness and hand it to him.

"Proceed to town and take the train to Plainston for your Task," he explains.

Another judge is approaching and they begin yelling about who sent a racer down the wrong track. An investigation will be conducted, and they go on and on. I silently back away from them and cross the empty parking area.

I have no idea where to go, but I see a sign for a town on my left. I find the sidewalk and proceed down the street. A street sign proclaims the town is about 2 kilometers away. With no cars in sight and nothing but ground and sky to view, it appears that I've got a nice little hike ahead of me.

Once I get close, I finally spot the train station just outside of town and walk to it. It has started snowing hard and I'm freezing. Thankfully, I find a café inside since I'm desperate for some hot chocolate.

In the café, there are only a few people sitting in booths. I slide into one next to a large window and watch the falling snow. I hope Archer is alright. I wonder where he went. I start to strategize my next move because I have to be in Kiruna by tomorrow night so we can get to Plainston the following day. There is nothing in Plainston but corn fields. Sounds boring. I guess I'll have to catch the next train. I ask my server for a train schedule. I am so relieved that I have an extra day on everyone else.

I look up from the schedule as the wind starts howling and realize that it's probably turning into a blizzard. The whipping wind and snow means that this storm is becoming quite powerful. The lights flicker.

I look around to see if anyone else is getting alarmed about the weather. No one seems to be noticing or fearful, so I sip at my hot chocolate. It tastes wonderful. As the server moves past, I stop her.

"Do the trains generally run in this kind of weather?" I don't want to be stuck here where the other teams could catch up.

"It depends," she shrugs her shoulders and walks away.

Mmmmkay. That was no help.

The door blows open and a man walks in. He's wearing a very nice fur-lined leather overcoat with a hood. He uncovers his head and shakes off the snow. It's Archer. He comes over, takes his snow-covered coat off, and throws it on the booth seat across from me. I see the tiniest wince as he slides in next to me. He puts his elbows on the table and blows into his hands. I notice he has a scratch just under his eye. He looks cold but the heat radiating from his body is very welcome.

The server comes over and sets a cup of coffee in front of him. She gives him a little flirt eye while she's at it. I can't really blame her; he is very handsome.

"You alright?" he asks after she walks away then takes a sip of coffee.

"Yes," I reply looking at him. "You?"

He sets his coffee down and gives me a stern look. Then he says, "You're lucky you only have that bruise on your forehead. You could've been killed. I really need you to trust me when I tell you something."

I reach up and touch my forehead. It's definitely tender to the touch. I had no idea there was a bruise, but I guess I should have known there would be. I look at Archer and concede. "I know. You were right. I'm sorry."

He turns back to his coffee with a grunt but doesn't say another word. He's definitely annoyed with me.

I try to make peace and apologize again with a little more flourish. "Look, we're partners, right? I know now that you were right and I'm sorry I didn't pay more attention. At the time, I didn't see the danger. But like I said, I now know you were right."

After a moment, he breaks his silence. "It's not about being right or wrong. I have a certain skill set. That's why I'm here. It's why I'm your partner. I know this race means a lot to you, but this race is extremely important to the Regions, too. It's all very politically and economically driven. There are many people who are going to go to great lengths to make sure our Region doesn't win. Our Region is willing to go to great lengths to make sure we do. Again, that is why I'm here."

Is he being condescending? I hate feeling belittled. I match his firm tone. "We were instructed to go down that track. What else was I supposed to do or even consider?" I am incensed.

"First and foremost, you need to listen to me," he scolds in his deep man voice. "It will be so much easier to take you out when you are not by my side." He's firm. "There was another starting point a short distance down. It would have met the demands of the race."

I turn away and look out the window. From my conversation with the judge, I know he's right. I just don't want to admit it to him right now. We sit in silence for some moments. I hear a train whistle blow in the distance.

"What happened to you?" I ask humbly still looking out the window.

I feel him turn toward me but he doesn't answer. So, I turn to face him.

"I know you got hurt. What happened?" I ask again.

He shrugs. "I was watching you go down the mountain when they broke a 2x4 across my back. We wrestled around. That's all."

I'm staring at him wide-eyed with concern and instinctively reach for his back. He saddles away from my touch with a warning tilt of his head. He must be in serious pain. I know there is more that he's not telling me. I can hear the protective quality in his voice through his abating frustration. He's not a good actor but he's proving to be a good protector.

"C'mon," Archer says with a little more patience. In fact, all traces of any frustration are gone. He tosses some cash on the table, "we have a train to catch." He gets up, picks up his coat and holds his hand out to me.

CHAPTER 6

Iwake up startled by an unusual lurch of the train. Then I hear a bang. I sit straight up and look around for Archer. He's not here. Many of the other passengers around me are on their feet. I can hear a woman screaming and a baby crying. There is a lot of murmuring all around me. Where is Archer?

"We have to move," Archer says urgently in my ear from a row behind me. Where did he come from? He is looking out the window as he reaches down and pulls me to my feet. I try to make my way into the aisle. Everyone is pushing forward but Archer has grabbed my wrist and is hauling me with him to the back. I look out, but all I see is water.

"Where are we?"

"We're crossing the Missouri. We have to go," he says over his shoulder still weaving us through the people.

"Go where?" I can feel my brows furrowing. "We're super high up and crossing this river. There's nowhere to go." I don't know what's going on, but Archer certainly seems concerned. He pauses to look down from the windows then looks up at the ceiling. He touches the frame under the window and then glances at the back door. I can see that he is thinking fast. I try looking around. What is it? I don't see anything. He tugs me toward the back door where there is already a mass of people standing and pressing.

Archer turns to me. "Stay here a minute." He begins to move away but then turns back to me saying, "This could happen very quickly. When we jump off this train, put your arms straight down by your sides, point your toes and keep your body rigid."

"Jump? Are you out of your mind? We can't jump!" I screech.

He leaves me standing as he presses forcefully toward the door. He tests the levers and seams. He and another big fellow look at each other seeming to size each other up. They only nod in some sort of guy communication, then both grab a side of the door. With gritted teeth, they force the door open enough for a large body to get through. A rush of air bursts through the car. Archer moves lithely away as the press of people pushes closer to the edge for the voluntary plunge.

They're crazy. I still don't see why we have to jump. I look over the edge from a near window. The water is so far below and barely visible through a light fog. I catch my breath. I turn to look out the front and take a step in that direction.

Archer whirls me around to look at him. He has his hands on my shoulders bending close to my face in order to hear over the rushing wind and yelling passengers. "You have to jump," he demands calmly but firmly.

"Why? What is it?"

At that moment, there is another lurch and an explosion. I fall into Archer's chest. He wraps his arms around me protectively as panic begins to set in with the other passengers. Something is very wrong but I don't know what. Smoke begins filling the car. I watch in horror as my fellow travelers begin hurling themselves and their loved ones out the door that Archer just opened. My feet, however, seem to be glued in place. Archer's lips are moving as though he is talking but I can't hear what he is saying. Everything seems to be moving very slowly.

Archer tilts his head so he's looking into my eyes. I see concern in his. He breathes out then lifts me and gently carries me to the edge of the train floor by the door. In my mind I try to jump, but I can't. I am frozen. I start breathing hard, the wind is whipping my hair sending little stings into my face. Smoke is filling the car; Archer is being pummeled by the other passengers because he is blocking them from me and I'm blocking their way out. I know I have to jump but I just can't move. Archer stands strong against the mob giving me room.

"Please Lily, JUMP!" Archer shouts in my ear so I can hear above the sound of the wind. I look at him and slowly shake my head. I see compassion flash across his face again as he looks at me. He's being pulled away from me. I can see hands on his shoulders, arms and around his neck pulling at him. He wrenches his arms free and moves his hands to my waist. Then he lifts me up and throws me out. I instinctively follow his directions and go rigid. I hit the water in a cold burst of sharp pain, like knives cutting through me as I go down deep. I swim upward finally breaking through the surface gasping for air. I see the train moving away in the distance, smoke is pouring out from the back windows. Other people are jumping making splashes and ripples at various places. For the most part though, the water is smooth and still. It's eerie. Where is Archer?

The other side of the bridge is still far away. I have a long swim ahead and start to panic a little bit. There is no one near to me. Where are all those other people who jumped? Did they get to a closer piece of land that I missed? I have never felt so alone. I begin to ask myself if I am going to make it? Then, as I look down into the dark wet depths, my new question is, are there any harmful creatures in this water?

I make myself breathe slowly. I'm alone. If I panic, it's over. I decide I should try to conserve energy as much as possible. I roll to my back and float for a while. I use my arms to softly guide me in a languid, controlled backstroke. I know I'm not going to last long if I surrender myself to the terror of this situation. I also know hyperthermia could set in soon, too. I must keep moving as quickly but as calmly as I can and try not to think of those things.

I alternate between floating then kicking and swimming hard. The shoreline is coming in closer and clearer. I just have to keep pushing. I finally make it to shore. Now that I swam for God knows how many miles, it looks like I get to climb this huge mountain of rocks to get back up to the tracks. Where the hell is Archer? Why didn't he jump? I'm so completely exhausted I can barely move. I sit on the closest rock trying to catch my breath but I know I need to get climbing. The air is frigid and I'm soaked.

Right now, I think I need to put together some sort of decent camp, get warm and get some rest. I try to move lower to the ground to get out of the cold breeze and lean against the rocks for a minute. I'm freezing and shivering. I wrap my arms around myself. I know I need to light a fire, but I just can't bring myself to do anything until I rest awhile.

I open my eyes as a train goes by on the tracks overhead. What happened? I sit up quickly looking around then fall back down on the cold ground. My entire body aches and I can barely move. I'm wet and shivering. I look at the water. Where's Archer?

I try to crouch down against a large boulder. It blocks some of the cold breezes, but I know I need to build a fire to survive. Why do I not see anyone else? There were so many people jumping from that train. Where are they? I flop over getting into the fetal position on the ground. I don't have the energy to budge. I've never experienced this before. I try to conserve as much body heat as possible. I see an orange glow in the distance. It must be the train on fire. My eyes fill with blackness as they close again.

I open my eyes. I feel quite cozy and warm. I look up. I'm under a shelter, lying on a thermal blanket with another on top of me. I turn my head to the left to see a warm fire burning nearby. My clothes are draped on a boulder next to it. I look under the blanket and suddenly realize I'm naked. My heart starts pounding. I turn to the right and my face bumps into Archer's chest. I'm snuggled up nice and toasty next him. At least he has pants on. I've never lain next to a man before, let alone naked. I need to grab my clothes, but he hasn't moved and I don't want to wake him. The heat emanating from his body is very warm. I'm still feeling somewhat dizzy and woozy and I just can't keep my eyes open. I'll have to think about this later.

I wake to the aroma of coffee and roasted chicken. I sit up quickly. The blanket falls from me baring my breasts. I grab it and cover myself. I look around; I'm alone. I see a few fish along with the bird and coffee pot on a grate over the fire. I reach for my clothes and quickly dress. Archer steps into the shelter a few minutes later.

"Good morning," he greets me. "Would you like some coffee?"

I shake my head. "No, thank you. I don't drink coffee."

He looks at me. "I wish I had known. I have water, too. I can heat it."

I smile. "I'll have water," I say as I run my fingers through my hair trying to pull myself together. I probably look a fright. There is no way I'm going to ask him about taking my clothes off. I know they were wet, heavy and cold. He did it so I could get warm. I certainly don't want to hear his opinions about undressing me.

"The fish smells very good," I comment. My stomach growls in agreement. I feel like I can eat all of it.

"I wish it were a pile of bacon," he smiles. His hair is a little damp; he must have bathed.

"Are there showers?" I laugh.

"There's a great big bathtub just waiting for you right outside," he smiles. "But I'll give you fair warning, it only has cold water today."

I laugh. "I'll keep that in mind."

"By the time you get back, your breakfast will be ready," he says.

I stumble outside. It is an overcast day but it seems to be afternoon already. I see smoke rising in the distance. I place my hands in the water. The water is as cold as ice. I splash some water on my face and run my finger vigorously across my teeth. I look back at the shelter to make sure Archer is not outside then quickly strip my shirt off, take a few quick breaths, then splash some water on armpits and torso trying not to scream. It is cold! I quickly decide that a full bath can wait. I waste no time. I shake myself vigorously to "dry off", pull my shirt on and go back into the shelter.

Archer is drinking coffee and reading something. He looks up me. "How was your bath?"

"Very brisk."

"Come sit by the fire," he requests as he takes another drink of his coffee.

I sit down next to him.

"I warmed the water for you. I wish I had brought along tea bags. Do you like tea?"

"Sure, it's okay. I prefer hot chocolate," I say smiling. I take a drink of the hot water. "The hot water is great though since it is such a cool morning."

He cuts the bird and hands me half of it. I take a bite. It is delicious! "Oh my gosh," I say putting my hand over my full mouth. "This is so good. What kind of bird is this? You should be a chef or something."

He chuckles. "You're just hungry because that is just a partridge," he says as he takes a bite of his portion.

"Where did you get the coffee pot and grate."

"I was able to find my pack before "disembarking" from the train. Your pack had completely disappeared. We'll have to get you some new supplies when we get back. We should make Plainston by nightfall."

He hands me two of the fish and he takes the rest.

"What happened last night?"

"The train derailed," he says between bites.

We finish in silence. I watch him under my lashes. When he finishes, he gets up and begins clearing our breakfast items.

"How did you know?" I ask him still nibbling the last of my fish.

He looks at me.

"How did you know it was going to derail? You seemed to know before anyone else," I ponder.

"All the signs were there," he says.

"What signs? I didn't see any signs," I say.

"I know. I keep saying this but you need to trust me," his voice is low but firm.

"You could've killed me throwing me from that train," I say lightheartedly.

He looks at me and squats down in front of me.

"Do you know anything about me," he asks kindly.

"I know a lot," I say in my own defense maybe a little more haughtily than I should have, accompanied by an arrogant chin tilt. I know some things.

"I have a certain set of skills. I'm here to protect you through this race. If you know anything about me, you know that I don't need to throw you from a train in order to kill you if that were my motive," he says softly.

I nod a little. He's rather scary when you think about it. He has killed people. But he's so gentle. I feel like an idiot, and he is right, he could break my neck at any time if he wanted.

"Just to be clear, you know I'm here to protect you, right?"

I nod again.

"Trust me when I say something is not right. I have much more insight into these kinds of things," he adds.

I know he is right about that, too. He's studied this stealthy, weird assassin stuff his whole life and here I am questioning who he is and what he does. I feel so ashamed. I turn away from him.

"I'm sorry," I whisper. "You're right. I'm just not used to working with anyone else. Please be patient with me."

He takes my chin between his thumb and finger and turns me back to face him. "I could say the same thing to you," he says gently and sincerely. "We both need to practice some patience while getting used to working with a partner. It may not be easy, but we'll get there, I promise."

CHAPTER 7

I meet Archer in the hotel's dining room. I see him sitting in a booth, drinking his coffee and looking out the window. He appears to be deep in thought. I slide into the booth across from him. On the table, there are hot chocolate and toast waiting for me.

"Lily," he says as he looks more intently at me, "Is it okay if I call you Lily? I probably should have asked before now."

"Yes." No one really calls me Lily. My family calls me Liliana. I don't know why I haven't ever been given a formal nickname. My cousin, Cari, calls me "L" a lot. Lily is okay, I guess. If Archer wants to call me that, I'll answer.

He smiles slightly and then continues, "I have been summoned to provide security to several ambassadors passing through this area. Most of the other Specialists have as well. I'll be back in a few hours. I must go quickly, but listen to me now." He lays out the small map in front of me. "On today's journey, to get to the corn maze, do not go through Kennett's Pass." He points to a large farm.

I agree as he stands. "I'll be back soon. I'll find you."

"Okay," I confirm. "See you soon." He gives me a parting smile and leaves. I watch him go wondering what's ahead for him. I only finish half of my hot chocolate and a few bites of toast. I want to get moving.

I hustle to see whether I can catch up with any of the others. After about 30 minutes, I see Poppi and Galina on the side of the road. They are looking at their maps. I don't see their Specialists; they must have gotten summoned also. They quickly hide their maps when they see me approach.

Poppi looks at Galina and then she looks me up and down like she's trying to assess me. For what, I don't know, but I guess she feels I'm okay because she lays her map back down.

"What are you guys doing?" I ask, knowing full well they are strategizing.

"We were told that there is a shortcut to the task using Kennett's Pass through his farm," Poppi says. Galina looks at her, then me and nods her agreement.

"Really?" I respond bewildered. "Archer said not to go through there."

"The improvements to the farm have been completed," she shrugs. "You do what you want, but since we're already behind, we want an advantage. Please just don't tell anyone what Galina and I plan to do. We don't want anyone else to know of this shortcut."

Galina grins.

"Okay, I won't," I promise as they take off running in the northwest direction. As I watch them leave, I wonder if maybe we can become race allies since I'm keeping their secret.

"See you at the checkpoint," Poppi yells over her shoulder and laughs.

I watch them disappear over the hill and wonder if I made the right choice. If I'm last, I will be eliminated. I definitely don't want to be the first to be eliminated from the race. I contemplate my options far too long and decide to go through the pass also. Maybe Archer didn't know that it's okay now. I take off running in the same direction the girls went. I hope I can catch up and we can all work together.

By the time I get to Kennett's Pass, there is no sign of the other girls. I look quickly at my map and see that the entrance to the shortcut is by the apple orchard. I run over there, but still no sign of anyone. I better not be last. I jump the fence and take off running through the trees. About mid-way through, the foliage changes from apple trees to some kind of garden with many dense plants. I consult my map. I need to continue through here. The exit is just beyond and the corn maze a short way from there. This could really save me some time. Going around is at least an hour longer. Once I get through this, I hoping that Archer will have completed his duties.

As I run deeper into this intense foliage, I'm rubbing against the leaves, vegetables and stems. While I don't appear to be getting scraped, it really begins to sting. I run faster to find a clearing, but my skin feels like it is on fire! It's stinging and burning! I lean against a tree in the clearing but the problem is getting worse. I'm running while involuntary tears stream down my cheeks from the pain. I can't see where I'm going, I have to find some relief. I see a fence and hurdle it. I collapse on the dirt road and start pulling at my clothes but then my hands start stinging and burning more. What the hell is this? The teary eyes are causing terribly blurred vision, but don't dare rub my eyes.

I hear someone running but can't see who it is. If it is an enemy, I'm so dead right now. I can't move. It hurts so badly. I don't know what to do.

"Lily!" It's Archer's voice! Relief floods over me. He bends down next to me and pulls off my shirt.

"Damn it," he yells. "You're covered in blisters. Why the hell did you go through Kennett's Pass when I specifically told you not to?" He's extremely mad.

"Poppi and Galina said they were taking this shortcut," I whine. He grabs some kind of lime green fluid out of his pack and begins to put a drop on each blister. "They said the renovations were complete."

Archer continues to dot me quickly with these drops easing the pain. "They lied," he answers angrily. "Damn it! Why do you trust them more than me? Mr. Kennett is sick of racers cutting through his fields. He sprays all his foliage and grounds with a highly caustic substance so that the moment it is touched, it causes these burning blisters which spread all over your body."

I turn away. How was I so taken in? Archer's tone softens while he continues to cover me in lime green speckles.

"The other racers want nothing more than to eliminate our Region early on. Please, Lily, just trust me so this kind of mishap won't happen again," he pleads.

The medication begins to work. While the blisters haven't gone away, at least they don't hurt as much. I put my over shirt back on and Archer lifts me to my feet, which also are blistered. I tip toe around trying to find a comfortable spot to walk.

"I can carry you," he offers but I shake my head. I got myself into this mess, I've got to find a way to get my act together since I still have a task to do. I just have to get there and face the humiliation of falling for Poppi and Galina's farce. They'll get a good chuckle at my expense. I'm so embarrassed.

"Listen, the blisters should be clear by morning," Archer says then adds, "Let me give you a piggyback. You're running out of time." He uses his deep man voice and it gets my attention. I know he's right.

He comes over and gives me a consoling half smile before turning around. I jump on his back and off we go.

"Thank you for the lift," I say into Archer's ear, "but I want to walk up to the task on my own. I don't want them to see the extent of my injuries."

Archer agrees. Right before we get there, he lowers me to the ground. I stretch out and walk around to find the most comfortable way to proceed. The pain is real, but I can't let them see it.

TASK: INSIDE THE CORN MAZE THERE ARE FOUR STATIONS WITH A PUZZLE ON EACH. YOU MUST COMPLETE THE PUZZLE IN ORDER TO MOVE TO THE NEXT STATION. IF YOU FAIL TO SOLVE THE PUZZLE, YOU MUST GO BACK TO THE BEGINNING OF THE MAZE AND START AGAIN. ONCE YOU FINISH, YOU MUST CHECK IN WITH THE JUDGE AT THE TOWN'S MUSEUM OF NATURAL HISTORY.

I look up to see Archer already walking away. Since it's not a team task, he is not allowed in the area. I head into the maze. The stalks are at least 3 feet over my head so there's no way anyone can cheat by looking over top of the maze. My feet really hurt but I start running anyway. After a few dead ends I finally find the first station. It's an old Sudoku puzzle. I love these! It's a tough one actually but I get through it. The judge checks me off and I move on.

I meet up with Ang at the second station. He looks up at me, then turns his back trying to keep me from seeing what he's doing. "I don't want to look at your work, buddy," I think to myself. The judge asks me wait on the other side of the stalks. I only have to wait a few moments before the judge says he timed out. My turn.

There is a mechanix builder set disassembled on the table. It seems to be a fairly basic robot that we have to construct with moving arms and rudimentary sprockets with metal links to move it forward and reverse. Just like war tanks in the old days. Once I get it working, the judge allows me to move to the next station.

I run through the maze. It's very complicated and difficult as I keep hitting dead ends. I can hear others in the distance now, and I know that there is at least one behind me. Hopefully, Ang will continue to struggle with that last puzzle. My feet are killing me.

I find the third station. Poppi looks at me and laughs out loud. Bitch! I hope she fails. I have to wait behind the stalks.

I'm finally called in. It's an old Constantin Puzzle. I only have to get these pieces to work together so a ball can move freely through. I got this. It is taking me some time though. Ang runs in. Shoot. He's asked to wait. Finally, I have it. The judge checks me through and I'm off to the final puzzle. I run into Lufti and Zara. Literally. We all crash into one another.

I arrive at the last station which is another mechanix build. I take a breath and go. I have to totally build this thing out of nothing more than metal pieces and rubber bands basically. It looks like some kind of toy. Again, it takes me longer than I hoped but I get it done. I find my way out of the maze and it's late afternoon now. I must find this museum before it closes. A woman getting into her vehicle asks me if I want a ride. You bet.

I run through the front door at the same time the curator is walking over to lock it. He directs me to the meeting room where we check in. The judge is just starting to put his things away but checks me in. I'm so grateful. Those who didn't check in will have to wait until the museum opens in the morning.

I'm slightly turned around after the check-in because I'm let out in a back-alleyway parking lot. By now, it's dark out and lighting is dim to say the least. I'm trying to find a path between the buildings.

"Hey, baby!" Startled by the strange male voice, I swing around. There is a guy about my age seated on a baseball bat trying to balance himself. He's a large, rather tall guy. He stands and carries the bat over his shoulder as he walks toward me. I look around but quickly surmise that behind him is the only way out of this alley.

I side step around him but he blocks my path.

"That's not a very friendly way to act," he grumbles with a fake pout. He takes another step toward me. I don't seem to have a clear way around this guy and take a step backward. I look for the museum door I just exited, but there is no handle on this side of it. "You're so pretty," he comments, "we could have a great night together."

"We could." A man's voice says. I whirl quickly around. Oh no, not two strange men! But then I see it's Archer sitting in the shadows on top of a delivery wall. He has one foot up on the wall with his arm resting on his knee, his other leg is hanging off the wall casually. I am so relieved to see him that I release a breath that I didn't even know I was holding.

The stranger laughs. "Well, what do we have here?"

Archer jumps off the wall and stands across from him. He's wearing a shirt that clings nicely to his torso. This man is built like a Greek god.

The young man warns, "Believe me buddy, your muscles are no match for me and my bat," and gives it twirl. "There is no need to mess with my game here or get involved. This is private between the pretty lady and me. Why don't you mind your own business and move along?" He flutters his fingers in a "get lost" motion.

"She is my business," Archer says calmly.

"Not anymore. Take a hike. She'll be leaving with me," he demands flipping his thumb at his own chest.

Archer just looks at him.

"I'm warning you, man. I know how to use this thing," he retorts gripping the bat and giving it another twirl. "I've put plenty of people in the hospital. Get lost!"

Archer just shrugs and stands there.

"Alright, you asked for it."

The young man starts twirling his bat then rushes at Archer. He swings the bat with all his might at Archer's head. Archer grabs it in midair. With a jerk and turn of the wrist, Archer easily disarms him. He gives the bat a quick twist and clips it around the back of the attacker's legs, lifting and flinging him in the air while flipping him onto his back. Then with a swift connection of his fist to the kid's jaw, Archer knocks him out cold. He stands over him, then drops the bat onto the unconscious aggressor's torso.

I run over to him. He glances at me as we start to maneuver our way out of the alley.

"I can't believe it," I laugh. "You beat him with his own bat."

"You call that a beating?" Archer asks.

I laugh and look at him. "What do you call it?" I wonder.

"Neutralizing the threat."

"Wait." I run back to grab the bat. "Don't want him threatening anyone else!"

When I catch back up to Archer, he places his hand in the small of my back and moves me through the dark alley.

"What happened? I thought the corn maze was the task," Archer says.

"I thought so too, but afterwards they brought us here to check through." I look at him shrugging my shoulders.

"Hmm," was all he said, he seemed a little distracted watching all the people and the general hustle and bustle. But I continue since I didn't really have anything else to talk about and he didn't seem very conversational.

"At the corn maze, they had us complete these builds and puzzles. We had to put these little mechanix builder sets together creating different types of toys."

Archer, who until then, seemed only mildly interested, stops and looks at me with a furrowed brow making his blue eyes narrow with a flash of icy steel.

"Did they give you a time limit," he questions as he stands to his full height, which must be about 3 inches above 6 feet, crossing his arms in front of his chest.

"Yes, we were being timed. I mean, they didn't say we were but at the first build I heard a judge tell a contestant that his time was up," I say gazing up at his face. "Why, what it is?"

"Have they made you do any other kinds of things like this?"

"Not here. We did during our year of preliminary contestant training. Archer, what is it? Is something wrong with that?" I ask.

He shakes his head. He's not going to tell me what he's thinking.

"Really? You're not going to tell me what you mean after questioning me about it?" I roll my eyes.

He purses his lips and shakes his head. "I'm not sure. It may be nothing," he says. He has almost a worried look on his face.

"Obviously something about it bothers you?" I try to encourage him to speak.

"Some," he replies. "In all your preliminary race work, did they mention that the race was in any way related to governmental recruitment?"

"No, not at all. It was never mentioned. I truly hope it's not. I don't wish to work for the government."

Archer smiles slightly, relaxing somewhat, then leans back against a post while we wait to catch the metro line, tilting his head as he looks at me. "What do you want to do?" he takes the bat from me then leans it against a wall.

"My goal has always been to win this race. My family is counting on me to move them up." I think of Colson and wonder for a brief second how he's doing. "Especially now," I add.

"Why especially now?" Archer asks.

"My brother has been diagnosed with a genetic heart disorder." I see sympathy in Archer's eyes as he looks at me. "We're only level 3," I shrug as my eyes glaze with tears.

He nods his understanding. "I'll do everything I can to help you win," he adds sincerely.

I don't want him to pity me. "I have always wanted to win this race. It will help my family. It will also give me better opportunities. I mean, I am hoping for an excellent mate selection that could move us up even further. I'd honestly like to place a career in one of the sciences, too."

He smiles. "A mate selection? What about babies?" he asks.

"Of course, when the time is right," I add. I don't know why but I can tell I'm blushing a little.

"You want to make your mark in the world first," he questions. "In one of the sciences? Which one?"

I take a deep breath, "I don't know if I want to make a mark in the world, but I'd like to make a difference to the people I love. I haven't quite decided which science, yet. I hope that what I end up doing will be fulfilling a need somewhere and helping others." I shrug.

"High aspirations indeed." He's still smiling and his eyes are like warm blue pools. I could get lost in them. A loud chime rings to announce the coming metro. Archer turns as the doors open and leads me onto it. We get off at our stop about 15 minutes later.

"Come, we're not that far from the checkpoint." Then he looks down at me. "It would probably be best if our conversation about your building test is not repeated."

I'm not really sure why he wants it kept quiet but I say, "Okay."

"Traitor!" I hear a man's deep voice yell.

It grabs Archer's full attention and he puts a protective hand in front of me. "Langt," he says and then we move quickly to a side street from where the yell seemed to emanate. I see Langt moving with clenched fists toward Byhed who is some distance away but he is facing Langt with drawn weapons and a smirk on his face.

Archer turns to me. "Stay here," he orders as he moves down the street at an angle to intercept Langt.

When he reaches him, he puts his hand on Langt's chest to stop him and says, "Tell me."

I can't really hear what Langt replies but when he is finished, Archer says, "I'm senior, I'll take the fight."

Langt pushes away from Archer and grits out, "The hell you will! This is mine!" Whatever Byhed did, Langt is red hot about it.

Archer moves aside. He returns to me. "I must stay for this. Both Langt and Byhed are in our Region's alliance. Go to the checkpoint immediately."

"Archer, I want to stay. I like Langt too," I argue.

He looks at me and sighs. "Please, Liliana. Go to the checkpoint. Please," he asks with lifted eyebrows.

I look around. Jannika and Elodie seem to be on pins and needles since their Specialists are about to fight. I can understand that. Other teams are there too, eager to catch a good bout, I imagine. I can beat them all if I leave now. I look back at Archer and concede. I start to walk away. Archer watches me for a moment, then moves toward Langt who now has a spear in his hand and is moving with genuine purpose. Byhed is moving toward him. This is going to be a good match.

I do have a fairly good view as I move to the checkpoint. Archer has made it "ringside". With arms crossed in front of his chest, he stands as overlord of sorts observing while the other two men circle around. As a crowd begins to form, Langt makes the first move. There is a titan clash between the men. They are so fast. Weapons are wielded. They move, dodge, strike, twist, bend, flip. It is amazing to watch. Byhed seems to have an advantage but then Langt makes some amazing move and he clearly has the advantage. He is incredible with that spear.

I have to turn away because the checkpoint is on the next corner. I take one last look and see Archer's searing blue eyes on me. Taking that as my clue, I turn away and move to the checkpoint portal.

"Ellis – Number 3" is called over the loudspeaker.

CHAPTER 8

Noswaref

As we disembark from the commuter, all of us are given an instruction card and a map. We are to go to the nearby Vianessa School of Dance where we will learn the steps to the Zauber Baum Waltz. We will be tested on it later in the race. In the fine print, the card says that our Specialists will meet us after class at Fredricksburg Park.

Jannika, Antonella, Zara and I gravitate to each other and walk together to the school.

"Do any of you know who got eliminated," I ask. I was so tired when I got to my room after the last leg, I took a shower and collapsed.

"It was Virandha. Region 2," Zara responds.

"Oh, wow. Really?" I am surprised. I thought he was a definite contender.

The other contestants are walking ahead of us. Antonella looks slyly over at me. "Perhaps Mirko will want to be your dance partner," she says and nudges her elbow into my side.

I just look at her. "What do you mean?" I'm puzzled.

She smiles at me. "For a smart girl, you are really oblivious when it comes to guys."

"She really is," Jannika adds nodding.

I look from one to the other and to Zara, who is also nodding. "What are you talking about?" I truly don't know.

Jannika laughs and winds her arm through mine. "Mirko has it pretty bad for you. Lufti told me he's on the Liliana train."

"He did? He does?" I try to think back at all my encounters with Mirko. Not once do I remember him doing anything out of the ordinary or extreme thoughtfulness or kindness to me.

"He's always staring at you," Zara whispers.

"Haven't you noticed that he is always sitting at your table or near you during the commuter moves?" Antonella laughs.

"He's trying to get close to you," Jannika adds wiggling her eyebrows.

I laugh out loud at them.

"No," I smile. "You guys are teasing me."

"Yep," Jannika grins. "Oblivious." The other girls giggle.

Once at the school, I can't help but look over at Mirko. He is watching us, but since we are the last ones in, I feel like everyone shot a glance our way.

We are all shuffled into a large dance studio and assigned an individual instructor. I am assigned to Mr. Jeppson. He's tall and thin with a long face and an equally long crooked nose that resembles a bird beak. He reminds me of an old cartoonish tutor. The head instructor claps his hands to get our attention and then motions for us to watch the demonstration.

We're told it has six basic steps but there is a lot of twirling around your partner. The trouble is, they aren't really explaining it very well. Sometimes you twirl once, sometimes you twirl three times and sometimes six times. There is also a lunging dip with a swing up in the air and then a dramatic bending dip. I don't know if I'm ever going to get this all down.

Mr. Jeppson begins his training with me. I'm not so confident about all that twirling and dipping in his skinny arms but I find myself surprised at his strength. We are going very slowly and he hasn't actually lifted me off the floor yet. But as our hour closes, I know it's coming.

The head master claps his hands and tells us to give it one good run through before our hour is up. The music starts and sure enough, my Mr. Jeppson seems to be struggling to lift and twirl me. I'm really frightened of the dip.

When we finally do go for the dip, Mr. Jeppson lurches me backward while he comes forward practically knocking into my face. I lose my footing and grab at him as I start falling. I can see his eyes get wide but instead of helping to steady me, he tumbles right on top of me. His long nose pokes me in the eye. I screech from the pain. Everyone is laughing at us as the head master hauls the man to his feet. I have to scramble to find my own way up.

Jannika comes over and wraps her arms around me in a pitying hug. I am grateful. When class is over, they basically tell us we are all terrible and that we should practice a lot in order to pass. I think we are aware of that. I just want to get out of here.

Since there is no sign yet of our Specialists, a few of us girls get together and find a secluded spot to practice in Fredricksburg Park. Jannika, Antonella, Zara and I pair up to try to remember all the steps. It's actually quite comical. We're running into each other, we definitely can't lift one another so we practice jumping for the lifts. We are a hot mess with this dance. We don't know how we are ever going to get it right. Finally, we just burst out laughing.

During one particularly bad twirl I think I see Archer. I stop to look around. In the distance, I see him and Langt leaning against a tree watching us. Once discovered, they walk over.

"What are you doing, exactly?" Langt asks. "We can't quite figure it out. Is this some kind of girl pretending that we don't understand?

We laugh harder.

"We're trying to practice the Zauber Baum Waltz," Antonella answers.

Langt and Archer look at each with raised eyebrows and scoff.

"I'm afraid you're doing a terrible job at it. I didn't recognize it all," Archer says smiling. He looks at Langt. "Shall we?"

"By all means," Langt answers charmingly motioning his arm forward.

Archer stands in front of me and Langt in front of Jannika. Archer flips his finger at Zara and Antonello indicating for them to pair up. Then he tells us the story.

"The Zauber Baum Waltz is considered a Christmas story because it is about a strong tree wanting desperately to be decorated with magical twinkling lights." He faces me, "I am the tree," he indicates himself by placing his hand on his chest, then turns his palm to me, "but you are the beautiful, magical, twinkling, twirling, ornamental illumination. You love the tree. The tree wants your happy twinkling near it always. It's a dance of magic and of love." He uses his hands in dramatic gestures. Langt is smiling. I can't help but smile too. He's very good at bringing it to life.

"The beginning and the end are always the same. I will bow. You will curtsy. I am stalwart and steadfast. You are the great beauty and wonder in my life." He smiles. He and Langt bow. Jannika and I curtsy. Archer looks over at Zara and Antonella. Zara bows and Antonella curtsies.

Archer lifts his arm to me and turns his wrist over inviting me to take his hand. The others follow suit.

"Put your elbow so it is resting on my shoulder. Then put your hand flat behind my neck but hold it out just enough so that it's not actually touching my neck. My hand is at your waist. It's a dance of love," he says smiling, "so I will tuck you in close." I suck in my breath a little as he pulls me gently in, close to him. I can feel the heat of his body and breathe in his wonderful masculine scent.

He holds his other hand out. "Put your hand on mine." I do and he closes his fingers around it.

"This is a six step. The tree always leads." He is talking loudly so the others can hear. He turns to me smiling, "You will step back with your left foot, then step back again. Step over once with your left foot, then front and front again, always with your left foot. Then I will lift your hand over our heads and twirl you around once. Let's try."

He's really good at giving directions. The "lights" move back one, two, then over one, forward one, forward two. The "trees" hold us firmly in their grips while pressing gently to lead our movements perfectly. Archer and Langt both are excellent "trees", so handsome and strong. Archer lifts my arm and twirls me at my waist. Then he stops to look around.

"Did everyone get that?" he's basically saying it to the ladies. It's clear that Langt knows exactly what he's doing. We all nod and smile. It was a much better lesson.

"Let's try it again, but this time after the twirl, the tree lifts the light a quarter turn and we start again." He leads me again. At the end, we all smile, we are getting it.

"The twirls are a progression of the tree and lights falling in love with each other. At the third stanza, the lights twirl happily three times. At the fifth, the lights twirl six times. Then we will practice the dips," he explains.

As we dance, he says softly to me, "Try to look at me. You keep looking down at your feet. It's a dance of love and happiness." He's grinning.

"Let me learn it first, then I'll look at you all day long," I smile.

"Fair enough," he laughs.

We get through it fairly well and clap. I think we are all getting it.

"Now, for the dips. Langt, would you and Jannika kindly demonstrate while I explain?" Archer asks. They both nod in compliance.

"The first dip is one of excitement. The tree has now made the lights an eternal part of his life. He's happy. He dips her down but brings her merrily right back up into the air. As he does, he realizes how much he loves her. The second dip is one of devotion. He brings her down slowing the pace and carefully cradles her in his loving branches." Langt performs a moving dip in which Jannika is dipped but quickly lifted into the air. He holds her there a moment and slowly lowers her while bending her back into the final dip as he bends over her body bowing his head. Everyone claps enthusiastically. Langt brings them both to their feet, steps back and bows. Jannika takes the cue and curtsies.

"Perfect," Archer says smiling. "Now let's put it together."

We go through the whole dance again. I keep looking at my feet as Archer keeps telling me to look at him. He must have said it a thousand times. He finally just wiggles his pinky finger and I look up.

Archer is such an excellent dancer. He lifts me so easily, and the last dip is so romantic. When he bends over my body, he looks me in the eyes before bowing his head. I want to eat him up. I'm really enjoying this time with him.

Once we have it down, Archer and Langt look at each other then go over to Antonella and Zara and help them finalize the steps properly. They are such good men. I watch what excellent dancers they are and so strong. Jannika and I just lean together dreamily as we watch. It's nothing for them to lift and move us girls around.

Espada shows up and takes over with Antonella from Archer. I watch him. He does move with great elegance and dances very well but he lifts his chin in an arrogant, aloof sort of way. It's rather unattractive. It's too bad because he's such a handsome man. But then again, all of the Specialists look like gods.

Archer walks over to stand next to me as we watch them dance. "Do you think you have it," he asks.

"Yes, I think so. Thank you so much for this," I add. "I know we all genuinely appreciate it."

He winks at me, puts his arm around my shoulders and gives me a little squeeze.

"I didn't do it for them," he replies and then adds, "Time to go."

CHAPTER 9

We find the road and make our way to the task. Up ahead there is a small table with the task envelopes. It's individual contestant only. I look up and see bikes parked nearby. They all have a small cargo trailer connected to the back-tire frame. I also see pallets of different items. Archer follows my eyes.

"I'll see you at the campsite," he says.

As he walks away, I open the envelope.

TASK: TAKE ONE OF THE BIKES WITH THE CONNECTED TRAILER AS WELL AS A RECEIPT POUCH. LOAD THE TRAILER WITH 50 LBS OF FLOUR, 50 LBS OF ONIONS, 50 LBS OF HAM HOCKS AND A 50 LB WHEEL OF CHEESE. USING THE MAP IN THE PROVIDED POUCH, YOU MUST DELIVER THE ITEMS AS FOLLOWS: THE FLOUR GOES TO THE STUREBATTEN BAKERY, THE ONIONS TO GRYGGERIKEREN RESTAURANT, THE HAM HOCKS TO HAGA CURING AND THE CHEESE TO BATINGULTA RESORT. FOLLOW THE MARKED PATHS ONLY. ONCE YOU FINISH, YOU MUST RETURN THE BIKE TO THE

STARTING POINT AND PLACE THE RECEIPTS AND POUCH IN THE MARKED BIN.

I look at the food at various stations around the park. I grab a bike and wheel it over to the closest station. I pick up a 25-pound sack of flour, which is heavy, and load it into the trailer. Then I grab another one. The next station has the cheese. Who knew a wheel of cheese could be so big and bulky? Another contestant has arrived giving me a sense of urgency. I grab the onions and move to the ham hocks.

Once I'm fully loaded, I scan the map to see my closest location. The closest location is actually quite far. We have to lug 200 lbs. of food items approximately 3 kilometers before we get to the first location. This is going to be a long day. Good thing it's a lovely day.

I see a station of water and food bars. I stop to grab an ample stash before heading out. I know I'll need the refreshment. The ride to the first location is slightly uphill so there is no break in pedaling. This is definitely a strength and endurance task.

I finally reach the first location gasping for air and needing a water break. This is the curing place. The delivery location sits on top of another small hill, but we are not allowed to use the bikes past this point and must carry the items the rest of the way up the hill to deliver it to the kitchen receiving area.

Lufti pulls up beside me. He easily hefts all the ham over his shoulders and makes his way up the grassy hill. I pull on the provided gloves and try to put all of it on my shoulders but that does not work for me. It's far too heavy, so I know it will be necessary to make at least two trips. I grab the maximum that I can carry and make my way to the bottom of the hill.

Lufti is already halfway up, but I can hear him grunting from here. The ground is wet and slippery. I begin the hike but fall almost immediately. I look around to see a barrier railing along the left tree line and go to it. It's clear I'm going to need at least one hand free to pull myself up this hill.

I hear swearing and find Lufti trying very hard to get to the top. He only has a few more steps to go. I stick a few ham hocks in my shirt and climb the railing hand over hand while my feet slip around on this wet hill.

I no longer see Lufti, he must've made it to the top by now. Poppi pulls up on her bike. She takes one look at me and pulls some string from her carry pack. She's prepared. She binds the ham hocks together and starts up the hill. She moves past me while giving me a very smug look. She takes another step but then slips and falls down the hill. The string around her ham hocks breaks and they go flying in every direction. Hmph! I can't help but chuckle to myself. That's what she gets for trying to be a smarty pants.

When I finally get to the top, I look down and see Poppi applying the same strategy I employed by using the railing to get to the top.

It takes me three climbs to get all 50 pounds up that hill and delivered. I'm already exhausted as I slip and slide back to the bike. I need a moment. I sit on the bike with my water and look around at the scenery. It is a beautiful Region. Poppi jumps on her bike and pedals away from me. I put the water away and get moving.

The bakery is about half a kilometer away. I park the bike and lift the flour in front of me. I get to the side door, trip over the curb I didn't see and smash the flour bag into a water spigot on the side of the building. The bag bursts and covers the sidewalk and me in flour. The manager, along with Poppi, comes out and starts laughing. He says I have to hose down the sidewalk where the flour is spilled and, of course, he won't accept my flour. I'll have to go back and get another bag to deliver before the judge will clear this delivery. I get up to try to brush myself off, then start hosing down the sidewalk. Poppi gives me a smirky little taunting smile as she gets on her bike.

Once the sidewalk is clean, I decide to proceed to my next delivery before going back for the bag of flour. Gryggerikeren Restaurant is just around the block. I pedal over to the restaurant. The manager tells me I have to come in to empty the bag of onions into a large bin. The kitchen is hot. The areas without floor mats are slippery. I find the bin and try opening the top of the onion bag but it won't come loose. I grab a cutter and cut into the mesh bag. I set the cutter down and lose my balance on the slimey floor. The bag breaks completely open with onions flying everywhere. I have to spend a lot of time running around the kitchen picking up onions and depositing them in the bin. I can't even remember how many times I slip and fall on this damn wet floor. The falls are taking their toll. My body is starting to ache.

The resort is a kilometer away. The weather has turned. There is a light, drizzling rain now. I'm cold and even more wet. Once I pull into the back of the resort parking area, I see that it also sits at the top of a small hill. There is no way I can carry that wheel of cheese up this hill. My heart sinks. With the cold, the wet and knowing that I still have to go all the way back for another sack of flour, I'm feeling very defeated. However, I only take a moment to feel sorry for myself. I can't let my journey stop here. Somehow, I've got to change my attitude and get determined.

I take a deep breath. I lay the wheel of cheese in front of me on the ground and inch my way up the hill. I may be moving very slowly but I'm getting there. I finally make it to the top and lift the cheese off the ground. One of my hands slips off the smooth wheel. It drops to the ground, then rolls all the way down the hill and lands against the fence. Noooooooooooo! I'm angry now and hastily start to make my way back down the hill but, of course, I slip and roll down the hill too. At the bottom, I lie there for a minute. Everything is aching. A security guard runs over and helps me up.

"Are you alright?" he asks searching my face.

"I think so," I reply with tears stinging my eyes. My thigh and back are very sore and I'm moving much more slowly, but I seem to be unharmed. I get up to repeat the process only this time, when I get the cheese up the hill, I don't lift it, but instead roll it to the back door. Only then do I pick it up. I hand it to the manager then make my way down the hill once again.

I return to the starting point and get another bag of flour. It's dark now. I slowly pedal the three kilometers back to the bakery. I'm exhausted, soaked to the bone, and can barely lift this bag of flour because I'm so sore. But I must fulfill my duty.

On the way back to drop off the bike at the starting point, I try to increase my speed and get a pretty good clip going. Another vehicle doesn't see me and swings close in front of me. I swerve to avoid the collision but hit a pothole in the road. The bike jerks to the right out of control slamming into the post of a wooden fence. I flip over the handle bars to the ground but my delivery bag with all my delivery receipts flies up in the air. I pick myself up off the ground searching myself for blood but there is none, thankfully. However, everything hurts. When I finally look over at the bike, I see that the handlebars are crooked, the frame is damaged, the chain is off and hanging on its spindle.

Then I spy my delivery bag with all the receipts through the fence. It's laying in a very large mud puddle. I stretch to grab it but it's just out of my reach. I climb on the fence and lift a leg over. I get my balance and start to lift the other one over but then the fence wiggles under my weight and I fall into the mud. My breath catches as I sink knee deep in the freezing cold mud. When I come out of my shocked state, I snatch up that delivery pouch and hurl it over the fence where I see it land near the bike.

I am furious! I want to scream but don't have the energy. It will take everything I have to struggle out of this mud. I begin to pull and pull but it's got me trapped like cement. I finally wiggle close enough to the fence where I can grab it if I lay across the mud with my upper half. I pull my legs free and climb back over the fence. The rain has stopped but I can barely move.

After a few minutes, I pull myself up, pick up the bike and walk it the entire way back for the two or so kilometers to the starting point. I fling my delivery pouch into the marked bin then turn for the journey back to the camp. The thought of going to group camp knowing I will walk in last looking like a muddy rat stops me in my tracks.

I am beat up, bruised and tired. I'm moving at a snail's pace. I don't want to talk to anyone, and I definitely don't want anyone to see me like this. I decide to move away from the road to walk through the woods, but it doesn't take long before the cold sinks deeply in and I start shivering. My body aches all over and it hurts to move. I don't think I can take another step as I lean against a nearby tree.

My thoughts get the better of me and I crumble in a heap to the ground. I have no energy. I don't think I can make it back to camp. I begin to sob softly into my muddy arm. Maybe I should just sleep here. One thing I do know is I'm last, I'm lost and I'm not sure if I will get to the checkpoint in time tomorrow.

"Hey," it's spoken so softly.

I look up to see Archer kneeling next to me. I tuck my head back in my arm. I don't want to see or talk to him either.

"C'mon," he says as he tries to help me up but I let out a small gasp from the pain of it. Every muscle in my body is screaming.

"I can't," I whimper.

"Are you hurt? Can you move?" There is deep concern in his voice.

"I'm not injured, but, yes, my entire body aches," I tell him in a very short and curt voice.

He reaches out and lifts me in his arms.

"Please," I beg leaning my head on his shoulder. "Don't take me to the camp like this. Let me just sleep here."

He doesn't say anything. He carries me to the train station in silence and sits me on a bench while he purchases tickets. I don't know where we are going and I don't care. He can take me to hell and I wouldn't be able to do anything about it.

He helps me onto the train where there are no seats left. A gentleman gets up to let me have his spot. Archer sits me down and gives the man a male "thank you" nod and stays close. There are two young women sitting not far from us. They look pristine and perfect as they give us a good looking-over. They are smiling and eye flirting with Archer. When they look at me, they whisper to each other in their language and laugh.

I turn away from them and find myself hunched over trying to "hide" from them. My hair is a ridiculous glob of mud sitting on top of my on my head, I am wet and completely smeared from head to toe in brown muck. I just had my ass busted on that task and right now, I only want to get off this train and bury my head in the sand. Archer says something to them in their language. Of course he knows their language. He seems to know everything.

As if reading my mind, he leans close and whispers "people will always come to conclusions and assumptions. They will judge you whether you are covered in mud or looking your finest. It is up to you to decide what kind of effect you allow them have on you."

The train rolls in to the station. Archer nudges my shoulder to communicate that we are disembarking. I glance over at the two women before I get off the train and they look very sheepish. I turn to Archer. "What did you say to them?"

"I told them that if they had to walk in your shoes today, they may not so easily condemn."

I let out a small laugh. "You're always so perfect, aren't you?"

"I've never known a perfect person," he answers.

The weather outside has turned extremely cold. I begin shivering immediately. This station is in the middle of nowhere. A few other buildings are all I see. It's starting to sprinkle. Archer leads me to a bench then disappears. He returns a few minutes later with a fully loaded wagon being led by a horse. A man is on the front perch of the wagon but there is only a few inches of room at the very back. Archer helps me to the wagon. I embarrassingly stumble but Archer lifts me and carries me the rest of the way. He places me on the back of the it and covers me completely with a wool horse blanket then jumps up next to me. I've never been in a wagon pulled by a horse before. This place must be far off the grid. I thought these types of vehicles were only for special events that boast old fashioned hay rides. Apparently, they really exist for real uses.

We ride for a while, and there is nothing but cold hard ground on this trail. Every lurch is painful torture. The wind cuts right through me, but I haven't the energy or inclination to complain. I just wish it were over.

We pass a barn and the wagon stops in front of an old stone house. It looks cold initially, but then I notice a yellow glow coming from the front window. That could be a very good indication that it's warm inside. I try to move but the effort is agonizing so I progress very slowly. Archer pays the driver then picks me up and carries me to the door. He knocks with his foot.

A large stocky woman opens the door. She's almost as tall as Archer and quite the formidable figure. Her graying hair is pulled back tightly. She is wearing a rustic shirt and skirt, covered by an equally rustic apron.

"What's this?" she asks gruffly in broken English. She has not moved aside to let us in.

Archer takes a deep breath. "She's had a rough day, Ruby."

"What did you do to her?" she asks still without moving to let us in.

"She's a racer. It just wasn't her day." He adds, "she's in need of a bath, a warm fire, some of your herbal tea, and by the way, we could use a room for the night."

She looks us both over and then turns to walk back inside without saying anything.

Archer walks in behind her. The house smells very inviting, like flowers and herbs and cinnamon. Best of all, it's warm.

"Set her there," she says without looking at us but her head nods to the large wooden table with heavy wooden chairs surrounding it. She barks some commands in her language to three young housemaids and they run up the stairs. She continues walking into the kitchen at the back of the home. Archer lowers me into a chair at the table.

He kneels next to me and whispers, "Ruby's a little..." his head bobbles as he seems to be searching for the right word, "crusty, but she can help you. Just do everything she says. I know we don't know each other very well yet but please trust me on this." I look at his face. He seems so very sincere, so I agree. I really don't have much choice. I can't move very quickly right now and I'm a guest in this woman's home.

He stands up as Ruby walks back over and roughly sets a cup of tea in front me splashing a little of it on the table. She's rather scary. She doesn't take her eyes off Archer. He seems so unaffected. He almost has a twinkle in his eye. Then he mentions, "About the room…"

"She'll have a room. You get the barn. Now go on," she nods toward the door.

He leans over to me and whispers, "I'll be in the barn if you need anything."

"She won't be needin' anything you have to offer, you horny bastard," she blurts out and flips her hand at him to shoo him out the door. I look at her in amazement, totally embarrassed, and then look at Archer who has his lips locked tightly together and is clearly trying to hold back his laughter. He turns to go to the door, opens it, looks back and smiles at me.

"Drink your tea," she demands.

I take a sip and gag immediately.

"Nobody said it was going to taste good. But you're not going up to bed until you drink down that whole cup," she threatens.

I hear Archer laughing as he closes the door.

I down it in a few gulps, gagging involuntarily after each.

I stand up letting the horse blanket fall to the floor and try to make my way to the stairs. I stumble to the ground as I reach them.

"Here now," Ruby says and helps me up. She walks me upstairs to a large bedroom where the three girls have been busy. There is a healthy fire going in the fireplace and a large tub filled with steaming water in front of it along with some other buckets. Ruby says something to them. They quickly run over and begin taking off my muddy clothes then help me into the tub. One of the girls leans me backward and picks up a bucket. She pours the warm water over my head into a smaller tub. It feels wonderful as it flows from my head into a waiting basin. After a few clearing buckets, she works a good lather into my hair and gently massages my head. She rinses with another two buckets of water.

Ruby hovers over me and gently begins scrubbing the rest of my body.

"Tell me about what happened to ye, today," she says in her accented English.

I sigh. "There's not much to tell, I failed miserably and came in last."

Ruby glances at me, "Let's hear all about it then."

As Ruby scrubs my arms and back, I tell her my whole sad story. Then I finish with, "Honestly, I don't even know how Archer found me under that tree in the dark."

"One thing I know, Archer is very good at what he does. You couldn't have a better partner." She pauses for a moment and seems deep in thought, then adds "You best not tell him this, but he's the only man in the whole world that I trust completely."

I smile. High praise indeed from this "crusty" lady. I wonder how they met.

"Are you going to give up?" she asks.

"I can't give up," I say softly and shrug my shoulders. "Not only have I been waiting my whole life for this race, but my brother is counting on me. His life is in my hands now to get the surgery he needs." Tears threaten as I think about him, but I hold them back. "I was truly humbled by what happened today. I've always done so well in all of my competitions. I didn't think anything could stop me. I thought I had all the answers. But I found out today that I'm not so great and I'm not as strong as I thought. I need help from others and I'm just as vulnerable as anybody else."

Ruby looks at me.

"There's never any use in dwelling on failures."

"That's just it, Ruby. I've never failed so miserably before. When I was sitting under that tree covered in mud and barely able to move, I realized a few things about myself. In the past, when I've had setbacks, I've always leaned on my family to tell me how great I am and pick me up afterward. Sometimes, I would find other people on whom to blame my problems or the circumstances weren't perfect. But today, I realized the competition is very formidable. All these people are very good. So many people are depending on me but I'm not so confident now," I confide.

"You have to reach deep down to find the strength to get through whatever comes your way. You can't depend on anyone else to come to your rescue. You must find a way to move forward," she says under her breath.

I agree with her. She must have been through a lot during her lifetime and learned a great many lessons.

The girls help me stand and then rinse me with another two buckets of steamy water. It's wonderful. I do feel somewhat more alive than I did when I came here.

They wrap me in toweling and sit me in front of the vanity. One of the girls starts combing out my hair while the others roll the tub and buckets out of the room.

A few minutes later, one of the girls and Ruby return with a canister of something, another cup of tea and a small tray of fruit, crackers and cheeses.

I nibble lightly on the offerings trying to avoid the tea.

Once my hair is finished, they have me stand up. They take the toweling away and start rubbing me down with some kind of white ointment that is in the canister. It applies smoothly and has a wonderful, herbal scent with cinnamon, like the house smelled when I first walked in.

They finish covering me with the salve, then pull the sheerest silk white nightgown that I have ever seen over my head. I look in the mirror and can see my entire body through this garment. They turn down the bed and have me climb in. The bedding is cool and so cozy. They cover me with a fluffy down-filled comforter. This is heaven. Ruby walks over with the tea.

"I'm not leaving until you finish this," she says handing me the cup.

I'm so tired. I just want to go to sleep. I take the cup and down the now cooled tea in one shot, shuddering afterwards. I hand the cup back to her.

"Nissy here will be back to sleep by the fire in case you need anything." She flips her head toward the girls. Nissy gives me a curtsy of acknowledgment. I smile back at her.

I wake up to the aroma of coffee and bacon. Soft yellow ambient light burns through the window. I stretch and sit up. I don't know if Nissy ever returned. I'm assuming she did because she was supposed to. I don't even remember them leaving the room. I slept very well.

I see my clothes, washed, pressed and folded neatly on the dresser. There is a bowl and towel on the vanity and it looks like a pitcher of water by the fire. Nissy walks in and smiles.

"How are ye feeling, Miss," she asks as she walks to the fire, picks up the pitcher and pours the steaming water into the bowl.

I move my arms and twist gently around. "Better," I respond astonished. I'm actually amazed at how much better I feel. None of my muscles ache at all. That tea and white salve are things of miracles. "I do need to go to the 'girl's room' though," I add.

"Of course, Miss," Nissy replies and opens a door that I thought was most likely a closet. The only thing inside is a toilet and toilet paper. It is made of stone and looks like it was cut right out of the wall. There are windows lining the top of the room. However, it is as cold as it looks so I waste no time in there.

I get dressed then Nissy twists my hair into a loose rope braid down my back. She is quite talented.

"I wish I could I do my hair the way you do it," I say to her. She blushes.

"You are so pretty, Miss," she mentions. I blush.

I can hear Archer teasing Ruby about something as I walk downstairs. They seem to be old friends. I peek around the corner. Archer is leaning on the kitchen countertop next to Ruby. She is laughing and pretending to get upset when he "steals" a piece of bacon from the pile. He looks so at ease, causally smiling and truly happy. I think this is the first time I've ever seen him this way.

"Good morning, Miss," one of the other girls says.

"Good morning," I answer as I walk into the full view of the room.

Archer stands and walks over to me.

"How are you feeling?" he asks; his mood light.

"So much better," I say sitting down at the table. There is a bowl of fruit in the middle of it.

"It's amazing what a good night's rest can do for you," he answers as he picks an apple and tosses it in the air.

Ruby sets a cup of tea in front of me. She's carrying a wooden spoon with bits of cooked egg on it. "You'll be drinking this before you walk out that door."

"Do I really have to?" I ask.

Archer lifts his eyebrows while sucking in air between clenched teeth in an "oh, no" kind of way.

"You must be feeling loads better with all that cheek you're giving this morning. Now you'll have two cups and one for the Archer as well," she says as she matter-of-factly nods to the girls to get a cup for Archer.

Archer looks at me, turns his hands up and shrugs with a funny "what are you doing" look on his face. I couldn't help but laugh.

"Bring that one the oatmeal," Ruby barks with a flip of her head toward me.

The girls set a bowl of oatmeal in front of me. It looks like it has local cloudberries, bilberries and some kind of nuts in it. I've never had cloudberries before so I'm hesitant but take a small bite. It tastes quite good. I'm so happy. Visions of horrible tea-flavored oatmeal were giving me the willies.

They set a big plate of bacon, eggs and pancakes in front of Archer which he wastes no time putting his fork into.

"We need to go as soon as you're ready. We are much farther north than the other teams right now, since we did our traveling last night, but they'll be making their way up here fairly soon," Archer says between bites.

I agree and drink down the tea. I cough and cover my mouth as I gag but I get it down. Once I finish the oatmeal, Nissy gives me a drink of water. I am grateful for her kindness.

Archer and I stand up and tie on our scarves since the weather has turned. Ruby is by the door. I can see through the window that there is a very cold wind picking up with snow flurries blowing around. "Take the buggy," she tells Archer. "Greta will ride with you to bring it back."

Archer smiles and gives her a peck on the cheek. "You're a gem, Ruby," he says.

"Get your nasty arse out of here," she grins.

I hug her. "Thank you so much, Ruby," I say standing on my tip toes to kiss her on the cheek too.

Once outside and the door is closed behind us, Archer turns to me, "How are you, really?" he asks seriously.

"I am so much better. Thank you for bringing me here. That tea and rub are miraculous."

"You got the rub too, eh?" Archer asks while pulling on his brown leather gloves, "There's nothing better. It really is miracle stuff."

I smile my agreement. "How was your night? It must have been cold in the barn."

"The back of the barn has a sizeable room with some beds for the field hands and other workmen. It's not fancy but it's clean and one can take a shower. There's a nice large central fireplace along with a generous stock of food and ale. I was perfectly comfortable, I assure you."

Greta brings the buggy and we make our way back to the train station.

At the checkpoint, I find that I came in second. Archer was right, our travels last night helped put us at the top of the pack. Ang was the first to check in and was enjoying some refreshment when I walked into the commuter.

He said that almost everyone last night got to the campsite in a sorry state and could barely move. He boasts with an egotistical flip of his head and snide grin that he decided to get a jump on everyone and head out last night while they were all sleeping.

Does he not realize that I'm his competition and he basically just told me that he is a sneaky bastard?

CHAPTER 10

Mocombo

We are lined up at the starting point, facing each other behind automatic barricades. I can see each one of my toughest rivals. The top group, which includes me, is now wearing a red emblem on our shirts. The next group is wearing an orange emblem and the bottom group is wearing yellow.

There are three countdown clocks. One is red for the first team, the red group, to be released; the second is orange for the orange group and the third yellow for the yellow group. I'm glad that everyone was as sore as I was at the end of the last task. At least I had the benefit of a Ruby and an early start the next morning to reach the finish line before most of the others got there.

I quickly look around to assess who got eliminated. I don't see Lyron from Region 9. Another guy. That's interesting.

When the red clock hits zero, the orange group gets released. All of us in the red group practically run into our barricades. The orange group stands there for a second, dumbfounded, then takes off. We are pounding on the barricades to no avail. The yellow group is laughing. The red clock resets to 15 minutes. I'm only going to be 15 minutes behind; I can catch up.

At the end of the second fifteen-minute period, the gates for the yellow group open and they take off while we watch until the last of them are out of sight. What the hell? At the end of the next fifteen-minute period, our doors still don't open and the clocks shut off. Are they having a technical issue? The clock restarts with 120 minutes on it. Two hours? I am going to be two and a half hours behind the orange group?

It's infuriating. That means we have to work twice as hard to fight our way out of the back and get to the checkpoint on time. They told us about switch ups and changes. I guess you just never know what is going to happen.

When we are finally released, I am still fuming. I am moving at a slow jog as a form of protest.

Archer joins me later in the day and asks what happened. In my frustration, I bark my answer at him. He leisurely strolls beside me in silence making me feel bad for treating him like that. I look over at him.

"I'm sorry I was a jerk. I'm just frustrated. Now I have to work twice as hard to get my place back. Why would they do that?" I question half to myself.

"Perhaps it's a test," he says. "Consider why they would put the top group at the back of the pack to claw their way out. Wouldn't it be just another way to prove your worth? The orange group gets a chance to lead, why not see what they can do in that position. The yellow, who have been last, may be more motivated with the opportunity to pass the leaders."

Ugghh! I hate when he makes a good point. I turn away from him and roll my eyes. He drives me insane with his logic. I know better than to respond because he would just hit me in the face with some more of his proverbial wise words. I bite my tongue and pick up my pace. He is right, and I know it. If this is another test for me, I need to perform rather than pout. Everything depends on my winning. It will be my own fault if I lose. I can't do that to Colson.

"The good news is," he continues, "I know a few shortcuts." I quickly look over at him. He steers us onto a foot path along the far left of the road leading behind some brush.

After a while, we cut to a more wooded area. When we get to the middle of it, there is a giant hole in the ground. It's very dark, I can't see into it. From one of the trees hangs a rope that disappears into the black hole. Wait, does he expect me to climb down into that abyss? My mind begins to race. I'm not very good with heights. My heart starts pounding as anxiety begins to set in. Everything starts running through my mind such as how deep is that? Are there bats? I'm already annoyed and extremely frustrated. This is not helping my foul temper.

Archer rummages around a very large tree that sits at the edge of this hole and pulling at some vines wrapping around it. The way it hangs off the side, the tree looks like it's about to fall into that hole. Archer locates and drags out another rope that has a slat of wood tied around the bottom. He pulls on it then brings it over to me as he holds it.

"Step on this," he says.

"Why?" I ask rhetorically. I know he's going to want to lower me down on that thing.

"This will take us down. It's a faster and a far better route to Biamong. We can catch up to the lead group and maybe even get ahead," he says.

I knew it.

"What's down there? How deep is it? What if I fall?" I question.

He looks at me. "It's deep. But please trust me. You're not going to fall. I'm not going to let anything happen to you."

"How are you going to get down?" I want to know how this is going to work.

"I'm going to ride with you."

"On this? Both of us?" I'm skeptical. "This doesn't look like it can hold both us. How are we going to get down there then? Climb?"

He stares at me for a moment with a disbelieving look. I guess he doesn't get questioned much but I gave my last idiot partner way too much freedom with decisions and it almost cost me this opportunity.

"This is a counter-weighted pulley system. It will not move with just your weight on it. You're not heavy enough. Once I step onto it, it will descend. Please trust me. I wouldn't do anything to cause you harm."

"How do you know how much weight is on the other end?" I ask.

I can hear some of the other teams that were behind us. They must be getting closer.

"We really don't have time for this," Archer replies in his more stern man voice as his arm wraps around my waist and tightens. He lifts me easily up and pulls me in front of him. His chest is against my back while the rope is against my face. He quickly steps completely onto the slat and we begin to descend gently down. I exhale loudly at his arrogance but bite my tongue and grab onto the rope. He sets me down so my feet are on top of his. There isn't much room on the slat so this is a very cozy yet irritating ride.

The cave is very dark but as we get lower, light starts peeking through an opening way off to our left. There is a rumbling noise that gets louder as we descend. When we get to the bottom and the slat is firmly on the ground, Archer reaches up with his free arm and pulls down some on the rope. He lets go of me and grabs the rope with both hands.

"Step off," he says blandly.

I step off. He uses both arms to pull the rope down even more. When he steps off the slat his arm muscles bulge as they bear the burden of the counter weight. He lets go of the rope and the slat makes a very quick ascent back to the top. Archer doesn't say a word but just steps in front of me and leads the way to the opening.

Okay. So maybe I should apologize because I was actually being the arrogant one and he knew what he was talking about; again. I don't know why I have such a hard time listening to him. I guess because of my previous experience, I just don't like going into a situation unless I know exactly what I'm getting into. Honestly, I've never had to before. My life is so different from this. I'm usually in control of what I'm doing or getting ready to do. Granted, I'm not on some journey around the world in my everyday life, but I'm a bright girl and I'm usually in control of where I go and what I do. Maybe I need to adjust my attitude.

As we get closer, I can see that the opening is actually quite large. The rumbling sound gets louder and louder and the air is getting much more humid. The ground below is damp and turning into a rocky foundation. When we get to the opening, I see a vast waterfall. The rocks below us are getting slippery. Archer turns around and holds out his hand to me. I grab it and he pulls me up next him. He keeps me near as we make our way out of the cave.

Once we emerge from the cave, I look across to the other side of the mountain. I gasp at its majesty. Torrents of white foamy water gush over the side of it for as far as I can see. I hold my breath at its beauty. The mist is so thick that I have no idea how far the falls descend down. Archer looks at me and lets out a small chuckle. He puts his hand on my lower back and nudges me forward. I guess we are going closer.

The thunderous sound of the falls is deafening and the spray from them is very heavy. Archer holds my hand to lead me to a small foot bridge near the base of the rocks where we can cross over the gorge. It passes close to the front of the falls. They are so magnificent. I have to stop for just a moment and take it all in. We stand there in the middle of that bridge getting absolutely soaked by the spray of those awesome falls. It is amazing. We look at each other and grin. I'm overwhelmed. I've never experienced anything like this before. I turn to Archer, lift my arms around him and hug him. I feel his arms close around my back as he embraces me. I'll never forget this moment. It is so beautiful. I can't thank him enough for bringing me here and letting me see this.

By the time we get to the other side, we are completely drenched from head to toe. Our clothes are clinging to us. I look at Archer ahead of me. What a view it is. He turns and holds out his hand to help me navigate the wet rocks. Water is dripping from his face and hair. I can see every muscle movement of his chest, back, arms and abs through his clinging shirt. Wow, what a man. He locates the path and we make our way across the side of the mountain.

CHAPTER 11

We are completely dry by the time we get to Biamong. As I look around, I realize there is really nothing here. I see maybe three old, archaic-looking, dilapidated buildings. We enter one of the buildings and I look out through the back window. It's a small airfield with a handful of ancient small planes that appear to have seen better days. I move to where Archer is talking with an attendant and stand next to him.

"Look me up, I'm certified," he is saying.

The attendant saunters behind the counter to his data device. We stand there for a moment waiting. I'm not sure why we're waiting.

"Okay, you're clear. We'll only need to take the girl in tandem," the attendant explains as Archer leads me over to a wall with some harnesses.

"She's going with me," Archer responds over his shoulder as he picks out a couple of harnesses.

"Sir," the attendant starts but Archer cuts him off.

"You just saw my level of clearance. I can take her," he proclaims as he pulls on his harness.

"Yes, sir," the attendant sighs and busies himself with something else.

Archer has me step into a harness. Then it dawns on me. The planes. The harnesses. We're going to jump. He pulls the harness up over my shoulders but I put my hand on his chest to stop him.

"Archer, no, no, no, no, I, I can't do this. I can't jump from a plane." I'm shaking my head while my knees start to get weak. I'm not prepared for this at all.

He lifts my chin to face him.

"Look at me," he says softly. His voice is soothing as I look up at him. "I will be with you. We will be hooked together. We will have a main chute and we will have a reserve chute. Please trust me. I won't let anything happen to you."

One of the attendants calls him over to talk with the pilot. I sit down on a nearby bench to stew about this jump. Every possible catastrophe goes through my mind. These are not even state-of-the-art air commuters; they are more like small old bush aircraft. I can't do this.

My heart is racing, my legs are bouncing, and tears begin rolling down my cheeks. By the time Archer turns back around to me, I'm a mess. He comes over, kneels in front of me and looks me in the eye. He exhales compassionately, reaches up and wipes a tear from my cheek with his thumb.

I fall into him and wrap my arms around his neck pushing my face in his shoulder. "Please don't make me do this," I sob into his ear. He wraps his arms around me and holds me close. I need that right now to feel safe here.

He continues to hold me, stroking my hair but he backs his face away from mine and gently says, "We have to do this, Lily. If there were another safe way into the basin, I'd take you that way. The only other way is through Cat Canyon but its four days to travel through there. Besides, you don't want to get eaten by lions, do you?"

I shake my head. I know he's only trying to help me.

"This is going to be easy. Please trust me."

I realize I'm not going to get out of this at all. I wipe my eyes and back out of Archer's arms. He stands me up and begins working on the task of clamping my harness together.

"I'm going to inspect the chutes, why don't you come with me?"

I can only nod. I'm so scared that I shadow closely to him like a puppy dog. He inspects and packs the chutes. This is something that takes a while. He's very thorough. I'm trying to stay calm but my nerves show through my prancing feet and fidgety arms. I don't want to cry again and seem like a crybaby so I focus on fighting it.

Once he puts the pack on, my heart starts pounding. We go out the door and start walking to the plane. There must be an inner me that knows I'm heading to my doom and resists my ability to walk. I stand almost frozen staring at the small plane. I swallow hard and I'm breathing faster.

Archer turns back to me and moves quickly to my side. He puts an arm around my waist and ushers me forward. I give him one last pleading look.

"I've got you," is all he says. There's no way around this!

Just as the plane takes off, I look out the window and see another team running to the airstrip. I think it's Kuzhan and Galina. Seeing them brings the reality of the race back in focus. Since I hate her for what she did to me at Kennett's Pass, I'm glad I'm ahead of her.

Once we're in the air and they open the door, I instinctually press my body against the side of the plane. Archer pulls me to him and places me in front of him clipping us together. Then he moves us to the opening. I'm frozen with fear.

"I've got you. I won't let you go; I promise."

He does everything. He puts the goggles over my eyes, lifts me to the side of the door, puts his hand across my forehead and presses my head back against his shoulder, then flips us out of that damn plane.

I scream and close my eyes. He lifts my arms straight out from my sides and holds my hands in his. Then something happens during that freefall. I can't scream anymore so I open my eyes and watch. I quickly realize how incredible this is. I don't think I'll ever volunteer to do it again, but while I'm here I might as well enjoy the ride.

Archer pulls the chute and we swing up higher then gently glide to the ground. He steers us around. I see the target landing spot just outside of a campsite. He takes us in perfectly and lands us on our feet. I hear another plane overhead.

When we take off all of our gear, he tilts his head at me. "Pretty amazing, huh?" he asks.

I give him a little "agreeing" smile as he leads me to the campsite. I sneak a look at him out of the corner of my eye. I'm beginning to realize that he's pretty amazing, too.

By nightfall, all the candidates have caught up at the camp site. A bonfire is going and most of us fall easily into conversation. Archer and the other Specialists busy themselves with the building of shelters. I can see he is just about finished but ask him if I can help anyway. He directs me to put the beds together. Once inside, I see the beds are already put together, they only need linens. I take care of it.

One thing I've noticed at the campsites, the Specialists seem to sometimes stand apart to some degree not even talking to each other. Well, I guess they do get together as a group and hang out especially the "allied" regions, but for the most part, they usually stay away from us and in the background. I wonder if it is just part of who they are.

Race attendants prepared a buffet for us. During dinner, I chat with other contestants. Many are still pumped up about the plane jump. I see that Archer and Langt have paired off more toward the outer areas. They seem to be laughing quite hard about something. I wonder what is so funny. I'd like to be a fly on the fence to hear what they are talking about. Those two are a couple of very handsome men. I smile. Their laughs are contagious.

I'm actually feeling rather tired and move to my shelter. My pack is lying next to my bed. I grab my toiletries and walk to the portable shower area. The water is cold but I don't mind. I get back to the shelter. Archer has done a nice job on it. He put the entrance on the side giving us a little more privacy. I like it.

I step in. He must have seen me coming this way because there is now a warm, inviting fire burning inside the small fire stove. I put my things away and comb out my freshly washed hair. My cot is set up along the far wall, away from the entrance.

I'm sitting on my cot reorganizing my toiletries when Archer makes an appearance.

"Hey, everything to your liking?"

"It's perfect. I should get some really good rest in prep for tomorrow's task."

He smiles while he grabs a few things and heads back out. I'm assuming to the showers. My suspicions are confirmed a short time later when he walks in wrapped in a towel with a wet head. I look up at his very fine body. Holy moly. The man is built. I turn away to give him some privacy while he gets dressed because he doesn't seem concerned about it.

A few moments later, I hear him lean back on the cot which can barely accommodate his long frame.

"Can I ask you something?"

He looks over at me with raised brows inviting a question.

"Do you have a name? I mean, a real name? What do the superiors of the temple call you?" I wonder.

He raises the corners of his mouth in a smile. "Right now? The Archer," he says amused but then adds, "Things are different at the temple. My parents gave me the name Arek."

"Arek," I let it roll off my tongue. "I like that."

"I'm glad you approve," he laughs.

"Do you remember your last name?" I ask.

"Yes," is all he says.

"Will you tell me?"

He looks at me and says, "Akecheta."

"Akecheta?" I ask rhetorically. I try to sound it out more slowly, "Ahka-Chayta."

He rolls to his side to adjust his pillow a bit higher.

"What was it like growing up in the temple? I couldn't imagine not being with my parents when I was a small child."

"Things are very different," he's playing with a string he pulled off his pillow as he talks.

"How do little kids train to be assassins?"

He looks at me very thoughtfully. Did I overstep my boundaries? Maybe I shouldn't have called him a killer to his face. I look away from him in shame.

"They don't exactly tell you from the start that you will one day be required to kill someone," he says with humor in his tone. I look back at him. His eyebrows are lifted and I see a glint in his eye, so I feel better.

He takes a breath and leans forward. "Training begins immediately, but in forms children understand. For example, everyone has chores. The little ones do little things like setting tables and running errands. But once a male turns 10, his loads begin to get heavier. This builds strength and our bodies grow very strong. We train in the form of games. To win, you must be very fast and very flexible. Most of all, you have to have quickness in the mind. Each game is played in a different language so you also have to understand what is being said in order to win. As you get older, the training becomes much more physically demanding."

"That's genius," I say.

He continues, "In the evenings, we are taught lessons by the great masters. They are usually in the form of stories when we are small and then we learn more hands-on strategic war games as we grow. Of course, we also have our studies." He lays back.

"How do you get so proficient with knives and things?"

"Even as small children, we have weapons in our hands. When we are young, they are not lethal, merely sticks or blow guns, but they must be with us always. As we grow, we have some form of weapon in our hands at most all times. It is how they become an extension of us. We almost feel incomplete without them at our fingertips. It's the same for most temples. We are raised to fulfill a certain purpose."

"Is it always about fighting?"

"Actually, no. Our main goal is preventing widespread violence and senseless slaughter. We are trained as we are to protect. We are a line of defense to prevent war so people like you don't have to fight those prone to violence or those who decide they want to rule the world." He looks at me and smiles. I must be looking at him like a pathetic little puppy.

"Please save your pity for me and the other Specialists. While we did not choose this life, we do have genuine purpose," he smiles.

"Is it difficult to kill people?" I almost whisper. He's quiet for a moment and takes a deep breath.

"Everything has a process, but the process has its flaws. For example, to save a life, there is another that is not saved. But sometimes, in killing one you save hundreds, maybe thousands. In the matter of kill or be killed, you really don't think too much about it. The question is never, 'am I going to die or how do I kill this guy?' The question is, 'how do I find and exploit his weakness in order to hinder his advancement'."

"What if there isn't a weakness?" I'm curious. I don't think Archer has a weakness.

"Everyone has a weakness. Once you engage in battle with someone, you find it quickly. If you don't, you'll have plenty of time to consider it while recovering," he adds quietly.

"How old were you the first time you killed someone?" I asked, then added, "It's okay if you'd rather not answer. You know, if it's too personal."

"I was thirteen."

"Thirteen? My gosh that's so young," I say appalled.

"Way too young," he says. "As a sort of rite of passage, boys who exhibit great promise during their thirteenth year are allowed to accompany a small group of Masters on a mission. I had earned a spot early that year because of my accomplishments. I sat in on all the mission briefings. I knew exactly what they would be up against and all the details. As it turned out, I went on a mission with one of my favorite mentors. He was Dea Master at the time. He has long since moved up into higher areas. They left me some distance from the mission's actual entry point where I was to sit and wait. It could've been hours or days. One never knows how long a mission will take. I was resigned to set up camp, hunt for food and sit tight. But after only 30 or so minutes, the Dea Master appeared and motioned for me to follow him. He brought me to the mission entry point. It was clear that a grown man could not fit into the entry opening. I realized I would be the one to take on this mission. I looked at the Dea Master and acknowledged my understanding. They quickly replaced my training blades with real ones and fit me with a wrist bow along with two lethal darts. Just before I was to go through, the Dea Master stopped me and broke the protocol of silence to whisper three words in my ear. Those three words have been my driving force since that moment."

"What were the words?" I ask amazed at this story.

"You. Are. Capable." He smiles.

"Wow! So, what happened?" I wanted him to continue.

"I found the target and eliminated the threat using lethal force." He shrugs nonchalantly. "When I came back and bowed to the Dea, he patted my shoulder." He chuckles thoughtfully. "You know, he still does. Whenever I see him, usually at some kind of fight, at the end of it, he will walk by and pat me on the shoulder. I guess it's his way of telling me I did well."

"That's really sweet," I say.

He continues, "From then on, I did not return to the training housing for juveniles. I was, from that moment forward, considered part of the junior elite. I was ranked as an A master, trained with the men's elite group and participated in missions."

"Were you the only juvenile?"

"No, there was a handful of us at the time. I was the youngest at thirteen. The others were fifteen through eighteen."

"So, you've been terminating people since then. Wow, that's an amazing story."

He's thoughtful for a few minutes, then adds, "Please understand me when I say killing is a last resort. Can we do it? Yes. But more often than not, we try to find other ways to keep the peace before resorting to any kind of assassination. Sometimes it's just a matter of helping someone misplace a piece of paper or deleting plans or instructions," he smiles.

"I like that," I respond and I mean it. It's nice to know that they go in with a peaceful plan but can make a change if it turns ugly.

He stands and walks out. I lie down and face the fire. I turn my thoughts to my own battles. They may not be life and death for me, but if I don't win, it will be like death to me because I'm essentially condemning Colson to a short life. Then I wonder, after all of this, how can I possibly return to the same life, the same people and the same home with nothing to show from my journey?

CHAPTER 12

I wake up as the sun is rising. Archer is gone, as usual. I smell the aroma of coffee and think that maybe it's later than I thought. I step outside and look around. Pink and purple paint the sky; light enough to see. I notice a small group of girls, some are contestants but some are race attendants gathered behind some trees in the distance. Curious, I sneak closer to find out what's happening.

I locate an opening and look through. There, in the clearing, are all the male Specialists. They are wearing some form of loose pants with no shirts. Espada is leading them in yoga-like stretches. I see Archer with his blonde hair and amazing body.

In their current stretch, they have a leg extended to the right while balancing their weight on the bent left leg then they slowly shift so the leg positions change in one fluid slow motion. One arm moves as though pulling a bow straight back and extending the other arm then bending backwards so the arm is pointing straight up. They come back to center, make a circular movement with their arms and do the same arrow stance using their other arm. Their backs, abs and arm muscles are clearly visible with the smoothness of the stretch.

I don't see the women Specialists anywhere. Maybe they have their own morning routine as well.

They continue with various bending and stretching exercises. Wow! Their male forms are beautiful to watch. It's hypnotic and soothing. They are so visibly strong. The final move is some kind of bending and twisting on one leg. They have to hold it for a period of time. Their muscles bulge from the strain. They start gritting their teeth and groaning from the pain of it. When Espada releases the move, they all breathe out and stand. They smile, slap or shake hands and congratulate each other and their instructor on the excellent morning routine.

All of us females disperse immediately so we don't get caught gawking like fan girls. I wonder if they do that every morning. Being who they are, I'm sure they knew they were being watched, but hopefully they don't know exactly who was watching them. I'll definitely try to catch that again.

***

When we get to the task, Archer and I see a sign saying: "TEAM HURDLE". We exchange glances and move closer.

There are several tables set up but there is a panel hiding the assignment behind it. There is a sign on each panel that reads: NAME YOUR POISON – SPECIALISTS MUST BE BLINDFOLDED BEFORE VIEWING THE TASK. ONE ITEM FROM EACH OF THE THREE CATEGORIES MUST BE INGESTED BY THE SPECIALIST.

Archer and I look at each other again. He raises his eyebrows. An attendant comes over and blindfolds him then removes the panel that was hiding the items.

I see a Task Card and read it to Archer. "THERE ARE THREE DIFFERENT STAGES TO COMPLETE. EACH STAGE HAS THREE ITEMS IN IT."

He says, "Go to the first stage and describe it to me."

I move to the first one. "There are three small glasses filled with colorless liquid. The note in front reads, 'One is a deadly poison. The other two will induce a heavy 30-minute coma."

"Hold each one up to my nose so I can smell them," he instructs.

I hold the first one to his nose. He inhales. He nods. I hold the second one to his nose. After a moment, he nods. I hold the third one to his nose, after another moment, he moves back.

"I'll drink the first one," he asserts.

"I'm scared," I say in a squeaky voice.

He smiles. "I'm not. Place it in my hand."

I give it to him and he drinks it. He holds the glass out and I take it from him. I just watch him expecting him to fall into a coma.

"Should you lie down?" I ask.

He smiles again, "No, I'll be fine. Let's go to the next one."

I stare at his blindfolded face for a moment. Why isn't he dead or comatose?

I move to the next set of choices.

"There are three small bowls full of red berries," I tell him. "The card says, 'one is deadly, one is hallucinogenic and one will induce a very long sleep'."

He exhales heavily. "Describe the berries to me."

"The first bowl is full of berries that are plump and squishy." I poke at one of the berries.

"Do they have black at the tops?"

"No," I answer after inspecting. "They are completely red."

"Are they round or oval?"

"Round," I answer.

He continues, "What's in the next one?"

"These are very small. They have a little yellow speck at the top."

He nods. "What's in the next one?"

"They are oval and very firm. All red," I say anticipating his questions.

"What size are they?"

"Medium size. They are not small but they are not as big as the first berries."

"How big is the bowl?" he asks.

"It's a finger bowl size, maybe a little bigger. About 2 inches high by 3 inches wide."

He inhales then exhales slowly. "Listen to me very carefully. In about five minutes, I'm going to go into a hallucinogenic state. It will last for several hours. I will be able to function somewhat but I will seem very off balance, ill and I won't be able to think clearly. This is going to slow our progress but at least we can move forward. You will need to take my hand and lead me from this place. Get a transport because we need to head northwest toward Meknes. We only have four hours to get there so move quickly.

"Okay," I acknowledge.

"Once I eat these berries, waste no time telling me about the next group."

"Okay," I agree.

"Give me the third bowl of berries."

I hand them to him and he downs them very quickly.

"There are three plates. It says these are Lachan village specialties one can be deadly, one can make you very sick and one is harmless. The first plate has two skewers of three scorpions each. The second has raw, sliced fish. The third is some kind of eyeballs."

"Give me the eyeballs." He's beginning to sway somewhat.

I hand him the dish while trying to steady his body. He gulps them down very quickly and asks me for a drink of water.

The attendant gives me a large glass of water then takes the blindfold off Archer. We are free to go. Archer is very slow. He blinks his eyes a number of times after drinking the entire glass of water. I take his hand leading him outside. He sways and supports himself using the wall.

"Give me a moment," he says bending over with his hands on his knees.

"Are you alright? Why aren't you dead or in a coma?"

"Hail the commuter," he directs while breathing heavier than normal. Beads of sweat are forming along his brow.

I hail the commuter then help Archer to it. I give the driver directions and we head off. I take Archer's hand. He is beginning to sweat profusely now. His breathing is staggered. The driver keeps looking at us.

"Are you all right?" I ask. I'm really worried.

He dips his head slowly but doesn't say anything. He bends forward and places his elbows on his thighs. I feel terrible for him and lay my hand on his back. I can feel his body tense. His hands ball into fists. He's fighting it. Whatever it is.

After a while, he leans back in the seat. His eyes are shut then open. He's sweating, his breathing is somewhat labored although his face looks relaxed. He's like a superman or something. I stroke his hair in an effort to soothe him. He turns his face to me. His eyes roll. His head drops down on my shoulder. His eyes close. I continue to stroke his hair. His mouth is very close to mine. Our warm breaths mingle together. It would be a rather sexy moment, if he weren't drugged and drooling a bit.

Although we've been driving for a few hours, the driver keeps looking at us. "What's wrong with him?" he demands gruffly.

"He's sick," is all I can think to say.

He pulls over. "He's on drugs!" he yells as he opens the back door dragging Archer out of the car.

"No!" I scream. I don't know what Archer will do like this. I just know he's a very dangerous man.

The driver slaps Archer on the side of the head and throws him down. Archer opens his eyes. They look stormy and wild. He is on his feet in the quickest of moments. Like a flash he strikes the driver knocking him out cold. I grab at Archer. He is on me in an instant. He grabs me loosely by my throat. His head shakes briefly as though he can see glimpses through the fog but he still has me gripped by the throat.

"No!" I scream. "Archer, no!" I put my hands on his arms and begin to softly caress hoping that the gentle movements will ease his aggression.

He's breathing hard and looking at me with crazed eyes. I reach up and stroke the tresses of the long hair next to his ear. He closes his eyes then opens them dropping his hands from my throat. He shakes his head. He's looking through me and breathing hard.

I suddenly feel how wide my eyes are and try to relax them by rubbing my forehead.

Why the hell would they drug an assassin? Are they trying to kill the rest of us? He looks like a caged animal. He closes his eyes again then leans over with his hands on his knees. After a few moments, he stands up, opens his eyes and looks at me again then blinks a few times. His eyes begin to focus but he is swaying and leans, half bent over, back on the vehicle.

"Lily," his voice barely audible.

"Yes!" I squeal enthusiastically as tearful relief runs through my blood. "Yes, I'm Lily." I confirm again patting myself on the chest.

"Water," he manages to choke out.

I reach in the vehicle for the water. He drinks it quickly without stopping, dribbling some of it down his chin and onto his shirt.

"We have to go," he murmurs while trying to focus.

"You punched the driver." I point to the crumbled man.

"Is he…alright?" Archer stands, still very wobbly, but at least he's more lucid.

"Yes, you just knocked him out," I explain holding another water canister.

"Why? Did he try to hurt you?"

"No, he thought you were on drugs. Rightly so, I might add. He was trying to throw you out," I emphasize.

"I have to get him in the commuter," he says quietly. He stomps forward and lifts the man easily, but he is by no means steady on his feet. His balance is dreadful and I'm afraid he's going to hurt himself or the driver.

"Wait," I coax touching his arm. "Let's sit down for a moment. You're not well yet."

He sets the driver down on the ground and seats himself on the backseat leaning out of the commuter. He has his elbows on his knees while his hands hold his forehead.

This is the first time Archer looks even remotely vulnerable. I guess "vulnerable" is not correct because even stoned he had his wits together enough to deck someone who was aggressive without killing him or hurting me. He sits unsettlingly quiet for some time.

After about 10 minutes, he asks, "Can you drive?"

"I've never driven one of these, but I think I can handle it." I shrug as I look into the window at the controls.

"Let me get this guy in the vehicle. We have to move." As he pulls himself up, he seems much more coherent. "How long have I been out of it?"

"About 2 hours," I tell him.

"Is there anything you need to tell me?" he asks.

"No, everything was fine."

"Why do I feel something happened between us?"

"Okay, you turned on me for a moment, but you didn't hurt me," I affirm.

"What happened?"

I tell him the details and he walks over to me. He reaches out to inspect my neck by pressing it here and there then turning my head this way and that way.

"I'm fine, nothing hurts. You didn't hurt me. You held me very loosely." I love standing so close to him while he's essentially caressing my neck.

"I'm sorry, Lily," he says softly.

"You took the driver out with one quick blow," I say looking down at the unconscious man then back at Archer.

"He deserved it." He's half grinning but still swaying slightly. I put my hand on his chest to steady him.

He lays his hand on top of mine and looks down at me. "Can I get him in the car now," he asks. "Can we go?"

I slowly pull my hand away from his body and move to the other side of the vehicle. He hoists and tosses the driver in the back seat.

CHAPTER 13

Archer jumps out of the bed waking me immediately. He pulls on a shirt and shoes then grabs his bow and a full quiver of arrows.

"What is it?" I ask scrambling around for something, I don't know what. My heart is pounding from being jerked awake like that. One moment I was warm and cozy, and the next I'm sitting but still half asleep. My stomach is threatening to heave from the suddenness of it all.

Archer turns to me. I hear a clinking sound as he holds up two blades for me to see and lays them on the ground next to me. "Get dressed. Stay here. Do not leave this shelter." He's very stern. Something terrible must be happening. Archer looks at me for a lingering moment then runs out.

I hear a distant scream. I run over to the shelter flaps which are magnetically sealed and push them open so I can scan the campsite but I don't see anything. There are some lights in the distance. I let go of the flaps and can hear the clicks as the powerful magnets snap back together. I get dressed and sit on the edge of my cot very still as I wait. I hear people running outside. I stand at the door again and peer out but I still don't see anything. Lights are popping on in shelters all around me. I sit back down on the cot listening.

It's been a while and I start getting fidgety because it has become very quiet. I move to look outside but stop. I begin hearing animal noises and panting. I can hear sniffing and growling right outside the shelter. I freeze. We're in Mocombo and there are wild animals outside of my flimsy shelter. I'm terrified.

Since Archer has deserted me, I have to think quickly. I have some fire here and I can get under the cot but that won't provide much help if jagged teeth and claws are trying to maul me. I look around and spy the blades Archer left with me on the ground. That's some real help except that the animal would have to be close. I slip to the ground and push the cot very slowly and quietly against the flaps.

I hear more sniffing and a low, ominous growl. The animal seems to be pacing around the shelter. I hear another growl and more sniffing. I think another animal has joined it. Now there's scratching at the shelter. Archer, where are you?

I pick up the blades as quietly as I can. I hear more sniffing. I think the number of animals has increased. In fact, I'm sure of it. I can smell them now. They are making more animal noises and growls. They are probably communicating some nefarious plan to devour me.

Suddenly, I hear a yelp. Then another. Then another. Archer bursts through the flaps.

"C'mon," he insists holding out his hand. "I'll take those," his eyes dart to the blades. I give them to him then take his hand. He pulls me out of the shelter lifting me up into a waiting open air vehicle. I didn't even hear it pull up. I look around and see dead dogs everywhere.

"What is this?" I say to him once inside the vehicle.

"Wild dog pack attack," the driver says.

As we pull out of the camp area, I see painted dogs running everywhere. There are so many of them. Several begin jumping ferociously at the vehicle. Archer shoves me down to the floorboards while he stands with one knee on the seat, sending arrows flying fast and furious. I'm awestruck watching him.

We pull up to a hotel. Archer jumps out and lifts me down, then pulls me quickly inside the building. There are a lot of people in here; some crying, some huddled together, but everyone looks somewhat bewildered. Archer turns me to look at him while holding my shoulders. "Try to get a room. I'll be back later. If I can help, I must. I'm sure I don't have to tell you not to go outside."

I shake my head defiantly scrunching my nose.

He touches my nose and smiles. "Stay here. I'll be back for you." With that, he runs outside, jumps back in the vehicle and is gone.

I run my fingers through my hair as I look around. I'm standing in the middle of this room filled with strangers. Where are all the race people? I move to the desk and ask for a room. The attendant says all the rooms are full. I walk away and find a hallway. There is a staircase. I decide to go up to the roof to look around.

The roof is after the fifth floor. I walk to the edge. There are fires lit all around in the distance. There is not much to this 'town'. It looks like this road is all there is to it for about five blocks. There are some shops, a small school, a tavern or maybe two, I can't honestly tell and maybe another hotel or larger building.

The streets are deserted except for dogs running in the shadows.

"It's crazy isn't it," a man's voice says. Startled, I turn quickly around. I thought I was alone. It's Mirko. I feel a little relieved.

"Yes, it is crazy," I say smiling. "I've never seen so many dogs."

"I know," he replies. "I was in the lobby talking to an older local man. He says the dogs are out of control and have been for some time. They travel all across the region doing terrible damage and eating anything that moves, including humans."

I shudder at the thought. "That's appalling," I say. "Can they not do something about it?"

"I asked the same question. They used to have an annual hunt to keep populations down, but some dog worshipping group stopped it. Without the necessary natural predator populations, the dogs are out of control," Mirko answers.

"No natural predators? What about the big cats?" I wonder out loud.

"The cats migrate during the seasons with the herds. He says the dogs move, too, but not with the herds. They usually stay in one area that has a lot of domesticated animals on farms for about a week devouring everything they can, then they move on," Mirko adds.

I think briefly about how my family would feel if they heard I had been devoured by a pack of dogs. I wonder how Colson is holding up. He needs me to get to the top three.

"What are we going to do about our race?" I ask. "We still have so much to do here. Do you think they will move us?"

Mirko shrugs.

We both look over the side watching the dogs run through the streets. I see other people on rooftops, too. I wonder how Archer is faring. I yawn. I'm very tired. I look around for a place to sit. I guess Mirko notices my movements.

"I have a couple of blankets in the hallway if you'd like to lie down," he offers.

"I would," I accept gratefully. "Are you sure you don't mind?"

"Not at all," he smiles. "When you go down to the fifth floor, take a right and go to the very end. I snagged the blankets and some pillows out of the linen closet and set them down there out of sight. I figured they would be gone quickly with all the people arriving.

"Good thinking," I say. "Thank you very much for letting me use a few." I walk inside leaving him watching the dogs and fires.

I find his stash and grab two blankets off the pile along with a pillow. I find a nice spot further down the hall and lay one of the blankets on the ground along with the pillow, then pull another on top of me. This is actually quite nice. I'll have to thank Mirko again. I'm drowsy and my eyes are heavy.

I wake to see Archer staring at me as he leans against the wall. He doesn't look cheerful. "Archer?" I question sleepily while I sit up on my elbows trying to focus. Why is he just standing there? Then, I feel movement next to me and look down. Mirko has crawled next to me and is sleeping soundly. I gasp and jump up and away from him.

"Looks like you had a nice night," Archer snidely remarks as we walk down the hall.

"What?" I ask as he holds the door to the stairwell.

"You heard me," he says with serious tone.

"We were watching the dogs from the roof. That's where I left him. What is this?" I say defensively. I'm still very drowsy and trying to wake up enough to keep up with Archer's brisk pace. He doesn't actually think Mirko and I...

"That's quite a pile of blankets you had there yet you only needed two," he says suspiciously. Now I'm annoyed. "Are you just wasting my time?" he growls.

"Archer, just what are you insinuating?" I question him angrily. I'm tired and want to get to the heart of his accusations.

He turns to face me squarely. "If you lost your virginity, tell me now so I can remove myself from this race. I have far more important things to do," he practically spits at me, then adds, "losing it on the floor of a hotel is so trashy and common."

I gasp at his insinuations, his painful biting words and the fact that he thinks I'm that kind of person. I don't know what came over me but I slap him across his cheek. It was hard enough that it left red marks. He doesn't move but instead just rolls his eyes and takes a deep breath. Then he grabs my wrists and pulls me right into him. I'm fully awake now.

"Tell me right now," he says slowly and deliberately in a mean sort of way.

"I'm not telling you anything," I spew with tears running down my face and I jerk away from him. "Think what you will."

He grabs my wrist and turns dragging me into the third-floor hallway. I follow willingly behind because, well, he's my partner and I don't know what else to do. Then I stop myself and jerk out of his grasp. I don't want to be anywhere near him right now. He looks at me, then walks ahead and unlocks a door to one of the rooms. For the briefest of moments, I wonder how he got a room…

"Get in the room," he fumes.

I'll be damned if he's going to treat me like garbage. I want no more of this. "No," I answer defiantly.

He comes back to me and gets right in my face. "Get in that room before I pick you up and throw you in it," he seethes between gritted teeth. At least he gave me fair warning, but I will not be bullied.

I push on his chest as hard as I can. He merely leans back a little. "I'm not going in that room with you. I'd rather sleep on the floor with Mirko!" I lash out at him.

His fists ball up and his steely blue eyes have a fireball of fury burning in them. He is breathing out of his nose because his jaw and mouth are clenched tight.

"Suit yourself. Go have another round with floor boy," he grits out, then steps into the room and slams the door behind him.

I gasp again at his accusations. He's acting insane. What's wrong with him? Someone down the hall opens a door. I just want to get out of there before anyone steps out. I run back to the stairwell. What the hell was that? I'm so irritated right now! Who does he think he is? Tears prick at the corners of my eyes, but I manage to hold them in check.

I run up to the fifth floor back to where I was sleeping. Mirko is still sound asleep. I grab a couple of blankets as well as another pillow and run up to the roof. Tears are running freely down my face. I look out and see some fires still burning. I don't see any dogs though. The wind has picked up some. The sky glints with shades of dark blue and orange. It's a little chilly, but the sun will be coming up soon. I find a cozy corner and lay a blanket down. I throw the pillow on top and curl up on it, then spread the other blanket over me. I can't stop thinking about my fight with Archer. He said some very upsetting things. I lie there allowing my tears the freedom to flow unchecked onto my pillow.

***

I wake up in a cozy bed and sit straight up. Archer is sitting in a chair looking at me. He's doesn't seem mad anymore.

"I'm sorry," he apologizes. "I don't know what came over me. Maybe I was just tired. I shouldn't have lashed out as I did."

"You have been with me practically day and night for over a month. I thought you would have known me better. I would not lose my virginity in a hotel hallway." I speak calmly wanting more than anything to clear my reputation in his eyes.

"Things happen. I really don't know what you're into or what your tastes are," he says and leans forward. "It's not something we talk about, nor should we."

I know he's right but his verbal cut caused me real pain. Sitting here with my eyes bugging out of my head, I realize that I have some genuine feelings for him and I don't want him to think I'm a sleazy woman. I was hoping that he had some real feelings for me too. Guess not.

"Well, my tastes do not run to Mirko," I say. "Honestly, I had lain down alone. I don't know when or why he came and laid next to me."

"I do," Archer says.

"Archer, don't forget that the sexual purity rules apply to him too," I assert.

He bobs his head. "Fair enough."

"It sounds like you don't believe me. Why in the world would you jump to such conclusions?" I ask.

He looks at me. "I'm a man, Liliana. Let's not forget that and I won't apologize for it either. I know what's on a man's mind. I know what his motives are. There's a lot that can be done without penile penetration."

I gasp at his reply. I'm so embarrassed. I know my mouth is gaping open. "Nothing happened," I defend shaking my head. "Absolutely nothing."

"I'll take you at your word. I really don't want to talk about this anymore," he says and stands.

"Nor do I!" I concur.

"I'm going for coffee. Would you like anything?" His tone is so cold and uncaring.

"Hot chocolate would be great," I answer shrugging. I really don't know what else to say. I miss my friend. This whole thing was my first experience with an outraged Archer and I don't like it one bit.

He heads out the door. I jump up. I want to get a shower before he gets back. I feel like we really didn't resolve anything. He seems to still suspect that something happened between Mirko and me. I have no idea how to convince him otherwise, but it is important to me that I do.

When I step out of the shower, my hot chocolate is sitting on the table, but Archer is not around.

He left a message that a late lunch is being served in the hotel's largest meeting room. I get ready and go downstairs.

I see Archer leaning against the far wall. His eyes are still a bit distant. I turn away from him and move toward the buffet. Since I'm not that hungry, I just grab some fruit and a small roll.

I try to find a table. I see Mirko and he sees me. He completely side steps around the tables and moves as far away from me as he can. Then he leaves as though he is afraid of me. I look over at Archer and he looks quickly away. Was he watching me? I'm getting a little suspicious.

I take my tray of food, walk right over to where he is standing, and I look at him. He looks down at me. I can't help but smile. "What did you do to him," I ask.

He shrugs his shoulders. "I may have had a chat with him," he answers calmly.

I scoff and concede, "Well, it serves him right for sneaking uninvited into my blanket like that." I turn and sit down at a nearby table.

Archer grins and joins me at the table. I think he finally believes me now. Maybe he was watching to see my reaction and whether or not I would get upset that he roughed up Mirko. Who knows what Archer is thinking except, Archer?

Before we leave the hotel, I spy a notice by the front desk that reads: "Because of the dog attack, the Rulers have made Mocombo a non-elimination leg. However, the last person to check in will receive a time penalty that will be administered at the start of the next leg."

CHAPTER 14

Franka

I was released in the fifth position. I see that Elodie is sitting in the time penalty area. She must have been last. I haven't gotten to know her very well. She's quiet and keeps to herself most of the time. If we both make it through this leg, I think I'll make more of an effort to get to know her.

Archer meets me about a mile from the starting point. "We have to make it to the ruins of Paris by early afternoon. It's a very dangerous place once the sun begins to set," he emphasizes.

"Okay," I agree.

"I know a fun shortcut to cross the gorge," he grins.

"I can't wait." I smile back at him.

We run off from the well-paved road into some dense woods. After about an hour of walking at a good clip, we near the gorge, where it's quite a good distance to the other side.

Archer walks into the brush lining a cliff and seems to be looking for something. He turns and looks at me with a bright, knowing expression on his face. He's found whatever he is looking for.

He looks back at the cliff again then freezes. I try to look past him to see what it is but he turns slowly around facing me.

He looks at me and then casually says, "Hello, Kali."

The beautiful Miss Kali slinks from behind the brush tapping a club to her hand.

"Archer," she smiles and faces him.

He looks at me then waves a finger and says, "No." I turn around. Roni is standing behind me. At Archer's veiled threat he takes a few steps back.

"I'm not here to start a fight," her voice is like silk. She's so pretty. She's wearing a cropped top and leather cropped pants that hug her hips. Her figure is absolutely perfect. She has skin the color of milky caramel. She's every man's dream. She glides over to Archer and runs her fingers across his chest. "I have a proposition for you."

"What's on your mind," he asks. She backs away from him and steps closer to me. Archer's eyes never leave her.

"I'd like to call a temporary truce. I'm in need of your…particular skills." Again, her voice drips with honey.

Archer makes a half smile. "You couldn't find it, could you?"

"No," she smolders, "but I'd like to make a deal with you."

"I'm listening," he says looking at me and Roni.

"You get me and the boy here across…," she starts but Roni interrupts her.

"Man, I'm a man, woman; how many times do I have to tell you," he huffs.

Her body doesn't move, but her eyes shift to him and then back at Archer. "Get us across the gorge and we'll give you and your girl a head start. If you don't cooperate, we'll throw her off this cliff right now."

Archer takes in the surroundings. Roni takes a step toward me. They clearly have the advantage being so close to me. Archer's jaw sets. "How much of a head start," he asks.

"What!" I shout. Why is he negotiating? Archer didn't even give me a chance to speak.

Kali looks at me and says in her super silky yet firm voice, "You're loud, girl," then she looks back to Archer. "I'll give you one hour."

"One hour?" Roni spits but Kali doesn't even acknowledge him.

"Done," Archer says as he pushes past her and grabs my wrist.

He pulls me with him to the cliff's edge and jumps down to a lower ledge then lifts me down next to him. He walks a few feet to the left then reaches up and pulls on a perfectly camouflaged wire. I didn't even see it until he pulled it. He slides his fingers along the wire following it back to where it attaches to the limestone in the mountain. He inspects and pulls on the wire, then looks across the gorge. I can hear the sounds of other teams in the distance but moving toward our location. Archer makes his way back to me.

"Get down," he says softly. I kneel down.

Kali and Roni jump down next to us. They crouch down so they too are out of the view of those approaching. Archer runs his fingers along the ground looking for something. Then he stops and digs up a small box. The box contains a harness of some sort which Archer quickly attaches to the wire and pulls. He straps himself into it and flips his finger at me to join him.

Kali steps in front of me and pushes me down. She quickly wedges her club against my neck. Her face is threatening. Roni grabs me and holds me down.

Archer looks at Roni and says with a very threatening tone, "You lay hands on her one more time and you will be the one at the bottom of this gorge within seconds." Roni steps back. Then Archer says to Kali, "I'll send the harness back over once she's safely across. You have my word."

After a brief pause, Kali steps aside and lets me through to him.

"Put your arms around my neck and hold tight," he says to me. Once I do, he lifts up his knee so I can easily climb onto his body and adds, "wrap your legs around my waist."

As I climb, I ask, "Is this harness one of yours?"

"No," he says backing all the way up to the limestone, "but we'll make good use of it." He puts an arm around me and holds me tightly against him then runs us off that overhang. The wire whizzes as we zip across the gorge. The view is so amazing! I squeal with delight. I can hear Archer chuckle at me.

We land on a small platform where the harness catches on a protruding limb. Whoever made that was a genius. In my mind, I couldn't thank them enough. Archer puts me down to unhook us. He grabs an arrow and pulls it through a knot in the harness. With a quick stretch of his bow, he sends it back to Kali. We don't waste any time moving back into the brush.

★★★

The ruins of Paris are very intimidating. There is a lot of overgrown concrete rubble. Walking through it, I feel like I'm being watched and tell Archer.

"You are," he confirms. I can tell his senses are heightened and he's on full alert.

This place is really a devastating scene. "All this from one war?" I ask.

"Take it all in. This is the result of a very violent war and why we try to avoid it at all costs. The eyes you feel are a network of black-market gangs. You can find anything you want here, for a price. The price is usually very high and most of the time, they don't want currency."

"Archer!" A man's voice explodes. The voice echoes through all of the empty holes and caverns of the crumbled buildings.

Archer licks his lips and stands still. "We only want to pass through," he yells back. It's then that I realize he's holding my hand.

"We want the girl," the man yells, but I still don't see anyone. I'm frightened that they want me.

"She's mine," Archer answers cooly.

"A trade," demands the voice.

"No trade," Archer maintains with a slow, deliberate shake of his head.

"You won't get far, Archer." The foe sounds confident. I'm scared.

Archer breathes in. I don't know what to do. He looks up at the sky, then scans the area around us.

"You didn't bring enough men, Bastien," Archer responds calmly.

There are several minutes of silence.

I look at Archer getting ready to ask him what to do but he only gives me a brief shake of his head, so I don't break the stillness. I get the message. I'm terrified.

"Leave the girl, Archer," the voice requests again.

"She's mine," he replies more firmly and pulls me closer to his body. "You force her from my hand and I'll slaughter you where you stand along with the rest of your family."

Archer is not messing around. He begins walking, still holding my hand firmly in his. After we have walked about a block, the voice tells us, "leave an offering."

At the end of the road, Archer flips a couple of gold coins into an old broken bowl. We walk out of the ruins of Paris in one piece. I'm so glad I have Archer.

***

After a few hours, we turn off from our path. I guess Archer knows a good place to make camp for the night around here. But at a bend in this dirt road, we wander upon a camp of gypsies. They watch us at first and then start walking towards us. They surround us, staring. This is scary. I move so close to Archer that I'm actually pressing against his side. The leader of the group walks over and faces Archer. He pushes Archer's shoulder and says something I don't understand. Archer looks down at his shoulder where the man's hand had touched and looks back at him. It has turned very tense.

The two of them suddenly start laughing and embrace. Everyone begins laughing and walking away. The man looks over at me and in very clear English says, "Welcome. My name is Calvin. This is my wife, Roweena." I smile at both of them.

I glance at Archer. He is looking at me, smiling. He puts his arm around my shoulders as we follow Calvin and Roweena into the largest tent.

"It's been a while, my friend," he says to Archer. "So, this time you come escorting this young lady through the game." He looks at me. "You have a very good chance of winning with this man is by your side." He winks at me and I smile at him.

"How's the High Tribunal these days?" Archer asks as we enter the tent.

Calvin's face takes on a more serious countenance. "Moralles is up to his old tricks. I think he may have enlisted the aid of Wynch as well. It's not certain yet, but we need to talk about it."

Archer agrees.

Roweena invites us to sit down on one of the futons then lays down a paper in front of us. "One of our operatives found this announcement earlier today."

Archer and I lean in to read it silently together. They're making the Specialists turn over their weapons. Archer scoffs. I look up at them.

"Is this normal?" I question.

"Sometimes. This one seems like an especially difficult situation," Calvin confirms.

"Why? Why are they making it so difficult this time?" I persist.

Archer leans forward and breathes. "When you take weapons away from the warriors, it's harder for them to fight."

Calvin looks at me and then Archer as he continues, "It's not going to be difficult for everyone."

"What do you mean? Why not?" I demand. That's not fair and I have a brother who needs me to succeed.

"What happens when you win the race? Who gets the real benefit? I mean, yes, you get opportunities and benefits. Specialists get their so-called freedom…"

"Temples," Archer interrupts. He takes a deep breath and sits back. Calvin looks at him and nods. They seemed to share an unspoken knowledge of what was happening.

"What is it? So what? The temples always benefit greatly. They always have." I shrug.

"If one particular temple receives all the benefit several years in a row, other temples will not. It would not take long for that one temple or temples to build a considerable army of assassins," Calvin emphasizes, "They are planning a coup."

Archer lets out a breath, "This explains a lot."

"What do you mean by that?" Calvin asks.

"Frankly, I have been surprised at the amount of combat I've encountered so far on this race. I knew there would be some, but it's been considerable." He looks at me as though he doesn't want to reveal something.

"Combat? What combat?" I ask.

Archer shakes his head as though there is nothing to tell. But it's clear there is something he doesn't want me to know. I look at Calvin and try a different direction.

"Who is planning the coup? Who is it they want to win?" I wonder.

"Obviously a few of the governments are working together, we just don't know which ones." Calvin adds, "It could be any of them."

Archer sits forward and says, "You first need to find out who is giving you that fake intel." Calvin and Roweena both look at him as he continues, "No Region would agree to allow their Specialist to be disarmed. Half of these Specialists are no match without their voodoo concoctions and tricks. They'd be taken out immediately. They need their potions and dusts to move forward. Whoever gave you that paper wants you to pass along this false information in order to disarm me, Langt, and Byhed who are clearly our allies. They may be feeding them the same bullshit."

Calvin and Roweena glance at each other. "We can get to the heart of it," Calvin says.

"Look at who has won the race in the last couple of years and build on that or their allies. Statsia hasn't won the race in a long time. This would not be a good starting point for them. Statsia being the instigator wouldn't make any sense. Once you take out Statsia and its allies, you've got your starting list narrowed," Archer says.

"Not necessarily," Calvin says. "There might be some inside work going on here. Don't let your guard down. They'll come for you first and keep coming."

Archer smiles. "I know," he says and then looks at me. "But it's not just me this time."

This is a little over my head. But since they are all looking at me, I smile.

Archer looks back at Calvin and Roweena, "Concentrate your efforts. Focus on the quiet cannon."

"Quiet cannon?" I ask.

Archer turns to me and explains, "The quiet cannon is a ticking time bomb."

Damn. That was profound. There is a lot said in that sentence. This is a very smart guy. I think my mouth is hanging open. "Are you always like this?"

Calvin looks at me and scoffs, "If you only knew who you were dealing with."

I look at Archer. "Who am I dealing with?" I ask more seriously. I mean who the hell is he anyway?

Archer looks at Calvin, "Can you give us a minute?"

Now what? What is this all about? What's going on? I wait for them to leave and we are alone. I look at Archer.

"You have no idea how ugly this might get. I think it's only fair to warn you," Archer says.

"I think I understand," I say believing I really do. But Archer is just shaking his head. I take a deep breath. I don't like to feel like I'm talking to my dad and being treated like a child.

"Enlighten me," I dare with a wave of my hand.

He looks at me. He seems to be searching for the words. Then he says, "There is no easy way to say this but the race is taking a serious turn. No, it's more than that, it's taking a deadly turn. With the rules on Specialist engagement being lifted this year, and now this, 'paper' I'm not exaggerating the danger. I know you don't understand the world I live in but let me make myself very clear. Right now, coming into this race, I am the top seed in not only my class, but also in this entire Specialist group. That means I am top target." He takes a breath and looks me in the eye. "If I'm the target, you're the bait."

That hits me. I flop back on the futon stunned by these jagged words. I'm going to get pulled into this Specialist war by association. And God knows what other Regional "war" might be in the works. But right now, he's unmistakably telling me if he's the target, so am I. I'm no match for his kind. I search his face and let his statement deeply sink in. I can tell by the look in his eyes that he knows I get it this time. I scan my brain and his eyes for options but I find none.

"What the hell am I going to do?" I say under my breath. "I've been waiting my whole life for a chance at this race. I've planned, strategized and trained for this. My brother and my family are counting on me! I can't quit this race and yet I'm bound to you."

"I can quit," he soothes. "You didn't ask for any of this. This is not what you signed up for. On your word, I'll withdraw," he says, "but then you'll be an easy target for them. Although, they may let you stay on for a while knowing you're no longer a threat to their plans. But eventually, they will take you out so their contestants' have the best shot."

"Wouldn't you get in trouble with Statsia leadership if you quit considering everything else you said is true?" I ask.

"Withdrawing from the race and withdrawing from the fight are two different things," he answers. I have no idea what fight he means.

I look away. I need some kind of solution and he's really not helping. I'm running everything over and over in my mind. I need him to make it through this. I know he's truly my only chance at winning or at least making it to the top three. Archer patiently lets me work things through.

"I know you're scared," he breaks the silence.

"Scared? That doesn't even begin to express how I feel. I can't go up against a Specialist," I whimper.

"You won't need to. Brute strength is no match for strength plus intelligence. We have both. Play the rules. If a Specialist kills a contestant, it is considered an open act of war. A Specialist won't come at you like that. Our actions are bound to our Regions. If a Specialist comes at you and you strike first, then yes, a Specialist can take you out. So, it's very important not to fight even if one tries to engage you. Leave the fighting to me. Statsia hasn't won this race in years. What they have in us this year is a very strong team and an excellent chance at winning. We have to play very carefully."

He is a very smart guy and he knows a whole lot more about the politics of this. He makes a lot of sense. Maybe we can do this.

"I can't quit. I also know I can't do this without you. And honestly, there's no one else I'd rather have as a partner." I take a deep breath. "If I'm going to be bait, it might as well be for the biggest fish," I shrug.

He laughs, "It goes both ways, you know. If you're going to be bait, they have to catch you first."

I smile and start to get up but he grabs my wrist. "There's one more thing," he says.

He's obviously not finished so I sit back down. He's serious again. "If we're going to do this, I can't express how important it is that you trust me."

"I do trust you," I affirm.

He shakes his head. "You trust me when you want to or when it's convenient to your plans. You came into this race knowing you're very smart and can probably out think most people your age and have done so many, many times. I have experienced firsthand that you think you know more than others and have even questioned me on more than one occasion. What I mean is, you have to trust me even when you don't understand why I'm telling you to do something. Remember Statsia? That track was sabotaged, you could've been killed. Make no mistake, they will try to kill me. Killing you in the process would be considered incidental. It's important that you LISTEN to what I'm telling you. Don't question me or argue. There will be times when seconds count and I need you to just blindly trust me. Can you do that? It could be a matter of life and death now."

I'm pretty sure he just slapped around my ego and it stings, but he looks very serious and this is a deal breaker for him. He's been right so far about everything. "I trust you," I say humbly and I know in my heart that I truly do.

"I also believe that it would be best if I take the lead from this point on. Can you let go of control," he asks with raised eyebrows.

I think he's right. He knows their tricks and traps much better than I ever would. "Archer, I can let go of control, it won't be easy for me, but I will. I do trust you, very much. But you have to trust me, too. When you're mad, you become rigid and can't see past your own anger. And like that mess with Mirko, it almost destroyed us as a team."

This time he looks away as if in shame. "I know. Not my finest hour, but believe me when I say I'm working on it."

I smile.

He pats my knee and stands. "C'mon, let's go enjoy the party they've prepared."

We walk outside and join the others.

"I need to borrow him for a moment," Calvin comments to me as he pats the back of Archer's shoulder.

The two men walk away but I keep my eyes on Archer. I guess I come across as a know-it-all. I'll need to work on that. If there's one thing I've come to realize on this race so far is that I don't know it all. I probably need to work on my patience and cooperation, too. My focus has always been to do what I want or need to do to get into this race. My family let me and never questioned me. They trusted me to get here and here I am.

Some of the women come over and take me by the arm. We walk over to a table filled with all kinds of foods. Roweena is there.

"Come," she says and walks me to the head of the table for a plate. "Eat, my dear."

The food smells wonderful and I realize just how hungry I am. I look up and see that a couple of ladies have taken plates of food to Archer and Calvin. I fill up my plate and eat with the rest of the group. Everyone is very nice and friendly.

After dinner, I help clear the leftovers with the rest of the women. Roweena claps her hands and some of the men begin to play instruments. Children start dancing while the women do the dishes. A few of the young women come over to me and hand me a cup filled with a clear liquid. They motion for me to drink it.

"What is it," I ask but they just laugh. I smell it and take a small sip. I cough because it is so strong. It's like burning fire going down my throat. They laugh at me again but seem determined for me to drink their brew. They each chug it back like water. They must think I'm a lightweight. I look over at Archer. He and his friend look very serious as they huddle by themselves. I see Calvin pouring drinks and handing one to Archer. Archer looks over at me and smiles.

I drink the proffered beverage and even kickback another to their delight. I start to feel very relaxed and happy. I don't know what this drink is, but it is magic. They pour me another and I drink it down. They pull me to my feet and we all start dancing together, just having some fun and blowing off a little steam. I needed this.

Roweena goes over and pulls Archer's hand.

"The young ladies wish to dance with you," she says pulling him to us dancers. Calvin joins too and soon everyone is dancing. I am pleasantly surprised to see that Archer has some moves. His shoulders are going and his hips are moving to the beat. The man can dance. Damn, he's sexy.

I feel so very carefree, like I'm floating on a soft, fluffy cloud. After a few more drinks and dances, Archer makes his way to me. He puts his hands on my hips and we shake our booties and move our bodies. He twirls me around. Everyone is laughing and dancing. I'm having the best time! What an awesome night under the stars!

***

I wake up with an incredible headache. I sit up and immediately feel like I'm going to throw up. I've been laying on the grass and have it all over me. I stand up and stretch. There are people sleeping all around me. It's like we just fell asleep as we danced. I don't see Archer.

I do, however, see a large stream and make my way to it. It's fairly deep and has significant width. I look around and see an area on the other side that has some cover by trees and rocks. There is a small sandbar that will allow me access to walk over there. I bend down and start splashing my face with water. Oh. My. God. It's so cold. I walk across the sandbar to the secluded area and strip. I lay my clothes on one of the larger rocks. The water is so cold but I have to bathe. I close my eyes and just go for it and jump in. Whew! The impact stuns the breath from me for a moment. Slowly, I get used to it. I undo my hair so it can get a good rinse. The water is so clear and beautiful. It reminds me of home. I swim a little bit. Of course, the water at home is a lot warmer. I never thought I'd miss it as much as I do, but I miss the sand between my toes and the blues and yellows of sunny days.

I glance over at the camp and note that people are beginning to stir. I guess I better get out to dry off. I stand for a few minutes in the sun, naked as the day I was born, and close my eyes leaning back on a large rock to dry briefly. The sun feels warm on my body. My head still hurts, but I don't feel like I'm going to throw up anymore. After a few more minutes, I smell coffee and bacon. I get dressed and go back to the camp.

Archer appears next to me. "Eat something. We have to go."

I grab some of the roasted bread, cheese and, of course, bacon. I drink a lot of water and refill my container before we go. I say my goodbyes as Archer puts his hand on the small of my back leading me away. He has a troubled look on his face.

"What is it? You look like something is wrong." I feel very concerned.

He looks at me then smiles. "I'm just far away in my thoughts," he continues, "we have to get to Burga before nightfall in order to make the train. Three other teams have been spotted traveling nearby. No doubt they are on their way to the train, too."

"Does that bother you? You really seem concerned." I wonder if Calvin told him some troubling news.

"As you should know by now, trains are tricky places to move about unchallenged. We must prepare ourselves for a confrontation," he warns.

"Do you know something I don't know?"

He smiles. "No," he assures and we continue to move.

CHAPTER 15

Halfway up the mountain we find a clearing with a small stream running through it. I lean against a tree at the end of the clearing to catch my breath. There is a chill in the air.

Archer takes a drink from the stream and looks around. He bends down, touches the grass then gazes up at the sky. "We need to make camp."

"Already?" That was a surprise. "It's early afternoon. What about catching the train?"

"The ground is very cold. The weather is going to turn. We aren't going to make the train today. We'll need to move quickly. We have to build a pallet so we'll be off the ground. Start gathering firewood."

He comes over to the trees where I have been leaning and starts digging a pit in front of them. Then he builds a large pile of moss. I bring the firewood over and lay it next to the pit.

I watch Archer as I gather the kindling sticks and twigs. He starts cutting down limbs carefully looking at size and length. He pulls down mosses and twists them together to form something that resembles a rope. He uses the makeshift rope to tie the branches together. It begins to look like a raft.

"What can I do?" I ask.

"Start laying some moss in an even layer all over the ground between the trees. Then gather rocks for the pit." He works quickly and deftly.

I lay the moss in a thick even layer as he gathers large logs and limbs. He lays them between the trees this way and that way and it starts forming a wall around the moss. He's like a survivor machine.

"Start gathering leaves and moss and lay them over the branches. We'll need a lot. I'll join you after I finish the top," he directs.

Since it's getting colder, I run more quickly around gathering the moss and leaves off the forest floor and throw them thickly over the entire shelter. Archer lays the pallet over the moss I laid on the ground and finishes the structure keeping the fire pit just inside the opening.

"Start the fire," he instructs.

I gladly construct the fire on top of the rocks in the pit. By now, it is very cold. I look up but I don't see Archer anywhere. I fill my flask with water and set the metal container in the fire to get it boiling as I huddle inside the shelter trying to get warm and wait for Archer's return.

When Archer finally returns, he's carrying a dead squirrel and some honey. He welcomes the now cooled water and drinks it liberally. I prepare the squirrel for roasting while he refills the flask.

As the squirrel cooks, we start to talk about the contestants. His point of view on them is so humorous; I can't help but laugh. He's right on target with so many of them.

After we eat, the wind starts kicking up and snow begins to fall. I look at Archer. He knew the weather was going to turn drastically. He's truly amazing.

I move the conversation to the Specialist group.

"What about the Specialists? Are there any whom you especially fear?"

He takes a deep breath and considers the question for a moment, "I'm not sure fear is the right word. Perhaps cautious or leery would be better. Every one of the Specialists is at the top of their game. That's why we're here. The winning Region is far more important than anyone believes. I would say each one is a very dangerous person in their own way. However, if I were to be overly cautious about anyone, I'd have to say, Peago." He looks as if he were deep in thought.

"Peago? She's so little, happy and sweet." I'm incredulous. The way she tries to hover around Archer and Langt when the group is together, I thought they were friends.

"Don't be fooled. She is deadly," he scoffs while stoking the fire. "She will try to lure you in with her kindness and sweet smiles, but one prick of her NARC dart and you will be wandering around in a hallucinogenic stupor for hours, or worse, if she hits you with her sleeping dart, you could be out for days."

"You sound like you speak from experience," I note. Now I am really wondering about Peago, but he seems disinclined to talk about her.

He glances at me with laughing eyes. "We better get some rest. We'll have to make up extra time tomorrow trudging through snow."

I lie down and turn my back to him. Did he and Peago have a thing? I'm a little upset by that notion. Am I jealous? I allow my mind to speculate about Archer. There is no doubt that he is amazing. He is good looking, built, has mad skills, he's smart and his protector personality makes him highly desirable and extremely sexy. What girl in her right mind wouldn't want to be with him? But if I'm being honest with myself, he has not once led me to believe he thinks of me as anything more than his charge. Does he ever think of me in an adult, relationship way? I wish I knew.

"Where were you born?" I wonder. I can hear him stoking the fire.

"Chenosekee," he answers.

"Chenosekee? No wonder you're an archer," I twitter.

"What do you mean?" he asks. I turn to face him.

"Maybe you were born to it. You know, Staticia ancestors? They used bows and arrows, rode around on horses and lived off the land. You could easily pass for one of them if it weren't for your blonde hair. You just need a feather headband and a horse. Don't you remember learning about them in history?" I smile to myself.

He laughs, "I may have been brought up in a temple, but believe it or not, we are highly educated. I've just never made that connection to my family or ancestors."

He is so interesting and even though I know he "works" for the government, freedom seems to surround him. He's good at everything.

"What about you?" he asks. "Where are you from?"

"A tiny beach town off the Floridina coast called Annamarine." I grow a little reminiscent.

"That sounds wonderful. What's it like?"

"It is wonderful for the most part. It's a great place for kids to grow up. My grandpa tells me that at one point years ago, it was built up and touristy, but with the higher frequency of hurricanes, the tourists stopped coming. Now it's just a small community where everyone seems to know everyone. You can't get away with much," I laugh.

He smiles.

"There's really not much in the way of opportunities. My dad is on the Beach Renourishment and Maintenance team to keep the beaches wide in order to protect the mainland and my mom is a school teacher at the local school."

"Why do I feel like there is something you're not telling me," Archer asks as though he is reading my mind. "It sounds like paradise."

"I suppose it is a paradise but sometimes it seems more like a prison," I reflect. "We can't leave. Ever. Unless I do well here, my future means I'll work at the local school or be part of beach renourishment. Same for my brother. He never really did well in preliminaries. That means he will either be a fisherman or water mechanic or become part of the refurbishment team also. There are no more dreams. It is up to me."

Archer nods thoughtfully.

"What if I can't do this?" I wonder aloud not meaning to be heard.

Archer is quiet for moment.

"Self-doubt affects everyone," he says.

I turn my eyes and look at him.

"I can't imagine that you doubt yourself," I scoff.

He smiles. "Tell that to a 12-year-old boy who was left in the forest and told he had to find his way back to the temple 100 miles away."

"They did that to you," I ask shocked. When I was 12, I was very sheltered.

"They do it to all of us during our 12th year. Yes, you'll find plenty of self-doubt in that situation," he adds.

"But you were a child. Of course, you're going to be scared," I rationalize.

"Not when you're raised in a temple. By 12, we can find our way 5 times that distance. But age really doesn't matter. What does matter is that self-doubt will cripple you and keep you from accomplishing your goal. If you choose to quit because of self-doubt, you will never know what you could have done. Quitting is a choice."

Why is he so wise anyway?

"You obviously found your way back to the temple," I reply thoughtfully.

"There are many who didn't," he rues.

"What happened to them?"

"I've never known. There are endless possibilities. They could have been eaten by animals, starved to death, froze to death or something else. Maybe they found a way out and just kept going," he reflects.

"How did you make it through?"

"It took a long time and hard work but I finally got there. You find out just what you are capable of when you really have to push yourself. I didn't want to die or worse, bring shame on my family, but I really wanted to prove to myself that I could do it. My goal was to become the best Specialist that I could be."

"And here you are," I add.

He gives me a half smile.

"How do you get past it? I mean, you are you, but I'm not sure I have what it takes."

He looks at me. The firelight creates shadow dances across his face, "You have what it takes. I have been training my whole life for who and what I am. You have been training your whole life to be here now. You have to put self-doubt at the back of your mind and just keep going. When you really doubt, that's when you need to dig deep and tell yourself over and over to just keep moving forward."

I swallow and consider his words.

"You're tired. I have always found that I have a better perspective when I get a good night's sleep." He reaches over and rubs my cheek.

I nod. I know he is right. I turn over again.

He lays down next to me and turns toward me. I can feel his chest rise and fall on my back when he breathes. The steadiness of it and the warmth of his body ease me to sleep.

When I wake up, Archer is not in the shelter. I look outside and see that there has indeed been a snowfall during the night. What I don't see are any tracks in the snow. That Archer is damn good.

I get dressed and start breaking down the campsite. We really need to get moving. Within seconds, Archer shows up with a bird and a cheeky grin.

"What?" I ask. "What is that?"

"Black grouse," he answers while wiggling his eyebrows.

He clearly likes the bird.

"Do we have time for chicken?" I ask with a smirk.

"This," he says in mock disgust, "is a delicious big grouse. It's no mere chicken. Look at the thigh on this bird, it's as big as a cow's."

I burst out laughing while rolling my eyes.

"And yes, we have time," he grins again.

He busies himself prepping and cooking it over the fire while I finish breaking down the camp. I really wish I could take a shower. I've got moss and leaves in low places. I walk behind some trees so I can drop my drawers and brush the dirt off my thighs. When I return, Archer motions for me to come sit by him.

"Now," he says gleefully, "take a bite out of this succulent bird."

I give him the "you're kidding me" look but take the branch with a piece of the so-called delectable item from him. He watches as I take a bite. I can't help but chuckle just before I sink my teeth into it, I chew. It is very good, but I want to make him suffer a moment so I tilt my head this way and that as though I'm trying to make up my mind.

He starts laughing. "You're a bad liar. I can see the 'this is the best bird I've ever eaten' look all over your face."

I swallow it down and start laughing. "It is quite good," I admit.

We finish breakfast and head out as more snow flurries begin to fall.

CHAPTER 16

TASK: TAKE ONE OF THE PROVIDED LANTERNS AND WALK THROUGH THE FIRST 5 KILOMETERS OF THE ICE CAVE. 11 WORDS HAVE BEEN HIDDEN BETWEEN THE START AND FINISH. YOU MUST LOCATE THE WORDS AND PUT THEM TOGETHER IN THE CORRECT ORDER AT THE FINISHING POINT TO COMPLETE A LOCAL ANCIENT PROVERB. ONCE THE JUDGE APPROVES YOUR PROVERB, YOU MAY PROCEED WITH THE RACE.

Archer reads the Task Card over my shoulder. I take a step toward the cave but Archer grabs my wrist.

"Wait. You're not nearly warm enough to go into that cave," he says.

I look down at the sweater I'm wearing.

"I've been walking in the snow wearing this sweater, I think I'll be alright." I try to understand his concern.

"That's right, you've been walking and moving in a very light snow in the sun," he says. "It's going to be freezing in that cave. You're going to be walking in it for five kilometers. That's a long time in an ice cave." He strips off his sweater. "Put this on over yours."

"Won't you need it?" I'm concerned about him now.

"I'll be in the sun and just fine. The end of this cave is a tunnel at a much lower altitude. It will be warmer there." He takes off his belt and hands it to me. "Use this to strap that lantern to your chest. Keep your hands free so you can use them. You don't know what or whom you'll be facing in there."

I pull his sweater over my head. It smells like him, which is rather comforting.

"Where are your gloves?" he asks.

I reach in my side pocket, pull them out and wiggle them in the air for him to see, then pull them on.

"I'll see you at the end," he smiles.

I smile turning from him and walk into the Task Area which is inside the entrance of the cave. There, I find the lanterns. I quickly attach one to my torso using Archer's belt. It works. That was a good call by him. It's always better to have your hands free.

The cave is extremely dark the further I go. The walls are narrow and made completely of ice. The walkway does have a metal banister on one side of it which is helpful because the ground is a bit slippery in places.

I've walked quite a distance and still haven't seen a word nor have I seen a person. I hear echoes from people either ahead of me or behind me. As the cave curves, I finally find the first word. It seems to be etched into the ice. The word is NOT.

I look around but I don't see any papers with the word on it. I also don't see any blank paper or writing implements. Great. I have to remember the words until I get to the end. So, I just start repeating the word NOT in my head and pick up the pace.

The next word I find is PUPILS. I start to think NOT PUPILS or PUPILS NOT. I see a small light up ahead, but it's still quite a distance away. Another racer! Seeing that racer motivates me to pick up the pace again. I hope I'm not last. I move more quickly. The cave has some pretty deep gorges on the other side of the banister. The banister is clearly not only a guide but a safety net too.

I'm getting a little closer to the light in front of me but that person must have seen my light and is moving away. I see another word, CONSTANTLY. PUPILS NOT CONSTANTLY. NOT CONSTANTLY PUPILS. It doesn't make sense but I continue to say them in my head.

I'm now on a decently long stretch of cave. The light in front of me seems to be moving at about the same pace as I am. I turn around and see a light coming from behind me and it's moving quickly toward me. I take off running but slip several times. On one such slip, I just about go over the banister. Safety first. What can I do about this? Maybe I can dim the light by putting it under the top sweater. I really am thankful for Archer's sweater. It is freezing in here, even moving almost at a jog.

No, dimming the light won't help. In a cave this dark any light will glimmer. I look back again. That light is still moving fast. Dang it. Oh, I see another word, BUT. So now I have PUPILS NOT CONSTANTLY BUT. I don't have enough yet to really make anything out of it.

The light in front of me has disappeared. Maybe there's a turn ahead. I check to see the light behind me has quickly moved closer. I still can't make out a person and I can't hear any footsteps either. If I run, I could miss the words but I have to move faster.

I finally see another word FIND. PUPILS NOT CONSTANTLY BUT FIND. I can hear footsteps now. They are moving quickly. I turn around. It's Roni. He's running hard. I can see his lantern hanging from his belt loop and moving haphazardly from side to side. I plaster myself against the banister so he can move around me but instead he stops in front of me and grabs my arms squeezing them hard.

"What are the words?" he yells at me.

"What?" I say disbelieving.

"What are the words you stupid bitch?" he demands.

I try to wiggle out of his grasp but he turns and slams me against the ice wall.

"Tell me or I'll throw you down the next gorge!" He shakes me hard.

I didn't know he was like this at all. He seemed so unmotivated before. Now, I have to think fast.

"I only have a few of the words. ALLOW EVEN STOP and WILL." I lie hoping this has been his plan since he saw me.

"Say them again!" he yells. I don't know if he's testing me because he knows they are wrong or if he is just trying to remember them.

"ALLOW EVEN STOP WILL. That's all I know. There was someone ahead of me, maybe they got more," I answer calmly.

He shoves me against the ice and takes off. He's going to be really pissed when he finds out I lied. I need to prepare myself for the confrontation. Prick. I breathe a few times trying to pull myself back together.

Now, I need to remember the real words. PUPILS BUT CONSTANTLY NOT FIND. PUPILS BUT CONSTANTLY NOT FIND. PUPILS BUT CONSTANTLY NOT FIND. There's another word, HISTORY. Can I make sense of any of this? HISTORY PUPILS CONSTANTLY FIND…NOT BUT. Okay, not much there. I keep repeating the words to myself.

I turn a corner and see not only another word but two lights far in the distance. One is still far ahead of the other. Whoever that is in front, I hope he or she kicks the shit out of Roni. Okay, new word

DOES. HISTORY PUPILS CONSTANTLY DOES NOT FIND. Wait, I'm missing a word. What was it? BUT! BUT, BUT, BUT. HISTORY PUPILS CONSTANTLY DOES NOT FIND BUT. HISTORY PUPILS CONSTANTLY DOES NOT FIND BUT.

Because the ground seems to be firmer, I start to run. If Roni was behaving like that because he knows he was last, I could be in trouble. HISTORY PUPILS CONSTANTLY DOES NOT FIND BUT. HISTORY PUPILS CONSTANTLY DOES NOT FIND BUT. I see another word ahead. MANY. Let's see what we have here. MANY HISTORY PUPILS CONSTANTLY DOES NOT FIND BUT. How many words is that? Eight. I need three more; I start running. MANY HISTORY PUPILS CONSTANTLY DOES NOT FIND BUT. MANY HISTORY PUPILS CONSTANTLY DOES NOT FIND BUT.

I see another light in the distance behind me. Excellent! I'm not last. I face forward. There is no sign of the two ahead of me. Must be a turn or maybe they decided to work together. If they did, Roni knows the truth by now.

I wonder what he will do when he realizes I lied to him. He'll try to sabotage my game. Why did I lie? I already have enough obstacles being bait for Archer. But why should I tell him and give him the advantage? I want to win! He wants to win by cheating. Asshole.

I see another word. IT. Great. Not much help there. MANY HISTORY PUPILS CONSTANTLY DOES NOT FIND BUT IT. Hmmmm. HISTORY PUPILS CONSTANTLY BUT MANY DOES NOT FIND IT. Nope. Just keep going.

I see a larger light ahead. That might be the end. I don't have 11 words yet. Shoot. I hope I didn't miss any. I don't want to go back through that again. I glance behind me. That light is still pretty far off.

I see another word. IS. Damn. Come on! That is not helping. I need something more substantial to fill in the gaps. HISTORY PUPILS CONSTANTLY BUT MANY DOES NOT FIND IT IS. Clearly my line of thinking is incorrect. I only have one more word to figure this thing out.

HISTORY IS CONSTANTLY…wait, I see the last word… TEACHING. Hmmmm. HISTORY IS CONSTANTLY TEACHING PUPILS, no the grammar won't work for the rest of it. This is going to take some time.

TEACHING PUPILS IS NOT CONSTANTLY..no that's not it.

HISTORY IS TEACHING PUPILS CONTANTLY DOES NOT… nope.

HISTORY IS CONSTANTLY TEACHING PUPILS BUT MANY DOES NOT FIND IT…no, but I feel like I'm close. I see the opening of the cave ahead. I don't have the answer yet. I hope they give us some time to work it out.

When I walk into the cave exit area, a judge is there. It's still extremely cold. I realize I'm shivering. It looks like the exit leads to a tunnel that goes to the outside. I take off the lantern and lay it on the correct table. There are only a handful of lanterns there. That's a good indicator that I'm not last.

The Judge hands me an electronic writer and directs me to choose one of the empty workstations to complete the task. There are a number of single tables and chairs separated by high fabric "walls". There is no one else here. I wonder what happened to Roni.

I sit down on an icy chair at a cold table and prepare to give it my best shot. I'll start where I left off. I push the words around in my mind a few times. Then, I finally think I've come up with something and write down, HISTORY IS CONSTANTLY TEACHING BUT IT DOES NOT FIND MANY PUPILS. That has to be it. It sounds like a complete sentence and it also sounds very proverb-y. I'm going with it. I cross my fingers as I hand the writer to the judge. She gives me a stern look before looking at my answer.

I watch her face as she reads my answer. She looks up at me with a smile. YES!

"Very good, Liliana. You have completed the task. You may proceed with the race."

CHAPTER 17

Oh happy day! That took forever! I'm so glad that task is over. I run through the tunnel to the exit hoping to find some warmth. Once outside, I need a second to allow my eyes adjust. I close them and open a few times. It's so bright and oh, so much warmer!

I can't see anything. I bend over to look down at the ground. I finally start to focus. I turn to my left and stand straight up again. I accidently bump into someone. I look to see who it was. Kuzhan is standing right in front of me. He raises his fist and I can see the flash of a dagger in his hand.

In the blink of an eye, Archer is in front of me. I fall backwards onto the ground as the clanking of steel on steel begins. I roll to the side and leap to my feet while Archer shoves him heartily away. I see Archer giving me a sideways glance. He must be making sure I'm clear of the area.

I move quickly out of the way and jump behind the wooden fence belonging to the cave's closed tourist center. Archer prepares for the fight. He reaches behind him and grabs another dagger from his arsenal and gives it a quick twirl of the wrist before making his stand.

The two men eye each other. Archer's movements are extremely slow and subtle. He lowers his chin a notch and holds the daggers back just a smidge. Then I watch as he lowers his shoulders ever so slightly. His eyes are laser focused.

Kuzhan makes some weird puffing noises. He's definitely trying to intimidate. Archer doesn't flinch. Kuzhan raises his arms and with a piercing yell, his arms come crashing down toward Archer and the clashes happen again. This time they don't stop. Their movements are quick and controlled. They move, swing, twist, and turn. They are well matched as they strain against one another. Finally, there is a step and a push and they continue the contest. They are so damn fast.

Archer finally disarms Kuzhan, but in his fury, Kuzhan finds another weapon and charges Archer. Archer's arm swings. Dagger to dagger meet in midair. The clang rings through my ears. Kuzhan reaches up and grabs Archer's wrist, but Archer is quicker and drops the dagger catching it with his other hand then goring Kuzhan in the abdomen.

The wound seems to infuriate him even more. He becomes reckless and wild. His arms begin swinging everywhere. Archer twists, turns and moves.

Suddenly, my ponytail is jerked from behind. My mouth is covered and I'm pulled behind the tourist building. I spin to face Roni. I see his fist come up and he punches me close to my ear while he has a big smirking smile on his face. The pain shoots through every nerve in my head. For a moment, my sight blurs but now everything is going black.

★★★

I wake up in a seat on a bus. I'm extremely groggy. For a moment, I have no recollection of anything.

"Oh, you're awake, dear," a kindly lady in the next seat over says. "Your companion got off the bus some time ago."

"My what?" I ask groggily. Then I come to my senses and jump up. It's night. I'm on a bus going who knows where. My head starts to pound and my jaw hurts. Why would Archer leave me on a bus? Wait, Archer was fighting.

"Where is this bus going?" I ask the lady.

"We're almost to Volkston," she replies sweetly. "You've been asleep since I got on this bus last night. I was starting to get worried about you."

I smile at her. "I'm okay." I'm trying not to act panicked, but I know Volkston is at least 700 kilometers south of where I was. I need to get off quick. My heart starts pounding in my chest when I come to realize I may have been out of it for a few days. That means I have roughly less than 24 hours to get to the next checkpoint. The only thing I can do is try to find a train in Volkston.

"How long to Volkston?" I ask trying to sound controlled.

"Probably about 2-3 more hours." She says looking at her watch, then whispers, "this bus is so slow.", as though she doesn't want the bus driver to hear.

"Thank you," I smile.

 She smiles at me and turns back to her reading device.

I can't believe I've been out of it for so long. She said I was asleep since last night. LAST NIGHT! Damn, that's a whole day plus who knows how long I was out before that. I've obviously been drugged. And who the hell was my companion? I need to get off this bus! I look out the window. There is nothing out there but darkness. Getting off the bus now would doom me for sure. No, I need to be patient and wait to get to the city. Then I can find the nearest train station. If an express is available, it will get me back within 13 hours. Shit! This is really cutting it close.

Dammit! I'm so pissed at myself for getting into this situation. Where the hell is Archer? Why did he leave me or didn't help me? I'm so mad! I stew about it for a moment. I calm down when I start to consider, actually, why didn't he help me? Is he okay? I drive myself nuts considering all the terrible possibilities that could have happened to him and have to stop thinking about it now.

Instead, I try thinking about what happened to me. I go to the bathroom and while in there, I look over my body. I don't see any wounds or major bruises. My outfit is filthy, like I've been dragged through some serious dirt or mud. I'm still wearing Archer's sweater. My hair is a disaster and my mouth tastes like it hasn't seen a toothbrush in a week. I'm pretty sure that terrible smell is me as well. I do my best to clean myself up some.

On my way back to my seat, I look around to see if there is anyone I know or anyone who looks suspicious. The bus is almost empty and I don't see anyone looking very seedy. I sit back in my seat and do my best to act normal.

When I finally get to the Volksburg Bus Station, it's 2 a.m. I take off to find the closest train station. I see a cab and ask the driver where to go. He won't give me any information; he wants me to be his next fare. I jump in and tell him to go. I don't have time to run around looking on my own.

At the station, I find out that my train leaves at 6:00 a.m. I have some time to kill so I go in search of some showers or at the very least some running water. After some searching, I see a ladies lounge ahead and dash inside.

I look in the mirror and cringe. I look absolutely horrendous. The lounge does have showers. I'm relieved to find there is no one else in here. I turn on the shower and get in, clothes and all. I figure that's the best way to get all this mud off. After cleaning my clothes the best I can, I take them off, wring them out and hang them on the towel rack. I turn my attention to my hair and body.

Once finished, I wrap myself in a towel and use the provided hair dryer to dry my clothes. I start thinking about the race. When I get back to Stromsin, I'll have little less than 2 hours to get to the checkpoint if I've calculated correctly. I just have to make it.

I wonder what Archer is doing. I hear the door open as I put my clothes on. They are still a touch damp. I walk out into a common area. Archer is standing there.

He lifts his eyebrows and lets out a sigh.

"You do know this is the Ladies Lounge?" I sarcastically ask smiling.

"Where the hell have you been," he questions smiling back.

I walk over and hug him. He gives me a warm embrace.

"I have been looking everywhere for you," he adds, "Are you okay? Did anyone hurt you?" Then he stops, his brows furrow and he touches a tender spot on my cheek.

I step away from him and shake my head. "I'm okay."

"What happened," he asks in earnest. "Who did this?"

I tell him what I can remember as he listens carefully until I finish. "Roni?" he questions half to himself.

I sigh my acknowledgement. I can see the wheels in his brain are in motion.

"A bus, eh," he says thinking about it. "That was a smart move. Makes it a bit harder."

"Really? You'd think they would be easy," I ponder.

"City buses are one thing. Little rural buses can turn into a logistical nightmare."

"I guess so," I consider all the stops at little burgs.

"C'mon," he says taking my hand. "We are going to have to travel swiftly to catch up with the others." He leads me to the correct train platform.

"Archer," I draw his full attention, "being bait sucks."

"I know, babe." He bends down to give me a sexy little peck on the cheek while stroking my other cheek. "You're enduring it very well. I hit the jackpot when I got you for a partner." He winks at me.

He always knows the right thing to say. I definitely hit the jackpot getting him.

CHAPTER 18

Lachan

At the starting area, I look around to see who is not there. I beat one person in the last leg and now I want to know who. I'm hoping it was Roni. That asshole. No such luck. I see him talking to Poppi a few yards away. But who I don't see is Galina. I start looking a little more frantically around. What sweet justice that would be if Kuzhan and Galina got eliminated.

"Bitch," Poppi says as she walks by me.

"Back at you," I respond. What's her problem? Maybe she's mad because I lied to Roni during the task. Who knows?

Jannika and Antonella walk over to me.

"She's pissed because Archer beat the hell out of her buddy's Specialist and took him completely out of the race. He's going to need a long recovery period," Jannika says casually.

I look up utterly surprised. I had no idea. "No! I didn't know." I'm shocked. "Did Galina withdraw then?"

Antonella leans in and responds, "No, without her Specialist, she got lost and went entirely in the wrong direction. Once you checked in, they had to practically go all the way to Medatilli to eliminate her."

They both laugh. Once it sinks in, I laugh too. How lucky.

"How do you guys know all this?" I wonder if it's the truth.

"Langt told me about Archer's fight. He said that Kuzhan was no match for Archer and that once Kuzhan tried to cheat, Archer completely laid him out. Langt said Archer has no tolerance for cheating in a fight."

"Espada told me about Galina. He was laughing so hard about it, I asked him what happened," Antonella said.

"Archer never said a word," I tell them.

"Racers find your starting points," a voice over the loudspeaker calls.

I wish them both luck and wander to the back of the pack.

Once I'm released, I see Archer leaning against a tree waiting for me.

"Sorry I'm late," I say exasperated. "I hope you have some ideas about how to move ahead."

"Actually, I do. You're not going to like it but it's what we need today."

I look at him skeptically, "What?"

Everyone else is taking these 2-seater scooters down to the valley for the task. We can beat them by at least an hour if we head about 15 minutes west and hang glide down.

I can feel my eyebrows shoot up. My breathing gets slightly labored at the thought. He knows I hate that kind of stuff.

"Archer…" I start shaking my head but he puts his hands on my shoulders.

"We have to do this, Lily. I wouldn't ask you if there was a better way. We need this right now to get ahead. I'll be with you. We'll do it together, just like the plane. Let's go for it," he pleads.

I take a deep breath and look down taking it all in. He's right. He usually is. I look up at him and give him the tiniest nod of agreement.

"That's my girl," he grins. We jump on the scooter and head in the opposite direction of the others to the facility.

We both put on our harnesses. Once he's strapped in, he motions for me. I look into his blue eyes one more time. If I'm going to die, I want one last look at him. When he's finished checking my harness, he looks into my eyes. He smiles at me then turns me around and clips me to his harness. They give us the bar.

"When I say three, you start running full speed off this hill," Archer directs.

I nod knowing he'll get that message from the back of my head. I definitely don't want him to see the tears of fear stinging my eyes.

"One, two, three!" he shouts.

We take off running and just like that, we're airborne. I feel Archer's happiness and excitement. I open my eyes which I didn't realize I was scrunching together and see a sight to behold. The glider's full extension is massive. I look at the lush green landscape as far as the eye can see. Field after field fill the countryside below creating interesting patterns of squares.

Archer steers us to the right. I see all the scooters travelling at different paces down the winding road of the hill. They have a long way to go. This really is beautiful. A gust of wind suddenly shifts us into an awkward drop. I scream but Archer compensates smoothly and gets us back on our placid float down to earth.

Once safely at the bottom I look back up at the large hill. It was very high all the way up there.

"Those scooters must wind around the back side of that," Archer says. "You chose well. You're now in the lead."

I look at him and smile.

"Come," he says, "we've got about a 10-minute walk. This is a no-vehicle zone."

After a few minutes of walking, I ask, "Why did Kuzhan come at me like that? I thought it would be an act of war."

"He claims you started it by pushing him. He's out now. You won't have to worry about him," he answers.

I look at him. Technically, I did accidently run into the man. If that's the case, I'll have to be extremely careful around these people. I guess he isn't going to elaborate on his fight. That's fine. I can let it go.

"Are the races always so political?"

"Political? Yes. But there's more to it than that. The second half of the race gets very difficult. The Specialists will become very aggressive in order to win their freedom." Archer kicks a random rock along the road.

I guess I never really thought about it or them. It just goes to show you how shallow and thoughtless I can be. I look at Archer.

"What happens if you don't win your freedom," I ask.

"We return to the temple and our fate depends on our standings. If we are close to the top, we may get another chance to win our freedom. Our winning the race does a lot to enhance the temple financially and also in awards and standings. A top temple is very lucrative. I won't say more than that. I will say that if a Specialist does not do well in the race, he or she may go back to find that they are demoted or put back through more training. Some won't be affected at all depending on where they finish. Our chances at freedom may come again much later or never." He was quiet for a moment as if his mind wandered to another place.

"What do you mean? I can't imagine that you get absolutely no life of your own, ever."

"Specialists are no better than indentured servants. We are working for the comfort of our families and temple leaders. We are given what we need but we are not given the chance to pursue our own interests, such as a family or a choice of other opportunities. We can only gain those things as we are promoted through lines. If we gain our freedom, that freedom is always limited. Yes, we can marry and live outside of the temple, but we also must continue to train and can be called to missions at any time."

I have so many questions about what he just said. Where do I begin?

"What did you mean when you said your freedom would come later or never?"

"If a Specialist goes back to the temple, he or she is constantly challenged by the next group looking for a place in the standings. We must continue to battle to keep our spots. There's always a chance that we could fall during a battle or worse, we could be maimed."

"So, you're saying that your life is pretty much a constant fight. It's kill or be killed? If you lose, your life is a big loser?" I was incredulous.

"Life is a fight for everyone. The fight for a Specialist is one of very physical violence. It's also much shorter than most," he smiles.

"I don't think that's funny. I think it's tragic. You may never know love or have children…"

"Oh, if you're very good, they want you to breed and produce more just like you," he interrupted.

I audibly gasp. I don't know what to say to that. First, he's little more than a slave and now he's like a horse used as a stud. And who are these women who put themselves out there to…well, shit! I don't know if I'm appalled or jealous. My mind is racing this way and that. I look at him. He means more to me every day. He seems so calm and accepting of his situation right now. Now I understand. He must be free.

"There's one more thing you need to know as we get closer to the final goal. The Specialists will come on strong and aggressive, but they are not the only ones. The last five legs of this race will be brutal. The general public may come out of nowhere to ensure either your defeat or victory. It's all about Regional pride and politics. Trust no one but me."

Great.

A boy greets us on the road. "Archer?" he guesses.

Archer smiles down at him. "Yes?"

"A Mister Calvin is waiting at Bonzi Gardens. I will take the girl to correct field," the boy stammers.

Archer gets down on his level and looks him straight in the eye. "What does Mister Calvin look like," he asks.

"He told me to give you this." The boy hands him a ring. Archer looks at it, then back at the boy. "Where is the field," he asks.

"At the red sign," the boy says pointing. Archer and I look down the dirt road where we see a red sign with some lettering on it. It's close, only a few more steps. Archer looks at me.

"I'll be back soon," he vows.

I tilt my head and smile. With that, he turns and goes his way.

CHAPTER 19

When I get to the task area, I see fields of rice paddy pods. They are sectioned and divided. Some are dry, some are properly flooded and some are in a muddy state in between. The muddy ones seem to be teeming with frogs. I find the task cards on a table along with hats.

TASK: PICK A POD AND WORK ALONGSIDE THE LOCALS TO HAND PLANT A CROP OF RICE SEEDLINGS.

As I look around, I see several groups of locals waiting for the contestants to show up. I'm the first to arrive. Excellent. I don a hat and pick a group of locals. They take me to one of the pods at the very backside of the fields. We start at the well and form a line so the buckets of water are passed from the well to the pods by one person handing the bucket to the next person until the water gets emptied into the pod. We hand the empty buckets back the same way. The area we will be working with is flooded some but the leader says we need to add some fresh water before planting the new seedlings. Once freshly "watered", we each grab a tray of seedlings and take them to the area. The only way to properly plant these is one stalk at a time. I have to bend over pressing the seedling into the muddy bottom to make sure it stays in place. The locals grab handfuls of seedlings so they are bent over most of the time planting. It's backbreaking work. Others continue to periodically add water.

After several hours, Archer shows up at the outer fringes of the Task Area since he isn't allowed any closer. He's leaning against a small tower of freshly bagged grasses for the farm's goats. I take a small break and walk over to him.

"Hey," he says looking fabulous wearing his sunglasses and clingy t-shirt while I'm splotched in mud and soaking wet. "What are you learning today?"

I smile. "I'm learning how to plant rice. I'm also learning that the back well is old and they could really use a new one."

He looks at me. "You think you can build a fancy new well," he asks with a twinkle in his eye.

"I can design a fancy new well in my sleep," I answer all smug with a grin.

He smiles. "Perhaps the best lesson here is not the fancy well, but what they really need," he says looking around, "is…"

"a better water distribution system" we say at the same time, then laugh.

"I knew you were a smart girl."

He looks around at the fields again deep in rice paddy thought. I notice he's leaning at the edge of a very muddy unused rice paddy. His ankles are crossed. I can't help myself; I give his chest a pretty decent push. He flaps his arms like a flailing bird trying to manage his balance but he begins falling backwards. I can't help but laugh. At the last minute, he grabs my shoulders and chucks me over his. We both go under in this cold, frog-ridden, clayish water, filled with mud. I look at him as he emerges from the mud on his hands and knees. All I can see are his blue and white eyes through all that mud on his face. I just start laughing. He looks at me and does the same. We toss some mud at each other and laugh again. I watch a frog jump off his back and get so tickled by it, I laugh harder. Then he laughs more. I love the sound of his laughter. We sit there a few moments laughing and enjoying each other's company.

I notice we are drawing some attention. Alas, I realize that I need to get back to my true purpose here. Archer holds out his hand and helps me out of the mud. We make our way over to the nearest well. There are four buckets of water already drawn and just sitting on the side of it. Archer picks one up and pours it slowly over my head. I wipe the mud from my face. He grabs another one and pours it down my back. I grab the third. He bends down and I reciprocate by pouring the water over his head and face. Then the fourth down his back. He refills the buckets and we rinse each other one more time.

When we are finished rinsing, Archer refills the buckets and leaves them where we found them while I grab another tray of seedlings. I start back to the paddy and look at him over my shoulder. I catch him checking out my rear end.

This is the very first time, that I'm aware of, that he has looked at me like I'm a woman and not a generic race partner. I'm thrilled.

When I finish the Task, the judge hands me a package marked "Homework" along with a map to a city park. I'm told to head over to the Star Oceana Bath House at the end of street. The judge tells Archer that this is going to take a while and he can meet me later at the assigned park. Archer acknowledges the directive and leaves.

I make my way to this bath house. I'm looking forward to it since I still have mud all over me. I feel I could use a good bath.

I walk in and am led to a changing area. They have me remove my clothes and then wrap me in a towel. They also take my wet clothes away, and tell me they will be laundered and returned before I leave.

I'm taken into a large room with very low lighting. There is a large pool of water in the middle of the room with very decorative elegant marble fountain figurines of various fish and corals lining the back of it. Water is flowing from each of them into the pool. Everything is made of a green marble. It smells fresh, like clean linen and sweet soap.

There is a low marble wall around the pool where wide marble beds protrude from it every few feet or so. A steamy cloud rises from the water. The water is very close to the edge of the beds. They have me get in the pool and soak in the hot water for some minutes which is very nice while they prepare my "bed". I move slowly around the warm water enjoying it completely.

They instruct me to lie down on the warmed marble "bed" they have prepared with the top of my head close to the edge and gently release my hair from the band holding it. My hair flows freely into the water. They very adeptly knead my head and wash my hair. This is heaven. The strokes are gentle yet firm and soothing. What a relaxing experience. I close my eyes and fully enjoy it.

From big black bowls, water is poured to rinse my hair. Then they roll me over and remove my towel. They lather up my back and shoulders with a delightful soap mixture that emits the most wonderful scent combination of floral and spices. They do it very slowly. It is almost like getting a soothing massage with soap. I close my eyes again trying to figure out what florals and spices they use. I wonder if I can buy some. After a moment, I let it go and just enjoy this pampering. They lift my arms and stretch them backwards just enough to stretch and loosen my muscles. They cleanse every nook and cranny. Then they roll me over and clean my front side. They clean my face, arms, legs and torso. Then two of them massage my hands and work their way up my arms. They rinse me with bowls of steaming water.

A girl on either side of me picks up a leg putting me in an awkward and very vulnerable position. My reverie is completely broken. I try to squirm away but they hold me tight. One girl puts a pillow under my backside.

"What the hell is this," I demand almost in a panic.

An old woman emerges from one of the doorways. She says something in their language that I don't understand. The women hold me even tighter. She approaches, dips her hands in the water and shakes them out. She very roughly inspects my private area; then proceeds with the virginity check. When she is done, she turns again to the water and washes her hands. She says something else to the girls and they giggle. One turns to me and says, "How can you still be a virgin with an Archer such as that? Does he like men? Do you?" They all laugh. The whole experience is very uncomfortable.

Then another one turns to me and asks, "Can I make you feel better? Here?" pointing to the area between my legs.

"No," I yell and jerk myself loose. I run to find my clothes. I can hear them laughing at me as I quickly dress. I just want to get out of there. Then I stop and sit down on a marble bench in the dressing room.

My lady parts are really sore from the rough treatment. I feel so violated. Touching me in that way without my understanding what is going on is just so wrong. I've had a few other checks like that in my life. They were done slowly and extensively by doctors who seemed to get some sort of weird enjoyment out of prolonging their inspections.

These people also seemed to take pleasure in my discomfort. Maybe they allow that in this part of the world but I'm very upset about it. That old woman may be registered by the race leaders but there has to be a better way to do the random virginity check than that. She was ridiculously rough. If my mother were here, she would be very vocal and write a strongly worded letter to our local health and wellness official. I'm definitely going to talk to Miss Terry about it.

As I walk away from there, I get even more mad. How dare they talk about Archer. But as I continue walking to the park, I think about what they said. In a way, their words do have some definite merit. I know I have wondered along those same lines. Not whether or not he likes girls, but whether or not he likes me. I have certainly developed genuine feelings for him. Maybe it is just the incredible intensity of this race. But I wonder if he does feel anything for me or is he just fighting for his freedom? Or just following orders?

I'll get myself worked up if I think too much about it, so I determine to let my mind wander in another direction about Archer. If he does gain his freedom, where will he go when he has it? What will he do? What am I going to do? If I win, how can I pursue the controlled life that I planned? I've grown very attached to Archer and I don't want to lose him from my life. I pull my hair up in a band and continue my walk to the park.

CHAPTER 20

The oval-shaped park is large with many beautiful green trees. It surrounds a clear blue lake. Benches dot the landscape around the lake every so often. On the far side, I see a row of shelters erected and head over there.

I find the one Archer put up for us. He's not here, so I sit down and open the "Homework" envelope. It says we have to crack a code. We are not allowed to show the code to our Specialists. I look over the instructions and the code very carefully. The code is not technical nor is it mathematical. It seems to be symbols and dots.

After I've been sitting for a few hours trying to figure this out, I know I clearly need help. It's not in my wheelhouse at all. I poke my head out of the shelter for a stretch. I see a few of the contestants with their envelopes lying or sitting on the grass trying to figure out their codes also. Who is the smartest person I know? Archer. It says I can't show him the code. Maybe if I describe it to him, he can give me a few pointers.

I go in search of him and see if he's anywhere in the park. I finally see all the Specialists have congregated at the beverage center and head in that direction. Peago has her hands on Archer's chest. I don't know how to react to that. I must have a desperate look on my face because the minute Archer looks up at me, he moves to my side.

"What's wrong," he asks.

"I need your help." I try not to sound miffed about Peago.

We go to a nearby bench where I tell him about the task.

"A code," he questions with a furrowed brow.

I confirm, "But you can't tell anyone. I'm not supposed to show you the code and I won't. But if I tell you what it looks like, maybe you could give me a few pointers?"

"Tell me about it," he affirms.

I describe to him the peculiar symbols and dots. I had memorized one row and tell him about it.

"What," he says slowly as he sits straight up looking at me. "Who gave you this?"

"The race judge at the end of the task. Don't you remember? It was in that envelope she gave me."

He takes a deep breath. "This is a top-secret code still in use today by a particular Region. I won't tell you any more than that. They are wanting you to crack this code?" He is shaking his head. "This is fire, Lily. Why the hell would they do this?" He is clearly upset.

I shrug my shoulders.

"Look at me," he commands.

I look up at him.

"I want to help you, but this could be considered espionage. I will not put you in danger of execution by this Region." He closes his eyes as he thinks. Then he opens them. "What are they doing?" He asks himself as he leans back thoughtfully.

"If a judge gave it to me, wouldn't it be okay? I mean it's on them, right? They gave it to me."

He looks back at me. "I can't help you. If you can't figure it out, it might be just as well," he retorts.

I know that tone. His concern for this has me on edge. "I understand your position," I concede. "I won't ask this of you. I just hope it doesn't end my race." I get up hoping that perhaps I can find another contestant to work with.

"Wait," he says gently pulling me back down. "You must understand, this isn't a simple thing to ask of me. I would do anything to help you win but this is extremely dangerous. If they were to pull you and send you off in chains for execution, it would fall to the government to negotiate your release. My problem is, I don't know what kind of game is being played here. I really want to march in there right now and knock somebody's brains out for doing this to you."

"Archer," I put my hand on his arm, "I know. I understand. You can't go beat anyone up, they'll know I asked you for help. If it ends my time here, it ends my time here. I don't want to do any political dirty work either."

He puts his hand on my cheek. "Please understand me. I won't knowingly put you in harm's way. I don't even want you to mess with this."

"I have to. It's my assignment."

I look back over my shoulder as I walk away. Archer is still sitting on the bench but he is rubbing his chin looking out into space. His jaw is tight indicating that he is angry. This is really bothering him. It must be very bad.

I find Jannika stretched out on a bench by the lake. She is facing up with her eyes are closed. She almost looks like she is sunbathing. She is casually chewing on her writing instrument. She has her code homework strewn across her lap. It appears to be the same as mine.

I'm assuming everyone got the same code. The shadow of my body compels her to open her eyes. She smiles when she sees me.

"How are you doing on the code?" I ask.

"Terrible," she replies. "I was considering cheating and asking Langt for help but it is such a beautiful day, I thought I'd enjoy it for a moment."

I smile. That is like her to seem so casual about life. "Do you want to team up to try to figure it out? They didn't say we couldn't work together."

"I'd love to," she says sitting up and clearing some space next to her on the bench for me to sit down. We are only given these instructions in the homework sheet: Each digit from 0 to 9 represents a dot, dash, or a divider. Two dividers are used to separate words.

"I think our biggest obstacle at first is going to be figuring out where the dividers are," I offer.

"Yes, once we do that, we'll need to assign a number to each of the dots and dashes," she adds.

"Then we'll have to turn the numbers into letters to decipher the code," I add biting my lower lip.

"This could take 20 years," she moans and flops back on the bench.

I agree.

"Let's get some snacks and go to my tent. At least we'll be more comfortable," Jannika suggests.

We lock ourselves together in her tent.

When the dinner chime rings, we think we have figured out a small piece of it. The code seems as if it might be about a location. It doesn't specify what kind of location. It could be the location of our next task for all we know. We're exhausted and ready for a break.

I go back to my shelter and hide the homework in my things. I don't want Archer to get upset.

After dinner, I decide to see if I can figure out anything more about this code location on a map. I don't have enough information. I don't even know what I'm looking for. While I'm looking, Archer walks in but he's very quiet. I suspect he knows more than he is letting on. He's probably already looked at the work I've done so far. It's incomplete, of course.

"You know, don't you," I ask.

"Of course, I do."

"How do you know? Did you look at the message I partially deciphered?"

"Of course, I did."

"Isn't that a breach of trust or something?" I ask rather snottily. Immediately, I'm slightly uncomfortable to hear his answer. Sure enough, he turns to me and grabs my arm pulling me right into him.

"Do you really think I'm going to let you get involved in this alone? I will know every step of the way what they are getting you into, especially with this kind of high-level bullshit. You can get as angry as you want, but I won't let you go through this by yourself," he informs me calmly but firmly.

At first, I get heated and I'm ready to fight, but then I realize, I'm actually glad he's so pig-headed right now. I don't know what's going on here. I'd rather have him by my side. He already knows what this code means. He is the one person in the world who I truly feel safe with. I look into his angry cerulean eyes.

"Okay." I want him with me especially if someone is trying to get me in trouble.

He lets go of my arm and I begin to walk outside to join the others.

"Lily, wait," Archer sighs. "I wish you would have told me so I wouldn't have to go behind your back and cause friction between us. We're partners. What happens to you is my concern," he soothes.

I concur. "I know. I didn't want to upset you."

"I may get upset but it's worse when you hide things from me. It's better if I know up front what is going on," he presses.

"I understand."

"C'mon. I have a plan, but I want to talk to Langt."

We walk to Langt's shelter where he is whittling a wood project outside.

"Have you had a chance to talk to Jannika about the code?" Archer asks quietly.

Langt shakes his head. He looks at Archer, then me and stands.

"Yoni!" he calls out in a deep voice that is uncharacteristic of him. I've never heard him like that before.

Jannika runs over. "What is it?"

We all go inside their shelter.

"Bring me your code paper," he demands.

She hesitates but she obviously must know her limits with Langt, too. She looks at us then rummages through her belongings to get the paper.

Langt looks at it.

"What the hell is this?" he asks furrowing his brow then looking up at Archer.

Archer nods.

"What is it?" Jannika asks.

The men seem to be in their own world.

"I have to do something. She'll be killed with this kind of information," Langt discloses solemnly.

"I think we need to know if everyone received a copy of this code or if they got different codes," Archer states.

Langt smiles. "Tonight then?" He beams with a lift of his brows.

Archer smiles his agreement.

"How in this world are you going to look at the other contestant codes without them knowing," Jannika questions.

Langt looks at us with his usual grin. "This is what we do best."

"Archer, won't it be difficult? I mean you're going up against other Specialists. Won't they know?"

He looks over at me with a half grin and winks. Perhaps it is an exciting challenge. The thrill of not being caught. This is their element and they seem very happy about it. The two pair off. I roll my eyes at Jannika while we walk outside.

"Yoni?" I ask her.

"Yes, it's how you say my name where I'm from in Noswaroff. Well, it's more like Yonka, but Langt calls me the short version, Yoni."

"Oh, I had no idea," I reply. "I guess I've been saying it wrong this whole time."

"It's okay. Every English-speaking person calls me Jannika. I'm used to it. If you started calling me Yonka now, it would be weird," she laughs.

I agree. We meander off to join the other contestants around the bonfire.

★★★

I haven't seen Archer for a while. I take a shower and get ready for bed. When I get back to the shelter, Archer still isn't here. I sit down to finish deciphering the code. It's definitely a location. I don't know what it is for and right now I'm too fatigued to look at the map. I put it away and lie down. Closing my eyes feels good and I drift off to sleep.

I wake up in the middle of the night to find Archer sitting next to our stove fire. He is shirtless and his hair is wet. He must've just gotten a shower. He is reading a paper. He obviously located my freshly deciphered code.

"Did the others have the same code," I whisper sleepily.

He shakes his head. "No, fairly basic cryptology," he says quietly.

He looks over at me and hands me the paper. "You cracked it. I knew you would because you're so smart. They probably knew you would too."

I take the paper from him. "Who are they? Who is doing this to Jannika and me?"

"I don't know right now, but I will identify the threat," he vows.

I look down at the paper. "Where is this place?" I wonder.

"It doesn't matter," he concluded. "You won't be turning that in." Then he adds, "When you get up in the morning, I want you to change it so it makes no sense. Then hand it in."

I swallow and nod my agreement. This must be really bad.

"Langt will have Jannika do the same. Don't compare notes. It's best if they think you did it separately and both failed."

"Okay."

"If we lose the race because of this, at least you will walk away unharmed," he says softly.

He takes the paper back from me and lays it on the hot coals.

I lie back down and fall asleep listening to the crackling fire.

CHAPTER 21

"Turning in the "homework" was a non-event. They basically put my name on the envelope and told me I was free to go," I relate to Archer as we walk away from the park the following morning.

"Interesting," he says. "They didn't look at it? They didn't say anything else?"

"No," I answer. "They just took it."

Lost in his own thoughts, Archer becomes silent. I know he's trying to figure out what they could possibly be leading me into. If I actually consider it, it is scary. Are they setting me up? And if they are, why? We both walk silently along for some time.

As the day moves into the noon hour, Archer stops and looks around then starts walking in another direction. He jerks his head in motion for me to follow him.

"Archer, where are we going? We're going off course," I mention.

He turns to me and smiles. "There is something I think you'd like to see."

"What is it?" I'm curious especially because he seems almost playful.

"You'll see," he leads.

I smile and walk along with him. Where could he be taking me? What is this all about? We stop at the edge of small dirt lane, where he turns to me.

"Close your eyes," he says smiling.

I look at him for a moment. By the look on his face, he is pretty pleased with himself. I shrug and close my eyes. He takes my hands and leads me down a path.

"Keep them shut," he urges.

"I am!" I giggle.

Then I begin smelling a fragrance. It is heavenly. "What is that?"

"Open 'em," he says.

I open my eyes. As far I can see, over the land and hills, are covered with different colored flowers. My mouth must have dropped to the ground. It's the most magical thing I've ever seen or smelled for that matter. I can't take it in fast enough. I keep looking and smelling. I don't want it to end. I twirl around looking in every direction, then at Archer. He's smiling at me. He takes my hand as we walk through the fields along a little path to the hilltop.

At the top, it's the same but I can see old golden statues of a fat man dotted across the landscape, too. This must have been an ancient place of worship here for these people. There are flowers of all colors, shapes and sizes as far as I can see. I could lose myself in this moment. I start moving through the flowers, trying to smell the different varieties. I put flowers in my hair, tucked in my clothes, between my toes and throw them in the air. I run over to Archer and put some in his hair too. He's such a good sport in my joyful moment. I run, leap and roll through the fields. I truly can't get enough.

I climb on the fat man and lie across his lap for a while enjoying the day. Archer comes over with some refreshments from his pack and we put together a little make shift picnic of dried meat, cheeses and fruit. After lunch, I run down the hill through the flowers and fall face first into them. I get up laughing and hear Archer laughing at me.

"Come, Lily," he calls to me. "We must go."

"I know, I know," I pout playfully. This has been such a wonderful distraction.

I start back up the hill. When I get almost to the top, I see Archer standing a short distance away from me. The smile has left his face. I look in the direction he is. In the distance, over the mountains, the skies are black. There are shadows of lightning running through them. The sound has not yet reached our ears but the message is clear. We need to find some shelter. This storm may take a while.

Archer looks at me and flips his hand gesturing for me to come quickly. We run for the closest road and find an abandoned cottage at the bottom of the hill just as raindrops begin to fall. We dash inside. It's rickety and old but there is a fireplace on one side. The roof has a massive hole in it on the other end with a light drizzle now coming in through it. There is dried hay everywhere. It appears that whoever owned this place was using it for storage or perhaps housing animals or something.

Next to the fireplace is an old bench along with a low table. It's dirty but it's all we have to shelter from the elements.

Archer starts a fire. He swipes off the bench and table with some old sackcloth he found on the ground. When it is wiped to his satisfaction, he pulls it closer to the fire and he looks at me. "Have a seat," he says.

I sit down.

"Thank you for taking me to those flower fields today. It was amazing. I'll never forget it."

"You're welcome," he answers sincerely.

I look at his back as he stokes the fire. The rain is pattering down through the hole. Thunder is becoming louder.

"Are Specialists higher than a General?" I ask.

He turns to me and smiles, "It's not a rank, Lily. I'm not military."

"So, you don't go into armed battles?" I ask.

"What I do is very different, but if I'm in an area of a battle between Regions, I may be called in to assist leadership in some covert way."

"Are Specialists as highly trained in firearms?"

"Of course," he replies.

"Do you ever use firearms on your missions?"

"Never," he answers.

"Is it because you're a Specialist as a bowman?"

He looks at me and lets out a small laugh.

"What?" I ask smiling but not knowing why.

"If you need a title, you could say that I'm a Dea Master of Strategic Combat, Top seed in the Archer Class," he says still smiling.

"Wait," I say. "I'm confused. So where does this "specialist" thing come in." I pause, I have to know. "Why are you called a Specialist? I mean, what is your specialty anyway?"

The smile fades from his face. He looks at me and answers, "Silence." He turns back around and goes back to stoking the fire.

What do you say to that? God knows what he has seen and done. I stand and walk over to the window.

"Try to get some rest," he calls over his shoulder. "We may be here a while."

I move back to the bench. I lie down allowing the sound of the rain lull me to sleep.

I jump up to a crash of thunder and a white blast of lightning. That was extremely close. Rain is pouring in from the hole in ceiling.

Archer is standing in about a foot of water on the ground. He has a very solemn look on his face.

"I don't know, Lily, this isn't looking good."

Suddenly we hear a distant rumble and the ground begins to shake.

"Shit!" he exclaims and runs to the window, then sighs with relief.

"What is it? An earthquake?" I ask jumping to my feet.

"Landslide. But it's below and to the right of us. We can't stay here," he says.

The shaking is dreadful. It might as well be an earthquake. The building starts to crumble all around us. Archer grabs my hand and pulls me out of the cottage. It totally collapses to the ground behind us.

The ground begins rumbling again and we can see another mudslide on the mountain in the distance. Archer is looking desperately around. The tiny road is quickly filling with water. The lightening is alarmingly scary. We seem to be getting trapped in this little corner between mountains. We see a barn nearby. We look at each other and run to it.

The ground is flooded. There are no doors and the roof leaks but there is a low loft where we can escape most of the water for now. Archer lifts me up to it and climbs up behind me. The lightning is terrifying. I cuddle close to Archer. He puts his arm around me, but I can tell his mind is elsewhere, probably trying to pull together a plan to get us out of this.

The water is rising higher and rushing into the lower area of the barn. Archer is very focused looking around the building. Sure enough it starts to creak and moan. He wastes no time. He jumps down and holds his arms up to me. I jump into them. The water is over our ankles. He sets me down, grabs some old looking rope off a nearby nail on the wooden wall and we start running the best we can on the flooded ground. We get to the edge of the land where the road was but it is now a raging river.

We're soaked to the bone. We've seen two mudslides so far. This river is absolutely churning while it rages out of control and lightning is crashing all around. Can it get any worse?

Archer finds a large tree nearby. He starts wrapping the rope around a limb. He takes the other end and ties it to an arrow. He shoots it to a tree across the river and pulls to make sure it's secure. Then he unties our side and wraps it around his wrist and hand.

"We're going to have to swing across," he yells in order to be heard above the rain.

I nod my agreement.

He pulls on the rope again. "Get on my back and hold tightly onto me!"

Water is pouring off his face. I don't know how we are going to make it out of this in one piece. He grabs the rope with his other hand and we swing across the river. About half way, the rope gives.

"Archer!" I scream.

He looks up just as the rope breaks. We both fly into the torrent.

I'm tumbled around in the rapids then finally breach the surface but the water is so rough that I'm taking a lot of it in. I try to steer myself to the side bank. Suddenly, I feel Archer's hand. He is holding onto some tree roots and pulls me to him. He helps me get to the top and yells for me to get on land. I run up to the edge of the soggy grass.

Archer begins to climb out but his right foot gets struck by a log throwing him back into the roiling waters. I run closer to the edge, screaming his name and looking frantically around. He is nowhere to be seen.

I feel the ground under me begin to give and try to lurch back out of danger but it is too late. I slide back into the churning mix myself. I go under and am struck by all kinds of debris. I make my way back to the surface. I'm choking and coughing trying to get some air. I see a log stuck on a rock up ahead. It looks dangerous but it's all I have and I'm quickly becoming exhausted.

I reach for the log. Sure enough, my grab maneuvers it back into the water. At least I'm hanging onto something. It keeps me afloat while I search for a way to the side. Still no sign of Archer. Where is he! I hope he's okay. I continue getting bounced around these rapids and almost get knocked off this log more than a few times.

I must have gone miles down this river.

I hear someone yelling and look around.

I see Langt up ahead on a low bridge. He's lying down on it with his hand touching the water. I know I'll only have one shot at this and bring my knees up in case I have to jump. I'm almost there. When I get close enough to the bridge, I reach up as high as I can. His hand wraps around my arm while he wrenches me clean out of the water in one fast pull.

"Are you okay," he yells. Rain is dripping down his face.

I shrug. I'm exhausted and have plenty of bumps and bruises, and I can't believe I'm still alive but he doesn't need to know that. "Have you seen Archer? He's still in the water," I yell over the rain.

He shakes his head but immediately begins looking around.

"I'll find him. Go to the checkpoint," he yells pointing to the right.

I watch him as he runs off, probably in search of Archer.

I begin running to the checkpoint. I'm not too far. I see Jannika a short way ahead of me. I hear yelling and can make out some more figures running behind me. I guess we all got caught in this crazy absurd storm.

I hope Langt finds Archer.

When I reach the checkpoint, I'm announced as Number 6. Jannika is just inside along with a few of the other contestants. We are told to go straight to our rooms where a hot bath is waiting for us. A doctor will come in to give us a quick inspection since many of us received injuries during our trek through the storm.

Some contestants are still missing and with all the landslides and the flash flooding in the area there is a real concern for their safety.

We will not be permitted to leave our rooms during the commute to the new location so that everyone's privacy and injuries are protected from the other competitors until the appointed start time at the next Region.

Wonderful. Well at least I'll have plenty of time to discuss what happened at that bath house with Miss Terry.

CHAPTER 22

Razatina

We are lined up at the starting gate and I'm in the middle of the pack. I keep trying to figure out who was eliminated. We had been informed during the commute that no one had been killed in that crazy storm. That was a relief, but someone was eliminated. Who was it?

Jannika is closest to me since she was number five. I try to mouth the words to ask her who was eliminated. She is tall so she starts looking around. She mouths Elodie and shrugs. She doesn't see her. I start craning around trying to see her as well. But I don't. That's disappointing to some degree. I liked her.

Our start times are staggered and by the time I'm released, Jannika is long gone.

During the commute, I've done nothing but stew about Archer. I feel like no news is good news. They would have told me if he had to withdraw for medical reasons or death. I keep anxiously looking around waiting for him to appear. I have to know for sure that he is okay. It's been a brutal few days wondering about him.

"Hey," Archer whispers behind me.

Relief floods over me. I run and jump into his arms. He laughs and hugs me.

"I've been so worried about you. Did Langt find you?"

He scoffs, "Yeah, he found me."

"What?" I say smiling. "What happened?"

"It took a while but I was finally able to grab on to some debris and rocks. It was a fight to get out of the water, but I was able to finally get out downstream. When Langt ran into me I was running back looking for you. He told me he pulled you out of the water which was surprising since I didn't know you were back in," he said looking at me with emphasis. "We found a small tea house that had excellent sake to get out of the rain. I had to endure several unbearable hours of endless berating by him for having to save my contestant." He rolls his eyes.

I laugh at him. "That must have been terrible indeed," I concur.

"You have no idea." He gives me that unbelievably handsome smile. "So, tell me, how did you fall back in the water?"

"I was running along the edge looking for you and it gave way," I shrug. "I plunged back in and Langt pulled me out."

Archer looks at me thoughtfully.

During our walk, he tells me that the upcoming Task area is considered a sanctuary and is a protected area. It is only open at a certain time one day a week. To make the next time frame, we have four days to get there. We can save a lot of time by taking the train and maybe take in some of the local sights, so we head to the station.

While we're on the train, Archer disappears for a period of time. He returns and tells me there's been a change of plans and we'll be getting off at the next station.

"What's going on?"

"We have to make a slight detour," is all he says.

We disembark the train and hike for about half a day to a river. We get into a canoe and slowly paddle on the calm water. It's beautiful. There are monkeys and different types of wildlife along the shoreline in the surrounding vegetation. After a while, Archer tells me to lay my paddle down. He rows us to the shore.

"Where are we going," I ask as he helps me out of the canoe.

"We need to make a stop," is all I get from him. Something must have come up that he's not talking about.

After walking along a path for a while, Archer stops.

"What is it?"

An older native steps out of the brush and greets Archer with a slap of some kind of shredded bamboo leaves. Archer bows. The native turns to me and approaches.

"Don't be afraid," Archer comforts, "he's only blessing you."

I let the old man slap me with his little brush thingy.

The old man then turns back to Archer. Archer speaks to him in his language. (Of course he does. He seems to know everybody's language.) The old man bows, leads us to a secluded village and into a large circular communal house where about 200 indigenous people seem to be socializing. Children of all ages are running around. There are several fire pits dotting the large gather space with fires blazing. The smell of food cooking gets my mouth watering.

As soon as we enter, little girls run over and cling to Archer. He smiles and cups their cheeks in his hands. The little boys are at the far end practicing their man skills with wooden "spears" and different games.

Archer walks over to them. Their eyes brighten. They all seem so in awe of him. He gives them pointers on their holds and aims. They laugh, play and roughhouse with him.

I'm not sure what to do so I stand in place and watch. Some of the women beckon for me to come sit by them. As I do, little girls come around me and start touching my hair and skin.

They are the most beautiful little girls I've ever seen. Their skin is a deep rich golden brown. They have piercing blue eyes and their long hair is light brown naturally highlighted with bits of pale yellow. They look like children whom the sun handmade.

"They think you are beautiful," Archer notes while making his way to me.

"I think they are," I respond.

Archer sits down next to me and the little girls climb all over him. I laugh and secretly wish I were one of them. One of the women gently pulls my hand. I walk with her to the amazingly large buffet of food where she offers me a plate and motions her hand.

Archer stands.

"Are we staying here tonight," I ask while I watch Archer play with the little girls. He looks at me.

"I've been summoned, Lily," he says as he tries to unwrap a little girl from one of his thighs. He picks her up in the air and then gives her a kiss on the cheek. When he sets her down, she runs happily to her mother. Archer begins untangling himself from the rest. They all get kisses and run merrily off. He grabs a plate and starts to fill it.

I'm feeling a bit disappointed. Summoned? Here in the middle of nowhere?

I place a few items on my plate and sit down on one of the floor pallets.

He comes over to sit with me. Others come and join us.

They talk to Archer in their language. Archer falls easily into conversation with them. They smile at me a lot make bowing gestures with their heads. I smile and bow back since I don't know what they are saying. The food is fantastic. I didn't realize I was so hungry.

After dinner, I help the ladies with their clean up. Archer stands and I can tell he's saying goodbye to the elders.

He comes over to me.

"I have to leave."

"You're leaving me here," I say slightly surprised and concerned. Geez, I don't even know the language of these people.

He places his hands on my shoulders. "I chose this place on purpose. I know you'll be safe here tonight. They will protect you. I'll return in the morning."

"Archer...I can't even speak to them," I begin to plead.

He touches my cheek, "You're in good hands. Please trust me." He's firm. I know that tone.

I can only quietly agree.

"Stay away from the Yakoana," he states smiling as he walks away. Who or what is Yakoana?

I sit and allow the little girls to play with my hair. They put lots of leaves and twigs in it, trying to decorate me. The adults seem to be packing up. Maybe that's the way they clean up. Everything seems to have a place.

Some of the men pick up large vessels and leave. When the women are ready, they call to the children. A group of men carrying weapons come and surround me. I'm frightened and I don't know what to do. I guess it shows on my face because a young woman steps in the circle with me and takes my hand. We all start walking together. I don't know where we are going but I do feel better having this girl with me.

We walk for some distance. The whole tribe is ahead of us while I'm surrounded by warriors. We end up at the base of a mountain cliff. It rises straight up in the air. Everyone walks through a well-hidden opening at its base. My guards stop and allow me and the girl to pass. When they enter the mountain, they stay at the base while we climb.

Inside is a winding staircase carved into the limestone to the top of this mountain. The journey to the top is amazing. There are many rooms and chambers also carved out of the mountain. Some of the caverns have mats on the ground clearly indicating sleeping quarters. One of the caverns is actually the back of a waterfall with water spilling all in the room like personal showers. This whole place is beautiful.

I try to imagine what it would be like to live here. They seem to want for nothing. All the women are terrific cooks from what I experienced of that dinner tonight. They have built a fantastic secure living quarters and shelter. They all seem very happy.

We arrive at the top and walk out onto a blanket of lush green grass. There are ruins all around. Whoever built this must have been a great community of people. The children run and play in and out of the stone "homes". I look over the closest edge. The whole side of the mountain facing the river running around the mountain below is carved into windows and patterns. It's awe-inspiring.

I can see the waterfall that I passed on the inside not far from this location. It's beautiful as it rolls through the mountain ruins. I wonder if this tribe is the decedents of the people who built this place.

It's getting dark. Fires pop up around the camp. Many of the men move into the cave. The women and I sit around the campfire and drink some kind of fruit juice which is very refreshing.

Some of the women stand, including an older woman who smiles at me then wraps her leathery brown hand around my arm and leads me into the cave. I see the men have taken guard positions around all the entrances.

This particular group of women goes into one of the caverns of the ruins. There are already some women in here. The floors are covered with comfortable skins and furs. The air is filled with a light pink smoke emanating from a small carved-out fire place that must have once been part of a kitchen. The fire has some sort of makeshift grill where different plants and flowers have been placed. They motion for me to sit down with them. They move their hands in a waving motion toward their faces, I'm assuming to get me to inhale the fragrance, so I do. It smells so good that I can't help but inhale it again. I'm soon feeling very relaxed and free spirited. My head languidly falls back as I keep inhaling. It's wonderful. I smell so much I'm getting a little dizzy. I need to lie back.

I can't get enough of that smoke's aroma. I feel so light, like I'm just floating around. My whole body feels so relaxed. I like this place! Many of the women have lain back too. They are smiling and happy also. The ceiling of this cave is speckled with crystals that glow as the light from the fire hits them. They are beautiful. My lips are numb. How strange. I don't feel bad. In fact, I feel very, very good. I haven't felt this good in quite a long time. Everything seems to be moving in a disjointed slow motion but it's so calming and lovely. It must be these ruins. Maybe they have special powers.

I open my eyes. It's the pink smoke. I inhale it again. It smells delightful. For a moment, I believe I see Archer's face. I must be dreaming. The cave is so beautiful. There is Archer's face again. He has a yellow halo around his head. Nope. Now he's gone again. I'm dreaming. The ceiling is twinkling. I love when it does that. It has such happy lights. It's like the ceiling is moving. It's so hypnotic.

I think I'm wet. It's cold. Somebody is stroking my hair. That feels comforting. My head is moving back and forth. How interesting. There is Archer's face again. There is Archer's shirtless chest. Wow. Look at those muscles. They are rock hard and wet. Are we in the shower? When did I get in the shower? I should undress. I can't get my shirt off. Something is pushing my hands away. It's cold. I see Archer's face. He's beautiful. I'm dreaming. The ceiling is moving again.

Oh my God! Where did this terrible bright light come from? It's so bright that I can't open my eyes. Someone is touching my face. I can't open my eyes. It's too bright. I'm tired and I need to lie here a minute more.

★★★

I open my eyes. I'm outside in the dark. I appear to be lying on a blanket on a dock next to a river. I jump up but fall back down. My head is so heavy! I do, however, manage to sit up.

"Hey, hey, easy," Archer says softly and rubs my back. He's lying down looking up at me. His arm is under the back of his head.

"Where are we? How'd I get here? I thought you weren't coming back until morning," I ask holding up my heavy head.

He scoffs at me. "It's long past morning, Lil. It's the middle of the next night. You've been out of it for some time." Then he adds jokingly, "I told you to stay away from the Yakoana."

"The pink smoke?" I begin to recall. "That's Yakoana?"

He nods smiling. "C'mon," he says patting the area next to him. "Lie back down. You need to sleep it off."

I snuggle in next to him. "They could make a fortune with that stuff." I say yawning. I close my eyes listening to the soft splashes of water against the dock as I drift back to sleep.

CHAPTER 23

I wake to the smell of freshly-caught fish frying over a campfire. I sit up and can tell immediately that my hair is going in every direction. My mouth tastes like a cotton ball. I rub my face. It feels weird. I must still be feeling the after effects of that fabulous smoke.

"Good morning," I hear from behind me.

I do not want Archer to see me this way so I keep my back to him.

"Do you mind if I take a quick swim in the river? I'd like to bathe."

"Don't jump in the water," he says. "There are crocs and other skin-crawling creatures in there." I can hear the humor in his voice but I also know that the warning is sincere.

Damn. I keep my back to him and do my best to run my fingers through my hair attempting to tame the beast. I rub my face again trying to figure out how to pull myself together into some kind of presentable state.

Archer kneels next to me with a cup of hot water. I am thankful for that.

"You look lovely," he says smiling. Nothing gets past this guy.

"Oh, my gosh. I must be such a horrendous sight right now. Don't look at me!" He's laughing at me. "I'm serious! Look away! Let me at least comb my hair and brush my teeth," I squeak.

He laughs handing me my pack. I quickly search its contents for the desired items and make good use of them.

"We have about an hour's hike to the valley base from here," Archer discloses. "We'll have to take horses up through the mountains to get to the Task area."

"Horses?" I am stunned.

Archer sips his coffee and nods.

"I've never ridden a horse before." My voice squeaks with concern.

"A new experience for you then," he grins.

Ugh. Does he have to be so happy about it?

★★★

When we get to the horse ranch, Archer immediately goes over to pat the horses. I check in with the crew and see about signing out two horses. I glance over at Archer to find him loving on those horses. They are loving him back. He's giving them treats and they follow him around like he's the Pied Piper of horses.

I don't know the first thing about horses which makes me uncomfortable. An attendant brings a horse over to me and lifts me onto it. I get the basic instructions for handling it while it skitters around. I'm swaying from this side to that trying with all my might to stay in this saddle and look composed.

Archer peeks over at me just before jumping on a beautiful black horse. He sits easily in its saddle making loving gestures to its lovely long neck like they've been friends for years. I watch him enviously for a moment, but it doesn't last long. The horse does seem to really like him.

I have to smile at his amazingly cool demeanor with his bow across his back and wisps of hair floating around him in the gentlest of breezes. He's walking his horse away from me on the far side of the barn while talking with one of the many riding instructors. I assume he is getting directions. He looks so powerful and strong on that horse. He reminds me very much of a portrait of an old Statsia native from way back when.

My horse on the other hand is acting slightly crazy. It's starting to prance around in circles and generally seems uncomfortable. I certainly am. I give Archer my best panicked look. I don't know what to do.

"Lily," I hear Archer yell just as my horse takes off.

I scream. I can hear a horse racing behind me. It must be Archer, there weren't that many people on horses outside of the fence. My horse heads for the forest. I get slapped around by a few branches and sit low on its back because I don't know what to do. I close my eyes and hold on for dear life.

I try looking back but I don't see Archer. I don't see anything but trees and shrubs. My horse is just running and running like its butt is on fire.

After what seems like miles, it finally starts slowing down. I feel somewhat queasy. I'm amazed I was able to stay on this animal. I begin to sit up but it sets the horse off again and it bolts. I almost fall off but manage somehow to lay back down on it and the brute calms. It finally starts to slow significantly but I don't dare sit up again. Then, gradually, it comes to a stop to graze.

I roll off of it before I try to sit up landing softly on the ground looking up behind me. No Archer in sight. I stand fully up brushing the dirt from me. I seem to be reasonably far up the mountain. I hear water and turn around to where the horse has moved.

There is a beautiful little waterfall in front of me. It's stunning. The flora and fauna all around it are in bloom. The horse is chomping on a bush with pretty little purple flowers. I move closer to the pool of water and dip my hand in. It's cool but not unreasonably so. I take off my boots and stick my toes in the water. A powerful stench hits me in the face and I realize that nasty, sweaty horse smell is me. Not only would it be lovely to take a dip, I feel it is necessary, especially due to the fact that I didn't get a bath this morning.

I strip down to my underwear and jump in. The water is incredibly refreshing. I know I'm in a race, but I think I can spare a few minutes to thoroughly enjoy this moment of bathing in an amazing place. I also know I have a little time to get to the Task. I lazily stroke my way around eventually managing to swim over to the waterfall. I look up at it for a minute. What would it be like to stand under it? Since there is no one around, I go for it. I climb onto the flat rocks at its base and let the water run all over me. I love it.

I spy a small hidden area behind where the rock has been carved out. It looks like a perfect place to sit and enjoy the backside of the waterfall. I wonder who did that. I swim under the falls to the back side, then basically play in them. I poke my face through them as well as my arms and legs. I let them hit the palm of my hands and splash all around. It's like being a 5-year-old again.

I jump like a mermaid through the falls and back into the beautiful blue pool. When I come up for air, Archer is crouching at the edge of the pool looking at me. He laughs and stands. He starts stripping! When I see him go for the underwear, I turn away and when I look back again he's diving in. I did get a glimpse of his fine naked rear end.

He swims over splashing around and laughing. We play for a short time having splash fights and kicking to see who can make bigger ripples. I go in for a big play but lose my footing like an idiot and go under. I end up swallowing a boatload of water. I come up choking and coughing in a very unladylike, embarrassing, sputtering fashion. I should have stayed under. He grabs me and pulls me to him. Out of reflex, I wrap my legs around his waist and lay my head on his shoulder while I catch my breath. He carries me back to shore.

"Stop," I cough just before we get out.

"Why?"

"Archer, you're naked," I sputter.

"Does it bother you that I'm naked? It's just a human body."

"It's, erm, a little distracting," I answer stammering a bit.

He laughs. "I see. So, it would be completely inappropriate to carry you out of here with my naked body?"

"I suppose so," I say shrugging.

"Well then," he says in a teasing tone while lifting an eyebrow, "if you'll unwrap your legs from my naked body, I'll cover myself to alleviate your discomfort."

I have to roll my eyes at myself because of the irony he just sarcastically tossed at me. Here I am all wrapped up on his nakedness and yet afraid to look at it? I feel so silly. I unwrap myself from him and climb out of the pool. I get dressed with my back to him while he dresses. I walk over to my horse and begin stroking its back so it won't get spooked again when I get on it. I feel Archer right behind me.

"No," he declares taking my hand. He lifts me onto his horse, grabs the reins of my horse and swings up behind me. I turn back to look at him and he tilts his head to me. His mouth is close to mine. There is definitely something extremely sensual about this moment.

The setting, the waterfall, the horse; it's all very romantic. I want so badly for him to kiss me right now but I'm feeling a self-conscience from our comments in the water, however I can't tear my eyes away from his very close, exquisite lips.

I don't know what made me do it, but I lean in to touch them with mine. The angle is all wrong and I end up brushing my lips against his chin. He brushes his lips very tenderly on my forehead. My heart starts pounding and I exhale. I didn't realize I was holding my breath until this moment. I don't know what to do next so I turn away from him and look ahead. He clicks his tongue and the horses begin to canter.

CHAPTER 24

A few of the other teams are waiting when we arrive at the task area. I sense eyes on me as we ride up on only the one horse. Archer doesn't seem to notice or doesn't really care. He jumps down and then reaches up and lifts me down.

There is a rope across the entrance with a sign that says it's an individual task. It's doesn't open until 2:00 p.m. Archer acknowledges the race attendant and leaves the area. We have to wait an hour. Other teams arrive, and it looks like everyone will be here. All leads will be gone. We'll be back to a level playing field.

I climb to the top of some rocks so I can look over the area. Then I see it. The side of the mountain has been carved into thousands of blinding sparkly bright white man-made ponds. Jannika, Antonella, Poppi, Roni and Banzi climb up also. We all stand in awe of this amazing site.

A race attendant, one of the older locals here, climbs up with us and looks over the site with pride. His gray hair, dark skin and squinty brown eyes tell a story of a long-lived life in this area. He's proud of it and his heritage.

"Underground there sits a salt filled spring," he begins in his raspy aged voice, and we all gather around him to hear more. "The shallow pans fill with this natural spring water. The heat of the sun evaporates the water leaving behind the salt crystals."

"It's incredible!" I respond.

"How deep are they?" Poppi asks.

"About a foot or so," the man replies smiling.

"How much salt is in each of those ponds?" Banzi inquires.

"You're about to find out," is all the man says. We all glance at each other.

I notice another race attendant closing in on the barricade rope below. It must be time to start. We all make our way back down the rocks. By the time we get down, the rope has been dropped and we freely walk to the task table.

TASK: CHOOSE A SALT PAN AREA. CAREFULLY SCRAPE ALL THE SALT CRYSTALS FROM THE EARTHEN SURFACES INTO A 5 KILOGRAM BASKET. ONCE THE BASKET IS COMPLETELY FILLED WITH SALT CRYSTALS, FLOOD THE SALT PAN WITH SALT WATER THEN BRING YOUR FILLED BASKET TO THE JUDGE.

I take the task card and pick up my supplies which include a basket, a scraping chisel, and a bucket. We all run in different directions to the marked salt pan areas. I start scraping and realize immediately that this task is going to be difficult.

The salt is as hard as a rock. It's more like a crystal growth. I really slam the chisel on the sides to try to loosen it. I also try to slam the chisel's pointy ends on the salt trying to break it apart. I'm only getting little crumbs off this thing.

I look around to see how the others are doing it. The guys seem to be doing fairly well with their man strength. It appears that many of the females are struggling. I see Antonella is doing some kind of sliding stab at the base of one of the salt crystals and chopping it into bigger chunks. I try that tactic. It works better for me too.

By the time I finish the task, all the guys have finished. I'm one of the last to leave. I see that Zara is still struggling quite a bit. I walk to the judge who approves my work. She hands me a card that reads:

JOIN THE LOCAL CELEBRATION OF THE FESTIVAL OF THE SUN. THERE WILL BE FOOD AND FUN. THE EVENING WILL CAP OFF WITH A CELEBRATION DANCE. ALL CONTESTANTS ARE REQUIRED TO ATTEND.

Archer is waiting at the end of the task trail to walk me to the hotel so I can shower and change.

"You look like you've been through the ringer," he laughs.

I actually feel that way too. My hair, which was in a ponytail, is now all over the place. I'm wet, covered in salt and dirty. My body aches all over.

"I'm sure I do," is all I answer. Well, he's seen me look worse, I try to rationalize to myself. We're both quiet the rest of way. He seems to be elsewhere and I really don't have the energy to try to maintain a conversation.

CHAPTER 25

Since the Specialists won't be joining the contestants for the feast or dance, we have to remain in designated areas because of some local political instabilities. We are told that Specialists will be posted around the area to keep us all protected and safe.

I head over to the celebration with the other contestants. The first thing that hits me before anything else is the smell of the food. Apparently, I am famished. My stomach confirms it on first whiff. I make my way to the banquet table.

I immediately see large trays of Lomo Saltado. The smell of the sliced beef stir fried with colorful fresh vegetables and seasonings is all I need to see. I'm in. I fill my plate, grab a fruity looking cocktail and find a table. A few of the girls join me and the night begins.

The music is inviting. I close my eyes. I find myself softly swaying from side to side and enjoying the unique cultural rhythm of it. I hear a bit of a commotion and open my eyes. I see Ruler Martinez and some of the judges making their way to the podium. The Specialists also file in and line up near the back wall. I see Archer. He has his hands clasped behind his back. He's standing next to Langt on one side and Peago on the other.

Peago. It just dawned on me that she seems to always turn up next to him when the Specialists are together. Hmmm.

"Contestants! May I have your attention, please," he begins.

We all look at each other dumbfounded. What is this? What now?

"As you may remember, back in Noswaref you learned the Zauber Baum Waltz. At that time, we told you it would be brought back during the race. Well, today is the day," he smiles happily.

That bastard. I have not even thought once about that damn dance. I look over at Archer. He winks at me. I can't help but smile. I hope I can make him proud. He did teach us this dance after all. I take a deep breath and then look over at Jannika. She looks fairly confident. She steals a glance at Langt and he gives her an encouraging nod.

The waltz challenge begins. The contestants must partner with a contestant of the opposite sex. The males choose. I see Archer standing next to Langt against the wall. When it's time for the challenge, Mirko makes an obvious concerted effort to get to me.

This can only mean trouble. I move away, but it doesn't work. As I side step, pretending to be suddenly in need of something to the right, he grabs my elbow and gently pulls me into his arms. I glance in Archer's direction while Mirko escorts me onto the dance floor.

Archer looks up. His back stiffens. He moves to take a step but Langt's arm very casually comes up at the elbow and flips his wrist into Archer's chest. Archer snaps his head at Langt, but Langt just looks at the group of dancers smiling. Archer crosses his arms and leans back against the wall.

"When the dance is finished, the judges will determine the winner. The winner will receive an evening in a first-class accommodation as well as have a financial benefit added to their salary card," Ruler Martinez announces.

There are gasps all around. The thought of sleeping in a luxury suite is enough to make me perform my best. I allow Mirko to lead me in this dance.

The music begins. I curtsy, Mirko bows. He puts his arm around my waist and pulls me in close. I don't even look in Archer's direction but I can feel his eyes on us.

The dance is actually going well. Mirko is a very good dancer. On one of the twirls, he whispers "look at me". I know what he is talking about. Archer would tell me the same thing. It's supposed to be the dance of love but I'm too busy focusing on the steps.

I try to be more attentive but I can tell Mirko is not very pleased. When the dance is over, we all applaud. I look over at Archer. He gives me a little smile.

Rule Martinez makes his way to the podium. "We have the winners," he announces enthusiastically. "And the winners are… Antonella with her partner, Ang." We all applaud. I'm a bit disappointed but not really surprised. Mirko simply walks away.

I walk over to give Antonella a congratulatory hug like all the other girls. She is glowing. The cultural celebration music begins again and we all laugh and dance. I look over at Archer. All the Specialists are gone. Back on their watch, they must be lurking in the shadows.

The rest of us dance and party the night away. This is exactly what we needed. By the time the last dance rolls around, most of the other contestants have left. Lufti made me promise him the next slow dance but I'm absolutely beat. We're the only two left as far as contestants are concerned. It's still pretty crowded with locals who seem as if they can go all night.

Archer shows up to walk me to the hotel. He is talking to some of the men but smiles at me as the band begins the riffs of a slow dance.

Lufti appears from behind and gently takes me in his arms. I look up at his face. He's not actually making eye contact which I find strange given the closeness of the circumstances. I mean, why did he want to dance with me so badly if he won't even look at me?

He leads me around the crowded floor. He's a great dancer. I look up to find Archer but it seems that a lot of men have grouped around his area watching a couple of guys playing some sort of man challenge game. Lufti starts pushing me a little harder leading me to a dark corner.

"What are you doing, Lufti?" I ask pushing back.

He pushes me off him backwards. Someone grabs me from behind and twists my arm. I yell out in pain. But the crowd, the music and shouting men are too loud. I know Archer didn't hear me.

"Shut up. You make a sound and I'll cut your throat," whispers a mystery woman as she presses something sharp against my neck. Lufti bolts into the shadows and is gone. The woman pulls me with her along a darkened wall then across the street. So, I'm bait again. Now what?

I look back to where Archer was. He is on his feet. His eyes are making a sweep of the area. Thankfully, it looks like he is looking for me. The woman moves us behind a wooden fence but if I squint, I can see everything through a crack between the slats. My captor is giving whispered orders to men in her language. I strain to glance behind me. There is a dirt alley road back there and a few rough-looking men milling around.

I turn to see if Archer is still at the cantina. He's there. But as he moves, the crowd moves with him. It's clear they aren't going to let him out. He appears to be outnumbered and overpowered.

I watch as a man tries to engage Archer but Archer moves quickly. As soon as he does, all hell breaks loose. People just start moving in on him. Tables get flipped and things are flying around. Archer's body moves as though it were a dance. He is calculated and precise yet smooth and fluid. Everything around him is useful. A waiter's tray becomes a shield then a weapon that crushes a man's Adam's apple. An umbrella takes a man off his feet then becomes an impaler. He uses forks, knives, plates, and glasses in gruesome ways. Even a broom practically takes a man's head off. Archer's arms are like cannons shattering noses and jaws. He grabs, twists, bends, blocks and rips. Glass is shattering. I can hear bones breaking and men screaming. He always seems a step ahead of them, like he knows what they are going to do before they do it. They don't stand a chance.

Another man charges. Just as he is about to make contact, Archer shifts sideways and swoops while rolling his shoulders. The man rolls across Archer's back and onto the floor beside him. A quick flick of his elbow and Archer's fist comes down like a hammer knocking the man out cold.

More men join the fight. Archer moves with swift elegance. He bends, twists, turns and is missed time and again, but his fists always find their targets. He is making quick work of it. I am mesmerized by him. I can't take my eyes off the entire scene. THIS. IS. A. MASTER.

He steps on the fallen without a thought or care, he's all about getting to the next offender. Within what seems like minutes he has cleared the entire area of fighters, except one. The one holding a blade to my throat.

She yanks me backward and I stumble over something. The trip makes just enough of a noise that Archer's head turns in our direction. He's moving very quickly toward us then kicks through the fence. Our eyes lock for the briefest of moments before he faces my captor and walks with purpose toward us. She pushes the blade tighter on my neck.

He slows. His jaw tightens and his eyes never leave her as he keeps creeping closer.

"Your fight is with me, Minsher," he says firmly. "You and I can settle this. Let her go."

"My fight with you, Archer, is long past. My mission here is to take you out of this race. But I only need to take her out to get you out. She's easy," she says slyly and mockingly.

Archer's eyes narrow as he points his finger at her. "If you take her, there is no place on this earth you can hide from me. I will hunt you down like an animal. Your death will be slow and tortured." His voice is deep, gritty and extremely threatening. I've never heard him like this. He is truly frightening.

"I will complete my mission, Archer. She will be dead long before you find me," she says loudly and rather haughtily.

Dead? She is going to kill me? I thought she couldn't do that. Fear is kicking in and I'm starting to panic. I can't stop it. My knees are getting weak and I'm stumbling a little. I see a blade flipping through Archer's fingers in his right hand. If I see it, no doubt she sees it too. She starts dragging me backwards. She is amazingly strong. A transport pulls up behind us. I want to fight or do something but I'm no match for a Specialist. She's got me tangled up, and I'm terrified. My heart is pounding out of my chest. Is she really going to kill me? I'm starting to breathe quicker.

"Lily," I hear Archer say softly breaking through my crazed thoughts, "look at me." He's only a few steps away. I look at his face. "Just me," he says.

The transport door opens. I search his eyes looking for an answer. I'm so scared and starting to breathe even harder. "Only me," he says softly.

As she pulls me another step back, Archer lunges. I hear a weird popping gurgle noise. The transport rushes away. Archer is in front of me holding the wrist that is holding the blade to my throat. The knife in his other hand is now through the side of Mincher's head. Her body drops.

Everything is going black. I fall into a very strong arm.

I open my eyes. I'm in the hotel room. Archer is lightly tapping my cheeks.

"Hey. You're okay," he says smiling.

"Archer?" I stammer.

"I'm here," he says as he helps me sit up.

Everything comes flooding back to me and I start breathing hard again.

Archer kneels in front of me. "Hey, easy. Drink this," he says softly handing me a cup. "It's over. Everything is okay."

I put my head on his shoulder and cry. "I'm not okay," I whimper.

He takes the cup from me. He puts an arm around me and his other hand on the back of my head and lets me cry.

"I can't promise you it will get any better. The danger is very real. We can end this now and drop out," he says in his calming tone.

I think very seriously about it for a moment. I don't know if I'm cut out for people killing each other. It doesn't seem to bother Archer at all. Of course, he's also doing the killing. I back away and look at him. I mean really gaze at him. This man is a killer. A murderer. I sniff and try to compose myself.

He's looking back at me. His crystal-clear blue eyes are not cold, but filled with compassion. He may be a killer, but he's also my protector. It's all so confusing. I know he'll do whatever I want to do. I lower my head. "I can't quit," I almost whisper. "Can you teach me how to not be affected by the killing and violence like you are?"

He tightens his lips and shakes his head. "I wish I could make it easier for you," he says as he runs a hand down my hair. "But I can't. I will stand with you and with your decision if you choose not to continue."

"Why are other teams not going through this?" I'm a little surprised by the bit of a whine in my voice as though I'm sixteen again and life is so unfair.

"That last team was affected greatly by the outcome of what happened," he explains logically. "That young man will not get very far without his Specialist. I plan to make sure of it."

That is the last thing I thought he would say. But his logical mind is truthful. I guess he's right. The more they come at us, the more they also take a chance of being disqualified, probably by the death of the Specialist. I shudder to think about it again.

We hear a loud knock on the door. Archer disappears to answer it.

"Because of what happened, and the rest of the political problems in this area, they are moving all the contestants to transports and taking them to the checkpoint. We have to go to the police station to answer a few questions."

He helps me up and stays next to me the entire time. Most of the time, he has his arm around me. He is so supportive. When they try to pull me away from him to take me to a separate room, I turn and cling tightly to him. Archer strokes my hair and smiles at me letting me know everything will be okay.

A race attendant stays with me during questioning. Basically, the police ask me what happened, and I tell them everything. They release me but I insist on waiting for Archer. They try to bully me into leaving, but I won't budge. I'm afraid for him. He killed someone in a foreign country. The policemen finally walk away down the hall. Archer returns to me moments later.

"It's going to take me a while longer, Lily, it usually does. They don't particularly like my kind, knowing I can clear their entire office handily." He smiles. "But don't worry, I'll be okay. I was fully in the right to defend myself and you," he says with smiling eyes. "Go with the race attendant. Get on the commuter. I will see you on the next leg, okay?"

"I don't want to leave you. You had to rescue me. This is my fault."

"It was not your fault," he says firmly, "it was Mincher's fault."

"I'm not leaving," I reply resolutely.

"If you do not get on the transport, you may forfeit your place in the race." The race attendant says flatly.

"I'm the reason he's here," I retort.

Archer takes a breath and goes to talk to the Police captain. They both come back to me.

"The Archer will walk you to the race commuter," the Police Captain says.

"Thank you, sir," I respond to the Captain then turn to Archer, "I'm not sure I should leave you."

Archer puts his hand on my back and walks me out. Not only is the race attendant following close behind but also four heavily armed policeman with their guns pointing at Archer.

"Don't worry," Archer says quietly, "I'm used to talking to police. I'll be with you on the next leg."

When I arrive at the commuter, the other contestants are still going through. I wonder why they are still outside.

I look up at Archer and he smiles.

Zara rushes over to me. "The commuter just landed. Some of the contestants still aren't here. Hurry!" Zara encourages pulling my hand. "Step through." She steps through while I try to get my bearings. I need to say goodbye to Archer but she hauls me over the checkpoint.

"Number seven" can be heard over the speaker.

I turn around but Archer and the police are already on their way to the station. Archer turns back and gives a reassuring wink.

I find my way to my room and flop on the bed. I'm still so shaky as I lie here remembering what happened. That knife sticking out of Mincher's head is something I don't think I'll ever forget. I get shivers just thinking about it. Something from this whole experience dawns on me again as though it's the first time, Archer is quite deadly and quite scary. I would hate to be on the wrong side of him. But then I think about his gentleness and kindness; like his trying to get me to focus on him and not the bad stuff going on. I wish I could have talked to him more about what happened but at least we're both okay.

CHAPTER 26

Scoterie

The commuter was delayed five days in Razatina because of the attack. I often wondered how long they kept Archer at the police station. I understand Lufti was detained as well for his involvement. Since that made him last, he was eliminated from the race. Good.

At breakfast before the race release, I sit down with my oatmeal and plum, while hearing some of the girls, led by Poppi, at the next table giggling. I lean closer but I can't hear what's being said. But then I'm pretty sure I hear them say Archer's name. Now, I definitely get closer and listen.

They are gossiping that Archer and Peago sneak off together whenever they can and have crazy sex together. They also announced that he and Peago would have gotten married if they could, but since they can't get married, they get together whenever they can and make mad passionate love to each other. Wait, what?!

I flop back in my chair, breakfast forgotten. For reasons I don't even want to think about right now, this news completely devastates me. I get up and walk back to my room, trying to look casual, closing the door behind me. As soon as I turn away from the door, my breath catches in my throat. My knees suddenly get weak as I stumble to my bed. I feel totally emotionally traumatized. I don't know whether to cry, faint, or just fall to my knees. This message is certainly clear, I have developed serious feelings for Archer and this attachment to Peago is like a bomb going off inside of me.

I rack my brain to see if there is any merit in the rumor. I know she puts her hands on him every time I see them together. I also remember that just before the dance Archer and Peago walked in together and stood against the wall watching the dance beside each other. Where had they been? What had they been doing? Shit! And here I was so concerned about him interacting with the police. Maybe he's been having a fling in Peago's bed for the last five days. Dammit!

What's worse, I know I can't compete with her. I will never be able to compete with her. She is possibly the most beautiful woman I've ever seen. What man wouldn't want to be with her? My emotional state plummets. I roll my face into my pillow and begin to shed giant, raw, stinging tears.

My intercom bell brings me back to life as the announcement that we are to be at the starting point in 5 minutes cuts through the room. I try to pull myself together by dragging to the bathroom and flushing my face with a stream of water. I have to find a way to get past this somehow so I can finish the race, I rationalize. At least now I know the truth. Or do I? I decide to watch their behavior at the next group campsite to see what happens.

We are released and the group mostly stays together until we get to the campsite. Our Specialists take off to build the shelters while we help prepare dinner, set up the tables and such. It was good to see Archer and know he's okay. He looks good. But it makes things worse too. My mind begins to think about Peago with him in romantic poses. Ugh!

After dinner, the contestants are to participate in a lecture of the Region's local culture and any new rules that pertain to this area. Tomorrow, we will begin at the Puckett Estate. It's a very large and well-respected establishment. We can get disqualified for any fighting or negligible acts while on the premises.

When we are released from the race information, I try to spy out where the Specialists are hanging out. Finally, I see them all relaxed, conversing around a large bonfire at the bottom of the hill.

I stand discretely at the top looking over to where they have gathered. They appear to be laughing and socializing quite a bit. I see Archer. His arms are folded across his chest and he appears to be having a good laugh. Peago is sitting next to him. She is very close, in fact, she is almost sitting on his lap! She is tapping her fingertips lightly on his knee. That's rather possessive. Anger wells up inside of me. That is all the proof I need.

I stand to leave then take one last look. Archer is on his feet looking straight right at me. His brow is furrowed and he is walking away from the others. Peago is watching him but looks up at me, too. I turn away and run back to the shelter. I grab my pack quickly and run full sprint to a nearby hotel.

I secure a room. Once inside, I lock the door. I barely put my things down when I hear a knock on the door. I walk to it and call out, "Who is it?"

"Lily? Will you let me in?" Archer asks gently twisting the door handle.

I lean against the door and take a breath.

"No, Archer. I need some time alone." I don't want to talk to him right now.

"What's troubling you? How can I help?" He's so sincere but the thought of him and Peago…I just don't want to see his face right now. I really need to get my emotions under control.

"Please go away, Archer. Let me get my thoughts together," I am strong in my resolve.

"Please, tell me. What is it? Let me help. We're a team," he beseeches.

"No, Archer. Leave me alone," I say firmly.

"You know I could bust this door down right now?" His tone is on the menacing side.

"I know you can. Please don't. Please just go away," I plead trying to keep things calm.

"I will give you your space tonight. But we will talk about this tomorrow."

After a few minutes, I look out the peep hole. He is gone.

I have a terrible, restless night. I don't know how to get over this. But I have to figure it out quick or my race is doomed. The best I come up with is to try to let it go. If he's in love with Peago, there is nothing I can do about that. Perhaps I can somehow keep a bit of an emotional distance until my heart heals.

I rise early and get to the ferry. There are a few race attendants there, and I sit with them until the other Specialists and race contestants arrive. Archer quietly stares at me as he leans against the dock railing at the back of the boat. Other Specialists soon surround him to engage him in conversation.

I find a seat on the ferry with the other contestants making small talk. I honestly can't focus on what they are saying because I'm so preoccupied with this whole Archer/Peago fiasco. I glance sideways noting that Peago found a spot next to Archer as usual. They are all laughing over there. I happen to look over just in time to see Peago's hand on Archer's chest. Her other elbow is leaning on his shoulder and she flips her beautiful hair as she talks to him.

I can't take it and I certainly don't need this in my face right now. Archer has a prerogative to love her but I don't want to know. I need some air. I get up to walk to the forward lavatory. Tears are pricking my eyes but I'm desperately trying to hold it together until I can get to the restroom. There is a small windowed door just beyond the lavatories and can see that it leads to a small room and then a passageway beyond it to the front deck. That's where I'll head next, but first I must splash some water on my face to clear the signs of my emotional distress.

I come out of the lavatory and head through the small door on my way to the front deck. Once through the door I hear "Hey." I turn quickly to find Archer leaning next to the door. I start to turn around but he puts his arm out and closes the door.

"Hey," he says slowly while reaching out for my waist. "C'mere." He pulls me next to his body and lifts my chin to face him.

"What's this all about?" he asks gently.

"Archer, I don't want to talk about this right now," I answer trying to back away from this iron grip.

"Oh yes, we will discuss it this very minute," he states not budging.

We hear Peago calling out to him. "Archer? Archer, where are you?"

"You better leave. Peago's calling."

He shrugs, "I don't care about Peago. She's not important to me."

I look at him. "But I thought…"

"You thought what?" he asks tilting his head. "Is that what this is all about? My relationship with Peago?"

Boom. He said it. His relationship with Peago. I try to wiggle away.

"Please, Archer, let me go." The tears start burning again but he holds tight. I don't want Peago to find us like this.

"There is no relationship with Peago," he answers shaking his head with his brow furrowed.

"They saw you," I return still wiggling.

"Saw me what? Who?" he questions.

I stop wiggling and say it to his face, "I was told that you and Peago sneak off together at night."

He scoffs. "Lily, I'm with you every night. When am I supposed to have gone off for a tryst with Peago? There's no truth to it. Who's telling you this? Another contestant? Don't you think it would serve a purpose to try to tear our team apart?"

"Archer?" We hear Peago just outside of the door.

He's searching my eyes but I can't answer him because Peago is so close, and I'm extremely uncomfortable. I turn away from him and won't say anything.

Archer breathes out of his nose in an annoyed sort of way while releasing me to turn and face the door as she opens it.

"There you are," she purrs.

"What is it, Peago?" he is not so warm.

"We're getting ready to start another game but it wouldn't be the same without you. Are you coming?" she asks with her pretty pout.

"No, I won't be joining you. Please play your game without me," he says coldly.

"Okay, how about dinner tonight? Can you get away?"

Does she not realize I'm here? This is very awkward. I start to leave but Archer grabs my fingers with his.

He turns back to Peago. "No dinner. Please excuse us," he answers.

She looks at me with a "scorned woman" scowl. Archer leads me through the next door out onto the front deck. It's a beautiful day.

There is a light breeze coming off the water. I lean against the railing looking away from him. Archer comes to my side. He leans on his side facing me. I glance over at him. His wavy blonde hair is blowing freely.

"Please don't be jealous of Peago," he requests softly. "It is entirely your imagination. I have no thought or care for her."

"Who said I was jealous?" I ask embarrassed. Am I that transparent?

"Your actions," he reveals smiling. "When you're jealous you like to avoid the issue, run away and sulk in silence." I look at him. This is not amusing to me, but he continues, "When I'm jealous, I lash out and won't listen to reason."

I gasp and look up him. "Mirko?" I ask astonished. "You were jealous?"

He nods his affirmation. "Very much so. When I saw him lying next to you, I wanted to break his neck. I think it's safe to say that we have a genuine fondness for one another."

I just nod.

"Having made that now known, if I see another man seeking your attentions, I'll safely assume he's uninvited. If you see another woman placing her hands on me, you can assume the same. Is that clear?"

I concede smiling.

I see Peago peering out the door's window.

"She's looking at us," I whisper.

"I know she is," he leans to me quietly while smiling. I'm looking into those blue eyes as he bends down and gives me a little peck on the cheek then brushes it with his thumb.

"Never run from me again," he whispers tenderly. "Talk to me first."

I agree still reeling from his affection. Peago is gone.

CHAPTER 27

We get off the ferry and, as instructed, head to the Puckett Estate. According to the posted sign, the gates will open in one hour, but more importantly that it's a team task. I stand at the starting gate with the rest of the group. We have plenty of time to look at the job ahead of us.

We can see marked-off sections which appear to be work areas. In each section, there are bunches of miscellaneous pieces of, I'm assuming bicycle parts, and a small box of tools. I think we have to build a bicycle. The gate opens and we all run to an unclaimed work area. I pick up the task card.

TASK: WITHOUT THE HELP OF YOUR PARTNER, CONTESTANTS MUST BUILD TWO BICYCLES FROM THE PARTS IN YOUR WORK AREA. ONCE THE JUDGE APPROVES THE COMPLETED BICYCLES, YOU AND YOUR PARTNER MUST RIDE THEM 2 KILOMETERS ALONG THE MARKED ROAD TO HUMTER FIELDS. ONCE THERE, FIND YOUR NEXT TASK CARD.

I get to work quickly. I've built many similar types of mechanical devices so this should be a breeze. I'm also sure it's probably a breeze for the majority of the field here.

Once I have my first bicycle assembled, I look around to see Jannika, who has already started on her second one and so has Zara, Banzi and Mirko. I need to move. As I'm finishing my second bicycle, I hear Jannika and Banzi call for a judge. When I call for the judge, so do Zara and Mirko. I see Jannika and Langt are peddling down the street and Mirko and Kavalaris are getting on theirs.

The judge approves mine. Archer is quickly beside me. We get on the bikes and waste no time leaving. My team is third out of the gate. I feel good about this but I'd feel better if we were closer to the lead. Archer keeps pace with me. He is casually peddling and enjoying the scenery while I feel like I'm working diligently and going nowhere. He looks cool while I'm dripping with sweat and completely out of breath.

I would like to look like I'm not a total sticky mess but a cute, exciting girl. How am I ever going to fully attract Archer when I'm sweating like a pig and snorting like a horse to catch my breath? I'm sure Peago looks fabulous as she rides the bike. I stop myself. I can't think about that right now. I know I shouldn't compare myself to her either. She may be beautiful but Archer doesn't appear to desire her the way she is going after him.

We get to the farm. It's huge. There's a table with some refreshment. Archer and I both step into the appropriate facilities to use the restroom. I don't know about Archer, but I also take a very brief moment to wash my face and clean up some.

When I step out, I see Archer at the refreshment table. He has a cup in one hand and a sandwich in the other. I do likewise. Then we move to the task table. We never know if it's something that only I do, or if both of us must participate.

TASK: TEAMS MUST TEND THE FARM. ROLL TWO BALES OF HAY FROM THE OUTER FIELDS TO THE BARN. DISTRIBUTE THE HAY THROUGHOUT THE BARN TO THE VARIOUS FEEDING TROUGHS. THEN FIND THE WATER VATS AND FILL ONE OF THE MARKED WATERING TROUGHS TO THE TOP. WHEN COMPLETE FINALIZE THE DAY BY SPREADING FERTILIZING MANURE DOWN 1 OF THE MARKED ROWS OF THE PLANTING FIELDS.

I look at Archer. He raises his eyebrows at me then grabs a pair of the provided work gloves for the men. I grab a pair of ladies' work gloves and we head to the outer fields. This place is huge! The outer fields must be a mile out. The hay bales are so enormous they rise over Archer's head by a good two feet. I see Langt and Mirko pushing one each while Jannika and Kavalaris, push one. it's not so easy for them as it is for the men. Archer gets behind one of the bales and pushes.

He looks at me. "They are heavy, Lily. Let's move it together. We'll make quick work of it and come back for the other." I agree.

"Let me get it started, then you jump in," he says as he begins to move the bale and then picks up speed. I have to jog to keep up but then he moves over so I can jump in to help. He is really carrying the load here. If truth be told, I'm barely touching this thing. We pass the other two ladies.

When we get to the first gate, he stops.

"Let's go get the other one," he says wiping the sweat from his brow. We jog back to the closest bale and push it to the first gate.

He maneuvers the bales through the gate then we take one at a time again to the second gate. Once through, we deliver them to the barn.

Archer rips the netting that holds the bale together with a mighty pull. I start grabbing hay and running it to the feeding areas. Archer moves to the next one and rips it open. He's been working hard. He's not running as fast as I, but he's getting the job done.

Once that part is completed, we look around for the marked watering vats. There are many close by but not marked. We finally find them at the farthest point away on the back of the building. We have to carry them by the bucket full to the water troughs in the front stables. Damn. We're going to be a while.

"Let's move together so we are filling at the same time," he suggests.

I agree while taking his lead.

We pass Mirko. Archer looks at him over his shoulder. He clearly does not trust him. Mirko stumbles a little and Archer smirks. No love lost there.

We finish the water and head over to the planting. We make a detour to the refreshment station for a quick water break. There are many teams here now at various stages of the task. All are looking very hot and sweaty.

Archer grabs one of the wheelbarrows and rolls it to the colossal pile of manure. I thought the place smelled bad before. As I stand next to this pile, I can't help but heave and gag. Archer ignores me and shovels it in the wheelbarrow. We take off to the planting rows.

We are assigned one of the rows. Small holes have already been made along this entire planting row. The row is unbelievably long. A farm woman demonstrates what we need to do. We have to use small shovels to fill each hole with manure to prepare the field for the coming days of planting. Then cap the hole with a dollop of soil.

Archer takes the wheelbarrow down the row. "You start at the beginning and I'll work this way. We'll move the wheelbarrow when you get to it," he informs.

I like his plan. We start dipping our shovel in the poop and get the job going. By the time we are finished, we are streaked with sweat and poo. Other teams are close behind. We run to the timeline to stop our clock. We are second. We passed Mirko up on the list! We are to make camp here tonight and will leave in second place in the morning. Four large tents are provided for contestant girls, specialist ladies, contestant guys and specialist guys. There are showers in another building. Archer and I don't even pause; we make our way there immediately.

Once inside the ladies' showers, I see a large bin where we can throw our filthy clothes. Towels and clean clothes are provided. I go to the shower area. Jannika is already there. I strip and jump into a vacant stall. The hot water feels sumptuous. The soap has a very clean outdoorsy scent. I guess that is what you'd expect from a farm.

After the evening meal, I go to the girl's tent and pick a cot to rest. Other girls start coming in. I'm so tired that their chattering doesn't deter me at all as I feel myself drifting off to sleep.

CHAPTER 28

After breakfast, Archer and I depart in second place. We have to catch up to the leaders. Archer leads the way through a trail among the trees. It's rather fun while spooky at the same time. This path cuts right through the forest. After a few hours, the path fizzles out and we have to make our way through it on our own.

When we finally clear the trees, we are faced with an immense white sandstone wall in front us. It must be over 18 feet high and spanning as far as the eye can see on either side. We look at each other. Another team breaks through the trees. It is Langt and Jannika. How did we pass them?

They, too, take in the view of the wall, then Langt and Archer look at each other for a moment.

"I got you," Langt says.

Archer scoffs. I have no idea what was just said between them, but as always, these two have an unspoken language all their own.

Archer backs up a good distance away and takes a deep breath. Langt looks behind him and shrugs, "You have about six." he yells. Archer nods his understanding. I'm assuming he means there is going to be 6 feet of clearance between Langt and the wall.

Archer runs full speed at Langt. At the last moment, just before impact he actually jumps with one foot landing into Langt's awaiting cupped hands. Langt gives him a heaving push as Archer springs in the air leaping several feet higher than he needed to clear the wall and easily lands on its ledge.

Archer disappears for a moment and then reappears. "It's quite a steep slope. The rampart is decent."

Langt looks at him. "Jannika first." I guess the competitor in them never really goes away even though they seem like good friends.

Archer agrees.

Langt directs Jannika to stand on his shoulders. Archer positions himself so he is gripping the top of the wall but then lowers his body so it is actually hanging down its side. That is the only way these men can get us to the top of this tall monstrosity. Langt speaks in their language to Jannika and puts his hands, palms up on his shoulders. Jannika climbs on his body and steps on his hands. He then extends his arms lifting her to Archer's legs. She grabs onto Archer and climbs up over his body to the top of the wall where she pulls herself over.

Langt turns to me and we repeat the steps until I am able to pull myself over the wall.

I know Langt can't reach Archer on his own and wonder how they are going to do this. I watch Langt back up further than Archer did. Archer moves to get a better grip. Langt takes off full speed at the wall. Just as he gets to the wall, he jumps and takes two steps up the wall then launches himself toward Archer. Archer's arm muscles bulge as Langt attaches himself to Archer's torso quickly climbing up and over the wall then turning and clasping arms with Archer as together, their impressive strength completes the task of getting Archer back on top of the wall.

We can hear more teams rustling quickly through the trees. We make haste to move to the other side of the rampart so we are not visible. It's getting cooler and the sun is losing its grip behind cloud cover.

Jannika and I look at each other.

"Why don't we work together?" Jannika asks but Langt is looking off in the distance and Archer has begun moving to the left.

He turns to me and holds out his hand, "time to go." I look at Langt who is still looking off in the distance although he is reaching for Jannika's hand. She looks up at him curiously.

"Come, Lily," Archer says. I take his hand not really understanding what is happening. These men continue in their unspoken language and it's clear that they want separation from one another. The competition must be fueling them to be the best.

Archer pulls me along quickly as we run on the ramparts of this wall which now reveals that it is connected at various places to turrets and towers of perhaps a long-ago fortress. I look behind but I don't see Langt and Jannika anywhere. Maybe they took to the ground or maybe they are so far opposite that we can no longer see them. The fact that I can't see them now stirs the competitor in me and I wonder if they got a jump on us.

"Archer? Why did you and Langt behave that way? I thought you were friends."

"We are friendly. This is a race. I'm not going to give it to him and he's not going to give it to me. At some point, hard choices will have to be made. It's best if we go our own way and may the best man get his contestant to the checkpoint first," he replies as we run along.

Scoterie is beautiful with its lush greenery and verdant forests. The air is getting much colder, and I can feel the bristle of a light drizzle.

It's as though the nights here have a life of their own, producing cold and damp conditions conducive to a good night's sleep.

Archer finds a tower with an intact roof and helps me inside. It's over grown with dead vines which he quickly pulls up twisting them together to make kindling for a nice, warm fire next to the back curve of the room away from the windows. We only have one small thermal blanket in our pack so I imagine our night will be cozy.

I look out the back window and down the tower to the ground far below. I feel like a princess in a fairy story wondering what it would be like to let down my hair so my true love prince can climb up and claim me. I laugh to myself. If only…

I look at Archer. He could easily be that prince. I want him to be that prince, but I don't think he actually thinks of me in that way.

He looks out the back window and I hear him let out a sighing breath. I can see his eyes scanning far and wide.

"What is it?"

He turns and walks to me. "Dinner appears to be slim pickins."

"That's okay. I'm not really hungry right now," I assure him.

The rain begins to come down heavily. After a few minutes it is accompanied by thunder and lightning. The temperature takes a dive as well. I sit in front the fire trying to get warm. Archer is moving around the tower pulling all the vines into a pile. Suddenly a snake slithers out from under them toward me. I scream, jump up, and run to the window.

Archer is fast. He is on top of the snake very quickly grabbing it just behind its head. He's smiling. "Dinner!" he beams.

"I'm not eating that," I inform him.

"It's not poisonous," he says looking at me. "This variety is actually quite tasty. Will you at least try it," he asks taking out a knife.

I let out a relenting sigh and nod in compliance.

He goes to the back window and dresses the beast preparing it for the fire. At least he's throwing all the skin out so there's not much in the way of blood and guts in the room with us. That was really thoughtful of him.

I happen to look up as he pulls the bones out of it and then look quickly away again. I'm not good with watching that. I mean, I can do it if I have to, but I'd really rather not. When he's finished, he brings it over to the fire. I stand and back away giving him plenty of room to work. I go to the window to watch the storm outside.

The snake begins to sizzle. I can smell it. I turn around to watch Archer's culinary skills at the fire. Either the snake doesn't smell all that bad or I'm famished. Archer's back goes rigid and suddenly he is fully alert. I know that look. He stands and moves to the front window. He pulls his bow in front of him and draws an arrow. He leans back against the wall and nocks his arrow blindly. He looks at me and motions his head down. I lower myself into a low crouching position.

I can't see what's going on but I'm not moving. Suddenly, a pair of rough looking men appear outside the window. They see me.

"What's this," one of them yells over the loud storm. He holds his coat close to his chin as the rain pelts down on him.

Archer moves quickly in front of the window with his arrow pointing at their faces. "Don't even think about it," he shouts.

Startled, they stop. One takes a relaxed stance. "Come now, lad. It's cold and wet out 'ere," he asserts.

"Move away or I'll move you away," Archer growls in a cold and calculating manner.

They back away a short distance, then stand there looking at him, then each other, me and lastly, the fire. It's clear they are going to try get through him. Archer knows also. He drops his bow and is out the window in one smooth, fluid movement,

The rain is beating them ferociously. Archer holds out his hands and gives them a smirk as he dares them to "bring it on". Sometimes I think he really enjoys fighting.

They look at each other and go for it. Archer's catlike movements are silky and lithe. He's quick and elegant. His opponents grunt and moan as he lands well-placed blows to their bodies. Then he helps them over the side of the rampart. I run to the window knowing that fall should have killed them but I see them run off on the mushy ground slowly and limping painfully. Archer is watching them even though the rain is saturating him.

He looks at me as he enters the window. "They didn't break anything," he says.

I don't say anything. Archer is dripping. I can smell the snake beginning to burn. He steps to the fire, flips dinner over and moves back to the window. He takes off his shirt and rings it out. He rubs and shakes his head, too. He returns to the fire and lays out his shirt. He takes off his shoes and lays them close also. He needs to get out of all those wet clothes. It is really cold in here.

"What about the pants?" I ask.

"There's nothing underneath," he says shaking his head.

"Well, I'll turn away so you can at least take them off and give them a good wringing."

He agrees. When he's finished, he calls me to the fire. Our snake is also done. As I eat it, it occurs to me that he was right again. It's actually very good.

Archer reinforces the fire. I can see that he is shivering. I check. His shirt is dry. I pick it up and hand it to him.

"Archer, please remove your pants," I request. He looks up at me with raised brows. "You're shivering. Put the blanket around you." I get up and grab the blanket.

"You need the blanket," he says pulling his shirt on. "I'll be fine. My pants will dry soon."

I kneel next to him with the blanket and look him in the eye. "I need you. Please take your pants off. We can wrap this blanket around your waist at least until they dry."

His lips curve into a slight smile and he agrees. He stands and I hold the blanket above my head to give him some privacy as he shimmies off his wet pants. I hear him walk to the window and wring them out again. I peak at his naked rear end. He's beautiful. I look away as he turns back. He takes the thin thermal blanket and wraps it around his waist. I see that he has lain his pants next to the fire.

He sits next to its warmth. "Come," he insists holding out his arm. I sit in front of him, snuggling into his arms and leaning my head against his chest. He pulls me onto his lap and holds me as we absorb the fire's heat mingling it with the warmth of our bodies.

★★★

I wake up all wrapped up in the blanket. The fire is still going strongly. Archer and his pants are missing.

I rub my face and stand. It's a cool morning but warming up, in fact, I feel very warm. I grab my canteen for a drink. I'm actually very thirsty. I fold the blanket and walk to window. I see some deer grazing. I turn in the other direction and watch a team in the distance running across the grass into the trees. It hits me with a sudden sense of urgency. I run to the other window and observe Archer moving quickly toward me from atop the ramparts.

"I found a rope nearby. We can repel to get underway," he says jumping through the window. He takes care of the fire and we pull our things together. He helps me out of the window and we take off running across this wall. I see the rope ahead.

Archer grabs it and checks the knots and gadgets. He gets into position on the wall making sure his grip is as he wants it. He motions for me.

"Wrap your legs around my waist and arms around my neck. Put all of your weight on my torso."

I climb onto him. As he lowers us down, I get a very good view of the surrounding area. It's very green and the forest looks lush and dense. I know we will have to get through there like the other teams.

Once on the ground, we race for the trees. It becomes evident that the forest is as thick as I imagined. We can hear other teams nearby but we don't see them. I wonder how far ahead Langt and Jannika are. I think the journey to the checkpoint is by boat but I don't see any water. I'm not sure where the checkpoint is but Archer knows. I'm guessing we must have a long way to go.

After several hours of walking, we finally see a break in the tree line. "Look, Archer. I believe I see the ocean in the distance." I begin moving more quickly.

"Lily, wait. I want to fill up the canteens first," Archer tells me as he side steps to a small stream. I give him my canteen but I don't wait. I run through the trees and burst out onto a beautiful grassy plain. A phenomenal ocean view welcomes me and I draw in a breath of its beauty.

I quickly walk the length of the greenest grass I've ever seen. I can't believe I'm standing on top of this cliff looking down at the magnificent ocean below. The view is amazing. The cliffs go straight down. Across the water, I can see a stretch of beach far ahead. It looks like a small white stripe between the surrounding orange cliffs and the aqua blue hues of the ocean. I stand on the edge and just breathe in the salty, fresh air. It reminds me of home.

I turn around to find Archer. He must see this. I observe Archer coming through the trees but Banzi is running at him from behind and tackles him just as he turns toward him. Where did he come from? Why is he fighting Archer? Is he crazy? I take a step toward him but Archer efficiently throws Banzi over his shoulder onto the ground.

Everything seems to move in slow motion. As Banzi is falling to the ground, Archer looks to his right and then turns to me with wide eyes as he is raising his hand. I feel the prick of the darts before I ever see Peago. I turn my head and watch as she lowers her blow gun. She tilts her head to the side as if to say, "oh sorry, too bad".

I feel a tingle in the small of my back. I can't move. What did she hit me with? I am paralyzed from the neck down. The slight momentum from her darts is just enough to push me backwards. I see Archer running in my direction, but he is too far away from me. I'm going over the edge of the cliff and there is nothing I can do. For some reason, I can't even scream!

I hit the water below with such force that the precious little breath I have left escapes. This is such a cruel way to die. I can't even fight to live. I can only observe my final minutes. As I sink, I start swallowing water.

CHAPTER 29

I'm on my side coughing up water on a beach. I feel someone rubbing my back and open my eyes. It's Archer. He looks like a train wreck. He's soaked and seriously gasping for air. I've never seen him like this. I still can't move below my neck. I can see the cliffs where I was standing at some distance over Archer's shoulder.

He stands up and looks around still trying to catch his breath. I see him start to press his wrist band.

"No," I say, but nothing is coming out so I try again, "No!" I try to yell but it comes out as a whisper.

Archer looks at me and comes to my side. He kneels next to me.

"I have to call in the evac, Lily. You need an ambulance. Peago hit you with some kind of neural debilitator and I don't know how long it will last. I've given you the antidote that I have and it's not working. The tide's coming in and we have nowhere to go like this. We have to get you thoroughly checked out."

"No. They'll take me out. Please, no." I beg him. My voice is a gruff whisper. I know this could mean the end of the race and the end of my brother's hopes. I burst into tears. To make matters worse, I can't cover myself and Archer is going to get the full effect of my ugly cry face.

He lifts me in his arms pushing my head to his chest so I can sob it out. He keeps looking up at the cliffs. I hope he's making some sort of plan.

Archer carries me to the base of the cliff and leans me against the rock. He stands, looking up then starts climbing to a ledge about 20 feet above me and tests its strength. I can see a water line very close to the top of it. I wonder if that is how high the water comes up to at high tide. Right now, I see the water touching my toes. He climbs back down to me.

"Try moving your fingers," he coaxes.

I try but nothing happens. They are not moving. Am I going to be paralyzed forever?

"No, nothing," I reply.

"Damn it! I could break her scrawny little neck," he exclaims to himself and paces a few more minutes.

He releases a sigh while running his fingers through his hair moving the wet strands out of his face. I look at his eyes. For the first time, he looks extremely concerned, almost worried. He looks back at me and stares at me for a moment. His face suddenly fills with compassion. He reaches down and moves a piece of wet hair from my face.

"There is a ledge," he starts softly and then takes a deep breath, "however, getting you up to it could be a problem. Without your ability to hold onto me you/we could fall off during the climb. But it is the only way without calling in the medical evac."

"I know. I am willing to take the risk if you are."

He stands and paces for several minutes. He comes back over and leans down. His hands are on his knees and water is still dripping from his hair.

"I don't know that I am," he says. "Do you understand the seriousness of this situation? If you fall, you could die, right here, right now."

He paces again. The water has made it to my heels.

"Archer." I speak softly but firmly. He looks at me. "If I can't complete this race, my brother will die and my life will be ruined anyway. Please try this for me."

He comes back over and kneels next to me. "You say that now, but you will recover from this. I don't know how long it will take, but I know you will come out of it and you will be able to live your life."

"What kind of life," I whisper as tears run down my cheeks. He and I both know that if I lose this opportunity, I will take my brother down too and I will never be able to move up in the world. I consider my paradise prison. No matter how great the location, it's still a prison if you aren't free. I have one chance and this is it.

I look down. The water is up to my knees. If we wait much longer none of this is going to matter anyway because I'm going to drown.

Archer stands. I hear him sigh. He looks up at the ledge again then bends down and takes the straps off of his shoes. He ties them quickly together. He puts the straps in his mouth and clamps down with his teeth, using his hands to pull them tight. He tests their strength and kicks his now useless shoes aside.

He kneels next to me and ties my hands together with the straps. He stands us both up with me in front of him and lifts my arms over his head holding me against him. I look into his eyes and kiss him lightly.

"Thank you," I say.

He shakes his head. "This could pull your arms right of out of their sockets. I don't know if it will work." He breathes deeply and starts to climb. I'm being jolted against the rock but I can't feel it. I know my back is going to take a beating today.

He's right, without the ability to help hold myself up, I'm just hanging in front of him. The pressure on his neck must be excruciating. No wonder he didn't hang me off his back, I'd be choking him to death.

He's definitely struggling somewhat to climb with all this dead weight on his neck, but he's managing very slowly. We finally get to the ledge. At least it is soft with green grass. He leans my back against the rock then unties my hands which are purple from the lack of blood flow. He sits next to me for moment leaning back against the wall of the cliff to catch his breath. When he has somewhat recovered, he lifts himself up on one knee and turns to me.

"Let's make sure we didn't dislocate your shoulders," he says. He feels and presses around my shoulders. "Everything seems to be just as it should be." He smiles. Then he takes my right arm in his hands and vigorously rubs it all over. Then he does the same thing with my left arm.

The sun is heating up and beating down on my face. I'm going to look like a lobster after all this. I hope I don't blister. I don't want to raise my concerns to Archer and I certainly don't want to complain after what he just did for me. He seems so very out of sorts.

After tending me, he stands up and looks up at the cliff way up high and then at me. I squint my eyes because of the sun. He comes over to me and turns me to my side trying to keep me in the little bit of the shade of the cliff.

"I'm going to climb up and see if I can find something that will lift you out without harming you in the process. You'll be safe here for the time being."

I look at him and agree.

He starts climbing up the side. He's making much quicker work of it without the addition of my weight. He disappears over the top and then looks back down at me. He disappears again.

I must've fallen asleep. I don't know how long he has been gone. At first, I think it could be that he's only been gone 10 minutes or so but the tide has come in considerably. It is more than half way up to the ledge I'm sitting on.

I try to move my fingers. They move! I'm so happy I start to tear up. I continue to try to move other parts of my body. I find that I can wiggle my toes as well. That's all so far but I have hope. It gives me incentive to keep trying.

The fresh air and sunshine must have taken its toll. I wake up again not realizing that I had drifted off to sleep. It's now late afternoon. I can move my arms which is great. I turn myself some still leaning against the rock. I can wiggle my toes and feet but I'm not able to move my legs quite yet. I'm worried about Archer. He's been gone a long time. Did he forget me?

I hear someone yelling below me and pull myself over to the side of the ledge. I peer over and see two men in a fishing boat. They are waving up at me. I wave back and smile.

"Ahoy there," one of them yells. "Do you need some help?"

I pause for a moment. Yes, I'd like off this rock but should I wait for Archer? Where is he? What if something happened to him and I'll be stuck on this rock forever?

"Yes," I call back instinctively. "My legs are injured."

"Understood," one of the men yells.

They maneuver the boat closer to the cliff then try to the throw up the life ring to me. After a few attempts, it lands close enough that I can grab it. I pull it over my head and around my waist and give them a wave.

One of the men jumps into the water and the other pulls the rope essentially pulling me over the ledge. I hit the water hard but manage to hang on to the life ring. The initial shock of the water's coldness stabs the breath from me and I gasp. The man in the boat pulls me toward him. The man in the water helps lift me into the boat.

They make me comfortable and give me some water then start the engines and head off. As we leave, I look to the cliff. There is still no sign of Archer. I turn away. What am I going to do now?

By the time we reach the docks, I am able to move my legs. The fishermen help me out of the boat. I stand looking around. There is nothing here. It took us a good two hours to get here and darkness is closing in fast. I have no idea where I am. At least I can now walk if I go very slowly.

"Can I drop you somewhere," The curly haired fisherman asks.

"Is there a hotel nearby? How far am I from Umberton?"

"Umberton," asks the blonde fishman. "That's at least 25 kilometers from here." My heart sinks. How am I going to walk 25 kilometers? I stand stunned.

"Let me take you home to my wife. You look like you can use some female companionship," he says.

I look at myself. I'm a disaster. I can barely walk, my clothes are filthy, my hair is matted, I'm completely sunburned from head to toe and on the verge of hysterical fit. No wonder he thinks I need a nursemaid. I just nod to him gratefully.

The man doesn't live too far from the docks. It seems like a quick 10-minute ride to his humble but comfortable looking home. We pull up in a dirt driveway and he helps me out of the vehicle.

His wife's name is Dandi. She says it's short for Dandelion. It suits her. She has a large volume of curly blonde hair that she pulls up on top of her head. It is just frizzy enough that it poofs out in all directions.

They help me up to the spare bedroom. The fisherman leaves and closes the door behind him. Dandi helps me out of my clothes.

"The back of your outfit is in shreds. I don't think I'm going to be able to mend it. It looks like you may need a few stitches on your back," she says. I'm not surprised. I know I was scraping along the cliff. But I don't feel anything on my back.

She draws me a bath and adds oatmeal and milk to the water. She helps me into the tub and has me soak for a while. It is very soothing. My mind wanders to Archer. What happened to him? How am I going to get back to Umberton? I decide not to dwell on these things tonight since there is nothing I can do. I'll face those questions in the morning.

Dandi comes back in and gently dabs at my scratched up back and arms. It stings a little, but I am happy that I can feel it. While I'm leaning forward, she brushes out my hair and then washes it. She is so good and kind. She tells me that she and her husband, Daniel, have a son, Lync. Lync has been away at the Carlsbad Festival in Umberton. They expect him home later tonight.

She lays out one of her long skirts, a blouse, some panties and a nightgown for me in the bedroom since my clothes are shot. I notice some more freedom of movement once I'm out of the tub. I dry myself and then try stretching out my arms and legs. I can walk a lot more freely. She has me sit down and gives me a few stitches on my back, then bandages the wounds and leaves the room.

I sit for a minute in my towel in front of the fireplace. The warmth of the fire is wonderful at first but then my sunburn stings. I keep thinking about Archer and wondering what he is doing. I put on the skirt and blouse and head downstairs.

Whatever Dandi is cooking smells heavenly. I head to the kitchen to see what I can do to help.

During dinner, Lync comes barreling into the room.

"Pops," he says excitedly, "you're not going to believe what happened. There was an incredible fight at the festival!"

His parents chastise him for not being more polite to their guest, but news about the fight has me eager to hear his story.

"My apologies," he says respectfully bowing and looking at me.

"No need," I smile.

"What's all this ruckus now," his father asks.

I know I should help Dandi clear the table but Lync's story has captured my full attention.

"Oh, Pops! Wait till you hear what happened. Jeks and I had climbed up the old Monterey Cypress tree in the middle of town to get a better view of all the festivities. We spot this blonde feller in a wagon who seems to be in a pretty big hurry. A group of men step in front him and he almost runs them over. He says to the big bloke in the middle that he's in a hurry and could they please move out of the way. He was real polite about it.

Then a woman wearing this crazy gold and silver thing on her head says, 'you're surrounded Archer, where's your partner?' He looks around with eyes like a hawk at everyone and he says, 'surrounded, Teever? You know me better than that.'

Everyone gets real still and then these little round saw blades start flying at him. He does some kind of flip off the back of the wagon and grabs a bow while he was at it and just starts taking them men out with his arrows. He was so fast; I've never seen a man do something like that. Other men come from nowhere and start running at him but he just beats them down one after the next. He used anything close to him to thrash these people. He's flipping around and jumping, he's twisting and turning. He steps on things laying on the ground and they flip right into his hands then he pounds people down with whatever he had. The group got a few licks in but this guy was just amazing. I watched him jump up in the air and slam a punch down on a man's face that just about crushed his skull. Then another guy shows up and starts throwing axes. One lands next to the blonde's ear on the fence and he grabs it. He flips around and kicks the ax guy right in the face knocking him out cold! He looks up at me and Jeks in the tree but then doesn't pay us no mind. I ask Jeks, 'What kind of superman is this guy?'

Then the woman yells again,' where's your partner, Archer? Did Peegro finish her off?' This Archer fellow stays real cool and starts moving slowly toward her; almost like a cat. Then she starts throwing those little saw blades again and a poor bystanding bastard gets hit with it. He falls into the blonde bloke. The superman lays him down real nice like and the woman throws more blades. I thought sure he was going to get killed but he ducked and rolled and jumped and flipped. He stopped some of them down with things he grabbed nearby.

Then he picked up a large spike from Kabbot's wagon and laid it on his shoulder as he looked at her with the piercing eyes of the devil. Before she could raise her arms, again he flipped his wrist with such power that the spike hit her right square between the eyes. It was a hell of a shot, Pops! She fell dead right there in the street."

"That's a hell of a story, son," Daniel says looking at me.

"Pops," Lync says in a lower voice, "I watched him break a man's neck with a bow then stand up flipping a blade between his fingers like it was a pencil. He was outnumbered 40 to 1 and he took them all down. Every one! What kind of fighter is he?"

Daniel looks back at Lync, "What you witnessed was a Temple Master, Lync. It's a rare thing to observe."

I pick up some dishes and go into the kitchen. I can hear Lync excitedly add bits and comments to his tale. Dandi is busy at the sink as I slip out the back door for some fresh air. I realize my hands are shaking, heart is pounding and I feel half sick. I'm so glad Archer's alright. At least now I know what happened to him. When Lync described his catlike movements, I could picture him so clearly. I know those movements all too well. I walk around for a few more minutes, but the temperature forces me back inside.

Dandi looks at me and tells me to go sit by the fire. When I walk into the room, Daniel looks up at me. I take a seat by the fire next to him.

"Lync, go get some more firewood," he says.

"There's plenty in here already, Pops," Lync protests.

"Do what you're told, son," he threatens.

Lync goes outside mumbling about life being unfair.

Daniel turns to me. "You're his partner, aren't you?"

It takes me a moment to answer not knowing how he might react but eventually, I nod.

"He'll be looking for you," he speculates. "I am sure of it."

I nod again.

"That cliff you were on would have been under water in another few hours at this time of year. You would have drowned if we hadn't happened along. Looks like you have a choice." I look up at him as he leans forward resting his elbows on his knees.

"There's a good chance they all think you're dead. You can stay dead and make a new start for yourself. Dandi and I live far enough off the grid that we could pass you off as a long-lost cousin until you're ready to move on, or I can take you back. I know where the checkpoint is. It's a good day's drive but I'll take you there if that is where you want to go," he offers.

I let out a breath I didn't realize I was holding. What kindness! I feel so blessed to know these people. I smile at him and touch his arm as an added 'thank you'. I lean back in my chair and look at the fire.

"You make such a sweet and tempting offer. The thought of disappearing had never crossed my mind before but it has now." I contemplate it a few more minutes remembering how I once thought it would be awful to live "off the grid". Now, I see that there is a certain freedom in leaving the modern world behind. They all think I'm dead. Could I disappear and change my life forever? I lean toward the fire and let the passing fancy of running away and losing myself in this world run its course. What would I do? Where would I go? Could I really put my brother and parents through that? Deep inside, I also know I have responsibilities to Archer, and his emancipation.

I look back at Daniel and smile. "If the offer still stands, would you please drive me to the checkpoint tomorrow? I must go back and see this thing through."

He pats my shoulder, then stands. "We best move early, love. Dandi will wake you at dawn."

Lync walks in with an armload of wood.

"C'mon boy, put that wood down. Let's get the transport ready," Daniel says walking out the door.

I make my way upstairs.

The trip to the checkpoint was extremely uneventful, verging on boring. Lync entertained us some with his stories of the festival and, of course, his reiteration of the fight. Daniel was right, it took us all day to get to our destination. He said the checkpoint was nowhere near Umberton, but southeast at the very southernmost point of this part of the region.

It's pitch black out when we reach the race transporter. The checkpoint is pretty camouflaged down here and surrounded by trees. It would have been many days walk from where I was.

"How did you know this was here?" I ask Daniel.

"Backwoods people know things," he smiles with lifted brows. "Make sure your partner knows, we meant you no harm."

"He knows," I smile.

They both wish me well and go on their way.

I grope around trying to find the entrance and finally manage to stumble through.

"Number eight" rings out over the loudspeaker. The doors shut behind me and the engines start. I am the last to arrive. I move into the living area. There is no one around. I hear the commuter engines as it starts to move. I wonder where Archer is then try to speculate where we are going next.

I finish my shower and Miss Terry comes in with one of the medics. They are both carrying a metal tray.

"The medic is going to look at your back," she says and motions for me to sit on the bed. The medic sets down a tray and lowers my towel in the back. He removes the bandages.

"The stitching is good. It is healing nicely. No sign of infection." He rubs some kind of ointment on the wounds and redresses them. I see Miss Terry point her head at the door.

Once he exits and closes the door, Miss Terry brings over a metal tray with the rounded metal probe device, a tube of something and some gloves on it. I know what this is.

"You've been off the grid, Liliana. You know what that means," she says while putting on the gloves. "Lie back on the bed and open the towel."

I make a snort of disgust in protest but I lie back and open the towel.

"You know what to do," she instructs while lubing up the device.

I do as she asks. I close my eyes until it's over. I hate virginity checks.

"Everything is fine. You may continue the race," she declares while standing.

I wonder what she says to those who are out of the race because they are no longer virgins.

"We'll summon your Archer. He'll continue the race with you at the next location." She picks up the tray and leaves the room.

Archer. I wonder where he is. I wonder what he thought when I wasn't on the ledge anymore. I hope he is alright.

CHAPTER 30

Carita

I see Banzi looking at me across the room. He's probably wondering how I survived. I wonder about that myself sometimes. Banzi is the last person I want to see. I turn and move to another table.

Antonella is sitting alone reading a book while eating an apple. She has glasses on. I didn't know she wore glasses.

"May I sit here?" I ask.

She doesn't look up but nods. Her book must be very interesting.

I sit down and eat a bite of my salad. I realize immediately that I'm actually not very hungry. I can feel Banzi staring at me which is so annoying. I try to avoid eye contact so he'll just go away. I push my plate aside and lift my cup of tea. He's still looking at me. I turn my chair trying to avoid his gaze.

Shit. He's getting up and walking toward me. I guess I'm not going to get away from whatever it is he has to say. He stands next to the table looking down at me. I take an exaggerated, annoyed breath and look up at him. I'm ready, let's have it.

"I want you to know that I had no idea she was going to do that to you," he announces. Antonella looks up from her book.

"Okay," I respond with a bit of a nasty tone and look away wishing he would leave, but he doesn't.

"I want to be like him, you know," he says dreamily. I look up at him as he brings his brown eyes down to meet mine. "He didn't hesitate jumping off that cliff after you. I've thought about it a lot. There could have been rocks, a boat, or anything at the bottom of that cliff but he just ran full speed right off it like he was jumping into a swimming pool. That was a hell of a drop! I thought you both were dead. I went to the edge and saw him dive down again and again looking for you. When he finally came up with you, he tried to get you to breathe right there while he was dog paddling to stay above water, fighting surf and holding you up all at the same time. I can't believe the strength of that man. I stayed and watched until you were finally breathing, but then I saw that he was going to have to pull you for miles to that shoreline in the cold water. You were unconscious and he had to keep you afloat the entire time while trying to swim and not go into hyperthermia. I didn't think you'd make it, but here you are."

I'm not sure if he's mad or glad about that.

He looks off into space, his face bright with inspiration and admiration then adds, "For the rest of my life, I'll never forget the man so willing to die for another. Truly, I want to be like that. I want to be selfless and willing to go to great lengths to do what's right. Wherever I end up in this world, I will strive to be that kind of man." He looks down at me. "I'm glad you're okay," he ends with a smile and holds out his hand.

I shake it, then he walks away.

I sit stunned taking in his revelation. I look at Antonella. Now she's staring at me. She puts a hand on my wrist and gives it a little squeeze.

"I'm not so sure Espada would jump off a cliff for me. What a great story. You must feel so lucky," she says and smiles. I smile back at her, then she goes back to her book.

I race through my mind trying to remember. I don't remember being in the water with Archer at all. I only remember being on the shore. I remember thinking Archer looked like a train wreck. No wonder. His bravery and courage continually amaze me. Run full speed off a cliff? Who does that? Archer.

I'm not hungry. Just as I get up, an announcement echoes throughout the commuter. We've been delayed. A hurricane went through Carita only a few days before we got here. The race officials delayed our starting time in order to move us away from the flooded areas. There are rumors that they may be tracking another storm right behind this one. We are being moved to the local convention center which is also a hurricane shelter.

Once we arrive, all the contestants get corralled into a meeting room with some refreshments. The entire back wall is glass that overlooks another room below. The lights are on, so I wander over to it to see what's in it.

It's a large long multipurpose room. It looks like they gathered all of our Specialists and other race officials in there. On the far end are refreshments laid out for them. I see Archer leaning against a wall not far from the door. It feels great to lay my eyes on him. He looks good; strong, healthy and unhurt. I can't help but chuckle to myself, he looks quite bored as well. He seems lost in his own thoughts. Langt is nearby.

Some of the other racers come over to check out the view also. Just as I am about to turn away, the outer door below opens catching my attention, then in walks Peago. Given that she almost killed me, I'm very curious to see just how friendly Archer will be with her.

She looks beautiful, as always. A twinge of jealously kicks me in the gut. She is wearing a skimpy cropped shirt and long skirt with slits going up both sides. Hair is perfect. Face is perfect, of course. Archer sees her walk in but then doesn't pay attention to her. She, on the other hand, seems to make a point of walking right in front of him to strut her cute little half naked figure. To my delight, he has no expression on his face and barely looks at her. As she passes by, she says something to him over her shoulder.

He is on her in a flash! It was so fast that I let out a gasp. His arm reaches around and he grabs her by the throat, then lifts her in the air by her neck roughly pinning her against the wall at his eye level. He is practically nose to nose with her.

I don't know what he was saying to her but his jaw is tight and his head is tilted. He doesn't seem to be yelling but he is letting her have it. She is grabbing, scratching and clutching at his hands to get him to release her. Her face is relatively relaxed but there is a certain amount of surprised fear in her eyes and she's beginning to turn a shade of purple. A voice booms over the loud speakers in their room. It must have been really loud to them because we could hear it.

"Specialists are not permitted to engage in neutral areas. Archer, you have 10 seconds to disengage before Statsia is disqualified from the race."

His grip on her throat didn't budge for a moment, and he didn't take his focus off her, but then he lets go by lifting his open palms straight up in the air next to his head dropping her to the floor. She lands like a crouched cat then lifts her head with a defiant look on her face and says something to him with a curling smirk.

He was back in her face in a split second although he didn't lay a hand on her. He just pinned her to the ground with this overpoweringly large masculine presence. I don't know what he said but he said it through anger-filled steely blue eyes and gritted teeth. Langt puts his hand on Archer's shoulder. Archer didn't seem to notice but after a moment of significant stare down with Peago, Archer stands and walks away. The entire group in the room down there had gathered around to watch the spectacle but moved aside as he went through. I realize the group in the room up here had gathered to watch it too.

Peago stands up and finds her way to the door. She opens it and slinks out. Both rooms full of people disperse. Archer walks to the other side of the room and pours himself some refreshment. I look to my right. Banzi is several feet away from me looking down at Archer. He looks over at me.

"She deserved it," he shrugs and walks away.

I turn and look toward the room below. I feel eyes on me and look over to where the incident took place. Langt is looking up at me. I walk away from the window just as Miss Terry and Ruler Martinez walk to the front of the room and ask us to sit.

Ruler Martinez then speaks. "We are allowing you to proceed. It is against my better judgment, but I've been overruled. The hurricane has left Carita in a shocking state. You may be the first on the scene in some of the more rural places. You may be somewhat taken aback by what you see. I know you are in a race and all I will say as you come upon these people and places, if you can help, you should try. Be very careful as you go about your business. Hurt people and animals can be very dangerous. Not only that, the land is full of broken items. There will also be sharp objects and other hazards." Ruler Martinez steps aside so Miss Terry can address us.

"Just do your best to get through this leg quickly. There is no major clean up or clearing in the works because there is another storm coming," she says.

We all look at each other and murmuring draws increasingly louder.

"We have been told that your commuter is leaving in seven days at dusk. Because of the treacherous conditions, this will be a non-elimination round. Just get through it and get to the checkpoint as quickly as possible. However, you can still be eliminated if you cannot proceed due to medical reasons or if you don't make it to the commuter before it leaves Carita." She steps back after her speech.

There is another round of loud murmurs and rebukes about the rules for this stage. Honestly, it's not much different from the rest of the stages. I don't know what they are throwing a fit about.

"You will be dismissed in the order you checked in during the last leg," Ruler Martinez says and moves away.

We all move toward the dismissal area.

Archer meets me on a muddy road to the task. Well, it is actually more path than road right now. We are both quiet as we take in the utter devastation of this area. The few homes along the way are absolutely destroyed and ripped off their foundations. The tree debris is everywhere. We are constantly fighting limbs and jumping over trunks. I also see a lot of dead animals such as squirrels, birds, dogs and cats. The stench here in a few days will gut wrenching.

"There is another storm," I say trying to break the silence between us.

He nods. I roll my eyes. Here we go. A silent leg. I decide not to ask if anything is wrong with him. I know what took place with Peago in that room. Maybe that's it and he needs some quiet time.

After a while, I decide to entertain myself by slapping at trees and kicking at rocks. About the time I realize how childish I'm being, Archer looks at me.

"You're being loud."

My patience is already at an end. "So what?" I respond shrugging. I mean, hell, I haven't seen anyone in hours and this silent shit is on my last nerve.

He moves close to me and cocks his head at me until I look at him.

"What," I exclaim.

This time he rolls his eyes. What the hell? Then he gets very close to my face and says softly, "We are being tracked right now." My mouth drops in shock, but he continues, "I'm trying to listen so I can get a better estimate of where this foe is. Do you think you could help me out by being a little more stealthy?"

I quietly agree. He moves ahead of me and I stand in place for a moment giving him some space so he can do what he does better. Geez. Now I really feel ridiculous. He's always got a purpose and reason for his actions. I feel so inferior. Just as I start walking, the earth below me begins to rumble.

Archer is beside me in five strides.

"What is it? An earthquake," I ask.

He smiles, "A large vehicle."

Within moments an extremely large heavy-duty hauler cuts a path out through the trees. Every so often it stops while workers jump down and toss large limbs into a machine that chews the pieces up and spits them into the back of the vehicle.

Archer moves in front of me as one of the workers runs up to us. "The path ahead has collapsed. We are cutting away an old road. If you want to climb into the cab, we can let you out about three kilometers up the road at the Paraiso Resort or what's left of it, anyway. There are other people there along with some food and shelter for the night."

Archer smiles and shakes the man's hand. "We're grateful. Thank you."

We move to the cab of the hauler where Archer helps me climb in. I catch his eye before I get in. He has a very serious look on his face. I realize he's mentally preparing for battle. Then I think about our circumstances. We're surrounded by strangers with a metal chomping machine. I should prepare myself as well. Archer climbs up next to me and pulls me onto his lap. He rolls down the window. I lean back against him. He has one arm tightly around my waist and the other hand on the door handle. He's ready for whatever.

The trip, thankfully, is uneventful. We walk into the resort. A lot of it is destroyed, but they have two full wings that seem relatively untouched. The place is mobbed with survivors. The sound is deafening. It's clear that we'd have to yell to hear each other which seems exactly what all these other people are doing.

We find a ballroom that has floor to ceiling pallets of storm survival fare such as bottled water, jarred items and canned goods. I help Archer load several waters into his pack. He moves to the food stores and I grab a box of crackers and a jar of peanut butter. He smiles as I shove them into my pack. He takes my hand and we head for the door.

We camp out in an abandoned home. We are both careful to only stay in the living room since we are basically trespassing. Archer said he wouldn't normally do this but he wanted us out of the elements since the animals and insects are displaced and it could be extremely dangerous on the ground.

We spend the evening eating our peanut butter and crackers and telling each other our stories of what happened to us once we were separated in Scoterie. He's not as elaborate in his telling of the fight that Lync was but he did say how concerned he was when I wasn't on the cliff and had started a full-scale search for me. He had made it to Daniel's home just as Daniel got back from dropping me off. He was in the home's shadows when Lync told Dandi that they got me to the checkpoint. His point of view was so interesting.

We get up. We are careful not to disturb the home's contents while getting ready to leave after a good night's sleep on a comfortable couch. They don't have running water or power so a bath will have to wait.

***

The Task area is only half a day's hike. It's in an open building. I see a race judge at the front entrance, two inside and one at the back. Inside, appears to be sectioned off into workstations separated by curtains or more like sheets hanging attached to ropes with some kind of clamps.

It's an individual task. Archer steps aside. I run into the work station and close the curtain behind me. I find the task card and read it.

TASK: USING ONLY TWO OF THE ITEMS ON THE TABLE, MAKE 50 FLAMING LIGHTS THAT BURN FOR AT LEAST 4 MINUTES. YOU MUST PUT THE LIGHTS IN THE METAL BOX TO SET THEM ON FIRE. A JUDGE WILL TELL YOU WHEN THE 4 MINUTES ARE UP. IF YOUR LIGHTS GO OUT BEFORE TIME IS CALLED, YOU MUST START THE TASK OVER AGAIN.

I look at the table and pick up the sectioned metal display tray. It has exactly 50 sections. Perfect. Then I look at the rest of the items. There is a dish, a large can of potatoes with a can opener, a large jar of petroleum jelly, a canister of paprika, a box of crayons, a nylon scarf, a flannel shirt and some string. I pick up each item and inspect them for any hidden secrets. Nope. They are what they are.

I can't seem to focus. The sound of another contestant running to a workstation snaps me out of my thoughts. I have to get serious. Focus! I look at the crayons and determine there aren't enough to make 50 candles so I move them away. I grab the flannel shirt and the petroleum jelly and set them in the middle of the table shoving everything else to the side. I start tearing the flannel shirt into strips. I count them to make sure I have at least 50. I grab the petroleum jelly and dump it in a pile on the table. I dip each strip into the jelly making sure each one gets covered. I squeeze out any excess and pile a strip into each one of the sections in the metal tray. I present the box to the judge who gives me a lighter. I light the strips then sit down to wait. At the end of the four minutes, my strips are still burning. The judge approves and I'm allowed to continue in the race.

CHAPTER 31

Archer shakes me gently awake. I sit up quickly. He puts a finger over his lips. I sit quietly trying to listen and also trying to the fight the nausea of being awakened so suddenly.

Archer is very still so I don't move. I have no idea what is happening. I only know to trust this man who, until a few months ago, was a complete stranger. Now he is my protector, my mentor, my friend and my constant companion. He makes me crazy but I cling to this connection like sustenance. This is what life is like with Archer.

"Listen," he whispers into my ear barely audible. "Trust your eyes, yes, but trust all of your senses just as much. Close your eyes and listen." I close my eyes and allow everything to get quiet. I try to hear everything around me. Then I hear it. Every time the stalker moves, he makes a noise. He sounds like a man to me. A woman would seem lighter somehow. It is like a swish of his clothes or it could even be the smallest of flicks from his shoelaces. I open my eyes wide and look at Archer. I can tell the spy is moving away. He holds up a finger to his lips, smiles and winks. He knows I got the message.

After several minutes, Archer motions the "all clear" and I let out a breath.

"Let's move while he has slipped away. He thinks he has us pegged and is probably setting a trap. I'll have you get on my back when we set out," he whispers.

"Why?" I question.

"He's tracking us."

"Who is it? He must be a very good tracker," I whisper.

Archer looks at me. "All Specialists are good trackers, but he's a Highlander. He was born to it. It's in his blood. Can you guess?"

A highlander? That must mean he's from Scoterie. "Foyver?" I guess.

Archer smiles and nods. I hate Poppi. I definitely don't want them to have an advantage over us. I start to take down the shelter but Archer stops me.

"Leave it," he says. "Let him think we're still in it for a little while longer."

Archer steps out first, then motions for me to follow. He turns so I can climb on his back.

"Won't this slow us down?" I question.

"He'll know I'm carrying you, but he won't understand why. When I find the right spot, we'll go into the river. I know this place. He'll still be quite a way back. We'll be alright." I climb on his back then we start our trek along the river.

I can tell that Archer is continually scanning the area. When he walks into the water up to his knees, I jump down. He leads me to a tree across the river and lifts me to a lower limb, then climbs up and motions for me to follow him.

"The trees here are old but sturdy. They run together so we can keep moving along without ever touching the ground."

I feel like Tarzan.

We move through the trees for quite a while. It's really remarkable. Then Archer stops. He jumps to the ground and reaches into some brush. I can see him twisting something metal. It makes a sighing noise as he opens it. He lights one of the small torches inside and looks around.

He stands back up and holds his arms up to me. I lower myself into his arms but then he covers my mouth and we crouch down. He puts a finger over his lips and lowers me into the tunnel. As my head passes his face, I look at him. The light from the moon reflects in his clear blue eyes. The light from the torch illuminates his chin.

"I'll lead him away. Follow the tunnel and don't emerge until you see the golden door. I'll find you," he whispers.

He lowers me the last bit and closes the cover. I grab the torch and start walking. It is so dark down here. There is a constant stream of water trickling in the middle of the tunnel. The smell is so bad I almost vomit a number of times. I can hear creatures scurrying and feel bugs dropping on me and falling off my body. What is this place? How does Archer know about it?

I must've walked for miles. I need some fresh air and some water. I long to sit down for even just a moment, but there is nowhere to sit, just this nasty smelling water. I trudge on. Then I hear something and I stop to listen. There is nothing more. Maybe I imagined it. I am just getting ready to take a step when I hear it again. It is slow, deliberate footsteps. Did the person hear me? I put the torch down in the water and continue to listen. It wasn't a large, heavy person. It was most likely a woman or a young man, or even possibly a child.

I lean against the side of the tunnel listening. The only thing I hear is the beating of my own heart and quick breaths. After a few moments, I begin walking more covertly. It is black in this tunnel. I have to feel the side of it to keep moving forward. Every so often my fingers run over bugs so I try not to slide them too much along the wall.

Finally, I see a flicker of a faint light. The tunnel opens out onto the beach. The light is the moon. There are some bushes lining the tunnel so I sit as close as I can to one of them and try to conceal myself as much as possible.

I drink some water and wonder where Archer is. Then I remember he told me to find a golden door. I couldn't see anything in that tunnel. I sure didn't see any door at all let alone try to distinguish a color.

I'm extremely tired. I lean over balancing my upper body on my elbows and stretch out my legs. Maybe I should try to go back through that tunnel in the daylight to find this yellowish door. Why is it golden anyway? Maybe there is treasure behind it. Wouldn't that be nice?

★★★

I wake up with the sun hitting my eyes. Archer is sitting next to me swigging water from his canteen. I sit up quickly.

"Where did you come from?" I ask.

"Why didn't you go through the golden door?"

"I couldn't see anything in there. I had to put out the torch because I heard footsteps and just ended up out here," I explain.

"I see."

"Did I take us way off course?" I feel bad now.

"No," he adds, "we're fine."

"Did you lead him away?" I ask.

He tilts his head at me. "Obviously," he smirks.

I stick my tongue out at him. Okay, dumb question on my part. He looks refreshed. I probably look like hell.

I stand to slap the sand off me as much as possible. I look into the sparkling blue water of the Caribbean Sea. It's so beautiful. It reminds me of home. Archer stands, also.

"Can I go for a swim?" I ask him.

"I think you should," he says almost laughing.

I look down at my muddy, stank shoes. I can tell my hair is full of sand. I feel a tickle on my cheek and reach up. Sand dribbles off my face. I start to laugh. I'm a mess.

We walk to the water. I wade in up to my waist then go for a full in dive. I float and swim around. Archer is in the water moving leisurely around.

I can see fish swimming below. It makes me hungry for seafood.

"I wish we could have a delicious seafood dinner," I say out loud.

Archer tilts his head and looks at me. "You want fish?" he questions.

I nod enthusiastically. "I would love some fresh fish cooked over an open fire," I reply.

"You shall have it," he smiles. "It does sound good."

We get out of the water, both of us dripping. Archer is looking up at the tunnel opening. Then he looks above the tunnel to the top of the hill.

"What is it?" I ask.

He looks down rubbing his chin. "Movement in the tunnel," he says quietly. "Climb to the top of the hill and wait for me." He motions toward a sandy path on the right side of the bushes where I was lying.

Archer nocks three arrows and turns toward the water.

"There," he says motioning in a northwest direction. I don't see anything.

He takes aim and lets the arrows fly.

"Excellent," he adds. "When you get to the top, look for a good place to camp for brunch. I'll go retrieve the fish and be back forthwith."

I agree happily. He takes off. He's so goofy sometimes. I'm really looking forward to this fish meal. I make my way up the hill. At the top, it's really lovely. The hill slopes down into a grassy area with large, shady trees. There are palm trees lining the area perfectly spaced out like it was once a community park or something.

I look over the side of the hill and see Archer coming out of the water with a fish on each of the arrows he shot. He's amazing. I turn back to the grass and decide the shade of the large tree across the "lawn" from me would be perfect for a picnic. It has several surrounding gardenia bushes and other overgrown shrubbery. Archer will be pleased about the concealment.

Before I get there, I hear some rustling in the bushes nearby. I move quickly away. Since Foyver was tracking us yesterday, I'm suddenly on high alert. I begin to move quietly backwards. I back into my enormous picnic tree and look up into it. Maybe I can turn it into a nice hiding place until Archer returns. The limbs are strong and spaced well so I begin to climb.

Suddenly, I hear a yell as Poppi jumps out of the bushes and grabs onto my leg trying to pull me down but I manage to break away and continue to climb. Poppi begins to climb too but she's on adjacent limbs. She's fast!

She passes me. At this point, maybe I should climb down. I start to move rapidly back down but she is on top of me quickly and shoves me. I fall but catch myself on the next limb. I'm hanging here realizing I'm in deep trouble.

"What do you want?" I yell at her, "Why are you doing this?"

"Why do you think I'm doing this? I want to win and you're in my way. I want you out." She sounds so butch, very manly. She climbs down to my limb and steps right next to my fingers. I look at her face. She is displaying an evil grin. I know this won't be good. I look desperately around trying to figure out what I'm going to do.

Then I see him. My Archer is standing on the hill. His golden mane whipping in the breeze. He has his bow and arrow aimed straight at me. Poppi begins kicking and stepping on my fingers. I look down. I am so high and about to drop. I'm sure to break my legs if I fall from here. Then I hear a whizzing noise. Poppi lets out a loud scream, She loses her footing, then falls through the branches to the ground as I try to climb back on the limb, but my arms are devoid of strength. She is screaming for Foyver.

Foyver. If he's close, I am in deep trouble. This could easily be seen as an attack on his partner and he would be free to kill me. I'm suddenly realizing how serious this situation is. Archer is too far away. I look back at the hill for reassurance from him. He's gone. Poppi is still shrieking.

I am scrambling to find a way out of this damn tree but I am too high. I can hear Foyver coming. Shit! My fingers give out and I fall a couple more branches before I catch myself again. I'm stuck and exhausted. I try frantically to hold on to this limb. I see movement. It has to be Foyver but I can't get down. I'm just hanging here like a big stupid target. Then I hear him.

"Liliana, JUMP!" It's Archer! He breaks through the bushes in full stride. He won't make it in time. I close my eyes. Should I let go? I take a breath. There's one thing I have learned and that is to trust my Archer. I let go of the branch not knowing what to expect.

I am caught in a full run over Archer's shoulder. I can hear Foyver behind us but I am afraid to look. Suddenly, I don't hear him anymore.

As I look up, I see him standing on a large rock looking down at us. I get hit in the eyes with the bright white reflection of his blades as he crouches for his throw. Archer is moving back and forth to avoid being hit. I take a breath and close my eyes. We're done for.

Archer grips me tighter, then leaps in the air. I hear the clang of Foyver's blades. I feel Archer go rigid as we are dropping into the cool wetness of a waterfall.

***

I wake up with a start and sit up. Where am I? What happened? I look around. It is dark, almost pitch black. I close my eyes and slowly reopen them trying to get them used to the bleakness of my surroundings. I am clearly in a cave. I stand and stumble around the cave until I get to the opening. It is night outside but lighter than it is in that cave. The air is cool and there is a decent breeze blowing. I turn back toward the cave to build a fire. Then I see him, not far from where I woke up. He is crumpled on the ground. I run to him and turn his face toward me.

"Archer?" I panic. I shake him. Nothing. I lightly slap him, then shake him again.

"Archer!" I am half screaming now. He's not responding. I can't see him very well. I put my hands on his chest. It is moving up and down, but barely. I scramble out of the cave and grab every scrap of wood I can find. I build a small fire close to where he is lying. I rip some cloth from the bottom of his shirt and wrap a few pieces around some sticks then light them on fire. I post the sticks around Archer so I can get a better look.

Frantically, I try to think. What happened? Then I remember. Foyver threw his blades at us. Oh my God. I pick up one of the small torches and start scanning his body. Then I see it. There is a significant gash on his left calf. It is ugly. There is a lot of dried blood on the ground. It looks like he tried to stitch it himself and did a pretty rough job of it. How long was I out? Why was I out? Did I get hit too? I don't feel any pain. I look at Archer again. He is cold and sweaty. I need to find some water.

I remember we jumped into a waterfall so there must be some water around here somewhere. I run out of the cave to look around. The breeze is picking up into a full-on wind. I can hear thunder rumbling in the distance and I see a few streaks of lightning. It's monsoon season here. I hope it is not the second hurricane they were talking about or we're going to be in deep trouble. I see a reflection not far from me. Water! Yes!

It is a good-sized body of water but unfortunately, it's at the bottom of a sloping landscape. I discover a path down to it and at the water's edge, fall to my knees. I plunge my hands in up to elbows to quickly rinse off the dirt. I splash my face and grab a quick taste to see if it's fresh or salt. It is fresh. I quickly get back to business. Archer needs a drink also. I look anxiously around for something I can use as a vessel. There is a curvy looking hollowed-out young branch nearby and I grab it. It won't hold too much but it is enough for now. I can come back for more. I rinse it out really well, fill it with water and head back to the cave.

I lay the branch close to Archer's face and put my fingers in the water. I let the water drip in his mouth and repeat it a few times. I wet a piece of cloth and dab at his forehead and cheeks. I untie his shirt and lift it over his shoulders. I roll it up and place it under his head. I wet the cloth again and dab at his neck and chest. Damn, what a specimen.

I can hear the wind really making some noise. The thunder is getting closer and the lightning more frequent. I hear something from the side of the cave and quickly turn. Villagers come around the corner carrying their items. When they see me, they proceed cautiously. I turn away from them and continue with my attentions to Archer.

One of the men with a torch slowly walks in my direction. I look up at him and he points to my fire. I bow my head for "permission" and he lights his torch. He returns a head bow as a quick "thanks" and goes back to his side of the cave where he lights their fires. In no time, the whole place is lit up and warm. I'm grateful. I can see Archer more clearly.

A few of the older women approach me. One of them points to Archer. I acknowledge her and move out of the way. She looks at his face and then lifts his eyelids and looks at his eyes. She runs her hands lightly around his neck, then his chest. She must have agreed with my earlier thoughts because she stops and turns her gaze to me, then smiles and winks. I can't help but chuckle.

She runs her hands lightly over his arms and then the women roll him over. She inspects his back and then his legs. When she gets to his wound, she moves her face next to it and examines it carefully. She motions for me to remove his shoes. She goes to her side of the cave and returns with a few of the larger men. They pick up Archer and take him down to the water. They gently place him in and remove his clothes. I look away when they remove his pants. I don't want to invade Archer's privacy without him knowing about it. As the men hold him, the women bathe him with some sort of soap. The smell of it reaches my nostrils. It has a very pungent earthy scent.

When they finish, they wrap some linen around his manly parts and carry him back up to the cave. A large pallet has been laid on our side of the cave and they lay Archer on it. The men go back to their side of the cave.

A group of men leave the cave carrying large vessels. Looks like they are making a water run before the storm hits. I decide I'd better get some water, too. I pick up my little branch and head out.

The sky opens up just as I get back. I am drenched but at least I have some water. I look over and the villagers are covering their water. I supposed I should too. I use a piece of Archer's shirt for the job. I know that if this is a cyclone, and I'm quite sure it must be or these people would not have showed up, we could be here for a while.

The women come back over. Their arms are loaded with items. I move out of the way. The old woman lays out a number of small vessels with different salves and liquids. She places a knife in the fire. The other carries a small bucket of water, some cloths and several blankets. She hands one to me. I am grateful. I must be a sight standing here soaking wet and shivering.

The old woman motions for me to sit next to her. I sit down and she moves the hair in my face to the side. She dabs the side of my forehead with a damp cloth and I almost hit the ceiling from the pain. I reach up and feel a significant bump that I had no idea was there until now. No wonder I have no recollection of Archer bringing me here or anything else. How long have I been here? I look down at Archer. What happened to us?

The younger woman sits next to Archer and places some linen under his leg by his wound. The older woman uses a small razor blade and begins cutting off the stitches he tried to sew and an amount of dead skin. It oozes a greenish brown color. I have to turn away. I'm not good with wound care.

A few minutes later, the old woman calls to the other side of the cave. A fairly large man comes over. He turns Archer and lifts his shoulders. The old woman drips a few drops of a clear liquid into Archer's mouth. I swallow hard but for some reason, I trust her. The man lays Archer down and leaves. The women pack up some of the vessels. The older woman looks at me. She puts her palms together under her cheek and closes her eyes. I smile in understanding. She gave him something to completely knock him out. The women go back to their side of the cave.

I sit on a rock next to the fire to dry off. I gingerly rub my bump and then look over at Archer's leg. From what I can tell, it is a very large sized gash. She had filled it with some kind of leaf concoction. It is smeared with a layer of salve. Her knife is still in the fire. I sit down next to Archer and stroke his hair. I run my fingers over his lips, cheeks and I even stroke his eyebrows. He is my partner and, dare I say, friend. I place my hand on his chest. It's moving slowly up and down. He just has to be okay.

As some time has passed, the women and the big man return. The old woman looks at Archer's eyes again then nods to the man. He comes over and gently lifts Archer. The younger woman quickly lays a blanket under him. The blanket is much bigger than it appears. The man lays Archer on one side of the blanket and then moves to the end and picks up Archer's wounded leg. He holds it steady while the older woman removes the leaves from the wound. She then picks up the red-hot knife. I know what is coming next and can't bear to watch. But I hear it. It is the sizzle of burning flesh. Then I smell it and have to walk away. I turn toward the opening in the cave. It is pouring rain outside. The wind and lightning keep me back somewhat from the opening. It is definitely a hurricane. The churning water in the lake is beginning to rise dangerously. I'm concerned that flooding could be a problem.

I feel a hand gently touch my back and turn to it. The old woman points to Archer. I return to him with her. She has cauterized and bandaged his wound. I turn back to her and hug her instinctively as a thank you. She hugs me back. She pats the blanket next to Archer. I smile at her. She takes the damp blanket off my shoulders and I lie down next to him. She covers us both with a dry, warm blanket then goes back to her side. She is the best surrogate grandmother anyone could ask for.

I can't help but nestle close to the warmth of Archer's body. I turn to him and gently run my hand across his forehead, moving down the side of his face to his cheek. I run my thumb across his lips. He's beautiful. I roll over and close my eyes for a moment. I need to think.

As I lie here facing the fire, I allow my thoughts to return to the race. Am I completely out of it? Were the other teams affected by the weather? How long was I out? How many days have passed? Will Archer be able to continue? Will I have to leave him here in the hands of these kind people to recover and continue? I know I will have to make a tough decision. But for the next several hours at least, the storm will hold me right here.

★★★

I wake up facing Archer's chest. I instinctively look up at his eyes. They are still closed. I reach up and touch his chest to check for breathing. My hand moves up as his lungs take in air then exhale. It's such a relief. I sit up slowly and look at him. I touch his cheek and sigh. I wish he would wake up. I miss him even though he is right here. I bend down and kiss his lips. Maybe my kiss will awaken this sleeping beauty. It does not.

A girl brings me a bowl of a cooked grain. I take it and thank her. The food is very good and I'm hungry. They are so kind to share. I can't thank them enough for their compassionate attendance to Archer and to me.

After a day and a half, the storm finally passes. The old woman has been checking Archer's wound every so often. The swelling has decreased and he is doing better. She's keeping him knocked out with that clear liquid. I guess she knows a strong buck like that would want to get up and carry on. I wish he could. I know she is doing the right thing, but I have to leave.

I think we have been in this cave for two days. I don't know how long before that. I really stop to think about it for a while. I guess I'll have to leave Archer here and get back in the race. The thought is just destroying me on the inside. I feel like he needs me and I'm deserting him. If he were awake, he'd tell me to go because we have to win. I easily owe him that much. I have to try.

I get up very early and make my way down to the water. I strip down and wash my clothes. I lay them over a rock to dry and then plunge headfirst into the water. I splash around and float for a while. I wash my face then take out my bright yellow hair band putting it on my wrist while I give my hair a good rinse. I sit in the sun for a few minutes while my clothes finish drying and then get dressed and return to the cave.

Young girls run over to me as I enter. They are carrying a basket with some hair ribbons and point at my hair. I smile and sit down. They braid and decorate my hair. When they are finished, I thank them and hug them both before they run to their side of the cave. I turn my attention to Archer.

I sit next to him and run my hands over his face and through his hair. Then I take his hand and hold it against my heart. This is such a battle. I have to go. He needs to stay. The old woman brings me some breakfast which I take gratefully. She sits down beside me. She must have read my mind about leaving. She points to the race emblem on my suit. She puts her hands on Archer's shoulders then points to herself and nods to me. She will take good care of him I know. I nod back and hug her tightly. Nothing can express my gratitude for her and the others. She holds my hand in hers for a moment, then she walks away.

I look at Archer again. He seems so vulnerable like this. God knows I hate leaving him. I should be the one taking care of him. I look across the cave at this group of people. They will guard him and take care of him. I'm sure of it.

I wish I had something to give him as a token of my appreciation for all he has done for me, but I have nothing. I want him to know that I was here with him and that I did stay with him. My brightly colored hair band catches my eye. I slip it around his wrist. My fingers move through his hair one more time. I look into his face and gently touch my lips to his. I caress his face as tears stream down my cheeks. I don't know if I'll ever see him again, but at least I know he'll be okay.

The walk to the checkpoint is very uneventful. The tree debris is an obstacle as is large areas of standing water. I finally see the checkpoint. It is still here. I cross over. The bell chimes and on the loud speaker erupts "Number 9". I'm last.

I get to my room and flop on the bed. The engines start. We will be heading to the next location within a matter of minutes. At least I know I made it within the 7 days. I wonder if it was a close call.

CHAPTER 32

Arbric

After my shower, there is a beep from the speaker in my room then Miss Terry's voice, "Liliana, please report to the meeting room."

I'm dreading this meeting because I know they are going to tell me that Archer is disqualified for shooting Poppi. If any good has come out of this, it's that Poppi is out of the race.

I dress and head over to the room. Ruler Martinez, Ruler Davies and Ruler Rockstanz are on one side of the room deep in conversation.

I see Miss Terry by another table organizing meeting tablets.

"Miss Terry?" I greet her trying to get her attention.

"Uh huh," she says absentmindedly not looking away from her work.

"Is Archer in trouble for shooting Poppi," I ask point blank. No beating around the bush here.

"What," she says still not looking at me. "No. Poppi attacked you. Archer was defending you within the confines of the rules."

What a relief. I'm so glad he isn't going to get reprimanded and doubly glad that Poppi is out.

"Is Poppi okay?" I wonder. "I mean, will her leg be okay?"

Miss Terry finally stops what she's doing and turns to me. She folds her arms in front of her and tilts her head looking at me over the top of her glasses.

"You really don't know how skilled your Archer is, do you?"

I'm a little taken aback by her reaction and just shake my head.

"Archer employed a thin Redux arrow to take down Poppi. It was a clean precise shot to the fatty part of her thigh. The intent was clearly meant to only stop her with no permanent damage which is exactly what it did. Poppi has had her leg checked and wrapped and can continue on in the race at the start of the next leg. The tiniest of scars would be the only permanent reminder of the incident, if any."

Damn, he is good. I just hope he is alright.

Ruler Martinez walks over to me.

"Hello, young woman. We'd like to have a few words with you. Would you please sit down," he requests and motions me toward a chair. "Can I get you something to drink? Coffee perhaps?"

"Water would be nice, thank you," I say as I take my seat.

An attendant brings a glass of water and sets it in front of me, then leaves the room.

Once the attendant leaves, Ruler Martinez and the others take a seat around the table. Ruler Martinez then turns to me and states, "This is the second time Archer has not responded to our summons. Ambassador Leman tells us that he has not been called on mission. Can you fill us in on the details of what may have happened to him?"

"Yes, of course," I respond and take a drink of water. I tell them the story of what happened and when I'm finished, they look at one another.

"Poison, obviously," Miss Terry emphasizes.

Ruler Martinez grunts his agreement. The other Rulers nod in union.

"Poison?" I ask. I wasn't aware of any poison. I certainly didn't mention the word poison.

Miss Terry looks at me. "If you have given an accurate accounting of what transpired, Archer had to have been poisoned by Foyver's blades. The injury alone is significant but not to the point of completely incapacitating Archer. He would have been able to thoroughly mend his wound and remain conscious through it all."

Ruler Davies speaks next. "Frankly, I'm amazed that he was able to get you to safety. The oozing you described from the wound as well as your other description proves that the poison was monoglifitricacide. It's deadly. Archer clearly gave himself a dose of antidote. That is what kept him alive. His fight then was not to bleed to death. But you said he tried to stitch his wound before he was overcome with the poison. Archer is an amazing man. His resolve is extremely impressive."

Miss Terry addresses Ruler Martinez. "Archer is one of the best assets in the world right now. It's clear he has become a target…" Ruler Martinez shoots Miss Terry a "shut your damn mouth" look. She slowly turns her head to me.

"Thank you, Liliana," she smiles. "You may go."

***

I'm the last to leave the starting point. I have to walk a mile to Marmakish which is the eastern entrance to the desert. When I get there, they dress me in a long white sheet dress and wrap my head with white fabric as well. The material is cooling. They have me put on some soft leather sandals, then they slather some sort of lotion on my face and give me a small vessel to take with me. I am handed a list and a map then sent on my way.

I find the supply tent about a half mile walk from where I began. None of the other contestants are present. I must be very behind. An attendant helps me gather the supplies in an area outside on a carpet. There are camels lying here and there or standing and feeding. I ask if I am going to be taking a camel across with me but the attendant just shakes his head. As I stand staring at the camels, the attendant taps me on the shoulder and directs me to a very rudimentary sleigh transporter.

It looks like a gigantic sled with a rope attached to the front. Am I going to have to drag this thing? I load it with the supplies. The water is very heavy, but I finally manage to get it aboard. I am ready.

I pick up the rope and pull. It doesn't budge. I put the rope around me to try to muscle it. How in this world am I going to make it across the desert like this? It will take me 10 years.

The attendant comes over, moves the water to the back of the sleigh and helps me shift things around. With all the weight more toward the back, I can move it more easily. It is still very heavy but at least I can move. I walk until I can't see the starting location any more. Then it gets really eerie.

I am alone in the desert. It is so hot. The sun is beating me down. I drink a lot of water which actually lightens the load. But the water is getting warmed by the sun and it isn't helping as much as I would like. If I have a three-day trek, I am in trouble. I take one of the large blankets and drape it over the water to keep it somewhat shaded from the sun's direct heat.

My lips are becoming very dry. I pin the sheet on my head across my face to keep some of the sun off. I am coming to realize that exposing myself to this heat is going to take me out. I am already dog tired.

I stop to look around at the golden hills of sand surrounding me. I've never seen so much sand in my life. This scene is very discouraging and a little scary. There is not one soul in sight. The good thing about it is that there are some tracks that I can follow but now I need some rest. There is absolutely no shade anywhere. I crawl under the sled and lay there for a few minutes. I can't stop thinking about Archer. Is he okay? I wonder what he thought when he woke up and I was gone. For all I know, that old woman may still have him in a coma.

When I wake, it's dark. I can't believe I fell asleep. I only wanted to rest for a minute. I crawl out from under the sled and sit for a moment trying to get my bearings. It's a full moon and the stars are bright and clear. With all this light, I can still see some of the tracks in the sand which will make it easy to navigate. It is so much cooler out now!

After several hours, I see a light in the distance. As I get closer, I can see a fire at a campsite. It must be Kamit. There are tents here and people. Hallelujah! I made it to the first oasis! After a delicious meal, I head to the showers. I haven't seen any teams here. I must be far behind. It is almost dawn.

They said I have to leave at dawn so I head out and walk most of the morning. In the afternoon, I crawl under my sled again to sleep. When I wake, it is dark but I am able to navigate although now there is some cloud coverage. By early morning, the wind has picked up. I am starting to get concerned. If I get caught out here during a Haboob, I could be in big trouble.

Dawn breaks and I see a slight reflection in the distance. It better not be a mirage. Hopefully, I am close to the next oasis, Dirisan. I am getting a bit troubled by the fact that I haven't happened upon it yet. The closer I get, the windier it is, however, it is the oasis! But this time, there is nothing. It's more like ruins. There are a few structures made out of some sort of white stone, but they are all well-worn. In the only structure with a complete roof, there is a covered well in the center. There is no one else here.

The wind is picking up rapidly. Small swirls of sand are making it inside the dilapidated building. I climb up on the roof to get a better view. Sure enough, in the distance I can see a brown orange wall. I catch my breath. I have no time to fall apart. I climb down quickly and pull the sled into the corner of the ramshackle and flip it on its side. I refill my water and drag it in the corner behind the sled. I pull two of my blankets around and over the sled, securing them underneath. I unroll my mat and lay it on the ground and secure some of the other supplies.

I run back over to the doorway and watch as the impending sand storm approaches. It's a very intimidating wall of sand, dust and debris all the way to the sky. My heart is pounding but the cloud is mesmerizing and lulling. I run to look out the back. There is no one coming. I see nothing but sand and it is kicking up a huge storm. I'm definitely alone. If anyone is out there, they are in big trouble. I turn around as the sand starts battering me. I run to the corner and crawl behind the sled. I tie some sheeting around my face as it gets very dark and very loud. I can hear the wind and sand slamming against the building and my sled. I close my eyes. This thing could last for hours.

I open my eyes to silence. As I sit up, a good amount of sand falls off me. I look out of my makeshift shelter. Sand is everywhere and has heavily dusted everything on the ground. I walk to the door and peer out. All tracks that were previously visible are gone. With all the fresh powdery sand I know my trek time is going to be longer. I better get moving.

Once I get my gear in order, I take a nice long drink of water, then head out. Just as I suspected, the new sugary sand is making my efforts slow and difficult. After what must be a few hours, I am really feeling the muscle pain in my back, arms, abs and thighs. How am I going to make it through the rest of this race? I'm going to need a week's rest from this.

I hear an electrical noise and look around. I see a black box protruding from one of the nearby dunes. It must be one of the spy cameras that keeps an eye on us. I haven't seen one before this. Hmmm, interesting. I mean, I knew there had to be some but this is the first I've actually seen. I wonder if the sand storm did away with whatever was concealing it. It must have. Since this desert challenge is a solo task, maybe they took extra measures to ensure we don't die alone out here. If we get off course and did die, they may never find us.

I see a reflection ahead. I continue watching until I actually see some buildings come into view. Hallelujah! I made it. Thank God! I made it!

When I reach the check-in area, I'm escorted to a bath house. I'm given water and a delicious meal. They tell me I'll be given a bath after I eat, then I'm to rest at least 8 hours. When they tell me I'm going to be given a bath, my mind immediately goes to Lachan and that creepy virginity check.

"Are the other contestants still here," I inquire.

"There are quite a few still here resting," the attendant responds.

So, I guess that means the leaders have already left.

"Am I the last," I ask.

He confirms with a bob of his head.

Shit! I knew it but it really sinks in after he responds. How am I going to get out of last place? I can't get eliminated now.

I'm led to a room with a large pool filled with steaming water. The air smells like a very complementary combination of fresh flowers, clean linen and soft spices. There are colorful metal "lily pads" floating in fixed locations in the pool. Some have washcloths, some have cleansing products in colorful bottles. There are powerful jets of water at either end, I'm assuming to keep the inviting blue water moving and filtering out the filth. It looks absolutely crystal clear. Along the sides of the pool are stacks of towels, refreshments and pitchers of cold drinks with chunks of various fruits in them along with iced metal cups. I guess the bath house is a social hang out as well.

After a quick look around, I see that I'm the only one here besides the female attendant walking over to me. She is beautiful with creamy dark skin and long black hair. She's wearing a white apron dress. When she reaches me, she bows.

"I'm Aaliyah," she says. "Let me help you get undressed."

I am grateful for the help to unwind out of this outfit.

I walk down the steps into the pool. The warm water is absolutely wonderful. I dunk my head under and take a little swim. When I come up and wipe the water from my face, I see Aaliyah standing on the side of the pool watching me in a friendly way.

"The yellow bottles have jasmine scented soap. The pink bottles have rose scented soap. The orange bottles have a citrus scented soap. The blue and purple bottles have hair cleansers," she tells me.

I look around at the bottles on the various lily pads as she describes them. When she's done, I thank her for the information.

"Do you require assistance with your bath or hair washing," she asks sweetly.

"No, thank you," I say, then add "I think I can take care of it."

"I'll just wait over here then." She moves toward a long mosaic tiled bench at the end of the room. "When you are finished, I'll hand you some toweling."

"Okay," I acknowledge then turn to swim to a nearby lily pad.

"There will be a physical with the race doctor after your bath," she adds before walking away.

I sigh. Another physical means another virginity check. I've been alone in the desert. "Why is this necessary?" I quietly ask myself as I turn my focus back to the lily pads again.

I decide to start with my hair. I grab the nearest blue bottle and smell the contents. It doesn't actually have any scent. I lather up my hair while contemplating which soap to use. I decide on the rose scented soap. I swim to it underwater in order to rinse my hair really well. Once at that lily pad, I take one of the white washcloths and work a good lather onto it. The scent is very light and soft. I scrub until I begin to feel like a woman again. This wonderful bath is just what I needed. I'm also feeling very tired. I hope I get to a real bed soon.

Aaliyah holds out a very large towel and I wrap myself in it. She then wraps my head and hair with another one.

Once I'm dried off, Aaliyah gives me a robe and slippers and leads me to an examination room.

"Take off your robe and lie upon the table," she says gently. She hands me a light paper-thin sheet to cover my nakedness. "The doctor will be right with you.

Within a few minutes, the doctor walks in. She is not what I expected. She is very Caucasian with blonde hair tied neatly in a bun at the base of her neck.

"Hello, Liliana. I'm doctor Saliba," She introduces herself as she walks over to me. "I'm going to give you a brief physical today."

"Okay."

"Most of the other contestants were experiencing some muscle soreness from the trek. How are you doing?"

"Yes, I have a little soreness. That bath certainly helped," I answer.

She smiles back and then puts on some gloves. I'm expecting another virginity check but she just pushes on my abdomen.

"Have you been feeling any pain?

I shake my head.

"Any unusual itching or burning?"

"Unusual," I question, "no." I shake my head.

"You've been in a lot of foreign soils and waters. That bath was not just for cleansing but there was an agent in the water to kill any foreign bacteria or parasites."

That's interesting.

"Let's proceed with the virginity check. Please lie back." I know the drill, and just follow directions until it's over.

"The males have their check here, too. A few are still recovering. It's tough on them," she adds making small talk.

She checks the rest of my body with a variety of squeezes, pokes, and pushes.

When the physical is finished and I have my robe on again, Aaliyah takes me up to a darkened luxury room where there is a very inviting bed. I drop the robe and just crawl in naked.

"Drink this," she says handing me a small glass half full of clear liquid.

I look at her as I take the glass and instinctively smell the contents, there is no odor.

"It's water laced with a mild relaxer. Doctor's orders," she adds.

I know she is not going to leave until I drink it so I down the liquid and lie back.

CHAPTER 33

I make my way to the yellow transporter where my guide's name is Qadir.

"Hi," I greet him as I get into the vehicle.

"Hello," he replies. "I'll be dropping you off at the Nazim Trading Post. You will have to bike the rest of the way to Kalil Springs." He hands me a small map with a bike path outlined on it.

"How far is it to ride a bike to Kalil Springs?" I ask.

"Not far," he tells me in a friendly way. "Should take about 15 minutes."

★★★

The bike ride was longer than 15 minutes. It was more like 30 once you bike through the Springs to get to the bottom of Kalil Hill. I see some of the other contestants, including Jannika, at the top of an enormous mountain of sand. I feel reinvigorated at the sight. I haven't seen anyone up close for almost a week. I must figure out how to get up there quickly and pass someone. I scan the area to spot the beginning of the path to the top. My plan is stalled as I'm directed to put on the special gear and shoes that are supposed to help me complete this task.

I begin and it's just more sand sloshing; a truly grueling effort. I think about how much I'm beginning to hate sand and this heat is unbelievable. I fall over numerous times in the hot sand. While I try to move quickly, it's very difficult to get back on my feet. Sand is finding its way into every part of my body. So much for the cleansing experience I recently enjoyed.

At last, I finally make it to the top and look around. I see hill after rolling hill of golden sand. I still hate sand, but this is truly a beautiful sight to behold from this elevation. I take a moment to let it set into my memory. I wish Archer were here to share it with me. I miss him. The sight of a few contestants fading off in the distance reels me back in. I need to catch up with them.

The attendant directs me to the far side of the hill. Once there, another attendant gives me a long wooden sled and leads me to the starting point. He tells me to lie down on my stomach. I look at him in disbelief. "Am I riding this down the sand mountain?" I ask. He smiles his affirmation as I grin back.

I lie down on the sled. "For a faster ride, keep your feet up," he advises. Then with a quick heave he sets me off on a super fast, amazing downhill run on this giant dune. I hold my feet up to get the most speed out of it. Sand rooster tails up from the back of my sled like a jet and I am flying! At the bottom it swoops and curves into a ramp like sand dune launching me into the air and landing some distance away eventually stopping in a small accumulation of sand. It is crazy awesome fun!

"Woohoo!" I shout as I get to my feet. "That was unbelievable," I tell the attendant who collects my now unnecessary gear. He smiles and gives me a thumbs up then hands me a walking staff. I feel myself frown. I hope this isn't an indication that I'm going to be walking through the desert again.

I find my way to the nearby refreshment tent. There's no one else here. I realize once again that I am last. I chug down water and start brushing the sand off myself. It's even in my ears but I have to get moving.

"Good day, fair princess," a familiar voice greets me.

Startled, I jump and drop my staff. I turn to see Langt. He's leaning against the tent post by the door. Where did he come from?

"You scared me. I thought I was alone," I respond.

He takes a deep breath and stands. "Archer's absence is causing a bit of a stir among our kind," he says with a touch of sarcasm.

I swallow. Is he friend or has he turned foe? I back up instinctually. My staff is on the ground.

He comes toward me and puts his hands on my shoulders. He is uncharacteristically serious. "Where's Archer?" he asks.

I look at him for a minute. He doesn't seem malicious but genuinely concerned.

I take a breath and tell him what happened. He drops his arms and leans back against a table. He looks away deep in thought as though a really terrible tragedy has just struck him through the belly. There is clearly something I don't know.

"What is it?" I ask after a few moments of his silence.

He looks at me as though he forgot I was there, then snaps out of it. He seems to be trying to figure out what to do or say. Then he adds, "Nothing. There is one among us that has been boasting of taking down the mighty Archer."

"Foyver?" I spit.

Langt nods, "This puts you and your Region in a terrible position."

It's true. Langt could take me out right now.

He continues, "Archer and I have been competing against other since we were kids. Given that our regions are aligned politically, we've been on many missions together. We've always watched out for one another. Right now, I'm on the owing side."

"Can you help him?" I plead.

He lets out a deep breath and shakes his head. "Not in the way you would like. My commitment right now is to Jannika and the priorities of Noswaref. I can't leave her no matter how many times he has saved my life. He understands this."

The disappointment of his words makes me nauseous. I turn and pick up another water.

"But I can help you," he pronounces as though he's looking right through me. Then, resolutely he stands. "Stay as close to the group as you can. I'll keep my eye on you and try to protect you through the rest of the leg. I'll do what I can to keep you in the race for his sake. Hopefully, Archer will be back for the next one."

I smile my appreciation to him.

He gives me a half smile. "Tell no one else about this," he warns smiling and pointing his finger at me.

"I won't," I vow, then reach down to pick up my sand staff. I turn back to him but he's already gone.

Those Specialists are amazing creatures.

At the exit, there is a race notice. ALL CONTESTANTS MUST MAKE THEIR WAY ON FOOT TO NAZIM HALL.

According to the map under the notice, Nazim Hall is about a kilometer away through more sand. I'm now grateful for the staff. I wrap some linen around my face and head to keep the sun from frying me. I pick up my staff and head out.

When I reach Nazim Hall, there is a task table out front with one task card left. I sigh. I've got to get ahead of someone quickly.

TASK: PROCEED TO THE ANCIENT ROOMS. THERE ARE THREE LOGOGRAPHIC SCRIPTS ON THE WALL. YOU MUST DECIPHER TWO OF THE THREE CORRECTLY IN ORDER TO PROCEED.

I'm excited! I love hieroglyphs. I have studied them for years during primary education. Maybe I can get through these quickly and catch up with the others. I practically run to the Ancient Rooms.

To my shock and amazement, there are still contestants here trying to work on this task. Excellent! A few have paired off to work together. I find the writing materials, make my way to a corner and get to work.

I'm moving along quite well when Antonella sits next to me, "I don't know what I'm doing. Can we work together?"

Shit. Here it is. A moral dilemma. If I help her, she could leave me behind and I'll be last. If I don't help her, she could be eliminated from the race instead of some of these other jerks. What do I do? I quickly find a compromise.

"Let me finish what I have. I'm almost done. If I'm correct, I'll tell you how to do it. If I'm not correct, we'll try some other way together. Okay?"

She chews on her bottom lip a moment, probably wondering whether or not to trust me. I understand that. I'd feel the same way. She nods, putting her faith in me. I'm touched.

I finish and run to the judge while Antonella, Banzi, Mirko, Poppi and Zara are still working. If I get this right, I can pull ahead. This is my chance.

I tell the judge: "The first one is: Knowledge is not necessarily wisdom." I wait to see if he tells me that is not correct, but he doesn't say anything so I go to the next one. "The second one is: People bring about their own undoing through their tongues." He smiles and hands me a completion pass.

I run back into the room to Antonella.

She looks up at me raising her eyebrows in question. I smile.

"I got it right," I whisper as I lean over her.

"That's great!" She seems genuinely happy. "Can you tell me how to do it?"

"Yes," I tell her. I'm not allowed to give her the answer so I try to explain how to solve it. "Hieroglyphs are written in rows or columns and can be read from left to right or from right to left. You can distinguish the direction in which the text is to be read because the human or animal figures always face toward the beginning of the line. Also, the upper symbols are read before the lower."

She nods in understanding and I continue. "Alphabetic signs represent a single sound and animals represent a combination of two or three consonants. Word-signs are pictures of objects used as the words for those objects. They are followed by an upright stroke, to indicate that the word is complete in one sign."

"Oh," she says as it sinks in. I can tell she understands, "so the bird is an ur sound?"

"Yes," I answer excitedly, she does get it! Then I add, "the bee is 'bat', the circle with the dot is 'ra'."

"Yes, I understand now." She points to the first panel, "that is reading right to left then?"

"Yes!"

"Okay, I think I got this now."

"Of course, you do," I concur. She's very smart after all.

Mirko running to the judge catches my eye.

"I gotta go," I whisper.

She looks over at the judge. "Yes, go."

I run through the doors and take a right down the hall. I'm not sure where I'm going but I think this is the way out. I slow down because the hall is getting darker the further I go down it. I start trying doors, but they are locked. I couldn't have gone the wrong way. I look left and it appears to be a dead end.

I find an open door to a room marked "Gallery". I go in and stand in amazement. There are shelves lining the high walls with colorful glass hookahs. They are beautiful. There are all kinds against the far wall that look very old. The ones closest to me look fairly new with brighter colors and designs. The lighting in the room is dim but I can see the vibrant colors.

There are four heavy, large wooden tables that look ancient and ornate before each wall. I assume it's so you take a hookah down and look at it or perhaps they smoke with them. I sniff the air, but It doesn't smell stale or smoky. There is a huge oriental rug that covers a redish carpet along the entire room.

I hear a noise and turn quickly back around to face the wall with the newer hookahs. I don't see anything out of place. I hear a few more tinks and clinks and walk a little closer to see what's causing that. Is it a mouse?

I scan the shelves. Now I can see a lot of them begin to move. As I look up, the entire rack begins to wobble from floor to ceiling. I stand frozen because it's coming down and I'm going to be killed.

I suddenly feel an arm clamp around my waist and tighten like iron as I'm whisked off the floor. My back is pressed against a very hard chest. We slide together as one under the closest of the heavy wooden tables. I'm on the ground completely covered by this body as the glass hookahs start breaking all around us.

I hear the table crack and then break as the heavy rack hits then falls to the side. A grunting snarl escapes from my protector's throat as he bears the full burden of the blow. When it's over, he lifts the table off of us and stands me up.

"You alright?" Langt asks but I don't get the opportunity to answer.

"I'm surprised to see you here, Langt," a man's voice booms all around the room.

I spin around but I don't see anyone. Where is he?

"Stay close to me," Langt whispers.

I look at him and wonder who is behind the voice.

"Hamar! I should have known," Langt calls out in his off-handed way to no one in particular.

"This one was an easy target to remove from the race," Hamar says, still hidden.

"My lady is fond of this one. She's not ready to part with her just yet," Langt casually responds.

"Are you taking Archer's part?" Hamar yells angrily.

"Now, why would I do that?" Langt jeers in a provoking tone.

"Where's your magic spear, Langt?" Hamar yells out snidely.

"Oh, it's never far from me. You know that. Would you like to get reacquainted with it, Hamar? I can certainly arrange it," Langt threatens but in a teasing sort of way. He hardly ever sounds serious.

"Leave the girl, Langt, and go on your way," Hamar demands.

Langt takes an exaggerated breath. "I thought I told you, my lady likes this one. I won't be leaving her with you today." He puts his arm around me and draws a long blade with his other hand. From where it came, I have no idea.

Langt leans in toward me. "He's going to charge," he says to me under his breath. "When he does, run for the door behind me and keep going."

I agree. I didn't know there was a door behind us, but that's where I'll go. He flips his wrist and the handle of the long blade extends to a full-sized rod. I stand amazed at the appearance of this spear by his side with a truly exquisite long blade at the top.

Suddenly, Hamar appears with a giant spiny sledge. He's such a big man. Sure enough, he is charging Langt. I run for the door with glass crunching under my shoes. I hope none of it breaks through the soles. I hit the door and it flies open. It closes behind me just as I hear the clashing sound of steel on steel.

The brightness of the sun sends me into a moment of piercing blindness. I cover my eyes and run sightless down the sandy street. When I regain my sight, I see another contestant running. Just ahead is the commuter. I pray I'm not last.

I'm almost there and the door is still open. Thank God! Number Five blares out of the speaker. I'm not last! This is even better than I thought given the whole Hamar thing. I feel very lucky today!

CHAPTER 34

Ingadeska

I scan the starters to see who was eliminated. The others are doing the same. I see Jannika, Roni, Zara, Poppi, Antonella, and Mirko. I don't see Banzi. Really? Interesting. But I'm glad Peago is out. Bitch. I wonder how Archer is doing. I miss him so much. I don't know if I can go much further without him. I know I'll be targeted again. I wonder if Langt will continue to try to help me.

Jannika is the first one to leave. I realize that she's about an hour ahead of me. That means by the time I leave, Langt will be long gone with her. I'm on my own.

At my start time, I'm given the information to make my way to the Great Tomb. At the fourth Taj Tower I will find a tree, and within the tree, I'll find more instructions. Okay, I have to get to Agra which is quite far from here. I need to get to the train station.

The station is so crowded I can barely move. The smell is horrendous. I make my way to the ticket window. People are touching me, but with all the pushing and shoving, it's not unusual. The sweaty bodies rubbing all over me and the stench of it is making me ill.

At the ticket window, the man won't even look at me. I keep asking for a ticket to Agra but he looks away. People are pushing and shoving me. Maybe he can't understand me. I'm practically yelling to him but he's not giving me anything. Finally, a man appears next to me.

"What do you want? You're holding up the line," he questions.

"I would like a ticket to Agra," I answer desperately on the verge of tears. "But he won't help me."

"He's not allowed to sell tickets to women," he says. "Have your husband buy the ticket."

Wow! This culture is ass backwards. I'm shocked but a good shove from behind restores my wits. I'm getting pulverized here.

"I don't have a husband," I plead.

He steps in front of me and orders two tickets. Once he gets them he hands one to me.

"Thank you," I say. I am very grateful.

"No problem. It saved me from waiting in that long line." He then gives my hip a little rub. "We can ride together."

I move away from him. "Sorry, not interested," I sputter as I push my way to the platform.

I am shoved onto the train by just being in the crowd. When the crowd moves, everyone moves. The squeeze on the train with multitudes of people is suffocating. The train starts moving. I can barely breathe from the crush and the smell. Men are all around me, staring at me.

I close my eyes for a moment, this is not good. Suddenly, I feel hands on me from every direction. They are groping my breasts, my ass and private parts. I have to get off this train, but I am not even near a door. I am scared, really scared.

I begin pushing and kicking. I just need some room. They are laughing, groping and pinching me. The train slows down so we must be close to the station. I am so glad I wore this one-piece outfit or I truly believe everything would have been ripped off of me by now. When I reach the platform, I notice my sleeve is torn and also a piece of cloth from my torso is ripped. Men start coming near again so I just take off running. I have to get out of here quickly.

Rain begins pelting me. As I try to find shelter, I see men watching me. I have to get out of this populated place. Thankfully, the rain makes it easier to run away without too much curiosity from bystanders. I run down a dirt road and find an old rickety shed without walls, just some wooden beams holding it up and a tin roof. I stand in an inconspicuous corner under that roof in the pouring rain. I have never felt so alone and hopeless. I knew this place was not a safe place to be. I hate this place!

I run back to the streets and down to the water's edge. There are many people here including women and children huddled under roofs. I see an abandoned rowboat and jump in quickly. I row myself out and away from the shoreline. Then I row along the city's edge while the boat starts to take on rain water. I just keep going. I see a bridge in the distance and pull up under it. I will huddle all night in this boat while it rains if that is what it takes.

I have plenty of time to think about what to do next. I grab my instruction sheet but because it is soaked, it just falls apart in my hands. I can't remember what to do once I get to the Great Tomb. Shit! I feel tears beginning to prick at my eyes but I refuse to be overwhelmed. I have to do this! I can't fall apart now. I just can't. I take a deep breath and try to relax.

I ponder my options. I'm not getting back on that train so I decide to take a bus the rest of the way to Agra to see whether I can catch the trail of one of the other teams. (Hopefully, buying a ticket won't be an issue.) Maybe if I follow their tracks, I will find the next assignment to get to the checkpoint quicker. I have four days left and I have not yet found, nor completed, the task.

Dawn is breaking. It's been another sleepless, uncomfortable night. The rain finally stops so I climb onto the bridge and make my way to the bus station. The buses are full but there are mixed groups of people and no one is paying attention to me. I buy a ticket from the bus driver. He doesn't seem to care about my gender, only my money. It is nice to get through that obstacle. It was really weighing me down. I lean my head against the window.

I doze on and off during the bus ride. I am jolted awake by the announcement that we made it to Agra. As we pull in to the bus depot, I hear a family of five tourists chattering excitedly about going to the Great Tomb and decide to follow them to the location.

Once I turn the final corner, the sight almost takes my breath away. The white marble is stunning. This is amazing! Before I can go in, I am required to drape my body and cover my head and neck with traditional dupattas because I'm a woman.

I don't mind. It puts me in a reverential mood and helps conceal my true identity as a racer so I can spy on the other contestants without being seen. Hopefully, they haven't all come through yet. I make my way to the edge of the property and sit on the ground in the shadows to wait it out. After several hours, my plan pays off.

I see Poppi walk in. I watch as she goes to the farthest corner of the tomb and disappears around the back of the building. Several minutes later, she appears with a small pouch wrapped across her body. I wait quietly in the shadows until she leaves.

I jump up and walk very quickly to where she disappeared. I continue walking and looking and then I remembered the bit about the tree. I see a few on the side in the shadow of the tower. Then, tucked away on the ledge of the backmost tree, I see two pouches. I grab one and move away from the area. Once clear, I open the bag. Inside are instructions for the next task. Hallelujah, I am still in this!

I am to go to the market in Samatispur. Find "Ali Baba" in the Genie Fortress to receive a good luck charm and instructions for the next task. I must bring the charm to the judge after I complete the task.

I jump on a bus to Samatispur. Again, no issues purchasing a ticket. After a few hours ride, there is a break in the landscape. There looks to be a decent sized town up ahead. As I get closer, I can see people everywhere. This Region is so populated. A flash of anxiety pulses through me.

I get off the bus and find my way inside the market. Vendors are selling everything from fruit to sunglasses. The smell is turning my stomach. I try to push through this mess, but the throng of people is making it difficult.

I'm asking everyone for the Genie Palace but the language barrier is not getting me very far. They just point in different directions. Finally, I see a vendor with a golden doorway which draws my attention. Sure enough, it's the Genie Fortress. The vendor holds up a selection of necklaces with a "Lucky Charm" for me to choose. I select one with a small cross feature surrounded by golden circles with small white beads dotted around it. It's dainty and sweet.

I step outside and find a place to rest my back against the wall while I read the new instructions. The task site is on the other side of the market near the blue and white tent.

I proceed there. I see a small track to the side of the tent. There are cooking stations. Mirko and Roni are occupying two of the stations. They are cooking something. I see the task table and pick up a card.

TASK: MAKE A POT OF ROGANJO USING INGREDIENTS ON THE LIST FROM THE SUPPLY TENT. ONCE COMPLETE FILL A BOWL OF THE SOUP THEN, WITHOUT SPILLING, YOU MUST TAKE A LAP AROUND THE ADJACENT TRACK AND CROSS THE FINISH LINE WITHIN 2 MINUTES. ONCE THE JUDGE APPROVES THE RACE AND FLAVOR OF THE SOUP, YOU CAN PROCEED AS LONG AS YOU HAVE FOLLOWED ALL RACE INSTRUCTIONS.

I can't help but laugh. Where do they come up with this stuff? Soup on the run, eh? The "followed all race instructions" I would think is about handing over the lucky charm.

I choose a workstation and pick up a list of ingredients. I walk to the supply tent. There are barrels and crates of unmarked spices, chilis, vegetables and raw meat hanging from large hooks.

I grab the items I know quickly, but the spices and the chilis cause me a great deal of pause. The problem is, the more I stand here trying to smell the spices to figure out which spice is which or what chili to use, my eyes begin burning and my nose is running from the heat of the chilis. I have to go outside numerous times to clear the air in my nose. I have to get moving. Those guys look like their soups are almost finished and I haven't even started.

I run back in and grab some of this spice and that spice. With the chilis, I grab a handful of the ones that don't tear my eyes up when I bend close. Next, I move to my workstation. I don the provided apron and get to work.

I lay everything out. The "stove" is actually just a fire pit with a grate over it. I grab a pot and set it on top to heat. I see some oil on the shelf and smell it. It's some kind of mild cooking oil. I pour a couple of tablespoons in the pot to preheat, then cut the lamb into chunks and throw it in the pot. I dice up an onion and the rest of the vegetables and throw them in to start cooking. I add salt and pepper and give it a stir.

The directions say to make the gravy. I don't see any milk, but there is yogurt. I sprinkle the vegetables and meat with a generous portion of flour and stir it around. I add some water with the yogurt, pour it over the veggies and allow that to cook down.

Now I have to take on the spices. The aromatic ones are easy; cloves, cardamom, cinnamon and of course, bay leaves. The chilis are not so easy but I manage to pull the dish together. Once the gravy is thickened, I add more water to make it "soupier" then give it a taste.

Whoa. The heat is extreme but this Region likes their food that way. It just needs a touch more salt. When I come out of my workstation, the two guys are gone but Poppi is at a workstation and Antonella is rummaging in the supply tent. Excellent. I'm not last. I have no idea how I beat Poppi here, but I'm glad. I go to the starting gate.

The air is very humid. That combined with the heat from cooking, the runny nose and sweaty body, I'm feeling run down. But now I have a race against the clock. The start judge has his stopwatch in hand. He takes a long look at me as though he disapproves of my appearance. A judgey judge. Who knew?

When he says go, I'm off. I try walking really fast so I don't spill but I don't think I'm making very good time. I try running on my toes to see if I can get a better, faster pace. I think I do but just as I come around the final bend, my time is up and I have to go back to the starting point. I stop at the water table and guzzle some water. I need a moment to recover. I'm really starting to feel sick. Maybe I'm a little dehydrated. I just don't have time for this.

I get up and start again. This time I go at a quicker pace. Even if I complete the time limit, I still have to face the tasting judge. I only have a few more yards.

I made it through in time! Now I present my soup to the judge. He takes a spoon to get a big dip of the soup. I swallow hard as I await his judgment. He's swishing it around his mouth for crying out loud. Why doesn't he just gargle with it as well?

"It's passable, Liliana," he says looking at me but he didn't pass me. Why?

Then I remember the charm.

"Oh, yes. I have something for you," I mention taking it off my neck and over my head. I hand it to him.

As he looks down at it, he smiles. "You have passed. You may continue on in the competition."

I thank him and move away. I'm so hot. I need to get this damn apron off but most of all, I need more water. I grab more and a seat but I can't stay long. I see Poppi at the starting point which means I have to move. I get up a little slowly, still feeling sick and grab an extra water.

I start walking quickly back through the market. I can barely breathe through the clash of body odor, animal droppings and cooking smells. Everywhere I turn there are hordes of people.

How do I get out of here? I pick up my pace and begin pushing through the crowd. I follow a road out as the shops begin to dwindle. I take a side path and see rows and rows of long concrete buildings with tin roofs. There are door openings every several feet and realize these are tiny residences.

I walk swiftly through the narrow passage way between buildings looking for a way out. There is a man standing against the wall. He watches me as I pass him. I get a sinking feeling. I turn down another narrow passage but it seems like a dead end. Then I see another small passage. The man is definitely following me. I turn down another passage but this maze of buildings seems never ending. The man has picked up some pals and now I have three men following me.

I start to panic. I keep hearing more noises behind me. Are there more now? I don't even look. When I turn down the next path I bolt into a full sprint. They pick up their paces too. I can hear them closing fast but I don't look back. One of them is very close now because I can hear him breathing. He grabs me from behind, and I start screaming and kicking. I reach up trying to scratch his face and drop to try to flip him.

He spins me around to face him in a bruising grip but I tightly close my eyes while blindly punching at his chest and kicking his legs trying to wrench myself free. He grabs my shoulders and gives me a shake. "Look at me!" he's firm.

I open my eyes and gasp. It's ARCHER! Oh my God, Archer! I've never been so extremely happy and relieved to see someone in my entire life. It overwhelms me. I completely fall apart. I'm half laughing and half crying. I start shaking uncontrollably and my knees begin to give way. I practically fall against him.

He holds me upright. "Whoa. Hey. Easy," he responds measuredly showing a genuine look of concern on his face.

I've never felt so alleviated and yet so incredibly on edge all that the same time. I'm shaking all over and trying to control it but instead I just lunge at him and hug him over and over. I start kissing his face. I'm having a hard time standing because I'm shaking so hard. Maybe the heat and dehydration have a little to do with it, too.

He slides one of his hands up my neck and places it on my cheek. He holds my head in place and looks into my eyes. His brow is furrowed. He is concerned. I can't seem to actually focus on him for very long. I'm trying to talk but my head bobs and I just keep pecking at his lips. I'm shaking and feel rather weird.

"Hey. Hey. Look at me. Easy. Shhhhhh," he whispers gently. He continues to look into my eyes as he is still concerned. He smiles at me then he bends down and presses his lips to mine. I can feel the soft warmth of his parted mouth. My hand moves instinctually to his cheek. His lips against mine as well as his shushing are soothing. His breath mixes with mine. The slow rhythm of his breathing and the heat of his mouth help me to slow down and relax. He continues holding my mouth captive for some moments.

"Shhhhhhh," he continues with his mouth lightly touching mine. I can feel myself calming. I stop shaking and have a better grip on my knees. He slides one hand down my back and I melt into his body like butter. He holds me close for a moment stroking my hair. I lean against his strength putting my head on his chest and close my eyes letting my body adjust to the safety of his nearness and the familiar warmth of his arms.

I have absolutely zero experience with men. After school, I spent every waking hour preparing for the tests and competitions in order to make this race. I never had time or even thought about romance. My only experience is a few clumsy kisses from schoolboys, but nothing like this nearness and feeling totally safe with someone. It is so affecting and I feel so protected. He pulls back a little but his mouth still lingers near my face.

"Are you through being hysterical?" he asks smiling. His voice is husky. The smell of his manliness awakens something deep inside of me. I'm so very happy to be with him again. I take a small breath and exhale. I look up at him and nod. His arms loosen. I want more of this closeness, but he's waiting for me to move back and reluctantly, I do.

I step away from him and try to focus more on our surroundings. I take a deep breath and stand on my own. I look up at him. He's still looking at me with a question on his face. But I'm okay, so I nod in acceptance again.

He pulls out a canteen and has me drink some water.

"I believe you have a touch of heat exhaustion. Let me know if you need more rest or if you feel well enough to continue."

"I can continue."

"That's my girl," he says smiling. He looks around determining the best course.

Suddenly, I have a thousand questions.

"Where did you come from? How did you find me? How's your leg? How did you get here?" I rattle off.

He looks back to me. "Later," he says. "We need to move."

He takes my hand to lead me out of this horrifying labyrinth.

Soon, we board a boat to cross the river. After finding some free space, we lean against the railing apart from the other people then turn to each other.

"I've missed you! I've missed you so much," I say hugging him.

He chuckles while hugging me back. "You've done pretty well for yourself," he says.

"I had help," I confess.

Archer looks at me and his smile fades slightly. "Tell me," he says. I watch his jaw clench ever so slightly.

"I am indebted to Langt," I say cautiously because of the look in his eye. "If you only knew what he's done."

Archer's jaw sets. "What has he done," he asks in a deep ominous voice.

I'm so taken aback by his sudden change. I stammer a little. "Archer, I..he…"

Archer takes my shoulders in his hands and asks again while tilting his head. "What has he done," he asks again gently but firmly.

A small breath escapes me. "Archer, you're imagining.,,"

"I can imagine quite a lot where an unprotected young woman is involved and the players believe me to be out of the picture." His eyes are flashing fire.

"Archer, please…" I try to finish but he interrupts me.

"Damn it, Lily," he spews loosening his grip on my shoulders, "Shall I find him myself and beat his confession from him?"

I jerk away from him.

"Do you think so little of your friend? Or of me?" I answer truly injured by this line of questioning.

He shakes his head. "No," he says pointing his finger at me. "My regard for you is of the highest quality. My question comes because you don't look at anyone's motives, only their 'thoughtfulness'", he explains frustratingly but calmly. "However, I lay no tactics aside. Do I have to remind you that this is a politically strategic race whose outcome is so important to the Regions this year, that it has taken a savage, deadly and, dare I say, deceitful turn?" His logic, as always, shines through. "As for Langt, perhaps I will consider that I have been unjust if you will only be more forthright in your explanation of what transpired between you in my absence."

"Archer, he paid me the kindest service! His concern for you was genuine," I answer finally finding my real voice while placing a calming hand on his arm. "Why in this world would jump to such conclusions?"

He ignored the last question. "Sweet words and a promise of love can change a contestant's mindset very quickly. I'm well aware of Langt's charm with the ladies," he pauses, looks out at the water for a moment, then turns back to me and sighs. "Perhaps you should start from the beginning," he suggests. I know he's not happy with this but he's fair.

I tell him about Arbric and how Langt came to my rescue. I told him how Hamar was determined to take me out. Archer stopped me.

"Hamar?" He furrows his brow and I can see a tightening in his jaw. "Did he hurt you in any way?"

"No, Archer. Langt fought him in the end and I haven't seen either one since. I don't know how either fared."

"Langt is fine." Archer says, "I glimpsed him earlier." Then he added, addressing me specifically, "I promise to thank him for standing in my stead." He tilts his head smiling. I smile my happy approval in return. Then he takes a deep breath. "Hamar…," he says thoughtfully, "our day will come."

"What do you mean?"

"He holds against me something that happened long ago," he says. "Whenever he is near, plaster yourself to my side. Is that clear?"

"What happened? I hope you don't mind my asking."

He looks at me with a half-smile. "Why would any man draw such a raging hatred for another man?" His lips tighten while he shakes his head. "Generally, only a woman can do that."

Shit. A woman. I'm not sure I want to know. "You don't have to tell me."

"It's not like that." He takes a breath and tells me the story. "We were kids, in our late teens, I guess. We were competing at a public temple match in his Region. There was a female present that he had taken a liking to. I guess she took a liking to me."

I could totally believe that. He's so damned good looking. I'll bet he was back then, too.

"Trust me when I say I did not encourage her affections at all. She followed me around to the point that I had to have one of the judges ask her to stay in the public areas while I basically hid in the back."

I laughed out loud.

"Hamar became quite offended and challenged me. I had no idea the lady had impacted his heart or that he even knew the lady at all for that matter," Archer added in his own defense. "I outranked him even then. I thought his challenge was legitimate, after all, he had home arena advantage, so I thought he wished to move up in rank. I had no idea he was trying to impress a lady."

He is thoughtful for a moment, then continues, "If I had known about the lady, maybe I would have given him more quarter, but when Hamar is roused to anger during a fight, he makes careless mistakes which I cannot abide, let alone allow someone to move up in rank. He profoundly faltered and I easily overtook him, right to the ground, embarrassing him exceedingly in his own eyes because it was in front of the lady. He was humiliated by my hand. He thinks I wanted to impress the lady."

"How can he hold against you the feelings he had for this girl? It is not your fault she was smitten," I sympathize.

"When you believe that you are diminished in the eyes of another, it stings you deeply inside and resentment grows. It's jealously at its base core. Whether or not you let it turn into a hatred, is something only you can control." He's still a walking proverb.

He continues, "The thing is, Lily, he believes his fight with me compelled the lady to pursue, or should I say, stalk me. It took two years before I didn't see her at every one of my public matches. I had to have her thrown out of my changing rooms many times."

I laugh. Then I notice my brightly colored hair band around his wrist. I am touched that he kept it there.

"Were you still in the cave when you woke up?"

"I was. There were some very nice people taking good care of me. They seemed very fond of you. They told me how sad you were to leave me."

I look at him smiling. "I was sad to leave. I don't think you would've left me. I still feel that I wronged you there." My smile is fading and turning instead to a shamed frown.

He lifts my chin to him. "You did the right thing. You can't win if you don't play. You would have been eliminated. I would never have forgiven you for ruining your chances on account of me."

"I thought you would say that, but it did not make it easier to leave you there."

"I was told that after numerous kisses, you dragged yourself away," he emphasizes dramatically and chuckles. "I'm not sure if they were embellishing the story for their matchmaking purposes or just the romance of the situation in that deep dark cave."

I laugh, blushing a little, then it dawns on me. "Wait! You could talk to them," I ask amazed, although, not entirely surprised.

"I could. I understand you took very good care of me, and I thank you for that." He smiles looking into my eyes.

"You know damn well that the old woman took very good care of you," I say.

"She may have tended my wound, but I understand you were most attentive. I am grateful," he says smiling.

God knows what kind of dialog transpired. My cheeks are getting flushed just thinking about how many times I had my hands on his body. I couldn't help myself. I touched him, had my hands in his hair, I kissed his lips, I stared at him for hours because there was nothing else to do. I'm so glad he will never know what thoughts I had, especially the naughty ones.

CHAPTER 35

This area is facing drought conditions; therefore, the road is hot and dry. They need some of the rain I was dealing with earlier in this leg. I'm so happy to have my Archer back. I look at him and feel so happy. I take a drink of water and look over at him again.

He's looking off in a distant direction and slowing his pace. I try to follow his eyes but I don't see anything. He has his super senses up and I trust them implicitly.

"What is it?"

"Langt," he replies.

"What?" I look all around and see nothing. "Where? I don't see him."

"Come," Archer says.

We walk to the edge of the woods behind a poverty-stricken building. I see Langt leaning casually against a tree.

"Welcome back," he calls to Archer in his charming way and holds out his hand.

Archer shakes it smiling. I am so glad. I was wondering if he still held him in some distrust. I guess maybe he distrusts everyone to some degree. But all seems well now.

"I hear your old friend, Moralles, has been recruiting," Langt says.

Archer scoffs. "No surprise there." He rolls his eyes. This person must not be a friend. "That's not why you're here," Archer cuts through.

Langt shakes his head. "I need a moment." He looks at me. I suddenly feel very unwanted and unimportant.

Archer looks at me. "Please excuse us."

The two men walk several yards away and speak in low tones. Langt's back is to me. Archer keeps me in his line of vision though. His arms are crossed against his chest and he's pinching his chin between his index finger and thumb as he listens. He nods and Langt walks away without looking back.

Archer returns to me and smiles. He puts his hand in the small of my back and leads me deeper into the forest. Must be a shortcut. He's quiet. Whatever Langt told him has made him very thoughtful.

We walk quietly for about an hour. The forest is filled with life. The sounds of animals, birds and the rustling of the leaves make the journey a little noisy so I don't mind Archer's silence overly much. He is lost in his thoughts and I let him be. We stop by a small stream that looks like it could've belonged to a much bigger creek or small river before the drought. Archer refills our canteens.

After a little while, the wind picks up and the air turns a little chilly. Through the trees, I see a bit of a clearing within the forest and a large campsite. A man walks over to greet us. He and Archer seem to be old friends. Archer talks to the man in his language. They look at me every so often. Then the man comes forward and shakes my hand, leading me into the camp. There are ground torches lining the path. It's really a pretty effect. I'm surprised the wind hasn't blown them out. They must have some kind of super oil or something buried underneath that keeps them lit. We enter his tent where his wife and a number of children are gathered around a cooking fire that sits in the middle of it. There is a kettle on it with something stewing and bread baking. My mouth waters from the aroma.

"This is my good friend, Anik. He's inviting us to sit down and join them for dinner," Archer translates. "This is his wife Korka and his children. The oldest boy is Jimson, then there is Dhanurashi, who is named after me," he proudly says smiling, "This is Adi, and Krish. The little girls are Chara, Estaa and the baby, Hasina."

I smile at them. They smile in return. They share their delicious meal with us. The children come over ready for us to play. I can't speak their language but we are somehow communicating and having a lovely time. The men are laughing a lot at whatever they are talking about. Every so often the tent flaps come loose from the wind and the children pretend to get scared until we tickle them.

After some time, Archer stands gathering his bow and things. I think I know what this means.

"I've been summoned," he states, "I'll be back in the morning."

I knew he was leaving me.

"You'll be in good hands here," he says rubbing my arms.

We step outside. The power of the wind catches us both absolutely off guard. My hair is beating my face. We duck behind a tent for a little relief. Archer is looking at those fire torches that are flashing this way and that and then up to the sky. The night is extremely dark.

"I don't know, Lily," he says, "This doesn't feel right to me."

"What do you mean?"

He shakes his head. "With the weather and everything, I don't think I should leave you here. I'm extremely concerned."

He pops his head back into his friend's tent. Anik comes out and looks around then gives Archer a wave, like "it's nothing" and goes back inside the tent.

Archer sighs. "I don't like it but Anik seems to think it's normal for them," he says.

"I'm already here now. I like your friends. Maybe this weather will make you return quicker to me," I tease smiling.

He looks down at me. His face softens. He bends close to give me a sexy little kiss right on the side of my lips. I'm totally shocked but happy. I wish it were more, but I'll take whatever I can get.

"I won't linger, I assure you." I can tell by the look on his face that he is very reluctant to leave me here.

"Then go, and don't let Langt keep you in the pubs all night," I reply smiling.

He breathes deeply as though he is thinking long and hard about it. His eyes are on me. He touches my cheek then runs off into the night. I return to the tent and play with the children for a while, then help with their bathing and putting them to bed.

It's been a few hours since Archer left, and the wind continues to press heavily at the tent. Every so often it really howls. I wonder if they get tornadoes here. I step outside for a breath of air before turning in.

I witness one of the tents on the outer edges of camp being pulled away from its pegs. Men and women are trying to secure it but one flap is dangerously close to a torch. I watch a blowing ember hit it, and to my horror, the tent catches fire. It goes up very quickly and then is swept around the camp by the wind. It touches other tents catching them ablaze and then is tossed through the air landing in a tree. Oh my God!

The tree is in flames immediately. It is like a domino effect. I run inside and start yelling but they can't understand me. Anik runs outside as others yell and chaos erupts around the campsite. I help his family members get out of bed, run to try to put out fires and find loved ones but it seems to be of no use. They disappear into the smoke. The flaming tents are pulled up and sent flying into the now well-lit forest.

The fire quickly surrounds us. Anik is yelling trying to get everyone out of the area and using his arms to motion "this way". By now, the smoke is very thick and trees are starting to fall. I try to follow Anik but somehow, I get separated. The fire and embers are floating in the air and falling on people's clothes and hair catching them on fire. I try to help but they run instead of dropping. The heat and the smell begin to overpower me.

I run in every direction looking for a way out but can't find one. The smoke is choking and blinding me. At one point, I find myself alone. As I bend close to the ground to get under the smoke, I see a very narrow path and I bolt for it. I'm coughing and my lungs hurt so badly.

I find a small clearing with the trickling stream running through it that Archer and I stopped at earlier. I drop on the damp dirt next to it and take a drink. I can barely breathe. My lungs want to cough but only a little raspy squeal escapes me. I'm trying desperately to get some air but the smoke and heat are burning my lungs. I lie on the ground with my cheek on the edge of the water. Its coolness soothes my face and the air, what little I can take in, feels fresher. My eyes are filling with black as I struggle to take in air. Am I dying?

★★★

I open my eyes. Archer's mouth is on top of mine. I try to breathe but it hurts. I just wheeze. It's light. There is no wind and no smoke. He pulls me up quickly with one arm. I see him pop a small bottle top off with his teeth. He squirts its contents into my mouth. At first, I think it is water and gladly swallow it because my mouth is so dry but then it starts burning. My mouth is burning, my lungs are burning and my stomach is burning!

He flips me over so my hands are on the ground. I pull myself up on all fours desperately gasping to get air. I'm gagging and heaving. He turns me back over and shoves some gelatinous goo pack into my mouth and then squirts in more of that burning fluid. The chemical reaction of it turns the goo into some kind of foam that quickly fills my mouth and throat. I start gagging immediately.

Archer flips me back over and I begin to heave and throw up. Every muscle in my body starts violently shaking trying to repel whatever he put in my mouth. I'm trying to vomit from the very tips of my toes. It continues to coat my throat. I vomit and gag and heave. When I don't think I can take anymore, Archer flips me over and holds up another bottle. I start waving my hands in front of my face gasping for air while choking on this damn foam. I can't do it again!

"It's water," he says quickly. "Just water."

I open my mouth as he fills it and flips me over so I can spit it out. He does it again. I spit out foam and more foam.

He turns me back to him and pours more water down my throat one final time. I'm catching a little more air. When he turns me back to him, he shushes me. But I'm struggling with all my might to breathe and I keep gagging. He wipes my face with a cloth then says, "Lily, be still and try to listen to me." He takes a few slow breaths, seemingly trying to calm me down, then adds, "I need you to try to take a deep breath for me, as deep as you can. Okay?"

I nod and take a breath. Surprisingly, it is deep. I can breathe! I can actually breathe!

I look at him and can see the relief cross his eyes. Archer drops his shoulders and takes a few calming breaths of his own. His arm is still around me and he is rubbing his forehead with his other hand. He leans back against a charred tree pulling me on top of him. He closes his eyes and continues to catch his own breath. I take a good look at him. He is covered in black soot, water and grime. He must have been fighting his way back to us. I realize that I'm soaked. I must have been laying halfway in that stream for a while. I lean my head on his shoulder. I can breathe. Whatever he did was a miracle.

I wake up. It's dark. I'm still on top of Archer. He is sleeping. I roll off him but he rolls at the same time. I'm caged between his body and his arm that was wrapped around me. He is still sleeping. He must have been exhausted. I don't mind my "cage". This is a safe place.

When I wake up again, Archer is gone. It's a beautiful albeit chilly morning. There is a deep fire pit with a fire burning in it nearby. I look around at the scorched and burned forest. It's very sad. I sit up and try to take a look at myself. My mouth feels like it is filled with cotton. I walk to the trickling stream and flush it out with water until it starts feeling normal again.

I can see that my clothes and arms are black with soot and charred. I splash water over my face and arms swiping at them to try to get it off but I'm just smearing it around.

Archer appears with a couple of dead birds hanging on a rope at his waist.

"Good morning." He looks very fresh, except for his sooty clothes, he looks like he's had a shower and everything.

I smile at him and return to my clean up attempt.

He has the birds dressed and on a spit over the fire in no time.

He comes to the stream and washes his hands then turns to me.

"Let's have a look at you," he says kneeling in front of me. "How are you feeling?"

"Okay. I can breathe again thanks to you." My voice is extremely hoarse, barely audible.

He moves behind me and presses on my upper back in different areas. "Take a deep breath."

I breathe.

"Do you have any pain?" he asks.

I shake my head.

He moves back in front of me and presses gently here and there on my throat.

"You have some minor swelling. That foam will leave traces of a healing agent in your throat for the next day or so. It's weird but it will pass."

"Okay," I grunt.

"You gave me quite a scare," he says smiling looking into my eyes.

I start to ask him about Anik and everyone else but he says, "Try not to talk today. Your vocal cords need time to heal. After we eat, we'll head out as we have a lot of ground to cover."

I just nod.

***

Late that night, we get to a decent sized city. Archer stops at a hotel where we take showers and grab a nap. Archer says we have to be up early.

When we leave the hotel, Archer takes us to a police station. It seems like everyone here speaks English. Most seem to be of Scoterie descent like some of the ancestry here, very fair and light colored.

"We have to report what happened," Archer states.

I can only nod my agreement and understanding since my voice is still a bit strained.

Archer spends a decent amount of time at the counter filling out forms about the fire. I'm fidgety. I still feel emotionally, and of course, physically drained from it all. I look up at Archer as he finishes with the forms. He is leaning with his elbows on the counter facing the Sergeant. His eyes, however, are looking at something else. I follow them and see an officer staring at me. He stands up from his desk and begins walking toward me. I step back instinctually toward Archer.

"You're very lucky," he says. "You're the only one who survived."

My heart drops. Anik and his family? All those people died? No one got out? Archer must be devastated. I look down and tears start filling my eyes. Archer pulls me to him and I silently cry into his chest.

"Thanks, man," he snarls at the officer.

"I'm sorry," he says defensively. "Did you know?"

"Yes, I knew!" Archer barks at the man. That emotional outburst confirms to me that Archer is hurting from the loss of his friends.

"Officer," the Sergeant interrupts, "you're not helping."

Archer rubs my back as I hold in another rush of tears. That just really caught me off guard. Anik, Korka, the children, all those people…I'm shocked no one escaped.

The sergeant asks us to wait a moment while he finalizes the report. Archer brings me to a chair where I sit down. He wipes the tears from my cheeks and holds me a little longer. After a while, he says, "I need a cup of coffee." He looks at me, "do you want anything?"

I shake my head.

"I'll be right back."

I watch him move through to the next hallway and disappear around the wall.

He's gone for some time. I stand and pace the floor. I look around the corner and see him take a drink of coffee while the Sergeant is talking to him. I sit back down in my chair.

After several minutes, the door opens to a commotion. A police officer walks in pulling a tattoo-covered man in handcuffs. The man has a decent sized nose ring and several other ornaments jutting out of the skin on his face. He is wearing a dark green overcoat over his clothes and is also sporting a leather spiked collar around his neck.

He is humorously disruptive. I smirk more than a few times at his antics. The officers are having a hard time controlling him. I look for Archer and finally see him coming through the hallway entryway. I stand but he stops. His eyes are very focused. I know that look. He's identified a threat. I suddenly realize the entire room has gotten quiet.

I turn to my other side to see what is going on. The tattooed man is standing right next to me almost in my face.

"Gawd, you're beautiful," he says loudly.

Where I'm from, I was born and bred to repay a compliment with a compliment.

"Thank you very much," I answer with my still raspy voice. "And that's a very fine nose ring you're wearing today."

The entire room breaks out in laughter. I feel a touch on my elbow and know it's Archer. The two men nod to each other in the way that men do.

"Come," Archer says. "We have a train to catch."

"We're free to go?" I ask looking at him. I see that his eyes are still on my new acquaintance. He nods his answer.

"No worries, mate," the tattooed man devilishly says to Archer. "I'm a little busy right now. I'll catch up with her another time. She's worth the effort." Then he winks at Archer.

Archer smiles, "Looking forward to it," he growls with a nasty undertone. He puts his hand on my hip and moves me out of there.

★★★

We arrive at the very populated train station and it must be rush hour again. There are men everywhere. I stop and turn to Archer.

"I can't do this," I utter shaking my head. My memories of being groped, fondled and bruised come hurling back at me. I am getting very freaked out and start shaking.

Archer looks at me and puts his hands on my hips. "Why not?" he asks.

I tell him my story of the last time I rode the train here. His jaw tightens. "Stay close to me. They will leave you alone," he says. "We have to catch this train, Lily. With everything that's happened, we're behind."

"Okay," I accept with a sigh. I'll do what he wants but I know they won't leave me alone. Their hands come out of nowhere.

Archer buys the tickets and we wait on the platform for the train. Men start closing in from every angle. Archer moves us closer to the edge of the platform then steps behind me. He has his hands on my shoulders.

The train arrives absolutely busting with people. The rush to get on is maddening. Archer muscles his way to push us through. Just as I thought, the crush is insane. We only make it as far as the entry platform, but with the open doors on each side of the train, at least there is some fresh air coming through. It smells terrible. Archer stands taller than most. He has reached up to hold onto a rail with his left hand. He has the other on my shoulder.

As the train moves, so do the hands. They are rubbing my thighs, my crotch, my breasts and anywhere else they can. I turn so I'm facing Archer and move in closer into him. He leans his head down. "They're touching me," I cringe.

He casually reaches up with his other hand and grabs another rail. Then I feel him pull himself up, lift his legs on either side of me and powerfully kick. About half a dozen men fly out of the other train door and land on the ground. Archer sets himself back down and yells something in their language.

All the men back away from us. Archer turns himself around so I'm behind him, crosses his arms and stands there while I hold onto him for the rest of the journey. When we get to our station, he yells something else and everyone clears the way as Archer pulls me in front of him and moves me off the train.

"What did you say to them?" I ask when we are walking on the road again.

"Just then?" He's distracted looking at a map and signs.

"Yes, but what did you say first on the train?"

"Roughly translated, the next man who touches my lady will be violently set to the tracks," he answers still reading.

I laugh shocked and amazed. This man is so brazen. "What about just now."

"We're getting off, move," he says. "It was effective," he shrugs.

I let out another laugh and glance at him. His mind has already moved on as he looks around for our next direction. I think he is incredible.

"Come," he tells me grabbing my hand, "we're going to need a transport. The checkpoint is about 5 kilometers yet."

CHAPTER 36

Panill

I wasn't the last to check in at the checkpoint, but I'm wondering who was. Jannika and I agreed last night to meet for breakfast, but she still isn't here. Antonella approaches with a plate of food and sits next to me.

"Have you heard who was eliminated?" I ask her.

"You don't know," Antonella replies sadly. "I thought everyone did."

I shake my head. "What happened?"

"Zara's specialist was so angry with her for falling behind in Ingadeska that he sexually exploited her. She failed the virginity test," she says tearfully.

"Oh my god! I had no idea! That's terrible!" I am so upset! Hamar is so brutal. "Did he get arrested?"

"He's supposed to be executed for rape. But he ran. They don't know where he is," she added.

Just then Jannika plops down at the table with us.

"You're late," I say to her. "Did you hear about Zara?"

"Yes, terrible tragedy for her." She doesn't seem as affected by it really.

We all eat in silence for a moment then I decide to change the subject or at least I thought I was.

"Why were you late?" I ask casually.

"Virgin check," she shrugs.

"I didn't get a virgin check," Antonella says. "I hope I don't. I hate them and I think we have had plenty already, but they may give us all one because of Zara," she adds shifting uncomfortably. When she does, she swipes her spoon accidently sending it off the table to the ground. She gets up to get a new one.

"Really, a virginity check? Gosh, that's the last thing I want today. The last one I had was Arbric, then the one before that at that creepy bath house," I shudder.

"The Lez House?" she questions rhetorically. "Oh yes, I had one there, too. After the old woman checked me out all those girls had their hands on me."

"Jannika?" I'm shocked. "What the hell? Did you report them?"

"No," she giggles. "I let them. I mean, what kind of life is that; always bathing someone," she says nonchalantly buttering her bread. "I guess they have to get their jollies somehow. If they want to fondle my breasts and touch my body, I let them. We are sexual creatures after all."

I realize my mouth is gaping open and close it. I try to focus on my breakfast.

"Besides," she whispers, "Langt has me so hot and bothered, I just imagined it was him."

"Jannika?" I smile at her. "Is something going on with you and Langt?"

She laughs. "Nothing really. We're just very flirty with each other and well, he's so damn beautiful, how can I help but have my hands sliding around on him from time to time. Everyone here seems to think there is something more going on though. They said the sexual integrity of our relationship is breaking down."

We laugh.

"I have had seven virginity checks already," she adds.

"Seven?" I gag on my food. "Are you serious? On my gosh, Jannika." I chuckle.

She laughs and continues, "this time, Manager Laurels says to me, my dear girl," she's imitating his voice, "you are a beautiful and curvy young woman. Do you have any idea of the effect your actions may be having on Langt? He is a man with strong needs and desires."

We both start laughing out loud.

"If you keep up with this behavior, you could find yourself out of this race. If you don't care about the race, think of your future. Do you really want to be living in the lowest conditions?" That last bit wasn't so funny.

Instinctually, we both look at Zara's photo on the racers wall, then back at each other and continue eating our breakfast in silence.

★★★

It doesn't take long to spot Archer. He's leaning against a tree reviewing a map of the area. He looks up and smiles but continues his perusal. It smells like salt and sea. The sky is clear blue and happy which reminds me of home.

"The task is at the Festival. It's not far from here," he says putting away the map.

"Did you hear about Hamar?" I ask him. It's really bothering me.

"What about him," he asks as we start walking.

"He sexually assaulted his contestant. She's out," I say with a sad pout. I hate the way she was eliminated.

Archer looks off. I can tell it pissed him off.

"Isn't he supposed to get executed for that," I ask with emphasis. I hate him.

"Yes," Archer responds with a nod.

"I heard he ran. He's a specialist. How do you find a specialist," I screech.

"With another one," he states calmly. "A better one."

"You?" I ask, frightened he's going to leave me.

"I'm committed. They'll find someone not involved with the race to go after him," he shrugs it off and I'm relieved.

We arrive at the Festival. I see Jannika and Langt in front of a large white tent on the beach.

"Look, that must be it," I tell Archer. We walk over to them.

As Jannika and I go into the tent, I look back to see Archer and Langt heading to the Tiki Bar in good spirits. Inside the tent, there is a canvas blocking our view from the rest of the tent, but there is native island music playing on the other side and people talking. In front of us is a table with the task cards. We each grab one.

TASK: CHOOSE A TEACHER AND LEARN A NATIVE DANCE. YOU MUST PERFORM IT ON STAGE WITH THE LOCAL DANCE GROUP AT A PUBLIC EVENT. COLLECT ENOUGH TIPS FROM THE ATTENDEES TO EQUAL 60 LIRKA. ONCE YOU HAVE RECEIVED ENOUGH LIRKA, HAND IT OVER TO THE JUDGE. ONCE THE JUDGE APPROVES, YOU MAY CONTINUE ON IN THE RACE.

"Great," Jannika sounds cynical.

I give her an encouraging pat on her back and we walk around the canvas into the tent.

There are a number of "teachers" standing just inside. They are all wearing grass skirts and bikini tops. I choose the one closest to me. Jannika chooses another. We each go to separate work stations.

The dance involves a series of steps including swaying of the hips and the fluid motion of the arms to the soothing rhythm of the music. The teacher instructs me that each of the movements represents a word and that the dance is actually telling a story. She explains when I hold my arms in a circle over my head it represents the sun and when I open my arms and turn them a certain way, it represents joy. She helps me understand that my story is about two lovers who were separated by a storm at sea but one day the lover returns and they are joyfully reunited.

I like that story so I focus on all the movements of my body to bring it to life. My teacher tells me I'm a natural and that my body moves perfectly. Once I feel confident enough to try it on stage, she takes me to get my hair styled and fitted with the correct wardrobe.

In that section of the tent, a group of attendants strip me down to my panties and bra then sponge me down with some sort of floral water. After that, they rub lotion all over me in the same scent. It smells wonderful.

"What flower is that?" I ask one of the ladies.

"Plumeria," she answers. "You are very pretty. Your figure is so perfect for this kind of dancing. You should make a lot of tips."

"Me? Thank you." I can feel myself blushing. I've never considered myself especially pretty. I don't think I'm ugly, but I've always thought of myself as just average looking. I think my hips are too wide and my grandpa always says I'm too thin.

They braid my hair from the top of my head all the way down my back. They pluck out a few tendrils to frame around my face and ears. They all smile at me. Then one of the women brings over a basket of the little plumeria flowers in pink and yellow which they place randomly in my hair.

I am given a grass skirt with attached bloomers. I step into it and they attach some flowers to it. They have me put on an orangy gold bikini top that is quite snug. It pushes up my boobs and gives me a lot of cleavage. They attach a few flowers to it too.

They wrap bands of flowers on both wrists and ankles while they complete my look with some light makeup accents on my eyes and lips. Then they drape a long lei over my head and across my shoulders. When they are finished, they have me turn around to take in their handwork. They all smile at me. A few of them suck in their breath and touch their hands to the chest.

"You look so beautiful. Those men don't stand a chance," one of the women exclaims.

"Well, if I look so great, it's all because of your handiwork," I say thankfully. "What men?" I ask.

"You will be dancing for the Male Sailboat Hall of Fame inductees tonight."

One of the judges stands at the tent entrance to walk me over to the stage.

"I'm ready," I answer and take a deep breath. I glance over my shoulder to see if Jannika is coming, but she doesn't appear to be here.

I spy Archer and Langt at the Tiki Bar in light-hearted conversation. Langt looks over at me and slaps Archer. Archer turns to me. His blue eyes shimmer. I must look good. The two men walk over to the pathway and Archer takes my hands in his. He leans closer and I can hear him smell the flowers.

"It's plumeria. Isn't it wonderful?" I smile.

"You're dazzling," he whispers in my ear and steps back from me.

The judge clears her throat.

"I have to go dance for these men now and make some money," I say twirling around happily. I feel very feminine and girly.

Archer's eyes snap resembling cold blue ice. "Like hell," he says firmly in a low, dangerous voice as he grabs my wrist.

The judge steps in front of me. "We will take care of her now. You go about your business, Archer."

Archer addresses the judge. "What the hell kind of task is this? You dress her up half naked like a damn goddess and you're going to parade her in front of a bunch of drunk, drooling men? I don't think so." He's really heated.

"Archer, what has gotten into you?" I ask. I can feel my brows furrow but do my best to relax in front of the judge while subtly wriggling my wrist trying to free myself.

Langt leans against the bar with his twinkling eyes and grin, taking in the entire episode in with a drink in hand.

"Archer, this is the reality for many women in this region. Liliana is getting a taste of this culture and how it exists right now. This culture has gone on like this for centuries. This is a lesson she will always remember. As in all tasks, these experiences will give her a more well-rounded knowledge of how the world works. She'll take the lesson of this task and use it to make the world a better place," the judge states calmly.

"Then I'm staying too just to make sure she doesn't get a thorough lesson in the harsh realities of how men work," Archer declares firmly.

Langt chokes on his drink. He's clearly enjoying this exchange. I don't think it's very funny.

"Archer, you know you are not allowed in the Task area. If Liliana doesn't complete this task, she will not be able to continue in the race." The judge isn't budging. She turns to me and asks, "Do you wish to withdraw?"

"Please Archer," I plead still trying to wriggle out of his grip. He's occupied in staring down the judge.

Langt steps in front of me and puts his hand on Archer's chest pushing back lightheartedly. "Come, Archer, let them have their lessons. We'll find a distraction of our own," he adds smiling in his usual sarcastic tone but there is a bit of edge to it. Archer grinds his teeth but lets go of my wrist.

His hands are in fists as he turns and walks away. Langt goes with him.

"What's wrong with him?" I say thinking out loud. "Has he had too much to drink?"

"He's male and he's human," the judge notes scoffing.

After the task, I'm escorted to the docks and directed to find my hut out on the water. It's a beautiful night. My body is sore. Archer was right, a lot of the men did grab me even though they were supposed to keep a distance. I'll probably have a few new bruises tomorrow. The light from the moon is reflecting off the water while the sound of the waves and splashes of water are so peaceful and calming.

I walk down one of the docks lined with huts. I'm excited to sleep on the water. I look at the end of the dock where Archer is sitting with his legs dangling over the edge looking out on the water. He sees me and stands.

"I just wanted to say I'm sorry," he says quietly.

"For what? I know you were only trying to protect me. If it's worth anything, you were right. The men did make unwelcome advances." I see his jaw tighten. A faint smell of cigar smoke and alcohol tingles my nostrils ever so slightly. He must have been hanging out in a lounge downing a few with Langt. I put my hand on his chest, stand on my tiptoes and try to kiss his cheek but he is so tall that I can't quite reach. I slide my hand around his neck and lower his head so I can reach it but he shifts and I end up pressing my lips to the corner of his mouth.

We both smile but neither of us move away. He moves closer and smells the flowers in my hair. I can't help myself, I shift to kiss his cheek but something comes over me and instead I lightly caress his lips with mine. He doesn't move. I can feel the warmth of his breath. His mouth, his lips, his masculinity…it's too much. I want so much more of him. I want to kiss him and I want him to kiss me. I press my lips to his again trying to evoke some kind of response but he doesn't move. Maybe this is a lost cause. I press my lips to his one more time. This time he moves. He slides his hand under my ear into my hair and tilts his head. He parts his lips caressing my lips with his. I part mine slightly more and he presses gently with his tongue finding the tip of mine. Our kiss is slow, leisurely and gentle as our tongues explore a bit deeper. He holds me tighter pressing my body against his. His lips tug gently on my lower lip, then his tongue slips back in. This kiss is the real thing. Archer is kissing me the way a man kisses a woman. Everything about this kiss is heaven. I do my best to give him a real womanly kiss, but I'm so under trained that I'm not completely sure what to do next. One of his hands slides down my back as mine slide up around his neck.

He pulls gently away from me. I look at him trying very hard to casually catch my breath. Why did he stop? I can't find my voice but just watch him.

He lets go of me and starts to say something but instead just turns back to the water. I stand there for a few moments staring at his back. Okay, this is awkward. What the hell? I know I don't have a lot of experience, but was it that bad? This is pointless and weird.

"I guess I'll turn in now," I declare.

"Okay. That's a great idea," he says over his shoulder.

"Are you coming?" I ask.

He whips around and looks intensely at me for a moment then his face softens and he smiles. He steps closer and plays with a piece of my hair. I put my hands on his hard chest. I'm hoping he'll kiss me again. I can hear my heart beating in my ears and the sounds of the party still going strong in the distance.

"You have no idea," he says under his breath as if to himself.

"No idea about what," I breathe happily but confused still waiting for another kiss.

He takes a deep breath and slowly shakes his head. "I'm not going anywhere near that hut with you tonight," he says and steps away from me. Boom. Moment shattered.

"What? Why? Where are you going?" I'm flabbergasted and a little annoyed. What did I do?

He leans in closer to me, gets right in my face, and speaks with the voice of authority. "Go in the room and lock the door. Don't let anyone, including me, in that hut tonight." He marches past me.

"What's wrong? Where are you going?"

"I'm going to take a long swim. Get a good night's rest. We have a big day tomorrow. I'll see you in the morning," he answers and trots off down the dock.

I'm so shocked. I don't know what to say. I'm just standing here gaping at his back. What just happened? A swim?

I go inside the hut and lock the door. I take the flowers out of my hair but I can't help thinking I did something wrong. After that fantastic kiss, why didn't he want to cuddle some more? Instead, he just pushed me away. Maybe he'd rather be with Kali or Peago. Maybe my kiss was unappealing. I'm so frustrated and embarrassed.

I throw myself across the bed and roll over onto my stomach. I want to cry but I don't know if it's because I'm mad or sad. He's so hard to read, damn him!

I hear a knock on the door. Maybe he's come back. I know he said not to open it for him but I don't care. Just before I get to the door, I gain a little bit of sense. What if it isn't him? I stop to take a deep breath. I look out the window. It's Jannika.

I open the door. She comes in and gives me a hug.

"I'm in the hut next door. I heard everything. You wanna talk?" She's so sincere. Tears begin to roll down my cheek. I wipe them away and tell her everything.

"Men," she says.

"Do you think we'll get in trouble for kissing?" I wonder.

"You don't get in trouble with the Rulers for kissing. The rules say we have to maintain sexual purity. I hate to say it but if you're going to keep kissing like that, your purity is definitely in danger." We both chuckle.

"That is true I suppose. After what happened, I'm definitely keeping my lips to myself from now on. I can't go through that rejection again," I confess tragically.

Jannika agrees. "But if you're going to get a good kiss before being rejected, you chose the right man. What a man he is," she giggles.

"What about Langt? Have you kissed him?" I ask quietly.

She nods and we giggle again like schoolgirls.

"I have an idea," she says mischievously, "Langt and Archer are off doing who knows what. Let's sneak out and have a little fun of our own." She lifts her eyebrows at me.

I know she's a bad influence but I need something to take my mind off of Archer. I don't need to sit here and cry about it all night. So, why not, I say, "What the hell? Let's do it." I know I'm flirting with danger, but the way I feel right now, I need a distraction from this race and my emotions.

Jannika leaves to get ready. I jump in a quick shower. I decide to put on my laciest, tiniest, panties with matching tiny, barely-there strapless bra just to feel like a "goddess" again as Archer would say. After some thought, I choose a sexy V neck spaghetti strap halter top jumpsuit in apricot. I bind a few of the orange and yellow flowers together and clip them just above my ear. Archer can eat his heart out. I laugh to myself knowing he'll never know.

We meet at the end of the dock. Jannika looks incredible. She's wearing a sexy gold and black jumpsuit with a shockingly low V neck that cinches at the waist and clings nicely to her body. She's very curvy. "Wow," I say. I also find it amusing that we both chose to wear jumpsuits.

"You look stunning. That outfit goes perfectly with your dark hair," she compliments.

"Me? Look at you! Girl, you are smokin' hot!"

We both start laughing.

"We should avoid the Tiki Bar since both Archer and Langt were there earlier," I say.

"I met a guy at the dance who said there is a big party at the Lowpi Estate up the road," Jannika is giddy.

I get a check in my soul and know we really shouldn't do this, but I inhale a deep breath and walk along.

The estate is an incredible mansion. There are a lot of people here. I begin to feel better about coming. With all these people, we should be alright. Once inside, Jannika's friend comes over and whisks her away. Great.

I mosey over to the drink table. A server gives me some kind of punch. It actually tastes really good. I meander through the crowded rooms and exchange pleasantries with different groups. I really want to look around this incredible estate. The art pieces and architecture are amazing. I amble through its halls. One painting is especially interesting so I stop to admire it.

"It's moving isn't it," a man says in a sexy island accent.

I turn to see a gentleman in a fitted navy-blue suit leaning in a darkened corner. The white of his shirt shines brilliantly in the shadows with the moon striking it through the window. The smoke from his cigarette dances in blue and black wisps across him. He's extremely handsome with his dark hair and tan skin.

"Yes, it is," I answer. I turn to look at it again but feel compelled to leave. Something in my gut tells me I shouldn't be alone with this man. I can sense his eyes on me as I leave but he doesn't say any more and he doesn't move in my direction.

It's time to find Jannika and get out of here. I look around in some of the other party rooms but I can't find her anywhere. I grab another cup of punch. It's strong but it is relaxing me. It's just what I need. I sit down on the couch to close my eyes for a moment. When I open them, four men are sitting around me. One on each side and two are across. They are just looking at me. There are still plenty of people here so I just smile and get up. I move to another end of the room, but I feel very uneasy now. I've had enough of men for one day. I wish there was some dancing at this party or something entertaining. I finally decide it is time to leave. I try locating Jannika one more time but I can't find her. I check the ladies' room but she's not there either.

I stand at the mirror for a moment looking at myself. This was such a bad idea. There is a knock on the door. I'm taking too much time, I guess. Someone probably needs to use the facility. I open the door to go out as a woman dressed in a dark silk dress with a matching scarf over her head bumps into me on the way in.

"I'm so sorry," she has an accent.

"It's okay," I respond and start out the door.

"No, it's not," she declares. I turn around. The woman drops her hood. It's Kavalaris. Shit! I try to run out the door but she grabs my hair and pulls me back inside. She closes the door and locks it. I'm alone and will have to face her head on. I have to think fast! I need to figure out some quick tricks to get out of this one. I know she has to come at me first or she's entitled to kill me. I can only wait for her move.

"Where's your Archer, little girl?" she laughs. She flicks her hand and some kind of glittery powder hits me in the face. Everything is going black. How stupid can I be? I feel myself being caught in her arms. Oh no.

CHAPTER 37

I wake up in a cabin on a boat. Jannika is asleep beside me. I sit up quickly. The headache hits me like a sledge hammer sending me right back down. Holy cow! What was that stuff? I roll to my side and lightly slap Jannika's cheek. She comes to and sits up with a gasp. Then grabs her head and falls back down on the bed too.

"I know. What happened to you last night?" I ask her.

"I don't know. Marco took me to get a drink and then we went outside. After that everything went black. That's all I remember. Who did this?"

"Kavalaris. She tossed some weird powder at me and it took me down."

"Kavalaris?" she questions to herself.

I make my way to the door and put my ear on it to listen. There doesn't appear to be any movement. I very gently try the door knob. It's locked, of course. I look out the window. We are moving close to an island. I wish I knew which one. I open the small window and a nice little breeze flutters my face. Judging from the placement of the sun, it must be midafternoon.

"Langt is going to be so angry," Jannika whimpers.

"We can't think about that right now," I answer knowing full well that Archer is probably beyond furious with me. I go to the other window.

"Do you think they'll be able to find us," she whines while still lying on the bed.

"Find us? How are they going to find us," I groan opening the window.

"What do you think Kavalaris is going to do to us," Jannika asks while staring at the ceiling.

"The only thing she really has to do is keep us roaming around on this boat for another day until we miss our checkpoint; then we'll be out of the race," I reason as I drag a chair over to the window.

The window is so narrow I can't squeeze through it.

"Jannika, we have to save ourselves right now and get off this boat. There is an island very close. We can probably swim to it if we can get out of here," I insist.

Jannika sits up on the edge of the bed. Her lack of urgency is severely getting on my nerves but I try to control it. I have a fleeting idea that perhaps she's part of this conspiracy to get me out of the race.

"What do you want me to do," she asks. My faith in her is restored.

"I can't squeeze through the windows. Do you want to try?"

"I'm bigger than you, especially at the hips," she grins.

"Okay, let's look around for another way," I say as I open the closet door. I notice a small access panel in the back. I move the latch around and hope there aren't any rats in there. I open the door. It looks like a crawl space leading to another room. Suddenly, I'm claustrophobic. This space is very tight.

"Jannika, there's a door in here to another room. Do you think you can get through?" I ask.

"Let me take a look," she says and goes in the closet. She slides through the door and gets to the other room. "I'm clear!"

Well, if she made it, I should be alright. I get in the closet and close the closet door. I slide through the access door. It leads to the engine room. I'm sure to close the door behind me so it's not obvious where we went. I look around for something to hold the door in place. I see a hammer nearby and lay it against the door. It's not much but it's something.

Jannika is crouched down behind one of the big white engine tubes. There is no one else in here right now. I crouch down next to her. I see only one door out of here. There are some small rectangular windows under the ceiling on the other side of the room. We are going to have to make a decision, either try the door or the windows.

"Door or window," I whisper.

"Window," she answers. Before I can blink, she runs across the room and climbs on top of the other engine tube. She stands up and looks out the window. I run over and climb on the third engine tube next to her. There is an island with a beach not far off the port side. It looks uninhabited, but at least there is land to swim to. There was an island on the other side of the boat also. If this is an uninhabited island, we're going to need a way to get someone's attention.

Jannika opens the window. It pulls out on the inside meaning it pulls out into the room. That's going to make it a little harder, but we have to try to get out of here quickly. I look around the room for something reflective. There are reading glasses on the desk and I jump down to grab them. I also grab a small metal wrench to use as a weapon, if necessary and shove them in my bra.

The window is not going to open enough to allow us to get through.

"We're going to have to break it," Jannika says. I nod in agreement. I see a greasy apron hanging in the corner and jump back down to get it. I give it to Jannika. She lays the apron across the window.

"Pull down on the frame on that side and I'll pull down on this side. Maybe we can break the hinges without shattering the glass and making a lot of noise," I say. She agrees.

"One, two, three," I whisper. We both push down on the window frame and it breaks clean. I slide onto the narrow deck and look over the side. Jannika rolls out next to me.

"We need to push off to clear the boat," I whisper. I shimmy around so my feet are pressed against the boat and my knees are up. I push off the side of the boat and gain good clearance into the water. I pop my head up quietly so I don't arouse any curiosities. I'm up just in time to see Jannika flop off the boat. No one on the boat appears to know we are missing. It's a big yacht from this angle.

We swim mostly underwater to get to the beach. Once there, we collapse on the sand to catch our breath. My party outfit is extremely heavy when wet and that swim took a good deal of effort.

"We better get off the beach before someone unwanted sees us," Jannika states emphatically. I agree and head to higher ground behind some trees. I take stock of this island. It is not large because I can see the backside of it. There are islands beyond that as well. There is also a closer island in front of us. If we are still here at nightfall, we'll be able to see which islands are inhabited by the glow of lights.

"Let's do our best to find some water and shelter," I say.

Our efforts are short lived as we hear the alarm from the boat across the water and run to the other side of the island. We jump into the water to swim to the next island. Then we run to the backside of that island and swim to the next one.

"I gotta take these clothes off before I drown," Jannika sputters.

"So do I. We need to get rid of them so they can't see where we are."

We strip down to our panties and bras and dig a hole to bury our clothes. My boobs are practically spilling out of this bra, but freedom to move is my main goal right now. I throw the glasses and wrench into the hole too. It doesn't look like we're going to be able to start a fire without attracting attention and the wrench, well, it's heavy.

After we bury our clothes, we hear our pursuers on the next island over and know we have to quickly depart. This time we hear the voice of Kavalaris also. We look at each other and make haste. We run to the backside of the island and start swimming to the next one. By this time, the sun is beginning to set. We can still hear our pursuers. I'm exhausted. Once we reach the island, we do our best to cover our tracks more thoroughly. The backside is dotted with rocks. We carefully walk only on the rocks to the water line and once again swim to another island. They don't call this the land of a thousand islands for nothing. While I'm grateful we're able to keep moving from island to island, I know we are also increasing our chances of being eliminated. I wonder what Archer is doing and most of all, what he thought when he realized I was gone. I hope he doesn't think I was mad and left on purpose or quit.

It's very dark by the time we get to the next island. I don't think I can swim another stroke. We both collapse on the beach huffing and heaving.

"I have to stop," Jannika says.

"Me too," I agree, "but we have to get off the beach."

We return to the water to rinse off our backs, then make our way to the interior of the island. This one is bigger with more cover. We hear a boat and crouch down. We see a spotlight shine nearby and lay completely flat on the ground. The spotlights move slowly on. They didn't see us.

"We have to get off this island," Jannika rattles.

I concur. There are plenty of islands to choose from and unfortunately there are no lights on any of them. This time we turn to the right and head down to that beach. We are moving more slowly because both of us are nearing exhaustion.

We have a long swim to the next island but we take our time. We also have to consider what might be in the water with us. Once on the new island, I notice the moon is high in the sky lighting up the night. It would have been a good night for it to remain overcast skies. We could certainly use the extra cloud cover. It must be the wee hours of the morning when we find a cluster of trees and climb in. The leaves, which provide some decent covering and branches, are large enough to support us. We lean into the trunk and relax. I'm exhausted and just can't keep my eyes open.

I am awakened by the sound of a thump next to my head. It's still dark out but there are pink streaks in the sky hinting of a rising sun. I hear voices not far from us putting me on high alert. I turn to see three arrows with yellow tips next to my face. Archer! I sit straight up and wake Jannika. I put my finger over her lips. She sits up as she sees the arrows too, then smiles.

I look around for Archer but I don't see him. After a few seconds I notice another arrow below me in the tree and then another one on the ground in front of the tree. He's made a trail of arrows! The yellow tips really help to recognize them in the dark. We follow the arrows down to the other side of the island. It's getting light now. I turn the corner of the tree line and see Archer and Langt on the beach. There's a speed boat in the water nearby. We both run to them.

I completely forgot I was in my tiny panties and tiny bra until I see the look on Archer's face. His eyes get wide and his jaw tightens. He is clearly mad. He has a right to be. We've been gone for close to two days. He takes his shirt off and holds it to out me.

"Get in the boat," he commands as I take the shirt from him. The voices are louder. Langt steps up next to Archer. They are clearly anticipating a fight. I wade out to the boat and climb in. Jannika is right behind me. I look and see Langt at the tree line. He looks around then looks back at Archer. He shrugs his shoulders and shakes his head like "the pursuers aren't worth the trouble".

Once on the boat I see a man tied to the side of it with a drape over his head. I swallow hard as I put on Archer's shirt. Jannika and I find our way to the front of the boat and sit in the chairs there.

A few minutes later, Langt climbs in the boat and makes his way to the captain's chair while Archer pulls the anchor off the beach. He wades into the water and easily pulls himself into the boat.

Archer unbinds the mystery man then takes the drape off his head. It's Mirko! He throws him over the side of the boat, which I know he probably enjoyed more then he let on, while Langt punches the engine to get the boat moving. Jannika I just look at each other. They kidnapped Mirko to keep us in the race? It was genius!

Once we clear the island, Langt tells us to buckle up to which we comply. I look back and see Mirko walking up on the beach.

Archer has stayed at the back of the boat as Langt opens it up. It's a Bullet Boat and I find myself plastered against my seat. I couldn't move if I wanted. We are flying across the water! This is probably the fastest I can ever remember moving.

After a while, I see a platform ship up ahead holding a heli-commuter. We pull up alongside the platform ship. Langt looks at me and Jannika.

"Let's go," he directs.

Archer has one foot on the platform and one on the boat. He lifts me out of the boat and onto the platform, then Jannika. A heli-commuter operative helps me into it and straps me in then helps Jannika. It's really loud. I see another operative go to where Archer is standing and the two slap hands. I read Archer's lips as he says the words, "Thanks, I owe you one."

Once we are buckled in, Langt and Archer climb in and take a seat. The heli-commuter takes off. I can't help but smile. I look out the window to view the islands and water. This is amazing! I look at Jannika and she's just as thrilled as I am.

I sneak a peek at Archer. He's staring at me but his face has softened. He looks down and then away. How long is he going to be mad? I turn back to the window for the rest of the ride. It takes a while but I finally see the checkpoint in the distance. If we had attempted this on foot, we would have never made it. Archer and Langt have been very busy since we went missing.

Once we land, the operator unbuckles Jannika and then me. It's very loud and the wind is flapping our hair spastically around. Langt helps Jannika down then points to the checkpoint. She runs in that direction.

Archer lifts me out of the vehicle and sets me down. His arms linger around me for just a moment longer than they should so I look up at him. He tightens his lips and does a quick shake of his head to the side letting me know of his disappointment but his features have softened. I look into his eyes. He's not mad anymore. He releases me and nods his head toward the checkpoint. I turn and run to it.

"Number Five" sounds over the speaker when I cross the line. Jannika and I watch as the heli-commuter lifts in the air and moves away. The engines of our own commuter start and we jump through the door before it closes.

Mirko is definitely out.

CHAPTER 38

Zealya

Jannika and I are released only one minute apart and last. Langt and Archer are with us quickly but we separate almost immediately. Archer is very quiet again. But this time, I know it's me. He's pissed.

"It seems like you are still mad at me."

"I'm not mad," is all he says but his attitude says more.

"I can tell, you know," I say exasperated. "You're acting mad."

Archer takes a breath before he replies. "If it seems I am mad, I am sorry. Perhaps I do get frustrated. How can I protect you if you run off from me? You open yourself to problems that can easily be avoided if you would just listen to me."

"Got it," I answer. I look away from him. Maybe he's right but his "constructive criticism" about it is making me a little annoyed so I start walking faster.

All he does is lengthen his stride a bit to keep up. Ugh. I hear him sigh and turn to him.

"I have a mind of my own, you know. I'm not helpless."

"You're very willful," he emphasizes. "I'm not arguing with you on that point."

"What do you want to say exactly?" I stop and stare at him.

He looks at me as though he's ready to let me have it. I'm ready, let's go. But instead, he turns away and looks out at the distance.

"I'm not doing this with you. You're smart enough to know why I'd be angry," he replies. "But perhaps part of my frustration is my fault, too. My assignments are not usually this long nor are they in such close proximately to a constant companion."

I'm genuinely taken aback by his cutting words. Wow. Does he hate being stuck with me? That hurt more than I would have ever thought it would. What do you say to that? I turn away as the tears flow uncontrollably down my cheeks. I enjoy his company very much. In fact, I thought we were at least friends. I start walking ahead keeping my head down so he doesn't see. But he knows. He touches my shoulder. I jerk away from him but he spins me around to face him. His brows furrow as though he doesn't know what he did. I jerk away from him again and start walking.

He moves next to me. "What have I done that has caused you pain," he asks quietly.

"Please leave me alone." I try not to sound weepy. "I'm sorry I'm a burden to you," I add with a touch of feeling sorry for myself.

"A burden? Where did you get that?"

"You just said it. You said I'm a constant companion as though you hate it," I choke.

He pulls me close and I try to push away from him but he tightens his grip. I bury my face into his chest to get a grip on the tears. "I'm sorry it came out that way," he apologizes talking close to my ear. "I'm really not good at this. My true meaning is that I'm not usually in the company of someone for so long. Maybe my solitude makes me an undesirable companion since I'm prone to doing things my way. I simply meant that I'm usually working alone and don't really have to consider another."

He steps back and reaches into his pocket pulling out a handkerchief and hands it to me. For real. I take it and look at him. I can't help but laugh a little.

"Nobody has ever handed me a handkerchief before. Ever."

He shrugs. "I'm working on my chivalry skills especially since my verbal communication seems to be lacking," he replies smiling. I wipe my wet cheeks.

"I'm sorry," he says as he kisses my cheek. "I've grown to care a great deal for you."

"I'm sorry, too. I'm bad about jumping to conclusions."

"I guess we both have things to work on," he responds smiling. He puts his arm around me and gives me a little squeeze.

***

The task is at an old Fort the locals call "The Castle". We get there in good time. It's basically a ruin of several high walls that have ramparts running on top. There are large openings in four of the walls that must have been huge doors long ago.

The courtyard is completely grown over with grass. Dandelions dot the landscape. Our task is laid out within its walls. Lining the walls are tables holding colored paints and supplies. In the middle, workstations have been set up. At the far end, in the shade, are refreshments and drinks. All of us get here about the same time. We all see a table near the far left doorway with the task cards and make a beeline for it.

TASK: PICK A STORY FROM THE STORY CARDS AND PAINT A STORY MURAL BASED ON TRADITIONAL ABORITIONAL DOT PAINTING METHODS. ONCE THE JUDGE APPROVES

THE FINAL PAINTING, YOU WILL GO TO ROODA HOTEL. DUE TO THE DANGEROUS TRAVELING CONDITIONS YOU WILL STAY AT THE HOTEL FOR THE NIGHT AND EMBARK ON THE JOURNEY TO THE CHECKPOINT IN THE MORNING.

It's an individual task so Archer and the other specialists wander off in different directions.

I settle in. This painting is going to take a while. I pick out a story about an old dog that turned his people's enemies into stone. We were each sent to an expert and given a lesson on dot painting techniques then pick a workstation to create a mural.

By early afternoon, our paintings are still far from finished. We stop for lunch and a general break. My arms are aching and my back is sore from staying in one position doing this tedious dot work.

By late afternoon, I am finally finishing up and so are some of the other contestants. The task is taking much longer than expected. All the Specialists begin arriving, probably to check on us since we've been gone all day. Since they aren't allowed in the Task area, they stand atop the "castle" ramparts looking down. The first one there is Foyver. His red hair is brilliant in the late sun. He's an imposing figure since he has a strong, toned body and commanding frame. He frightens me every time I see him. His hands are on his hips and he's looking down at us. If he were my partner, I would be making haste because he seems to be terribly put out at having to wait.

Kali shows up next. She looks fantastic, as usual. Gorgeous hair blowing in the wind. Espada and Langt show up about the same time. Both of them are extremely handsome men with amazing bodies. Both are wearing body hugging shirts.

When Archer shows up, I spot him immediately at the far end. He's looking off in the distance. His blonde hair and dark sunglasses make him easily standout. Interestingly, he has a small quiver strapped to his thigh. I can see a reflection off the small arrows, indicating they are made of some kind of metal. He's also wearing a wrist mounted crossbow on a black leather fingerless glove. He too is wearing a body hugging shirt.

His wrist crossbow is mainly used for closer ranges. The small size of the arrows and the power of that trigger can penetrate just about anything at close range. I wonder what he has been up to today. I see that others have noticed his crossbow as well. He turns my way. I force myself to look away from him to concentrate on what I'm doing. I need to get this finished.

I return my focus to completing the task. Within minutes, I hear a commotion and look up. I can't tell what's being said but it appears that Foyver is doing some trash talking at Archer. Archer is just shaking his head and ignoring it. Then I realize these two haven't been in close proximity of one another since Foyver hit him with the poison blade in Carita.

Foyver keeps talking. He's really obnoxiously egging him on. I look at Archer and realize his patience is wearing thin. Foyver continues while walking in Archer's direction on the top of the wall. Archer is now moving toward Foyver. I can read Archer's lips. He is holding out his arms. I think he is exclaiming, "I'm right here!"

The men are closer, chests are out as they get face to face. I can't tell what Foyver is saying because his back is to me. But it looks like Archer is asking, "What are you doing?" He's shaking his head. "You want this right now," I can hear his deep voice now. He's motioning his arms into a shrug. His ire is up but he is calm.

A voice over the loudspeaker announces, "Specialists are not allowed to engage in the Task area. You have 10 seconds to put 25 feet between you or your Regions will be eliminated."

Archer glances at me. I shake my head pleadingly hoping he won't get us disqualified. He turns and walks away. Foyver, on the other hand, continues to agitate.

Foyver says something. All the other Specialist's backs get rigid and they are at full attention as though they heard something shocking. Something happened, I just don't know what. Archer turns quickly around to face Foyver. He has enraged, focused, steely blue eyes and an angry mouth. It looks like, though, he is very calmly saying, "let's go," and he's motioning his hand to outside of the Fort.

"Asshole," I hear Poppi say under her breath. I'm not sure if she's talking about Archer or Foyver. Foyver hasn't been inclined to de-escalate the situation at all. He seems perfectly willing to let Poppi get disqualified.

I'm almost finished with the task. All the Specialists have left. What is going on?

Poppi and I finish at the same time and scurry to the judge. We both get approved and then run outside of the Fort. Foyver and Archer can be seen in the distance. They have squared off. It appears as though they haven't been fighting long. We race to the tree line where the fight is taking place.

Foyver is very quick and efficient. The two men are very well matched. They bend, swoop, and avoid. Fists, wrists and arms collide as they block, roll, twirl, dodge, and move over each other's backs like aerial artists. They are lightning fast. Foyver suddenly has his round blades in each hand clanking them together and taking his stand again. Archer brings his wrist up and nocks a small metal arrow then puts his arm behind his back. I'm on edge, scared to death!

The other Specialists have no expression on their faces, but they seem to be getting aroused by the action. It's like their adrenaline has kicked in. Their eyes are sparkling. They are breathing a little harder. They all have blades in their hands in some form and all the blades are moving. They are tapping or flipping or twirling. It's like nervous energy that they want to be in this so badly but they can't get involved. Perhaps it's their silent outlet for the desire to fight. Langt is especially entrenched in the action. I can see it in his eyes but he isn't moving. They only watch quietly. There seems to be some sort of Specialist code of conduct going on here.

Foyver makes a charge but Archer sidesteps and manages to wrap his arm around Foyver's pulling his arm back at the shoulder until there is a small crunch sound to which Foyver grunts and drops the blade in that hand. Foyver takes a step around and tries to swipe Archer with the other blade but Archer bends and twists away from the blade at the same time unlocking their arms. The two men stand apart facing each other once again.

Foyver lunges at him but Archer jumps back in the nick of time before the blade catches him. I'm sure he suspects that it is poisoned again. I know I do. They go at it again with lightning speed: moving, dodging, punching and weaving. Archer is avoiding the blade as much as possible. Foyver is sweating profusely and seems to be getting tired. He makes a shitty move by grabbing the back of Archer's shirt and twisting it to choke him but Archer grabs the front of it at his chest and rips it completely away catching Foyver off guard. It gives Archer that split second advantage. He spins Foyver, grabbing him by the throat then lifting him in the air and slamming him forcefully to the ground. He has his knee on Foyver's arm with the blade and his fist with the crossbow squarely in the middle of Foyver's chest tilting slightly to the left. It's very clear where this is going. Foyver starts to move but Archer tilts his head and tightens his lips in a "don't do it" fashion. But Foyver reaches up anyway with his free hand to grab Archer's throat as he starts to twist clearly trying to break it. Archer's muscles bulge as he pushes his body down on Foyver's digging in his fist as he presses it harder against Foyver's chest. Foyver tightens his grip on Archer's throat. Archer pushes back lifting his body away from Foyver and squeezes his fist mechanism triggering the arrow. It sounds like a nail gun as it echoes through the trees. We all know what that means. Foyver collapses and is dead within moments. Archer moves to the side and rolls to the ground on his back to catch his breath. He has visible bruising on his throat.

The other Specialists start breathing normally again, the blades have disappeared. Langt walks over to Archer and offers his hand to help him up. Once on his feet, he bends over with the shreds of his shirt hanging from him. His hands are on his knees still trying to get his breath.

"I bow to the Master. That was a hell of a fight," Langt says slapping Archer's back. "One of the best I've seen in a long, long time." Archer just exhales and nods.

Poppi walks away.

I also turn to walk away. I sense that Archer needs some time to decompress. Langt is a far better companion for that than I right now. I could use a little time to myself, too.

I find my way to the hotel room and jump in the shower. My emotions are in rags and I don't know how to react to this. It's not easy for me to witness someone being killed. Before I came on this race, I never saw a killing. It's such a deep moral dilemma. I mean, I hate the killing but I'm so glad it wasn't Archer that was killed. In fact, I'm overjoyed it wasn't Archer.

I turn the hot water up and let it flow off my shoulders and down my back. I allow myself a bit more time to work this out in my mind before finishing my shower.

Archer walks in hours after I do. I'm in the bed furthest from the door with my back to him. I'm glad he's here, but I really don't want to talk with him right now. I only want to sleep or pretend to be. I can hear him stripping. Then the bathroom door closes and the shower turns on.

After several minutes, I hear the shower turn off and I hear him come out. A few seconds later, he lies on my bed next to me. I can tell he's on his back looking up at the ceiling.

"Can we talk about this?" he asks.

So, he knows I'm awake.

"About what?" I ask. I really don't need a conversation about anything right now.

"About the fight."

"No. I don't need to talk about it. I'm very glad you're okay," I say.

He rolls so he's facing my back. I feel his hand on my hip.

"I know you don't understand the Specialist world. I outrank him. He challenged me. I had to take the fight."

I roll over and face him. He's only wearing a towel. "You're right. I don't understand your world. But I trust your judgment," is all I can say.

He smiles and picks up a piece of my hair. He plays with it as he talks to me. "He was so foolish, Lily. All he had to do was get his contestant through this race."

"What do you mean?"

"He let his pride get in the way of his logic. There are only five teams left. He had a definite shot at winning," he says thoughtfully.

"I guess I really don't understand."

Archer looks at me. "In the Specialist group, I outrank every person here. I'm a Dea Master. I know you don't know what that means, but the only way for them to move up in the ranks is to challenge me and win. This is not the time nor the place for that. He became cocky because he got a nice shot on me with his blade when we were in Carita. He let it go to his head that he could take me out anytime or anyplace. Apparently, he's been running his mouth about it for several legs now. He never stopped to consider that he wasn't really fighting me. He essentially shot me in the back."

"Couldn't you tell him to challenge you later?"

Archer shakes his head. "No. If I'm challenged by a lower ranking Specialist, I'm honor bound to take the fight as long as I'm not medically handicapped."

"Did you have to kill him?"

"No," he says with a little shake of his head while looking at me. "If this was strictly hand to hand I could have let him go. When you break out weapons in a fight, you must be prepared to kill and prepared to die. In this case, with the weapons in play, he was bested by a superior. He could have yielded to me and walked away. He knew that, but given our audience, I guess he wanted bragging rights."

Archer pauses and is thoughtful for a moment, then he continues. "He chose a fatal path, Lily. He went for the kill knowing I had him locked down. The fight was already over. Checkmate. I even allowed him a little extra time to stop but he didn't. He kept coming. At that point, I did the only thing left to do, I gave him the benefit of a quick death. He was a good fighter. It's regrettable because it was so unnecessary that he do this right now."

I stare into his thoughtful blue eyes for moment. I guess his years of training allow him to just step away from this and assess it like it's a sporting event. A man died today. It's a tragedy.

Suddenly, there is a knock at the door.

Archer gets up and answers it, then returns to get dressed. I turn away as he drops the towel.

He comes over to the bed and leans over me. I roll toward him. He gives me a peck on the lips. "I've got to meet with the local authorities. This might take a while; I'll be back later. Please stay in the room."

I agree and watch him head out the door.

CHAPTER 39

The journey to the checkpoint is a quiet one and we are almost there. Archer is the one this time who breaks the silence.

"Lily, you've been unusually quiet. Are you still upset about my fight with Foyver?"

"No, I'm not upset. But I have been running it through my mind a lot."

"Can I help?"

"Not really," I answer, then add, "Well, maybe you can answer a question for me."

"I'd be glad to if it will help," he says sincerely.

"You have no fear. Aren't you afraid of dying?"

"Death always stands close to me. It's something I've been conditioned for. If my time comes, it only means my purpose has been fulfilled."

"That's kind of a deep spiritual attitude," I say not really understanding it.

He laughs. "I was raised in a temple…"

I laugh with him. "Okay, fair enough." Then I add, "But look around. Isn't all this worth living for?"

"You're asking the wrong question, Lily." He says almost distractedly. He suddenly seems very interested in the trees.

"What's the right question?"

He looks at me. "The right question to ask is, is it worth dying for?"

Now, I hear something in the trees, too. Archer puts his hand on the small of my back and is propelling me along at a quicker pace.

"We have to move." He grabs my hand and we start running.

"What is it?" I pant getting scared.

Archer stops us behind a large tall rock that sits close to the edge of the canyon where the trees break and whirls me around to face him.

"The checkpoint is up ahead in the distance. Do you see it?" He asks while drawing out and adjusting some of his blades. Then returning them to his person.

"Yes, I see it. What is going on?" I'm so frightened now.

"No matter what happens," he commands, "keep going. Don't stop! Get to the checkpoint! Promise me you will keep going." He gives me a little shake.

I turn to look at his face. What the hell? He's looking at me with angry eyes. "I'll keep going," I vow.

"Good girl. Now head out," he's calm again.

"What is going on?" I ask him searching his eyes.

"I'll fill you in later," he rushes. "Please run now."

I turn away from him and begin to move.

"ARCHER!" A voice booms. It echoes throughout the canyon below.

Startled, I whip back around. Archer's back is just ahead of me. Hamar is standing on a boulder at the edge of the trees. I know at once he has the advantage. Archer turns his head to me and says, "Keep going! Get far away from here!"

I turn away. I can't be Archer's distraction, so I must go. I start running. I finally make it to the other side of a row of large rock formations. As soon as I'm out of sight, I double back. I have to see what's going on. I find a very tall rock that has a hollow hole in the middle to peak through.

"I am right here, Hamar. I thought you were out of this race. Would you like to settle an old score," Archer provokes. Hamar is down on Archer's level now.

"Your arrogance is so annoying. I'm going to smash that smirk off your face with my bare hands," Hamar spits.

I see Archer's face now. He's facing his opponent and he does have a certain half smile on his face. His jaw is set as though he is ready for anything. Eyes focused, sharp and just a touch squinted, he looks and moves like a lion ready to pounce. His left hand is clutching his bow although his finger is tapping it nonchalantly.

"No weapons then?" Archer shrugs. He really does seem to be provoking Hamar.

"I don't need to waste weapons on an asshole like you," Hamar grunts.

Archer has a satisfied smile on his face and drops his bow. Maybe he just wants to kick this guy's ass. He lifts his hands up to his shoulders and waves them back and forth to show his opponent his empty hands. I'm befuddled that he is acting this way. He is intentionally provoking him with arrogant and cocky behavior. I've never seen Archer act this way. It's more like a show Langt would put on.

Langt. Then I remember. Langt said something about Hamar losing control and getting sloppy when provoked. That must be Archer's tactic, too.

They are both staring each other down as they start circling one another. Archer smiles again and winks at him. Unbelievable! Hamar's fury is unbridled as he charges Archer like an animal. Archer stands, his eyes focused, no smile now as he waits. Just as Hamar reaches him, he twists to avoid impact but swings his elbow back around and smashes him mightily to the ground with a grating blow to the upper back.

In an instant, Archer turns facing his opponent. Hamar is on his feet quickly and charges again. Archer twists again, comes back around with another slamming fist to the side of his jaw. Hamar stumbles but is on his feet again, prepared to charge. He doesn't seem to be thinking or have any sort of strategy. He seems blinded by rage and hate. Archer eggs him on again.

"I'm still here, Hamar, waiting!" Archer teases. He acts nonchalant, but his eyes are penetrating and there is a certain tension in his jaw. Maybe this is his strategy. Maybe he's trying to get the idiot to wear himself out with his careless maneuvers. He charges, Archers knocks him off his feet again.

Hamar begins to stand. He has his back to Archer, which is weird. He's definitely moving a bit slower. It appears that he is not moving at all, actually. Then I look at his face and his eyes are on me!

I gasp and jump back. How did he see me this far away? He starts running in my direction. I hear a muffled "dammit" from Archer. If I live through this, he's going to kill me. I start running in the opposite direction but ahead of me is a lot of open space to the far-off checkpoint. I have nowhere to hide and I don't know if I can outrun this guy. Why did I put myself in this type of danger?

I glance over my shoulder to see Archer pointing his bow at us. Behind him I see Kavalaris, Byhed, Porrah and another figure creep out of the shadows. It's an ambush! Kavalaris flips her whip of chains from behind him sinking a hook in his arm. My heart is racing. There is nothing I can do but move. Oh my God, Archer. Please be okay.

Hamar is coming directly at me. I face forward running as fast as I can. I can hear him snorting like a bull behind me. My heart is beating so hard it hurts to breathe. I'm not going to make it unscathed. This guy is going to run me down like a dog. I look over my shoulder, he's closing fast. He seems to be on a mission. I run harder but I can't last much longer.

Just as I look over my shoulder one more time, I see Hamar is almost upon me. My side hurts so badly but I keep running. He leaps at me and catches my ankle. I go down hard on my knee. I try to kick out of his grasp but he's clawing and grabbing at me with a wild look in his eyes.

He crawls quickly on top of me and pins my arms under his knees. I begin screaming and kicking and kneeing him but he is unfazed. He slaps me hard across the face. My eyes begin to water from it, then he slaps me again from the other side. My face is numb from the blows. I feel a split on my lip and taste the blood in my mouth. He hits me again and bites my shoulder. I scream from the pain. He shifts his body and moves lower but I'm still pinned under him. I scream again and he punches me in the head. My eyesight keeps fading in and out and I'm dizzy. He starts choking me. He reaches down to punch my chest knocking the wind out of me. Then his eyes light up. He gropes my breast, then squeezes it so hard I scream out again.

He starts tearing my clothes and unbuckling his pants. OH GOD, NO! I find some fight left in me and wrench one of my arms free, I start clawing his face and kicking trying to get him off me. He punches me in the head again and pins my arm under my back. Something in my arm pulls creating a searing pain down the length of my arm. My vision blurs as my eye is swelling shut and blood is running into it. He is continuing to free his loins and take full advantage of my incapacity to do anything about it. If he doesn't kill me after this rape, I'll do it for him. I know I won't be able to live with myself at the very depths of society in ruination and despair because he has had this victory over my life. Burning tears mixed with blood are freely flowing down my face now.

He laughs while he puts one hand on my throat and squeezes. No amount of self-defense training helps when you are so completely overpowered. He slams his hulking knee between my knees to open my legs and starts fumbling around my thighs ripping at my clothes there. He moves to the side and seems to lose his balance. It's my opportunity as my adrenaline kicks in. I free my unhurt arm and punch him in the ribs. He falls to the side of me. I somehow find the strength to roll away from him. I jump to a crouch so I can leap up and kick him but when I look over at him, I see an arrow sticking through his head and two more through his face with pieces of fleshy meat attached to the ends of them. There is also another arrow protruding from his throat. His body is twitching while his blood drains from his body.

I look up to see Archer in the distance standing on top of the rock I was hiding behind lowering his bow. I fall back down and sit there humped over for a moment but then slowly get to an upright position. The pain kicks in. I make it up on my feet, sort of, as best as I can. I look up and watch as Archer drops to his knees then I see his head slump as he falls off that rock. God knows what he's been through.

I take one last look at my would-be rapist. I want to kick his ass and rip him to pieces. The best I can manage to do is kick a little dirt his face and dibble spit some of my blood on him. I've never hated anyone more in my life.

I turn to make my way to the checkpoint. My clothes are in shreds, my legs are hardly moving, my arm is hanging weird and I can barely see but I finally make it there. There is a medical team waiting for me. I'll get disqualified if I don't cross on my own. I hear indistinct yelling and look over to see two other teams far off to the left running this way.

"Number 3" sounds as I drag myself across the checkpoint. A large male nurse lifts me onto a gurney and they wheel me away.

CHAPTER 40

I can barely crack open my eyes, but I'm clearly in the medical part of the facility. While I'm lying on a table, the medics are cutting off my clothes and everything goes black.

I crack open my eyes and I'm under a scanner. I'm very cold. I'm naked. Everything goes black.

I crack open my eyes. A doctor is doing something to my shoulder. I reach up and feel my ribs are wrapped. The doctor looks at my face and starts to say something. Everything goes black.

I crack open my eyes. My legs are in stirrups and two medics are down there. One seems to be doing something to my thigh. The other is inserting a probe. I try to move but I have no energy. Everything goes black.

I open my eyes. I'm in a recovery room. Miss Terry is sitting next to me reading a book.

"Miss Terry?" My voice is no louder than a whisper.

She jumps to my side. "Hello, young lady. You gave us quite a scare."

I close my eyes. Everything goes black.

I open my eyes to see Miss Terry looking out the window. I feel more awake. I try to move to a sitting position but pain stops me.

Miss Terry comes quickly to my side.

"Slowly, Liliana. You've been through quite the ordeal," she explains.

She helps me sit up. If I'm such bad shape, can I continue? I have to continue!

"Miss Terry, am I out of the race?" My eyes are already watering.

She runs her hand down my hair and looks very motherly. "Not yet," she smiles.

I release a sigh of relief.

"However," she adds, "it will be very difficult for you to continue. We have postponed the start by three days while officials investigate the incident. The doctors won't release you for at least five. That means you will be two days behind the other racers. It will be very challenging for you to overcome that especially given your condition."

"What is my condition?"

She sits facing me on the bed. "It's bad, Liliana. You suffered a cracked rib, some minor nerve damage in your shoulder, many contusions on your breast, neck, eye and jaw. You needed stitches on your shoulder where you were bitten, also on your thigh and just inside your labia where your skin tore from his grabbing and pulling."

I spring up breathless even through the pain. "He didn't…"

"No," she assures me pressing my shoulders lightly back down. "There was no penetration."

I lie back and breathe trying to let it all sink in and overcome the pain of springing up like that. Then I spring up again.

"Archer?" I'm panicking now.

She gently presses me back down again. "We don't know of Archer's condition. As you are aware, he has his own team and they are very guarded about releasing information on the nature of his injuries. I do know that he was ambushed by four eliminated Specialists. He prevailed, however. His team will only say that he has not withdrawn at this time."

I'm very quiet. I can't tell Miss Terry how much I love and care for him. I wish I knew how he is really doing.

"I want you to rest now. We'll talk some more later."

I concede. I am feeling tired.

***

I wake up and I'm alone. I glance at myself in the mirror across the room. My eye is purple. My neck is purple. I have yellowish bruises on my cheek and chest. I feel the wrap on my shoulder and ribs. There is a bandage on my thigh. I consider my near rape for some time. Tears stream down my face as I relive it in my mind all over again.

Miss Terry passes by the door but then she rushes to me and sits on the bed. She wraps me in her arms and holds my head against her shoulder. I start crying. My crying turns into hard, bitter screaming sobs. She's stroking my hair and rocking me while I let it all out. I'm crying so deeply that my breath is shaking as it comes out. Tears run down her face as she shares in my pain.

She holds me the whole time and lets me have my screaming fit. Once I calm down, she sits back away from me and says, "Don't ever mistake this vicious attack for the real beauty of what can transpire between a man and woman in love with each other."

I look at her not really knowing what to say.

"This was a monster who was doing everything in his power to cause you pain. But a real man in love with a woman is gentle and kind. He will put you first and allow you to be in control of his advances," she says.

"Why did he do it?"

She brushes my hair to my back. "Studies will say all kinds of things about why men rape, but the truth is, each man rapes for different reasons. In this case, Hamar had a pretty distasteful history with Archer. Rumor has it that he has gone all over the world and has been in constant search for Archer trying to take out his revenge, but he has never been able to do so. One might think the attack on you had something to do with that. But then we have to remember that Hamar did rape Zara. Zara had nothing to do with Archer. I don't think we'll ever know the real truth behind his attacks or what motivated them."

"What will happen to Zara?" I ask. "Will she just go into a ruined life?"

Miss Terry takes a breath. "We really aren't allowed to talk about it, but since you had a similar experience, I'll tell you in the strictest of confidence." I pledge my discretion. "Race officials are working to help Zara. I'm hopeful they will be able to relocate her to an off-grid community where she can start a new life. The rules of society are more relaxed in places like that."

I smile thinking of Daniel and Dandi. I like that. At least it's some kind of hope for her.

"I'm going to send Dr. Windslow in for a few sessions with you. She'll be able help you work things out in your mind somewhat," Miss Terry says as she stands.

I agree. Maybe I need it. "Thank you, Miss Terry."

She smiles at me. "I will always be here for you if you need me. Now, I know of two young ladies who are very eager to see you. If you eat all of your dinner and get plenty of rest, I'll let them come see you tomorrow."

CHAPTER 41

Ruska

Surprisingly, Archer is waiting a few yards from the checkpoint door in the snow when it's time to go. He looks good. He looks strong. Nothing about him indicates that he has suffered any kind of injury. He's wearing a heavy winter white leather and fur cloak. A medic walks out to him and they converse quietly for some time. I look at Miss Terry.

"Why is Archer here?" I ask. He usually meets me on the road.

"Circumstances are different this time. He was summoned to meet you here today so the medical officer could talk to him about the extent of your injuries."

"Why would you do that? I'm doing so much better. He doesn't need to know all that," I respond now upset, embarrassed and annoyed.

"He needs to know, Liliana. It is important that he understands the extent of your injuries to determine what you can and should not do right now. Not only that but he may have to redress some of your wraps. If you should incur another injury, he needs to know what is already wounded. He is a doctor after all or have you forgotten that?" Miss Terry is so blunt in her manor.

"I didn't know that," I say amazed. "He's a doctor?

"He's not trained at the university in the way you would be, but yes, he is a degreed doctor of medicine, botany and I believe some type of chemistry or physics. I'd have to look it up," she says matter-of-factly.

"He's so young," I say half to myself.

"Yes, yes," she says looking into her satchel. "He has a few other degrees too that are not doctorates in various areas like astronomy and some kind of science. He is also certified in many, many things. Temple people start their higher degrees when they are in their teens if they have the aptitude for it," she adds distractedly.

I'm shocked. Why didn't I know that he was a doctor? I should have, I mean, how many times has he kept me alive or checked me for injuries?

I watch him. He has his arms crossed but I can't tell if it because of the cold weather or if he is annoyed. The wind is strong. Since he wears such a poker face, it's so difficult to read. He hasn't looked over at me yet. Then I see him take a deep breath and nod to the medic. The medic is returning.

I walk out and Archer looks at me then looks away. My guess is he's still mad at me for staying when he told me not to. He probably thinks it's my own fault I was beaten. The sad truth is, part of me knows he's right. I put myself in harm's way.

"Are you sure you're up to this?" he asks when I get close enough not looking me in the eye. That's all he says. There's no 'good morning or how ya doing or it's good to see you'. I guess he is mad and all business now.

"Yes," I reply. That's all he needs to know. I can be cold too.

"Okay," he affirms and turns to the path leading the way.

I follow Archer in silence for some time. He doesn't seem to want to look at me or talk to me. He must be angry at me for not leaving when he told me to. Oh yeah, and I nearly got him killed, too!

I do feel bad about it. He has a lot to gain by my winning this race, too. It was my fault for not leaving earlier. I put myself in a horrible situation that could have been even worse than it turned out to be.

Archer stops. There is a frozen lake which is so blue it looks like glass. The trees reflected on it on the other end are amazingly beautiful. It's like the ice has weighed down the branches and created a flowing ice shield around it. The effect is gorgeous. I've never seen anything like it, not even in pictures.

Archer squats down and flicks the snow ahead of him with his fingers. There are a few clearly defined tracks underneath the top snow. He scoffs and stands up. He turns to me and removes his white fur cloak.

"We just can't catch a break," he says quietly while tying his toasty warm cloak around me, then moves me behind a tree. "Stay here and don't move," he emphasizes that last part and even added a firmness to his tone. Will he ever forgive me?

"What is it?"

He takes out his bow and nocks an arrow. He leans back, aims very high, and then lets it go. The arrow makes a high arch and comes back down. It hits the very top of the first tree of ice with a decent amount of force. The ice shatters revealing a maze of ice branches behind it.

A small growling sigh escapes from Archer.

"What the hell?" I gasp.

"Nirvkh," Archer says while scanning the area.

"What is that?"

"Indigenous tribe. They use the snow to cover their tracks and hide their numbers," he says while grabbing a fist full of arrows. "Food is scarce here. They have a healthy appetite for human flesh when available."

"What?" I gasp. "Can we go around them?"

He looks at me. "We have two choices. We can go around which will take much too long for you to remain in the race or we can take a chance that this outpost is not heavily guarded and make our way through this territory which could make up for the two days we're behind."

"What kind of choice is that?" I ask. He just looks at me again, briefly, of course. Great. I have to either drop out of the race or try not to get eaten by some freakish cannibals?

He walks a few feet back from the frozen lake edge and nocks another of the arrows. He holds the rest of the bunch in his hand. "Once I'm across, wait for my signal, then follow quickly behind me. Take a running start to the ice and slide your way across. Most of all, stay quiet."

"Wha…" I start but he is already running. He slides quietly onto the ice and drops to one knee while shooting arrows faster than I can see. Everything is silent except for the cracking of the ice as the perfectly placed arrows free the limbs. A few of the men are exposed and run toward the lake waving their weapons.

I can't even describe what I'm watching. Archer is truly magnificent as his body, so strong, glides silently across the ice while his arrows find their marks. It is incredible. I am proud and in awe at the same time. I can't take my eyes off of him. He's taking out the majority of the "guards" before ever reaching the other side and no one is the wiser.

Once across the lake, he jumps to the snow and flips a dagger in each hand then starts engaging his opponents. He seems to have a primal ferociousness in his fighting today that I have not seen before. He's ruthless and brutal. He stabs, punches and slices, cutting them down one after the other. He's shredding them. It is all very fast.

He waves his arm motioning for me to move. I run like he said and hit the ice. I fall flat on my face wincing at the pain it sends through my already-sore body and ribs but manage to quietly get up on all fours. It seems like it is taking me forever to get to the other side. When I finally reach the edge of the lake, Archer grabs my hands pulling me quickly and completely off the ground and onto the snow. His fur cloak drapes around me.

He picks up a few axes dropped by the other men who are now laying in red snow with pieces of their bodies strewn around them. I try not to look. It's so gross. I don't think I could ever get desensitized to this.

Archer puts a finger to his lips signaling for me to stay quiet while he motions his hands downward signaling for me to stay put. He creeps forward. A few seconds later I hear the crunching of a bone breaking then another like the cracking of a skull.

Archer comes out from behind a tree and flips his head signaling for me follow him. The outpost was not heavily guarded and we pass through without many more incidences.

Once we get clear of the area, Archer turns to me and I hand him his cloak.

"Do you need to stop to rest?" he asks then looks away while putting his cloak on.

"No," I answer, I just want to get to camp. I can't take his standoffishness. I feel myself getting hurt and angry at the same time. It's probably best to try to walk it off.

When we finally get to camp, I do need a rest. I sit by the fire pit while Archer lights it.

"Stay here and get warm. I'll get the shelter set up."

I look around and it doesn't seem as though anyone has been here yet. Everything here has been put in place by the race officials, but there is a light dusting of undisturbed snow on everything. Could it be possible that we are the first? If we have trimmed off this much time, I'll be very impressed with Archer's navigational skills.

Before long he's back and heating some water in a tea kettle. He doesn't really look at me or say much. I'm getting seriously annoyed. He prepares a cup of tea and hands it to me.

"This should help," he says but doesn't actually make eye contact with me.

Finally, I'm at the breaking point.

"Are you so mad at me that you can't even look me in the face," I yell.

He looks at me startled and steps back.

"Mad at you," he answers incredulously but more on the calm side. "Why in this world would I be mad at you?"

"Because I didn't leave when you told me to. Maybe if I had Hamar would not have, have…" I can't even finish.

"What he did is not your fault," he responds in his deep voice while pointing with his finger.

"Then why is it so hard for you to talk to me? It never was before. You won't even look at me," I screech.

He is clearly struck unaware. He steps backward and almost falls over a seat. Instead, he manages to just sit down hard. He chooses his words carefully.

"If you sense any reticence on my part, I am sorry," he says.

"Reticence? Why won't you look at me?" I'm yelling again. I'm so insecure about what he thinks of me. "Am I so hideous that you have to turn away?"

He looks down.

"See what I mean?" Tears are burning at the corners of my eyes.

He sighs. "It's not you. This was my fault. When I look at you, I see my failure to protect you tattooed across the bruises on your throat and face. This never should have happened," he replies sadly.

I'm boiling. "Well," I answer sarcastically, "how about we take a moment to feel sorry for you?"

"Ah, shit," he snarls and turns away.

Now, I let him have it. "Look at you! You're so big and strong. I can never beat you physically! I will never win against you!" He turns around to look at me. I get right in his face and I continue, "You will never know what it is like to feel so absolutely powerless and helpless at the mercy of someone so much bigger and stronger that the only thing you can do is lie there and let him beat you or worse! I would have welcomed death over being raped!" He closes his eyes briefly as though the words cut through him. "There is a reason they call rape a fate worse than death because it is! You have no say as to what this big, strong man does to your body! There is no choice but to be pinned down while he does whatever he wants!" He wasn't Archer at the moment, he was every man everywhere and I wasn't Liliana, I was every woman who has ever been physically harmed at the hands of a man. Archer sat there and let me spew forth all the venom and hatred inside of me with spit flying out of my mouth and tears running down my face. He didn't move. He took it. He took all of it. When I was through with my rant, I paused.

He was himself again and I was me.

"You'll never know," I tell him shaking my head at him. "I survived that brutal beating and when it is all said and done, you won't even look at me. Failed me? You're failing me now!" I cry and run to our shelter. I'm exhausted, cold, hungry and completely emotional. I cry myself to sleep.

I wake up during the night. I'm a little cold but Archer has laid his cloak over me. I see him staring off into space on the other side of the fire. He is leaning against a fur on the icy wall of the hut. His long frame is stretched out; he has no shirt on. His arm is still wrapped where he was hooked. He has a variety of just-about-healed cuts on his shoulders and abs. One knee is bent and his other arm is hanging over it. He's chewing on some green twig, very deep in thought. The light from the fire dances across the shadows of his face. I get up and drag his cloak with me as I walk over to him.

He looks up at me. I lie down next to him and place my head on his chest. He covers me again with the cloak as I close my eyes. The warmth and protection of his hand settles on my back. I feel him lean toward me so I open my eyes.

"You are right. I may never understand what you went through that day, but you'll never know how tormented I am that I wasn't there for you. I would have ripped him apart with my bare hands," he tells me softly.

I lift myself up and now I'm very close to his face.

"Not there? You saved me that day," I said tenderly. He makes a face like it wasn't enough, but I continue, "Don't you understand? You did so much more than just kill my assailant; you truly saved me. I had just about given up. I had made up my mind that if he didn't kill me after raping me, I would have killed myself. I really wanted to kill myself because I knew that beast was about to ruin my life forever and essentially dooming my brother to death, too. When I was recovering in medical, I spent a lot of time reliving those moments in my mind again and again. For a while, I was so lost about what happened and wondered how I would ever get over it. The thought of being raped consumed me. But the more I thought about it, the more I realized that yes, I took a really good beating but, in the end, that is all. Not only was I alive and not raped, my life had not been raped either. That was because of you. So that day, you saved me."

We look into each other's eyes. He's still searching for absolution. It is clear to me that we both need some kind of reckoning about what happened but I don't know how we are going to accomplish it. I just wish this man in front of me could realize that he is my hero. I will always take that memory with me of how he fought against his own injuries to save me.

I reach up to stroke his cheek with my fingers. I realize now that I truly love him. I lean closer and we kiss each other lightly on the lips and then again. We search each other's eyes once more and go in again. This time our mouths are parted and our tongues get involved. It starts slowly but we give that kiss the freedom it needs to go as far as it wants to go and find some ground to reconcile everything that happened. His mouth is hot and starving, mine is seeking and thirsty. Our kiss builds up out of fiery, heated, pent up, raw emotion. He pulls me into him and holds me as tight as he dares. I wrap my arms around his neck letting my fingers crawl through his soft hair and we let it keep going. The intimacy of this moment between us is powerful. We let everything out in those kisses. There is love, pain, anger, understanding and even forgiveness pouring out of us as our mouths make slow passionate love to each other. When we stop for air, he stops it there. He searches my eyes, then gently lays me back down on the fur, kisses my forehead, gets up, grabs his shirt and walks out into the snow.

***

I wake up. I'm nestled into Archer's body facing his bare chest. His arms are behind me. I don't know when he came back. I smile inside and think for a moment about kissing him. It was amazing. Kissing him is so rare that when it happens it is a major treat. He's such a good kisser. I shift my eyes to look up at him. His eyes are closed. His breathing is steady and deep. He sleeps. I don't want to move and wake him. He needs rest too.

Just as I start to doze, I hear a distant noise. I lie very still trying to see if there is more to it. Archer's muscles tense a smidge but he hasn't moved. I shift my eyes again to look at his face. His eyes are open and he's fully alert. I hear another noise. He closes his eyes. I guess whatever we hear is not important. His breathing becomes steady again and he is relaxed but I want to know what it is. I try listening again. The noise is getting slightly louder and closer. I hear voices. It must be another team or teams. No wonder he doesn't care.

I wake up. It's light and cold now. Archer is gone. I hear a flurry of activity outside. Several teams must have come in last night. I sit up, yawn and stretch. Then I lie back down on our cozy little bed and rub my fingers in the fur where Archer was lying. It is so soft and it smells like him.

He peeks his head through the tent opening.

"Rise and shine, Lily," he says and hands me a cup of hot chocolate. "Everyone made it in last night. Breakfast is ready." With that, he is out.

He seems bright and cheery this morning. Maybe everything that transpired between us has allowed for some adequate healing to begin. There is a knock on the tent post. I pull a fur up to my chin.

"Yes?"

A young man sticks his head in the tent. "You are expected at medical in ten minutes, miss." I smile my acknowledgement and he exits.

I take a drink of the hot chocolate, then get up.

Once I'm dressed and ready, I head over to the medical tent. There are many people at camp. I see the contestants including Jannika. She is in the buffet line. Langt is making her laugh about something. As I walk, I'm scanning the area for Archer. Finally, I see him. He's leaning against a tree on the far side of camp. He's holding a plate of food, but he's not alone. Kali is talking to him with her pretty, silky smile. She's standing close to him. My breath catches in my throat as she laughs and lays her hand on his chest. She then turns her gorgeous mane of hair. Ugh! Archer is smiling and talking casually to her. I'm getting upset.

"Miss?" brings me back to reality. I'm standing in front of the medical tent and the young man is holding it open. At his word, I step inside. Doctor Barrett looks up at me.

"Miss Ellis," he says walking over to me, "how are you feeling?"

"Fine," I answer, but secretly I'm seething and want to get back out there and poke Kali's eyes out.

"I need you to sit on this table and let me have a look at you."

I comply. A nurse comes over as he closes the curtain. The nurse lifts my shirt over my head and covers my shoulders with a blanket. The doctor comes over to inspect my bruises then unwraps my arm and ribs. He stretches and pulls on my arm but I don't feel any tenderness.

"The nerve damage in your arm is almost completely healed," he says, then he puts his hands on my ribs. He pokes and pushes around until he finds the one spot that sends me through the roof when he touches it. "Guess that's a sore spot," he smiles.

I'm not amused.

"We'll do some special wrapping for it, but you seem to be doing quite well. Do you have any pain or problems that we should talk about?"

I shake my head.

"Okay then, let me get you wrapped up and you can be on your way."

When the doctor finishes, he asks me to send Archer in.

"Yes, of course." I'm not sure if he's getting checked out or briefed on my condition. Maybe both.

When I step out, Archer and Langt are each holding a cup of coffee and are deeply in conversation. He looks over at me. I flip my thumb to the medical tent. He nods and stands.

I walk to the buffet table.

"Hey!" I hear behind me. I turn around as Jannika is catching up to me. I smile at her.

"How are you feeling? You look good. The bruises have almost faded."

"Just got checked out. Everything is good," I answer as I spoon some eggs on my plate. "How's everything going with you?"

"I'd be doing a lot better if some certain beautiful Specialist would quit putting her hands on my man," she whispers sarcastically.

"You too?" I ask. "I saw Kali pawing at Archer earlier. I wanted to rip her hair out."

"Oh yeah, I saw that, too," Jannika says. "She's really been laying it on thick this morning. She must want something."

We walk to a table and sit down.

"How are Archer's injuries healing?"

"He's doing really well. Pretty much healed," I answer. I don't want her to feel that Langt has any sort of advantage. I know they're friends, but…

Antonella joins us.

"By the way, are all Specialists doctors," I ask. I want to know if I'm the only idiot who doesn't know things.

"Yes, I think so. Langt is a doctor of medicine, botany and mathematics. He has several other degrees too just not doctorates although he may be close to earning another one. I think he is currently working on some sort of bioscience. In my Region, the Specialists are highly esteemed because of not only what they do, but that they are highly educated and pursue advanced education their entire lives. It's just part of who they are. They have to know a lot of different things. To be paired with such a person is a great honor," she admires.

Antonella adds to the conversation. "Espada is a doctor of medicine also. He holds a doctorate in engineering and some other kind of science. I was amazed at how highly educated they are. He said they have to be for what they do. He said that most people work all day and then fill their evenings with different sorts of entertainment. He said when they are not on mission, they work all day on their temple master activities but their evenings are filled gaining knowledge whether pursing another degree or studies about warfare and subjects that appeal to them. But apparently, they are always adding to their knowledge. He said that is their entertainment."

"They are so young. They must be incredibly intelligent. I feel so inferior," I add humbly.

"Yes, they all have a number of doctorate studies. I think they are all, at least in this particular group here, doctors of medicine. Not really sure, though. They are all around 30 so they aren't that young," Jannika says thoughtfully.

"That's very young for all that education," I laugh.

"I suppose," Jannika says shrugging.

I realize that I am very pathetic on Specialist knowledge.

I look over at Archer. He's still standing there but appears to be getting ready to go to medical. He's taking a drink of his coffee while he listens to Langt. He glances over at me and winks.

CHAPTER 42

TEAM HURDLE

There are many tables loaded with a variety of items on them. There is a sign that reads: BLAST FROM THE PAST – SPECIALISTS MUST STAND BEHIND THE YELLOW TABLE AND INSTRUCT PARTNER ON WHICH ITEMS TO PUT IN THE BASKET FROM THE BLUE TABLES TO CREATE A BLAST FROM THE PAST. THE BASKET MUST THEN BE HANDED TO THE SPECIALIST WHO WILL CREATE THE FINAL ANSWER IN FRONT OF THE JUDGE. ONCE THE BASKET IS HANDED TO THE SPECIALIST, THE CANDIDATE CANNOT GO BACK TO THE BLUE TABLE TO RETREIVE ANY MORE ITEMS. IF THE ANSWER IS NOT SATISFACTORY TO THE JUDGE, THE TEAM MUST WAIT 30 MINUTES BEFORE MAKING ANOTHER ATTEMPT.

We go inside the work room. Archer stands behind the yellow table and I go to the blue. The blue tables are absolutely filled to overflowing with so many items. I'm afraid if I touch anything it will bring some of it falling down to the ground. I'm completely overwhelmed and haven't a clue where to start or even where to focus my attention.

"What do you see?" Archer inquires.

"Well," I begin with a shrug, "there are paints, papers, shreds of cloth, powders, crayons, candles, pencils, party favors, buckets of sawdust, rocks, marbles, string, streamers, bamboo, charcoal, matches, trays, pens, cut out shapes, scissors, a pocket knife, fork, spoon, stickers, poster board and just about everything else." Then I walk over to him. "A blast from the past? Are we supposed to create themed party items?"

"No, you wouldn't need my help for that." He spends a few moments looking over at the blue tables. "What is that big jar of white powder on the end? Does it have a label?"

I look at it closer and find a small label on the bottom. "Potassium nitrate," I reply.

"Potassium nitrate?" he asks surprised. "Now, what's that doing there?" He tilts his head to the ceiling while crossing his arms. I can almost feel the wheels of his mind in motion. After a few minutes, he smiles. "The irony," he says under his breath. He looks at me. "Do you see a jar with a yellowish powder?"

I look around. "There are three. One says saffron, another says sulfur…"

"That one. The sulfur. Put it in the basket. Put the potassium nitrate in, too. Didn't you say there was coal or charcoal?"

"Yes, there is a pail of it."

"Put it in the basket. What about a pestle and mortar?" he asks.

"Yes, I found two. Stone or stainless?"

"Stone."

"Now some string, the pocket knife, the matches, a package of the marbles, and do you see any kind of open container? What about that bamboo? Does it have a bottom?" he asks.

I grab everything quickly then look for the bamboo he's asking about. I see and reach for it. "No, but there is a smaller wooden container next to it that has a bottom," I answer.

"How big is the opening?"

I hold it up for him to see. "It's not big, but it's not small either."

"Perfect. Bring me the basket."

I bring it over to him and he unloads the items on his work table. Using the mortar and pestle, he crushes some of the charcoal. When he gets it to the consistency he likes, he sets it aside and then starts assembling something. Using the knife, he carves a small hole in the wood and laces the string through it until a good amount accumulates on the bottom leaving several inches still on the outside. Once he assembles his item, he gets the jars of powders in front of him and the coal. He looks up at me.

"Lily, go stand over there."

I don't know what he's doing but I move far away from him.

He dumps the crushed charcoal on the table. Next, he roughly measures a portion of it and returns it to the mortar bowl as well as a good amount of the white powder. Then he carefully adds an exact amount of the yellow. He mixes them gently together and attentively pours the mixture into his handmade device. He seems to be very cautious as he packs it down. He places a package of the marbles inside. Then after a final inspection, he hands it to the judge.

"Your work appears to be satisfactory, but now we must test it. Let's go outside," the judge says. Archer looks over at me lifting his eyebrows and grinning.

When we get outside, the judge asks us to wait while he checks clearance.

"What is it?" I whisper to Archer who looks like a little boy with a new toy.

"A blast from the past, baby! Gunpowder. Let's see if my homemade cannon works." He winks at me merrily.

The judge gives us clearance. Archer sets up the cannon and tells me to stand back when he goes to light it. It explodes perfectly sending the marble "projectiles" flying in the air. He smiles; very pleased with the explosion. The judge appears to like it, too.

"Well done, Archer," the judge comments then turns to me. "Your team is free to proceed."

I smile my approval also.

Once we're out of earshot, I ask, "How did you know that?"

"Once you said Potassium nitrate, I wondered why they would put saltpeter in the mix. I had a few directions to go. Sulfur was the clincher. If it was on the table, I knew I had it. Then it was a matter of basic chemistry. All the elements were there," he laughs.

For a moment I just stare at him realizing just how amazingly smart he is. He's so impressive. Gunpowder, I would never have even thought about that. No wonder his kind are the best in the world.

"I heard you say, "the irony". What did you mean by that?"

"They don't allow the use of firearms in the race, yet they want us to make one even though it's a bit old fashioned." He just shakes his head.

I snicker.

"We have a long journey to the checkpoint," Archer announces.

"I know. How are we going to get there?"

"We'll have to take a train. We have another mandatory rest stop in Balakova," he adds pulling out his instruction cards.

"Really?" I'm surprised. "Are we meeting up with the other contestants."

"Apparently."

That's interesting. I wonder why. I mean, we're getting down to the last few of us left in the race. I feel like I'm one of the leaders at this point and I don't want to be on another even playing field.

Since it's going to take 22 hours by train to get to Balakova, Archer secures accommodations on a sleeper car so we both can get a good night's rest. Thankfully, the train ride is uneventful.

★★★

We check in at the State Museum. I guess we're all going to stay here in their basements tonight. How interesting. We go downstairs and see Langt and Jannika at the refreshment table. The men nod to each other while Jannika and I wave happily.

Archer and I move to the area where cots are set up by team. Ours is close to a corner at the far end of the room. I sit on one of our allotted cots and look into our team trunk. We have clean clothes and bathing supplies.

"Do you see a shower?"

"No, but there must be bathing rooms here somewhere. Would you like me to find out?" he offers.

"No, not yet. You must be hungry. Let's get some decent food."

He agrees happily. I thought I heard his stomach growl when we arrived. I guess I didn't realize we haven't eaten in a while.

"I'll set up the room separators after we eat," he offers.

I look around to see a small pile of supplies. Those must be the room separators he's talking about. It's more like curtain rods and a few fabric dividers. We better not talk strategy since the "walls" will be paper thin.

Langt and Jannika have moved to one of the tables with their food. When we get ours, we sit down with them. Langt gets up and goes back to the refreshment table.

Antonella and Espada walk in. Espada does the man nod thing. Antonella smiles at us. They go to their corner of the room and inspect their supplies.

Langt returns and hands Archer a bottle of ale. He takes it gratefully. I wonder who else will come through the door. Then I realize, we're down to the final four. It's just Kali and Roni left.

"We're the last four," I mention to Jannika. "Can you believe it?"

"I know, we only have about 10 days left," she confirms. "It will be strange going home. I feel like I have been away so long and have experienced so many adventures."

"Me too. Can you believe that there are three girls left and only one guy?"

Jannika and I look at each other and then at Archer and Langt and just smile at them. Girl power all the way!

"Here we go," Langt comments rolling his eyes. Archer just smiles. He has a twinkle in his eye.

"Does it surprise you?" I ask

Archer shakes his head smiling.

"Why would it?" Langt responds smiling. "You have the best Specialists!"

"Fat heads," I laugh. "I should have known they would take all the credit."

Jannika throws her napkin at Langt.

"You're not the last, you know," she teases. "And there is a woman Specialist keeping right up with you boys."

"Does it surprise you that Kali is the last woman standing?" I ask.

"Not at all," Langt says, "she can kick ass as well as any man."

Archer agrees.

"Has she ever taken you down?" Jannika asks looking at Langt.

"She hasn't yet, but the day may come when she finds the right move to take me down. Based on what I've seen here during the race, it could be sooner than we think," he says.

Archer nods in agreement while taking a swig of his ale.

"It must be amazing to take down a man like a warrior. Most women I know wouldn't be able to do that," I add.

Both men laugh at me.

"What?" I ask wondering what I missed.

"You're a little hard on your sex don't you think?" Langt asks.

"What do you mean?"

"If there is one thing I know," Archer declares, "a woman doesn't have to be a warrior to bring a man to his knees."

"Preach it, brother!" Langt agrees.

They clink ale bottles and return to the refreshment table.

I roll my eyes. Men. Jannika just laughs.

Suddenly Archer's eyes become very focused as Roni walks into the room. Langt and Kali see it also. Archer makes a bee line for them. Kali pulls two "stick" clubs from her arsenal and stands in front of Roni holding the sticks at arm's length in front of her.

Archer moves right in. She presses the sticks against his chest as Langt moves cautiously over as does Espada. Kali stands tall but shifts her eyes to Langt then back to Archer.

"Archer?" Kali quizzes. She is standing firm but there is a question in her voice.

Archer's steel blue eyes are focused on Roni as he addresses him. "You harmed my partner in Franka. Prepare to defend yourself."

Kali tilts her head to Roni with a wide-eyed "you picked a fight with Archer?!" look on her face. He looks at her terrified. She faces Archer.

"I'll take the fight, Archer," she speaks calmly but firmly.

Archer takes his eyes off Roni, looks at her, then gives her a curt nod.

Archer moves away from her in a half circle. When he turns to face her, he is also armed with two stick clubs. His eyes are focused on her.

"Archer, you've had opportunities to address this with me since Franka," she notes. "Why now?"

"This was the right opportunity to teach your boy a lesson," Archer determines. "You can still step aside, Kali."

She doesn't answer. She takes a stand then moves in. Her sticks fly fast and furious. Archer's are just as quick. They both swing, strike, move, twist and twirl out of each other's way. Stick fighting is very fast and amazing. I've never seen or heard anything like it. Kali moves in fluid, elegant movements. She matches Archer's cat like dexterity perfectly.

The fight is incredible. I can see why they have such a great respect for her skill. She gets him with a couple of extremely good cracks to his torso and jaw. He gives her a congratulatory half smile after each but it only intensifies his fight. She's beginning to wear down some but he is coming on stronger.

Then, in one smooth movement, Archer spins and with a mighty swing smashes his stick with an excruciating blow straight down on Kali's wrist knocking her stick completely out of her hand. She lets out the smallest of groans from the pain of it while her wrist begins swelling immediately.

Archer charges pinning her against the table. He holds her arm in one hand while with his other he holds one of his sticks pressing hard on her throat.

"You won't win today, Kali," he says quietly but sternly. He lets go and steps back from her. "Choose," he demands. He is slightly bent forward as he takes a fighting position with one hand in front of him and one behind him.

She stands up. With contempt in her eyes, she holds out her last stick and drops it. Archer stands and bows but keeps his eyes on her. She walks away with Roni in her shadow. As she turns the corner, I can see her grab her swelling wrist and begin rubbing it gingerly.

CHAPTER 43

I sit straight up out of my sleep. I'm breathing heavily. I'm just sitting here in the darkness with the faint glow of a low wall sconce trying to figure this out but, I'm pretty sure I just had a sex dream about Archer. I look over but he's not here. Thank goodness. It must be early morning because he was here when we went to bed. Maybe he and the other specialists are off doing their morning stretches.

He walks into our sectioned-off area moments later and looks like he just had a shower. He has a towel around his waist and one around his neck. I find myself looking at his naked body from top to bottom and back up again. He's so nicely put together. He has broad shoulders, a fantastically toned body with clearly defined abs, nice chest, strong arms and very strong legs. He's not bulky looking at all like many of those body obsessors are. He is just perfectly put together. After a dream like that, my eyes linger for a second longer than they should on the healthy bulge under his towel.

"Is there something you want to see?" Archer asks humorously. He misses nothing, dammit.

I look up at him and he's grinning at me. "What? No!" I stutter.

He's laughing. "I can drop the towel so you won't have to wonder what's under there," he teases.

My mouth is gaping open and I'm at a loss for words. I was totally caught gaping at his man bulge.

"Archer! No! No!" I'm nervously laughing. If he only knew what just happened in my dream.

"Should I find separate sleeping quarters tonight," he jokes.

"Stop. No, why," I say wondering if he can read my thoughts.

"You're breathing rather heavy and checking out my body." He's enjoying this.

"Archer!" I giggle.

"Well, Lily, you've got a hungry look in your eyes and it's not for food," he shakes his head smiling.

"Oh my God, Archer! In your dreams!" I'm fully laughing now. If only he knew my dreams.

He tilts his head smiling and puts his thumbs under his towel wiggling them. "Last chance. Towel is coming off."

I squeal and turn away falling face down on my cot. He just laughs as I hear his towel hit the floor.

He puts on his pants. "All clear, now," he teases.

I turn back around.

He's smiling at me. "What was that all about? Curiosity?" he asks.

"No," I say trying desperately to hide the real reason I was staring at him. I have to come up with something quickly. "You Specialists always look so great and perfect. Do they teach you that at temple?"

He looks up at me. "Well, we must always be presentable and in the best shape. I'm not sure what else you mean."

"I mean, why are Specialists so beautiful?"

He looks at me like he's been struck dumbfounded. "I've never heard that before," he says shrugging his shoulders.

"You haven't? A woman has never complimented you on your extremely good looks?"

He furrows his brows and shakes his head.

"Bull! Women come on to you all the time." I've seen it firsthand.

"Women come on to men anyway regardless of good looks," he says emphatically. "Women are always touching me."

"So no one has ever told you that you are a handsome guy?" I say with real sarcasm.

"No," is all he says and starts putting on his shoes.

"I can't believe that. Are you a virgin?" It just slips out. My mind totally went there.

"No," is all he answers. He's distracted with the shoes.

"Really?" I ask even more than a little incredulous. I don't know why but I'm genuinely surprised. "I didn't think they allowed you to, um…you know, at the temple."

"Actually, it's part of our…" he looks up at me and stops himself.

"Training?" I finish his sentence staring at him with shocked surprise. "They train you to have sex?" I ask all wide-eyed and interested.

He tilts his head, sucks in some air between clenched teeth and seems to be looking for something to say. Then he starts stumbling, "This um, is really not, um, a good topic."

But I'm all in it now. "Can you get over being bashful? I really would like to know. They train you in how to please a woman?"

This time, his mouth is hanging open and he clearly doesn't know what to do. Finally, he flips his wrists in a resigned fashion as he struggles to look for the right words, "We are thrown into a lot of social situations. We can't be distracted by, um, unknown territory… we always have to…"

"Give a peak performance!" I finish his sentence again and burst out laughing. He turns shaking his head with a smile and I could swear I heard a chuckle as well.

"Okay, okay, say no more, I'll let you off the hook," I grin. "Let's talk about something else."

He exhales and looks genuinely relieved. Secretly, so am I.

A race attendant pops his head in our area.

"Archer, a Specialist meeting has been called for changes in today's journey," he says.

Archer acknowledges, "I'll be right there."

He pulls on a shirt and looks over at me.

"So, you think I'm totally gorgeous, huh?" he snickers and winks.

"What? Stop. We're not talking about this anymore. Get out!" I laugh throwing a pillow at him.

The rest of the journey to the checkpoint is easy. When I cross the threshold "Number One" is announced. I'm first? I'm so excited! I'm first!

CHAPTER 44

Medatilli

We begin our Medatilli leg in the ancient city of Venice. We have arrived during their Spirit Festival. Everyone is decorated in colorful masks and brightly colored costumes. The aroma of the food and the exuberant laughter of the participants is exhilarating. Archer wants to move through it quickly. I understand. There are a lot of people squeezed together in these narrow lanes and alleyways. It could be dangerous, but we could actually have some fun, too.

I think the Venice canals are so romantic. There are boats and gondolas also decorated in fabulous textures and bright colors carrying happy couples slowly down the waterways. I wish we had a carnival like this back home.

I am happy about this carnival, but mostly I'm happy because Kali was eliminated in the last leg. Antonella told us that Kali and Espada squared off in a fight. Roni watched while Antonella ran for the checkpoint. Roni was last and got eliminated. While Antonella was happy she also revealed the strategy that she and Espada employ. I'll have to watch for that one.

But mostly, I'm happy because I made it to the top three. That means my family's medical services have been upgraded. Colson can get the surgery he needs. Now, we'll need to find a way to pay for it. We'll figure that out. I know we will.

As we jog through the carnival. Archer stops and grabs me. He looks around. He is more than a little concerned. He pulls me into a back alley and takes a breath to compose himself while stretching out tall. Then he looks at me. I've never before seen that look in his eyes.

"Archer, what is it?" He is scaring me.

He seems extremely stunned. "Get down," he says slowly and quietly.

I crouch down on my knees immediately. "What is it?" I have never seen him like this. I'm truly terrified but I stay low.

"Don't say anything," he says very quietly touching the top of my head. He is still looking around. He is extremely unnerved.

I'm looking around but I don't see anything, however, he is genuinely, seriously agitated.

He drops elegantly to one knee and bows his head. Within moments we are surrounded by a force of people dressed all in shiny black. They are wearing black oriental type masks. Most of the masks are accented in yellow. All of these people are armed and pointing guns at us. I didn't think they allowed guns on the race. I'm terrified, but Archer isn't moving. This is so unlike him. My flight reflex begins to hit me but as if reading my mind, Archer discreetly places his hand around my wrist. I stay still, albeit breathlessly.

Then another group of black clad people come forward. Their masks have red and yellow markings. They are unarmed and take a stance directly in front of us. One person in particular has a larger mask. The markings are all in red. I am about to flip out but Archer isn't moving. He's just bowing his head while on one knee. What's wrong with him?

A large commuter pulls up to the side several yards away. The door opens and Calvin walks out wearing very formal black robes with thin purple, red and gold stripes down the front. What is going on here? Obviously, this is not race related. He steps in front of Archer facing the person with the biggest mask, holds his hands out slightly to the side, palms up and bows.

"Esquire, please remove the bystander," a woman's voice says from behind the large mask.

Calvin looks over his right shoulder and nods at the commuter. Two men run out, grab me and take me into Calvin's commuter. Archer didn't move except to remove his hand from my wrist. There is something very serious happening here. He just let them take me. Once inside the commuter, I struggle to free myself. But the men holding me basically drop me and move to the front viewing window. I realize very quickly that I'm not the target, for once. I take a quick look around and notice that the commuter is very luxurious. I move forward to the viewing window and find a chair next to Calvin's men. I perch myself on it to watch the proceedings. More of Calvin's employees run forward to watch also. One of them flips a switch and then we can hear everything, too.

"Dea Master Archer, disarm. Prepare for battle," the woman's voice orders.

Archer stands, bows and moves to the side. He removes his over vest and shirt, clasps his hands behind his back, looks straight ahead and stands very still. Without his shirt, I can clearly see how tense his muscles are even though he looks relaxed.

"Honorable High Priestess, on behalf of Dea Master Archer, we respectfully request the reading of the charges the High Temple Tribunal has brought against him."

Charges? Against Archer? This is bad. No wonder he was so unnerved.

"The charges against Dea Master Archer are a 1:1 Weapons Infraction," the High Priestess responds.

"We respectfully request to face his Accuser," Calvin declares.

"The Accuser is Dea Master Moralles," the High Priestess announces.

I see the tiniest of tightening in Archer's jaw. Other than that, he does not move and stares straight ahead. I remember that name. Calvin and Langt both have mentioned it to Archer before.

A man steps forward. He is built very much like Archer, he is tall, very strong, but he is bald and older. He sports a lot of body art.

"Dea Master Archer, your battle with Dea Master Moralles will commence shortly. You will not be permitted to use weapons to defend yourself. If you should disarm Dea Master Moralles, you must hold up the weapon and not use it in any way. Are these instructions clear?"

Archer acknowledges with a brief nod.

Wait. Did she say disarm? So, this Moralles guy gets to use weapons but Archer doesn't. That hardly seems fair.

"Mark the arena," another masked person calls. People clad in the same black suits and masks with yellow markings run in carrying red lighted devices. They gather in a circle and attach all the devices together forming a large circular area on the ground.

"Dea Master Moralles and Dea Master Archer, this is a Yield Prerogative fight. Step into the arena," the Highest Priestess demands.

Both men step into the lighted circle. Archer's eyes narrow with intensity as he looks at Moralles. If ever I saw Archer extremely pissed off, this is it. They bow to the High Tribunal then bow to each other. Archer doesn't take his eyes off the man. The starting bell rings.

Moralles comes right at Archer brandishing blades in both hands. Archer lets him charge then at the last moment produces a powerful kick right in his chest lifting Moralles off the ground and sending him flying several feet backwards. Archer is on top of him in a flash. He holds up a blade.

"Dea Master Archer, disarm," commands the priestess. Archer tosses the blade outside of the marked arena.

The fight continues. It is insanely fast and furious. The two men are incredible. Archer holds up another blade.

"Dea Master Archer, disarm," blasts out through the arena. This goes on throughout the fight. Every few minutes, "Dea Master Archer, disarm!"

His opponent is savage-like but Archer is too. I've never seen him so intense. Their movements are extremely fast. Their punches so powerful yet they are so agile moving, blocking, flipping, twisting and maneuvering. "Dea Master Archer, disarm," I hear it again and again. I see blood dripping down Archer's torso from several slashes. His opponent has massive bulging wounds on his face and purplish bruises on his arms. After every call for Archer to disarm, someone says a word in a language I don't understand. Both men are dripping with blood and sweat. I hear, "Dea Master Archer, disarm." Again, then a word. At one point, Archer goes back in on one maneuver and rips the other man's shirt completely off. Two more blades fall to the arena. Archer moves quickly to retrieve both. "Dea Master Archer, disarm," I hear again and then two foreign words.

"Dea Master Archer, stand down," the priestess says. Archer moves to the side.

Moralles stands and moves to the side.

"Dea Master Moralles has been fully disarmed. This battle is now hand to hand. Step into the arena," the woman continues.

"Hand to hand?" I think to myself. Both men are gasping for air and both are wounded. However, once in the arena, both men stand tall, focused and seem ready to proceed.

The bell rings to start the fight. Archer seems to get renewed energy from somewhere and he strikes like a man on a mission. The power behind his blows is awe inspiring, lifting Master Moralles entirely off the ground with some of them. He takes his opponent completely down within moments.

"Dea Master Archer, stand down," the priestess directs. Archer moves to the side of the arena. He is breathing very hard, sweating and has blood dripping from his body. He looks like a man who has been in a dogfight but again, he still stands tall and looks straight ahead with his hands clasped behind him.

"Dea Master Archer, you have earned Yield Prerogative. Will you exercise it now," the priestess asks.

"No," he declines.

"Dea Master Moralles, Yield Prerogative has not been exercised. This is now a fight to the death," the priestess tells the combatants. "Prepare yourselves. Mercy is contracted."

Master Moralles does not stand but only makes it up on his knees. The bell sounds but he still does not get up. Archer finally approaches him guardedly. He stands arms length away from the man. The man still does not stand. He looks at Archer defiantly with blood dripping out of his mouth and nose. Archer takes a breath and gets down on his level. Moralles strikes out but Archer catches his fist, gives it a quick twist and breaks it. He looks him straight in the eye and delivers a fatal blow. The man falls lifelessly to the ground.

"Dea Master Archer, stand down," the priestess instructs. Archer stands and moves to face the Tribunal. He takes a knee in front of them again and bows his head.

"The High Temple Tribunal will now deliberate," she adds.

The non armed people walk off somewhere.

Calvin comes back into the commuter. His people flank him and start excitedly talking about the fight. Apparently, it's more incredible than any of them have seen either.

The back door opens and Langt walks in.

"Langt? What brings you here?" Calvin asks.

"I was summoned and physically brought here," Langt answers. "I don't enjoy being manhandled by Tribunals. You could have just summoned me. Why am I here?"

"To bear witness, I imagine," Calvin explains.

"Do you have any idea how terrifying it is it be suddenly surrounded by Tribunal clansman," Langt rhetorically asks Calvin.

I feel like saying I know all too well how that feels but I keep my mouth shut.

Langt looks out the viewing window.

"Archer? Archer was brought before the Tribunal on charges," he asks in disbelief.

Calvin confirms.

Langt flips a thumb to the lifeless body on the ground. "Who was his opponent?"

"Moralles," Calvin says.

Langt's eyes get wide. "Moralles? Moralles!" He seems to be in serious disbelief. "What was the charge?" Langt, of course, knows all about the proceedings here.

"Weapons infraction," Calvin confirms.

"Weapons infraction?" Langt continues to be shocked and surprised shaking his head. "That prick. He knows no shame."

"How many," Langt says after a moment.

"Ten." Calvin looks at Langt with a smirk, almost pride.

"Ten? That must have been a hell of a fight," Langt is shocked. The other men in the room are all scoffing and grunting.

"All right, all right. You are dismissed," Calvin says to his employees. He looks at Langt. "I can't even describe what we just saw."

Langt crosses his arms "I'm so sorry I missed it." He seems truly disappointed. He looks out the window at Archer kneeling. "He's suffered some decent injuries. I guess that is to be expected given his opponent. He looks like he's been through the ringer," he assesses, then looks back at Calvin. "How long have they been deliberating?"

"About 30 minutes," Calvin concludes.

"Why so long? Was it clean?"

Calvin nods, "You're talking about Archer, of course it was clean."

"Of course," Langt agrees nodding.

They are quiet for a moment just looking out the window.

"You don't think his status is in jeopardy? They won't demote him?" Langt is suddenly very serious.

"Only they can determine that," Calvin answers with a sigh.

I look out the window to see Archer on bended knee, drenched with sweat, surrounded by these people in black wearing their masks. He hasn't moved. I wonder what's going through his mind.

"Why would they demote him," I ask.

The men turn to me. It's almost as if Langt is just beginning to realize I'm there.

"Archer is a Dea. He's a very high-ranking Master. There are only four in the world. Well, three now that Moralles is gone. The High Temple Tribunal will determine Archer's fate based on whether or not he proved himself in battle and in character. The charges brought against him were serious and they came from another high ranking Master. It was a 1:1 charge, meaning there are no witnesses and no evidence against Archer except for the word of another highly respected Master. If the Tribunal finds Archer lacking in any respect, he could be declassed," Calvin explains.

Langt sighs, "Moralles has had it in for Archer a long time. He may yet have the final word."

"Why did he have it in for Archer," I wonder.

"Archer has always performed beyond his years. Archer and Moralles became Deas at the same time. Moralles was offended because Archer was so much younger. He felt Archer should never have become a Dea and has set out to ruin him every chance he got to prove his point. If he and Archer were ever in close proximately, there would be a fight. Archer always showed the upmost respect for Moralles. He never did consider him a peer but a superior. No matter how many times Moralles tried to screw him over, he always looked the other way," Langt explained. "He should have taken him down long ago."

The Tribunal returns.

"Bring forth Cee Master Langt and Esquire," the priestess announces.

Langt and Calvin walk into the arena. I see Langt take a knee next to Archer and bow. Calvin stands on Archer's other side. His hands are folded in front of him and he bows his head in respect and then faces the Tribunal.

"Cee Master Langt," the High Priestess begins, none of the men move, "you are the ranking Cee Master in this area. You have been summoned here this day to bear witness to the Tribunal's judgment of Dea Master Archer."

"Dea Master Archer," she repeats, again nobody moves, "you have been brought before this Tribunal on charges of Weapons Infraction.

From this day forward, you will no longer be known to this Tribunal as Dea Master Archer," the High Priestess announces.

Oh no. Are they demoting him? The only movement from anyone I see is Archer closing his eyes. Tears begin to form in mine.

"From this day until further notification, you will be known to this Tribunal as Jei Master Archer." Archer opens his eyes. This is the only movement still from all the men. "Your exemplary skill not only proved that you did not need to commit a weapons infraction in order to defeat your opponent but it has exceeded and impressed this Tribunal's elevated expectations. Your character before, during and after the battle was of the upmost respectable and merciful. Rise, High Master, this Tribunal wishes to salute your superior abilities."

Archer stands. "I am truly honored," he says and bows once again. The entire group, including the high priestess all bow to Archer as well.

"Esquire," the high priestess addresses Calvin, "you will receive notice of the Tribunal's ruling. You will then have 48 hours to submit this ruling to the Regions."

Calvin bows his head in acknowledgement.

As they turn away, Archer returns to his knee and bows his head. There is no expression or movement on any of them. One member of the Tribunal retrieves Archer's shirt, lays it over his neck and gives his shoulder a pat, then he walks way. I am instantly taken back to Archer's story about his first kill at 13 years old and how his Master patted him on the shoulder after a good fight. I wonder if this is the same person.

A crew dressed in black runs out and removes the dead body and all traces of their presence here.

Once every last one of the people in black are gone, Calvin turns to the men. He smiles, "Rise High Master."

Langt leaps to his feet. Archer is a little slower but both have smiles across their faces. I run outside. Langt and Archer embrace and then Calvin shakes Archer's hand. I run over. Archer grabs me and picks me up in a tight embrace and sets me back down.

"Jei Master!" Langt says astonished, "Holy Shit! I can't believe it."

"You?" Archer says. "The whole thing was unreal. I've never been called into battle by the Tribunal. It was really unsettling. I can't believe that just happened." He pulls his shirt over his head.

"Moralles?" Langt says disbelieving.

"That fuck. I just wanted to kick his ass so bad. Calling my honor and reputation into question and dragging me in front of the High Temple Tribunal on a weapons infraction when he was the one who pulled that stunt on me in Jenvaia last year. I should have killed his ass then," Archer says emphatically.

"Ten blades?" Langt laughs. "Ten blades?"

"It was unbelievable. Did you see that?" Archer asks.

"I wish I had seen it. I missed the entire fight. I was summoned and brought here after it was over," Langt answers.

"He must've been pulling blades out of his asshole. Who the hell does that?" Archer asks. "When I disarmed him yet again and they called huche, I didn't know if I was going to make it. I was so spent at that point I just ripped his shirt off of him to find out if he had any more of the damn blades hiding."

"What is huche?" I ask.

"Eight," Langt answers.

"Oh. I remember hearing something like ninduc."

"That's nine and ten," Archer says. He looks at Langt, "at that point, we went hand to hand."

"Was it Yield Prerogative?" Langt asks.

Archer nods. "I refused."

"I would have, too," Langt says.

"I just had to end it. His obsession with me had to stop," he affirms. Langt nods. Then Archer adds, "They did make a mercy call though so I had to do it much quicker than I would have liked. I wanted to just shred him."

Langt agrees.

"I think this calls for a celebration drink," Calvin chimes in. "Let's head over to the bar."

The men smile and take a few steps. Does nobody notice the blood seeping through Archer's shirt but me?

"This man needs medical attention," I say pointing to his blood-stained shirt. They all finally notice Archer's wounds.

Langt takes a closer look. "Lift your shirt." Archer pulls it up. "Looks like you'll need a lot of fusion stitches. You have some deep lacerations on your chest, torso, back of your right shoulder and the back of your left arm. You also have a pretty nasty contusion on your lower left side here. He pushes lightly on it. Archer winces. "Hmmm. Anything else? Broken ribs?" he asks.

Archer shakes his head. The men laugh and walk to Calvin's commuter. I roll my eyes. Men.

Once inside, Langt gives direction to one of Calvin's men and comes back over. Archer removes his shirt and sits on a high stool. Calvin disappears.

A tray is brought to Langt with a variety of medical supplies. He puts on gloves and begins to clean Archer's wounds.

"As your physician, I'm going to run a scan to make sure there is no internal bleeding, but as your opponent, I'm honor bound not to read it. You will have to do that and make your own decisions."

Archer agrees. I'm a little surprised. I guess I forgot that they are also opponents.

He scans Archer with a hand-held device then gives it to Archer. Archer reads it and wipes the scan. "All clear," he says handing it back to Langt.

Calvin appears with a bottle of brown alcohol. He pours four glasses and hands one to each of us.

"To the new Jei Master," he announces and we all take a drink. The men down the glass but I choke on it. It's so strong and tastes terrible. I cover my mouth with the back of my hand as I cough. They smile at me.

"Give me that," Archer reaches out for my glass. I gladly hand it over. "I need it more than you do," he adds smiling, then slings the liquid to the back of his throat and swallows.

Langt brings over the fusion device to stitch Archer's wounds but Archer doesn't even seem to notice anything is happening. He must be so used to getting stitches.

"What is a Jei Master?" I ask.

"There hasn't been a Jei in over 50 years," Calvin answers in awe. Archer smiles. "In the eyes of the Tribunal, our man here stands above reproach in skill and respectability. He is the highest-ranking Master in the land right now. Well, working Master, that is," Calvin adds.

Langt finishes with bandage wraps. Archer pulls on his shirt and jumps down. "Thanks, man," he says to Langt and they slap hands.

"His wage card just tripled as well. Let's not forget that. You're looking at a very wealthy man," Langt says to me back to his usual winks and grins.

"Shall we continue the celebration? Calvin asks. "Archer is paying." We all laugh.

"I've got to get Liliana to the shelter location. She's going to be very behind. We'll have to continue this later," Archer answers.

"One more thing," Langt says to Archer, "as your attending physician, I declare that you are medically unable to participate in challenge battles for at least 3 days or until your regular physician gives you an all clear."

"Got it," Archer says. "Thanks."

"Esquire?" Langt says formally.

"I'll make the proper notices," Calvin says waving us all off.

CHAPTER 45

Archer and I are lying in the shelter on our sides facing each other. He has his hand on my hip. I'm caressing his bruised and bandaged chest. Every now and then when he moves, I can see the tiniest of winces.

"That was crazy today," I say.

"Yes, it was," he responds.

"Does this mean no one can beat you because you're so good?"

"I wish it did. It's like any competition, even the best have off days." He looks thoughtfully away for a moment. "I made a huge mistake today," he confesses quietly.

"What was it?" I ask. I thought he was magnificent.

"I entered into a fight in anger. Extreme anger, actually." He looks down at the ground contemplatively. "That's a rare thing for me."

"I would think it's hard to fight if not in anger. Why would you fight if you weren't mad?" I ask as he meets my eyes.

"Emotion can sway judgment and control. Remember Hamar," he reminds.

I nod.

"It's not so bad as his emotional fighting but I suppose I will always wonder if I would have exercised the Yield Prerogative if I weren't so damn mad. By not doing so, I made the choice to sentence him to death and by my own hand." He held my gaze. What was he hoping to find in my eyes? "I was the judge and executioner."

"Aren't you that all the time?" I ask. This isn't his first kill.

"No, the choice to die is left up to my opponent. This time, I chose not to yield. I didn't give him a choice at all to walk away. I chose that he would die and I would do it."

"But didn't you say that he had been obsessed with killing you and you had to end it? And didn't you also turn the cheek numerous times in the past? And did you say, everyone has a right to defend themselves?" The corners of his mouth turned up a little at that but I continued. "Haven't you proven that you are worthy of the rank despite the bit of emotion you held closely inside? Will you not be feared more than ever now?"

"Feared is not my goal. Respected is the object I desire. I suppose I've earned that in the eyes of the Tribunal, but it's more than that, too. I, or should I say we, at least until the race is over," he says stroking my hair, "will need to be prepared. I don't think my challengers will come at me in the race. But there are a lot of Masters now who would love to take on a Jei to beat him. Remember when I said I was top target?"

I nod.

"It's only going to get worse. Right now, I'm going to have two Deas breathing down my neck and most likely several Cees. Moralles also had a lot of followers who may strike back. Just as in anything, you're going to learn from your experiences and failures. These Masters are going to be looking for new ways to be better than I and overcome their competition. All these Specialists considered to be my so-called inferiors are hungry. Their goal is to take me down. Taking me down would elevate them as long as they keep it honorable."

"Are you worried?"

"No," he answers shaking his head with a slight smile. "It's all part of it. The key is that they have to beat me first. I'm confident in what I can do. I, too, am always learning ways to improve my abilities. I know I'm tough to beat, but I also know it is possible," he adds.

I love his humility. He doesn't underestimate anybody. I really love him for that.

"We can't let this get us distracted from what our real purpose here is," he adds. "My commitment to our Region's priorities will always be more important than the next guy trying to up his game," he says and rolls onto his back.

"Can I ask you one more thing?"

He nods.

"After Langt's scan, if something more were wrong with you, would you have told him?"

"No," he says shaking his head.

"Is there something else wrong?" I ask.

He looks at me then smiles. "Hairline fractures to a few of my ribs."

"Are you in pain?"

"I've lived with worse," he answers shrugging.

"Can I help you wrap them? Will it make you more comfortable?"

He looks at me and sits up. He grabs some items from his gear.

"They don't need to be wrapped but if you could help me press these core supports on my lower back, it would help with the healing process. It shouldn't take long to heal."

He directs me on where to put the supports. When we're done, he looks at me.

"Thank you," he says sincerely. "I've never trusted anyone with the knowledge of my injuries before. I hope you'll keep my secrets."

"Always," I confirm.

He bends his head down and our mouths meet. I tease his lips with a flick of my tongue. He nibbles on my bottom lip just before our lips and tongues unite for a little sweet play. Then we lie down next to each other.

"I guess I'm not the invincible man you thought I was," he estimates.

"You are so much more," I murmur.

He's quite a man and so down to earth. I lay my head on his shoulder. We both need to get to sleep. Our journey to the task point is a few days away. That will give Archer time to heal.

CHAPTER 46

TEAM TASK: TEAMS MUST SUCCESSFULLY COMPLETE THE TARGET OBSTACLE COURSE USING AN ARROW, A SLING SHOT, A SPEAR AND AN AX. THERE ARE FOUR TARGET AREAS WITH A SEPARATE SKILL. EACH TARGET IS APPROXIMATELY 50 FT OR MORE AWAY FROM THE STARTING POINT. A JUDGE WILL DETERMINE WHEN THE TEAM CAN MOVE TO THE NEXT OBSTACLE. TEAM MEMBERS MUST COMPLETE TWO SKILLS EACH TO FINISH THE COURSE.

I glance at Archer.

"Have you shot or thrown any of these?" he asks.

"I took archery as a child, but that's a no brainer for you."

"I think I should do the spear and the sling shot," he contemplates. "I can coach you through the other two."

"Okay, whatever you think is best."

We are directed to one of the competition areas. They are wide fields divided by large hedges so we can't observe if other teams are nearby.

We walk over to the first obstacle which is the arrow. I survey the target down the lane. I pick up the bow and nock the arrow. I've watched Archer a thousand times. I should know this. I place the bow higher and take aim.

"Use this part of your hand as you grip the bow," Archer reminds me, tapping his palm right under his thumb. "Pull the arrow up to your cheek to get a better aim. Bend your knees a little and I'd say give it about a 15-degree angle. Then let her rip."

I readjust my grip and my stance; I give it what I think is a 15-degree angle and I let it go. I watch as it drops right in the front of the target. I look at Archer. He is smiling.

"You did great! You just needed a little more power," he says. "Give it a 25-degree angle. Do everything you just did."

As I stand sideways, I make certain my grip is right, then I nock my arrow. I pull the string back to my cheek and point it at a 25-degree angle.

"Breathe, Lily," Archer coaches softly.

I take a deep breath and exhale, aim and release. It hits the target. It's not a bullseye, but its on the target. I squeal happily jumping up and down. Archer is laughing at me. The judge approves it and we move to the next obstacle.

The next obstacle is the spear. The target is very far away. I look at Archer. I can see in his eyes that the wheels are in motion and he is calculating everything. He looks at the judge.

"Is this a standing throw or running?" he asks.

The judge nods. Obviously, no help there. Archer turns to me, lifts his eyebrows and shrugs. I laugh at his expression.

Archer turns around and picks up a spear. He throws it up lightly and catches it to get a feel for the weight. He absent-mindedly rolls it on top of his hand like it's a baton as he looks at the target. He is very focused. After a moment he takes several long steps backward. Then he takes a stance and moves the spear into position over his shoulder. He inhales and exhales, then he runs a few steps to the starting line and forcefully hurls that spear. It flies through air so fast with such power that when it hits the target, the impact lifts it and knocks it completely over.

The judge looks at Archer with a nasty smirk. I guess he's upset because he has to walk down there to see where Archer hit the target and if it's within the boundaries. We all walk to the target. It's a bullseye, of course. Archer lifts up the target and sets it back where it was supposed to be. The judge grumbles his approval for us to move on. Just before I turn the corner around the hedge to go to the next obstacle, I look back to see the judge struggling to remove the spear from the target. He lifts his leg to place his foot on the target, pulling with all his strength. I gaze at Archer's profile. He is something else indeed.

The next obstacle is the slingshot. I see a small target that, once its hit, will release a basketful of birdseed. That's rather nice, if you hit the target, you feed the birds too. Archer walks over and examines the slingshots.

"What are you looking for?" I ask.

"I'm looking at the reference points and the anchor points on each of these slings," he says while picking them up one by one. I have no idea what that means. Weapons are his thing, and he knows what he's doing. Before he commits, he looks at the ammo, which appear to be acorns or something similar. He tosses one in the air and catches it, then goes back to choose his slingshot. He takes a stand at the starting point, places the ammo in the slingshot then holds it straight out in front of him while stretching the band and pulling straight back to his cheek. It almost looks like he is shooting an arrow without the bow…and I suppose, without the arrow too. He lets go of the band and easily hits the target letting the birdseed fall to the ground. The judge approves us and we move to the next obstacle.

When we arrive at the ax throw, the target is a log standing on its side making it a rather narrow target. I'm worried immediately. I've never thrown an ax. Archer is walking ahead of me. He stops and crosses his arms, probably thinking the same thing. He looks back at me.

"You can do this," he encourages as I walk in his direction. "The key is going to be to throw it overhand. Hold the ax with both hands over your head. The target is farther than I'd hoped so you're going to have to release it on the upward part of the throw. About here…" he says demonstrating over his own head so I can watch.

I agree with him, but I'm not very confident.

I pick up an ax.

"Get your grip," Archer says balling his fists in front of him as if to demonstrate how I should hold it.

I do my best to hold it similarly to his demo. I lean backward and release it with a great heave ho but I miss the target completely.

"You're doing great," Archer comments supportively. "On your next try, remember to keep your body straight when you throw."

I make the adjustments but I miss again. We may be here a while. Archer smiles at me. Finally, on my fourteenth attempt, I hit the target.

"See, I knew you could do it," Archer says smiling.

The judge approves us to move forward in the race. Unfortunately, I glimpse the shadow of another team leave before us. We need to move quickly.

The exit judge hands me instructions with a map. He tells Archer to meet me at the Maltanese Plaza Resort.

"That's far from here," he discloses to the judge seriously. "And in the middle of the Sea."

"Archer, she will be completely safe. She will be accompanied by a race attendant to the port. There she will be taken to one of the islands by a nautical transport to complete an additional task," the judge explains looking a little frightened by Archer's stare down.

Archer looks at me and then back at the judge but doesn't move.

"Another contestant is still waiting for the transport, Archer, you may escort Miss Ellis to the race attendant at the transport location," he is sweating now.

Archer steps closer to me. "I'll do that," he states laying a hand at the small of my back and maneuvering me away from the judge.

Once off the grounds, Archer asks me for the instruction card I was handed.

"What is it?" I ask.

"I just want to be sure that it's not more secret codes and building government gadgets," he says scanning over the instruction card. "Looks like you're going on a diving quest to retrieve some secret items."

"Are you worried?" Because now I am a little.

"No," he answers smiling. "Have you ever been diving before?"

"Yes, my home is near the water."

He looks at me a moment. "That's right. I remember now. I guess we'll be home soon," he smiles again.

Home. I haven't really thought about the race ending. I've been so busy on this crazy race adventure. What am I going to do when I go home? Life there will seem so boring compared to all this. I don't want to go back to how it used to be.

Archer is such an integral part of my life now. What am I going to do without him? I get emotional but pull myself out of it quickly when Archer grabs my hand and runs me across a busy street to the commuter and awaiting race attendant. He says he'll see me in two days at the resort. Two days? I'm shocked and look over my instruction card again.

Once I'm aboard, the large commuter leaves. I run to the ladies' room and then find the deck to enjoy the boat ride. I make my way to the railing. I love the salty sea breeze caressing my face and wind blowing my hair. I look about and see Antonella sitting on one of the lounge chairs reading a periodical.

"Hey!" I exclaim as I get near.

"Hello," she squeals. "I thought I was all alone. This is so strange, isn't it? I haven't been away from Espada this long during the race outside of commuter time."

"I know what you mean. It does seem weird," I add while claiming the chair next to her.

A server brings us a couple of fruit drinks. I try mine and it's delicious.

"Is Jannika aboard also?"

"I haven't seen her. I don't know if she's ahead of us or behind us."

Wow. That really hit me in the face. Both Antonella and Jannika are my biggest threats right now. They are also the two I've bonded with the most.

"What do you think we'll be doing for the diving task?"

She takes a sip of her drink then answers, "I wish I knew. I hope we're not expected to collect specimens like Octopi or Squids." She shudders slightly.

I can't help but laugh at her but, truthfully, I hope we don't either.

CHAPTER 47

Antonella and I meet on the deck in our swimwear. She's wearing a white one-piece which looks great on her. I just threw on my tangerine bikini. We are anchored offshore of a nearby island. It's a beautiful day with clear blue skies and azure water.

We are told to sit for our safety briefing before we get decked out in snorkeling gear. So, it's not a formal dive, which is good in my book. I'd rather not have to go deep. Still, it sounds like it's going to be a long day in the water.

I feel well rested. The night on the boat was wonderful. I spent it mostly alone and fell asleep as soon as my head touched the pillow. Jannika is not with us so I still don't know if she's ahead of me or behind me which means I absolutely have to beat Antonella. She is probably thinking the same thing about me.

Captain Flavin's booming voice brings me out of my thoughts. "Your task card is on the beach just ahead." We look in the direction of the beach. I see the table that seems to also have other items as well. The captain continues, "on my mark, you will jump off the boat and swim to the beach to retrieve your task card. All other information will be on the cards. Make your way to the dive platform at the back of the boat."

TASK: THERE ARE THREE MARKED BUOYS OFF SHORE. AT THE BOTTOM OF EACH IS A BOX WITH YOUR NAME ON IT. INSIDE IS A KEY. COLLECT ALL THREE KEYS AND SWIM TO THE RAFT WITH THE BLUE FLAG. ONE OF THE KEYS YOU RETRIEVED WILL OPEN ONE OF THE THREE BOXES ON THE RAFT. INSIDE YOU WILL RECEIVE FURTHER INSTRUCTIONS.

I jump in the water before Antonella and start swimming out to the first buoy. All the bouys are at different distances from the shore. The one I chose is the farthest away. She quickly jumps in after me. The race is on. I glance back. She is heading to a different buoy. Smart girl since I'm already ahead on this one. She's going to be tough.

By the time I reach the first buoy, Antonella is on her way to the second. I'm out of breath but I definitely feel a sense of urgency. I dive below, this box is quite far down. I have to come back up to catch my breath before attempting it again. I dive down again, this time I get there, open my box and grab the key. I better not drop it. I head to the next one. Antonella is headed to the same one. She'll get there first.

We pass each other just as I'm getting close to the buoy. She's heading out to the third. I have to get this quickly. I dive down. Key number 2 is sequestered. Heading over to the last buoy. Antonella still hasn't made it to the last one but she's close.

I get to the last buoy and dive down. I grab the last key and come up for air. Antonella is on her way back, too. I have to move. I get to shore first because my last buoy was closer. As much as I want to just fall on the sand and lie there to catch my breath, I drag myself along the shore to where the raft is floating then jump in and swim to it with keys in hand. Antonella is not far behind. She looks as wrung out as I feel.

I pull myself up on the raft. The second key opens my box. There are several items in here. I grab the task card and fall back into a seated position to read it as I catch my breath.

TASK: USING THE LAMINATED, WATERPROOF CARD, SEARCH FOR THE 10 OBJECTS LISTED UNDERWATER. THE OBJECTS ARE DISTRIBUTED THROUGHOUT THE MARKED AREA AT THE BACKSIDE OF THE RAFT. I look up to view the marked off area. Shit. It's huge. This is going to take forever. I'll have to pace myself. ONCE YOU'VE FOUND ALL THE ITEMS ON YOUR LIST, TAKE THEM TO THE JUDGE LOCATED AT THE "X" ON THE MAP ON THE BACK OF THE LIST CARD.

The items listed on this card are crazy: an old boot, a golden butterfly, a large colorful jewel, a round pearl, a mesh bag, a small treasure chest, a blue seahorse, a rainbow coral, and two replica fishes. That might make it easier, but they do seem a bit obnoxious.

Antonella, still dripping, has retrieved her card. She's breathing heavily. I've only got seconds to get ahead of her so I jump in the water and swim to the task area. I hear her jump in behind me. She's smart. She's trying to stay with me. One of us could be eliminated today.

I arrive at the designated area and tuck the card in my swimsuit's top strap. That should keep if secure while I dive down in search of these items. I make my first dive. Of course, it's deeper than I hoped. There are no items near me. This is going to be a long swimming task with lots of up and down for air. Shoot. I'm exhausted just thinking about it, especially since I'm already tired from just getting the list.

I begin. Maybe if I swim to the center of this vast area, I'll find stuff randomly along the way. Maybe I should treat it like a pie and swim in slices. I shrug, telling myself, what the hell? Let's do it. I bob up and down as I swim toward the center. Sure enough, I begin to see items on the sea floor. Unfortunately, they are not what I'm looking for. I do a quick check and see Antonella swimming some distance behind me. I wonder if these items are hers. I hurry myself along. The third item I see is a blue seahorse. Excellent. I grab it but, it's a bit bulky to carry. I need to find that mesh bag.

Now, I find more items, I gather the butterfly, the treasure chest and one of the fish. It's getting hard to carry this stuff while I dive. I see a clam. I'll bet the pearl is in it. Then, from the corner of my eye, I see a bright yellow item and swim to it. It's the mesh bag! Hallelujuah! I snag it and dog paddle while I try to shove everything into it. I secure the string around my wrist and return to the clam.

Yep, the pearl is in there. I'm half way there! I swim to the far side and find the coral. There are many items that are not on my list. Wait, I see another fish. I grab that and put it in my bag. Now I just need the jewel and the boot.

I cut across the area toward the middle back. I see Antonella come up for air across the way. I dive again and swim underwater. Nothing. I take a breath then head in another direction. I swim underwater desperately trying to find my last two items. I see something that looks like a rock and am about to pass it by but something about it catches my eye. I revisit it and see that it is not a rock. It's covered with a lot of sand. I pull it up. The boot! Geez, I could've been looking for this for hours. I'm so glad I found it.

Fatigue is beginning to set in, I have to locate this jewel. I turn in the direction where Antonella is searching. That's my last "slice of pie". I dive deep. There is a giant fake green "jewel". I grab it and put it in the bag. I dog paddle while I make sure I have everything on my list then turn the card over to the map. I now have to find the judge. I'm really tired and starting to even feel a little sick from it.

Just then, Antonella pops up. Her breathing is labored and she seems to be struggling. I live by the water and swim all the time. If she doesn't have the stamina, she could be in real trouble. A very dirty little voice in the back of my head reminds me that if I help her, she could pass me and I'd be the one eliminated from the race. I have to admit, it did cause a brief moment of pause, but I know I wouldn't be able to live with myself if I let her get hurt or worse.

I swim to her and take her arm trying to help hold her up. "Float on your back for a minute to rest," I instruct.

"Let go of me," she snips and jerks her arm away.

"I'm sorry," I'm shocked. She's never acted like that before. "I thought you needed help."

"If I need help, they may delay me. Let me alone," she demands splashing some water in my face then dog paddling away.

I can't believe she just did that. I was only trying to help. "You got it, babe," I think to myself then also think, "Drown for all I care." I swim away to locate the judge. I look back to watch Antonella floating. She's still breathing hard. She also seems to be crying.

I finally find the judge on the back side of the beach. He clears me to continue. He says the motor boat will take me back to shore where I will find refreshments as well as a change of clothes. An attendant helps me on the boat. I am so spent, and my legs feel like lead. I collapse into one of the seats in the shade of the canopy. I wonder how Antonella is doing. A female attendant hands me a water and an energy bar.

"You might as well relax," she says smiling. "The trip to shore will take a little over an hour."

I smile at her. I lean back to enjoy my delicious energy bar.

As the boat returns to shore, I see a gorgeous guy wearing white swim trunks with a blue coral design running through it. He has blonde hair and is wearing dark sunglasses. The white band of the trunks against his tan abs is quite stunning. A limp white shirt hangs from his hand. He's talking to a man at the tiki hut.

As I come closer, I see it's Archer! What's he doing here? I run over to him. He's still talking in the man's language but he slips his hand in mine. The man turns to grab something and Archer leans over to me and pecks a kiss on my lips then turns his attention back to the man. What an awesome day!

He throws his shirt over his shoulder as the man hands him an ignition disk and points out on the water. I look over and there is a Jet water transport nearby. Archer thanks him and we start walking to the transport.

"I was told the fastest way to get to Meteora from here is by boat. I rented this man's jet transport for the day." The man meets us at the water's edge and hands us safety vests. I pull mine around my bikini and clasp it. Archer is ready too. The man says something in his language to Archer. Archer looks at him for a moment, then nods.

"What is it?" I ask. Archer didn't seem to care for that last bit the man said.

"He said the ambassador's entourage is making its way through town today for an engagement parade. The parade has not been announced so it won't attract unwanted attention, however, the roads and ramps will be closed for about an hour," Archer explains.

After some time jetting through the water, we see many watercraft anchored or floating by the off ramp. Archer slows us down as we approach to wait the parade out. I hope this means everyone is getting sidelined.

I see a secluded beach surrounded by crystal blue water. There are a few of the watercraft there. It's beautiful and I don't want to only sit by the ramp in the hot sun baking. I poke Archer on the shoulder and point to the beach. He pulls over there.

"Can we rinse off for a minute?"

He turns off the transport. I take off the vest and jump in. Archer does likewise. We swim around splashing and playing. He lets me stand on his shoulders then he springs in the air letting me dive from them. I feel like a little kid. It's such an awesome time.

We see other people pulling up anchor. The parade must be over.

"We better get moving," he finally says. I knew it was coming, I just wanted to spend more time with him. But in the back of my mind, I wonder where Antonella is.

"May I drive," I ask enthusiastically like a little teenager. He scoffs but agrees.

We climb back on the transport. He's behind me. He leans in close as he shows me the controls. His chin is just over my shoulder. Then I'm ready. I take one last look around.

"It's so beautiful."

"So are you," he says and gives me a peck on the neck sending shivers down my back.

I turn to him and kiss his lips. He moves a strand of hair out of my face and smiles at me. I move hair out of his face and laugh. He moves in and we kiss again. That kiss morphs into another, then another, then he turns me completely around so I'm facing him. Our next kiss turns into a glorious make out session. His hands are on my bare back and mine on the sides of his bare waist. Our kisses are scorching and exciting. I can't get enough. I can feel that his finger somehow got hooked just inside the side of my bikini bottoms from our movements. I try to move a little to dislodge it as we are kissing, but it's not helping so I try leaning in even closer. This move tips the transport somewhat on the water. Archer adjusts his balance and we tilt backward. I fall into him. He catches us but in doing so his hand slides all the way inside my bikini bottoms cupping my butt cheek. His finger tips are dangerously close to my lady parts. He freezes. I gasp at the surprise of it. My fingertips are nervously scratching at his abs and I'm afraid to move. His mouth is parted, while his breath is hot and shallow. His hand has not moved and he has not corrected it to essentially take it out of my pants. I look into his eyes. There is a terrible war going on inside of him.

After the briefest of moments, he lets out a breath and flings us both back into the water.

When we come up for air he says, "I'm driving. "

That was that. He drove us to Meteora without another word or touch. Once there, he didn't lay a hand on me. We walked side by side the rest of the way through town making small talk and avoiding any mention of what just happened between us.

CHAPTER 48

We stop outside of town and change into more appropriate attire for the hike to the checkpoint. I am still wondering about Antonella. It keeps eating at me. I'm pretty sure that Jannika is ahead of us which means…

I tell Archer about my concerns. He listens thoughtfully. He doesn't say anything but he does pick up the pace.

We turn the final corner. The checkpoint is at the end of this very long and dusty trail which is dotted with large trees and rock formations. But my biggest concern is that I see Antonella in front of me. She is casually walking. She doesn't know I'm behind her. I think I can outrun her.

I peek at Archer. He has stopped. He has that look on his face that his senses have picked up something. He glances down at me.

"Go," he says quietly. "You have to beat her."

I take off running. Antonella finally turns around to see me coming.

Suddenly, I see a flash of Archer just before his hand hits me squarely in the back shoving me to the ground. A blade barely misses my cheek. Archer slides to the side but springs to his feet, yet hunched down looking very much like a panther on the prowl, before I even get my face out of the dirt. I stay down sensing the danger but not really knowing what it is. I just watch Archer. His eyes are narrowed and fixed on his opponent. Blood is dripping from his upper arm where he took the blade instead of me. He flips his head signaling for me to go.

I get up to run quickly away but once I'm clear, of course, I have to turn around to see what's going on.

It's Espada. He's brandishing his richly embellished sword at Archer. I should have known.

"You're no match for me and my sword, Archer. You know I can easily best you here. Yield to me and walk away," Espada gloats.

"As you can see, I have no sword today. Perhaps a different weapon would suffice," Archer negotiates in even tones.

"What? You want me to pick up one of your little arrows? A sword is a weapon for real men," Espada taunts. He twirls his sword around very close to Archer, but Archer steps casually to the side.

"Hand to hand would be just fine with me," Archer offers nastily.

"How about a hair cut?" Espada teases waving his sword around Archer's head.

He steps closer, clearly confident in his abilities and begins wielding his sword around like he's playing with it but then takes a quick jab at Archer and laughs as Archer twists away from him.

Archer's eyes are laser sharp and alert. He's watching every move but not backing away. Espada continues his game of whirling the sword and randomly jabbing at Archer and laughing.

"Hey, girlie," he yells at me, "when I'm done with your little friend here, I'm coming for you." he laughs again. I bristle involuntarily at his words remembering my near rape by Hamar and experience a moment of panic. I try to get a hold of myself.

I can see in Archer's face that it hit him too and he has had enough. At the next swing of the sword, Archer moves in quickly and claps his hands together trapping in the blade between them. Then with a mighty pull, he swings down with his arms and flips his wrist snatching the sword right out of Espada's grip. It turns in the air where Archer catches the hilt with a bleeding hand, then places its point squarely in front of Espada's heart.

Archer's eyes are focused and angry, his tone is menacing. "You won't be besting me today, Espada."

Espada curls his lip and leans forward pressing the sword tip into his own chest.

"Do your worst," Espada dares in a low throaty tone.

"My worst?" Archer lifts his eyebrows and scoffs. Then he stands tall, lowers the sword and sneers with a note of sarcasm, "Live with the shame of it, Master Swordsman." Then adds a provoking, "I'll keep the sword as a souvenir."

Espada screeches and charges Archer wielding two knives that came from God knows where. Archer's ready for him. He twists full circle as Espada is about to hit him. His palm comes around and clasping the back of Espada's head, he lifts him up by the neck, then slams him face first to the ground in a crushing blow. Blood begins to puddle around him. Espada jabs blindly at Archer's leg with the knife getting in several good slices. Archer snarls and with a flex of his bicep lifts Espada's neck by the hair off the ground, exposing his throat. Then with a quick twist of his left wrist flips the blade of the sword as he goes in for the kill.

"Noooooooooo!" Antonella shrieks catching Archer's attention. He looks up at us, strands of blonde hair blowing across his face. Antonella starts running toward them, but I grab her and hold onto her as she screams and cries. Archer's eyes meet mine and for a moment we're locked, each learning a little bit more about the other. He's savage and brutal with his enemies yet compassionate about what we will witness. I let go of Antonella. She runs toward Espada, blood gushing from his broken nose.

Archer keeps his eyes on me as he lowers the sword but his jaw tightens and he viciously squeezes the back of Espada's neck letting him cry out in pain until he drops the knife. Then he digs his knee into Espada's shoulder as he stands and I hear a disgusting popping crunching noise. Espada screams out again. Archer may have very well taken him out of the race with that. He looks down as Antonella falls next to Espada crying and rubbing his hair. Archer looks up at me again, he raises the sword and allows it to rest on his shoulder. Blood is dripping down his arm, hands and leg, then he turns and walks away.

So do I.

CHAPTER 49

Sionetel 2

When I crossed the checkpoint, I was confined to quarters. During the commute to Sionetel, I was informed that Medatilli was a non-elimination leg. That means there are still three of us vying for the victory. I also know that Espada may have extensive injuries which means he might be out of it which also means Antonella would be going through last part alone.

Now, as I'm getting ready to be released, I am told that we are all starting about 15 minutes apart. I ask if I am in first place or second but a smile is all I get. No one is telling.

We will cross the finish line tomorrow.

When I'm released, Archer is waiting for me.

"This is it," I exclaim. "We just have to make it to the final temple."

"I want to reach Nyona today. We will be able to rest then head to the temple to the finish line," he smiles. "It's almost over, Lily."

I smile back but…oh my God, it dawns on me that I may never see this man again after tomorrow. What am I going to do? How can I be without him? I glance discreetly at his profile. I can see him crack a smile. He knows I'm looking at him. He doesn't miss anything.

We walk quietly along for some time. I guess Archer's thoughts have been in the same line as mine because when we stop to eat he asks, "What is the first thing you're going to do when you get home?"

"I don't know. I haven't really given it much thought. I guess it all depends on what happens here."

I'm a little sad, I guess. I don't really want this to end. I've taken a journey all over the world with a man who has become my protector, provider and loyal, trustworthy friend. He is also an excellent kisser. I think I just want to marry him. He's everything a girl could want in a man except the whole killing thing. I wonder how his life will change after all this.

We finish the meal in silence. Each of us seems to be lost in our own thoughts.

At Nyona, Archer creates a simple but sturdy, warm, comfortable shelter for the night. We haven't really said or done too much at all today. We just traveled here and have gone through all the motions as we have so many days before.

It's unusually quiet though. There is no hustle and bustle of having other contestants or race attendants around. I'd like to think that Archer is contemplating his life without me but I know Archer. He is most likely thinking about his upcoming fight. The first two Specialists at the fight arena in the morning will battle it out in a closed setting trying to give their contestant an advantage to the finish line. The third or last contestant and her specialist to arrive is automatically eliminated at that point. So close, but out of it.

We both eat very little. I retire early leaving Archer to his thoughts outside of the shelter. I manage to doze a little here and there but I can't sleep for too long at a time. Maybe it's the finish line jitters. I can't stop thinking about it. I can't believe the race is almost over. The same questions roll through my mind continuously. What am I going to do after this? How can I go back to a normal life? How can I be without my Archer?

I awaken in the middle of the night. I roll over to watch Archer as he sleeps. I feel the press of his arm around me. His breathing is steady and warm. He seems so peaceful and so beautiful. This is our last night together. I lift my head and kiss him lightly on the lips. He opens his eyes. We just look at each other for few moments. No words could express how I feel about him.

I put my hand on his face and I kiss him again. He kisses me back. I roll him on his back and climb on top of him. I clasp my fingers in his next to his head and kiss him again.

"Don't do this," he says quietly.

"This is our last night together. It should be something special, something we can take with us forever," I reveal.

He shakes his head. "This race will soon be over. It won't take long and you will find someone through the selection process. Then you will regret anything that happened between us here."

I can only exhale. Doesn't he understand? My feelings are genuine. No one in this world could compare to him. I look into his blue eyes and mine start to fill with tears. "I'll find another? Is that what you think? I want you. You're torturing me," I'm terribly sad.

"Torture," he exclaims and rolls me on my back. Our hands are still clasped together but now they are next to my head as he leans against me. "Look at you," he continues, "you're so beautiful. You're lying here next to me with the softness of your womanly curves pressed up against me. You freely give me your precious kisses and sweet caresses. Don't you think I want you? My God, I'm a man, Liliana! You're a willing partner who has my heart wanting me to make love to you and I'm the one saying no. That's torture!" he lets go of me and sits up moving away from me. He leans back looking away.

I sit up and hug my knees looking at him.

He turns to me. "You're not thinking with your brain," he says angrily as he runs his fingers through his hair. "As usual, you're only considering your heart. If that's all it took we would be sharing a night of incredible passion!" he spits.

I put my cheek on my knees and look at him. His eyes bore through me then he exhales and softens.

"What if you win," he asks. "Let's suppose you win but then it turns out you're not a virgin because after months of being thrown closely together and even sleeping wrapped up in each other's arms, we can't control ourselves for one more night. Your life would be in ruin and it would be my fault. There's nothing I can do about it. I can't save you from that. I'm not free! I'm a warrior at the mercy of politics bound for life to the temple. Right now, there's a very real threat out there and I don't yet know what it is." He stops for a moment and looks at me. "I've already been summoned. I will have to appear at the Council League right after the race. Our time is over."

He steps outside. I go after him. His back is to me as he seems to gather his thoughts.

"This is about the temple winning the race isn't it," I ask.

He turns to me with a look of exasperation on his face like I'm the most illogical person he's ever known. "Since before you were born, this race has been about the temple winning. That has never changed. What changes are the players. But this," he says flipping his wrist back and forth so his fingers point from me and back to him, "this is between me," and he takes a deep breath as though it's difficult to say and places his hand on his chest, "Arek and you, Liliana." He turns away from me again.

I realize that it's probably been years since he referred to himself as himself, Arek and not Archer. Finally, it's personal. He's having a hard time with this. He's everything to me right now. He's not only my hero, but he's also the man I'm in love with and then not only that, he's become my best friend. I can't lose him. I can't be without him. But I don't know what to say.

I walk to him and put my hands on his shoulders and press my face against his back. "I'm sorry," I tell him. "I just don't want to say goodbye. How can I? I want to be with you forever."

He takes a deep breath and turns to face me. He takes my hands in his. "This is not what I ever thought I'd be talking about with you tonight. But here's the truth, plain and simple, yet ugly. I'm a killer, Liliana. Don't you understand that? I not only have blood on my hands, sometimes I crave it. There is a part of me that is stone cold. I've done things and I've seen things that I will never share with you or anyone. That will always be a part of who I am and can't be undone no matter how much you fantasize that I'm your perfect man. You could never have all of me. You may dream of a husband who comes home to you every day, makes babies with you and then grows old together with you. I dream of perfecting the fight. I want the fight. It's who I am. You deserve so much better than me and a life far greater than I can ever offer."

He's treating me like a child. I know who he is. I've known all along. He's just making excuses for why he can't love me back. Maybe that makes it easier for him. I take my hands from his and walk back to the shelter. I'm hurt, angry and embarrassed. He just gave me the big-time rejection talk. I'm not going to beg him to return my love.

If it so easy for him to walk away, then so be it. Tomorrow we race to the end. That's all I need to think about right now.

CHAPTER 50

I open my eyes and see Archer staring at me. "Good morning," he says softly.

I just roll over. I don't need his beautiful face mocking my love for him.

"Hey," he says rubbing my back, "we need to talk about last night."

"You've made your point. There's nothing left to say." I'm already in so much pain from his words. I don't need to rehash them again.

"There is one thing more that I think you should know. Please look at me."

I take a breath and roll back over to face him.

"What is it," I ask curtly.

"Last night I was harsh but everything I said was true," he starts.

I can't hear this speech again. He's lying next to me about to give me the same rejection. It's unnecessary. "I get it," is all I can say and start to roll back over but he puts his hand on my hip to stop me.

"I'm not very good at this, so please let me finish," he says.

I look him in the eye, exhale a sassy, exaggerated sigh and then give him my full attention.

"It's our last day together. I don't know who our opponents are going to be today and there's always a chance…well, we just need to be on top of our game." I agree with him then he continues. "We can't allow any unspoken tension between us hinder our progress." I'm definitely listening. This time he swallows and takes a deep breath. "Last night I said what I had to say," I nod for him to continue, "and it doesn't change anything…because I won't be able to say the words you want to hear. If I say them, you will hold on to them and I can't lead you into false hopes…but I have come to care deeply for you."

I exhale in shock. Is he professing his love for me? I can't believe he said it. That must have been very hard. "I am so in love with you," I breathe. I reach up and kiss him. I'm not messing around about it either. This may be my last chance to kiss this man. I kiss him with a hungry mouth and greedy lips as I squeeze myself closer into him with all the love that can emanate from my body. He returns my kisses with the same fervor, pressing me against his rock-hard chest and thighs. One hand is behind my head, his other at the small of my back. I never want to forget the feel of him holding me like this while knowing that he truly loves me. Our bodies move together with kiss after kiss. Then he gently pulls away. As we catch our breaths, he looks me in the eye, reaches up and slowly unwraps my arms from around his neck with a "no more" look in his eyes and slight shake of his head. Then he lies back next to me and we both just look at the top of the shelter.

"Lily, there's one more thing. I've been thinking about this for a long time." Archer turns to me. I turn to him. "I don't want you to be anxious about failing your brother and your family. If we don't win, I'll pay for Colson's surgery."

I'm overwhelmed by his generosity. I stare at him for a moment. I don't really know what to say.

"But I think we can win. You've come so far and done so well. I really need your thoughts and your focus to stay here with me. Don't worry about your brother's health right now. He's all set."

I gaze into his blue eyes. They are so understanding, kind and warm. My hand moves to his cheek and I let my thumb trace over his strong jawline. Who is this amazing man? Assassin? Killer? Gentleman? Friend?

His lips find mine and we kiss the lover's kiss. It is strong, determined and possessive. He has changed my life forever and now that of my brother.

The sun peaks through the shelter's entrance opening as a gong is heard in the distance. We look at each other and get up. We scarf down a quick bite. I'm not hungry at all but I know I need the strength to finish this thing.

We dress quickly and run to the arena. We stop just before we go inside. This is where the Specialists will have their final battleground. We have no idea who is going to be waiting for us in there. It could be Langt and Jannika or Espada and Antonella. I'm hoping the latter. I feel fairly confident in taking them down.

Archer and I look at each other as he takes me by the hand.

"Are you ready," I ask him.

"Always," he replies and smiles. I'm not sure I am.

We walk inside. Langt and Jannika are there. Oh no. I really love them both. But more importantly, they are going to be tough to beat.

"Specialists, prepare for battle," says the voice over the speakers. They aren't wasting any time.

Archer and I walk to one side of the arena while Langt and Jannika walk to the other.

"Listen to me," Archer says while taking off his bow.

I nod my acknowledgment but he reaches up and holds my chin so I'm facing him and looking him in the eye.

"Listen to me," he says again slowly. "I know Langt, probably better than he knows himself. He can be a cold-blooded killer when he needs to be." I nod again shifting my eyes down to the ground. I think it's sad that they might have to kill one another, they are friends, but Archer turns my chin back up so I'm facing him.

"But in this case, he doesn't need to be." I just look at him. What does he mean by that? "He just needs to beat me in a foot race and he knows it." I let out a breath. I feel my eyes get wide in understanding.

"If I know Langt, he's going to ask me to settle this like men," Archer says while tying his laces. "What that means is he is challenging me physically. In most cases that would be hand to hand combat. No weapons. But I think that once we step into the ring to wait out the 30 seconds for the starting gong, he's going to take off running to the finish line."

"Can he outrun you?" I ask.

"Possibly. He's very fast. And he's just arrogant enough to believe he can," Archer grins. "When we are called to take our places, move casually to the back of the arena, closer to the back door. The minute we step into the circle, you run. Run as fast as you can and don't look back." Archer stands up and places his hand on my chin again.

"Promise me you will cross that finish line, with or without me," he demands. I nod my agreement but he bends down and puts his face right in front of mine. "Promise me. We can't have gone through all of this for nothing."

"I promise," I confirm and smile at him. "But how can you be so sure that's his plan? Maybe he'll surprise you this time," I say as Archer picks up a few blades and tucks them into the back of his leather vest.

"Because in all this time that we've been talking, he hasn't picked up a single weapon," Archer smiles and winks at me.

"Specialists take your places," booms across the arena speakers.

Archer kisses me on the forehead and whispers "good luck" in my ear.

As Archer moves to the starting position just outside of the fight circle, I look at Jannika. She is leaning over a railing looking at Langt. I start making my way to the back. Jannika is still watching Langt. I look at over at Langt and see that he is watching me. He looks over to Jannika and jerks his head toward me. I turn away so they don't think I'm up to anything and just casually wander in the far direction. I look out the corner of my eye to see Jannika moving in the same direction.

Langt reaches the starting point and just as Archer predicted, Langt says, "We both knew it would come down to this, brother," Langt continues "Why don't we settle this like men?"

Archer doesn't even glance at me. I know he doesn't want to disclose our plan. He just smiles at Langt. "I agree to your terms," Archer answers formally. I know what's coming and my heart starts beating faster.

"An agreement to settle without weapons has been made," the voice over the loudspeaker declares. "Specialists, remove all weapons."

I watch as Archer disarms whatever blades he has on him as I continue to back up closer to the door.

"Step into the ring and wait for the gong to sound," the voice directs.

I stop to watch them step into the ring. I have 30 seconds before they can move. I take off and hit the back door flinging it open. I start counting, one, two, three, four, five, six, seven, eight, nine, ten, eleven, twelve, thirteen…then I hear the door behind me. I have about 13 seconds on Jannika as I run across the grassy mall toward the temple stadium.

My heart is pounding and I'm running as fast as I can. I race through the temple doors. The gong rumbles and the crowd erupts into cheers, one, two, three, four, five, six, seven, eight, nine, ten… the gong rumbles again indicating Jannika has come through, but she's gained a few seconds on me. Damn her long legs! I can see the finish line platform at the other end of the stadium.

Specialists aren't allowed to enter through the temple doors, only on the outside doors so I have no idea if Archer and Langt are nearby. I glance over my shoulder. Jannika is catching up to me. I kick it into gear and run as fast as I can.

The crowd suddenly starts going wild. It must be Archer or Langt. I look to the side and I see Langt at the top of the stadium. Shit! My heart sinks but I have to win this. Then I look over my other shoulder and I see Archer! He jumps down from the top of the wall and continues down the next levels, running toward me. The roar of the crowd is earsplitting. I can hear Jannika now. She must be only steps behind me.

I keep going and try to pull ahead. I have no doubt of Archer's ability to catch up to me. The crowd is going absolutely wild. The race between Archer and Langt must be incredible. I can hear them all behind me coming fast. I'm almost there! The roar is deafening. I'm so close! I feel Archer's arm wrap around my waist as he launches us in a great leap across the ribbon. We all land in the center of the Winners Circle.

All four of us are lying on the ground on center stage. The crowd is cheering riotously with the majority of the spectators on their feet and stomping. Ruler Martinez helps me up, then Jannika. We all stand on the platform looking up to the big screen but there is no name on the board. A red notice "In Review" flashes across the screen. A hush fills the temple stadium while the finish is being analyzed. We all trade glances.

After a few agonizing moments, Ruler Martinez holds his ear piece as he tries to listen to the final judgment. He steps back to the center of the platform. Silence fills the arena. "How exciting was that?" he questions the crowd who erupts again in cheers. "This is the closest finish we've ever had and probably the most exciting. By the narrowest of margins, the winner is….Liliana Ellis!

I jump into Archer's arms. He lifts me in the air and twirls me around. Langt and Jannika also give both of us a congratulatory hug. Then Archer and I turn to each other once again. He wraps me in his arms in a jubilant embrace and squeezes. I am so happy!

"We won," I whisper in his ear.

"This time," he breathes into mine.

CHAPTER 51

We are led off stage. Jannika and I have to pass our final virginity tests to make our placements official.

Calvin stops me before I go into the examination room.

"Hello! Congratulations, Liliana! This is quite an achievement!" He takes my hand and shakes it, smiling. I smile back and hug him. I'm so happy.

Archer and Langt walk up behind him. He turns and praises them too. "I knew both my boys would be winners," he congratulates. They all happily shake hands.

Archer looks at me and winks as the attendants usher Jannika and me inside the room.

We both pass our tests and are moved to the Ruler's office.

"Congratulations, ladies," Ruler Martinez offers. "You will both be sent home for a week, then you'll be going on a victory tour. Jannika, as first runner up, you will be expected to step up and take over if at any point Liliana is unable to complete her duties as reigning champion."

Jannika smiles her understanding.

"Liliana, your tour will also include the meeting of potential suitors. You will be going on outings with these suitors and eventually you will choose one in the selection process as your mate." I smile. This is what I've always wanted, yet somehow, in light of my feelings for Archer, I no longer want to choose anyone else. I really just want to get through this meeting so I can go back out to him and be with him as long as possible. I think briefly about one more kiss goodbye before I return home.

When we emerge from Ruler Martinez's office, Ms. Terry is waiting for us. "We have to get you two all dolled up for your appearance on the Winner's Circle show." She smiles as she holds her arm out in the direction we are to go. There are two attendants waiting and we follow them to hair and makeup.

I keep looking around for Archer and Langt but the halls seem to have become deserted while we've been busy.

We are showered, made up, dressed up and have our hair coifed. I look at Jannika, she looks great! She tells me I look beautiful, too. We find our way to the studio. I still don't see Archer.

"Here we are, ladies," Miss Terry sings in front of the door marked "Studio Entrance". "I'll be waiting right here when you get out."

I look around again for Archer and Langt but don't see them.

"Is Archer already in the studio," I ask. I mean, he's a winner too.

"Archer?" Miss Terry has a confused look on her face. "Why would he be in there? His job is finished."

"Archer is a winner too, Miss Terry. We both won," I remind her while realizing that the Specialists are never really remembered as part of the winners. I frantically look around for him.

"Archer and Langt have already left. They were sent back to their Regions immediately after the race." She smiles as if this were everyday news and nudges me through the studio door, but it rips my heart out.

He left. He's gone. I didn't even get a chance to say goodbye. No goodbye kiss. No nothing. Will I ever even see him again?

THE END

ABOUT THE AUTHOR

Sharen grew up and raised her family on beautiful Anna Maria Island which is on the south side of Tampa Bay in Florida. Sharen has always been an avid reader, writer and teller of stories. Sharen considers her family to be most important to her and spends much of her free time enjoying them. She loves learning new things and traveling. Sharen spent the majority of her career in the corporate world. She was finally able to return to her love of storytelling and focus on her first full-length novel, Running with the Gods.

www.ingramcontent.com/pod-product-compliance
Lightning Source LLC
Chambersburg PA
CBHW060942190726
48286CB00005B/1394